Welcome to the Ridge!
Marcia M

Wake-Robin Ridge
A Darcy's Corner Novel

Marcia Meara

ISBN-10: 1494255774
ISBN-13: 978-1494255770

DEDICATION

To Rebecca, who said it's never too late.

CONTENTS

ACKNOWLEDGMENTS

So many people have helped along my writing journey, I hardly know where to begin. Every single one of them told me I could do this, and I should do this. And then they cheered me on when I finally said I *would* do this. My heartfelt thanks goes out to the following people.

First and foremost, my Beta readers who read my rough draft, chapter after chapter. I learned something from each and every one of them, but two have gone above and beyond the call of duty. Kathy Hahn and Felix Becerril read every single word of this book, not once but many times, from draft to edited (and re-edited) chapters. They have been amazing in their dedication to helping me fulfill this dream.

Nicki Forde, who loves everything I do, picks me up when I'm ready to quit, and used her excellent graphic art skills to design my book cover. You are a Force of the Awesome, Chickie!

My editor, Caitlin Stern, who has worked long, hard hours, cleaning up my excess verbiage and keeping me honest about my characters. She has taught me so much, and made me a better writer, though hyphens are still my enemy.

And of course my family, starting with a huge thank you to my husband, Mark, for stopping at the grocery store to pick up deli dinners on far too many nights, and never complaining about my long hours at the computer. My son and daughter, Jason and Erin, who have always been a source of inspiration to me. And who have gifted me with my much-loved grandchildren, the beautiful and funny Tabitha Faye, and the very precious Kaelen Lake. And finally my mother, who is waiting impatiently to see the print version of my book, not trusting this whole eBook thing at all.

I can't wait to see what happens next!

Prologue

~∞~

Wake-Robin (Trillium erectum): *A species of flowering plant native to the east and northeast of North America. Named for its deep red bloom, the wake-robin is among the first flowers to pop up in the spring, covering the shady forest floors of the Blue Ridge Mountains with carpets of wine-colored blossoms.*

~∞~

FRIDAY, JANUARY 22, 1965
WAKE-ROBIN RIDGE, NORTH CAROLINA

LLOYD CARTER CRIED OUT, sending a startled white-tailed doe wheeling off through the dark woods. *"No, Papa! Please don't! I'm sorry, I'm sorry! Mama? Mama, help me! Please? Please, Mama!" But Mama looked away. She always looked away, and then the strap would come down,*

1

*over and over, crisscrossing his bare back with fire, and ripping
scream after scream from his throat.*

Lloyd was curled in his sleeping bag, knees drawn up
to his chest, and arms wrapped tightly around them. He was
awake now, but still whimpering with fear. The nightmare
always reduced him to his ten-year-old self, helpless, as his
father whipped him with a narrow leather strap cut from a
horse bridle. It had been "Papa's Instrument of Atonement,"
and he had used it for the slightest infraction, leaving rows
of bloody stripes behind. Lloyd's youthful transgressions
had called for a lot of atonement in his father's eyes, and his
back still bore the scars after all these years.

Shivering and choking back tears, he sat up in his small
tent, waiting for his breathing to slow down, and his fear to
turn to rage, as it always did. A slow anger built, consuming
him, and burning away the lingering reminder of childhood
trauma.

*Bastard! Damn, stinkin' bastard! And her no better! Why'd
you let him do it, Mama? You could've stopped him! Why'd you
hate me so much, always turnin' away like that?*

He closed his eyes, shutting away the last memories of
the searing pain, and let his hate take control. Hatred and
anger were old friends to him. They hadn't let him down,
yet. Snarling, he laced his boots, ignoring both the terror of
the nightmare, and the bleak misery of his childhood.

*It don't matter, now. Neither of you matter anymore. You're
both dead and gone, and no one the wiser on that score.*

He thought about how easy it had been to fool people
when the "big tragedy" happened. A few pitiful tears and a
scared, wide-eyed look of confusion, and they couldn't do
enough to comfort him. He had been twelve—just a skinny,
baby-faced kid—but a kid with a box of matches can be as
deadly as a man with a gun.

2

So sad, Papa. So sorry, Mama. You two are gone to glory, but guess what, Papa? Guess what, Mama? I'm still here. And guess what else? Nobody raises a hand—or a whip—to Lloyd Carter these days an' gets away with it. Nobody!

Lloyd crawled out of the tent and stretched his muscular arms over his head, shivering in the pre-dawn air. The icy chill of a January night in the North Carolina mountains cut right through him. He glanced at his duffel bag, and smiled. *Good thing I came prepared for everything, isn't it? And I do mean everything!*

He pulled on his heavy parka, and made a cup of instant coffee over a small, single burner camping stove. Sipping the scalding liquid, his lip curled up into a nasty sneer, as bloody visions of what he planned snaked through his mind.

I know at least one more person who's gonna learn pretty soon that you hadn't oughta screw with me, an' I'm gonna have fun teachin' her that lesson, too! He shivered again, this time in anticipation.

Packing up his small knapsack with beef jerky and a couple of granola bars, he clipped a canteen of water to his belt, then selected two of his sharpest knives from his duffel bag. He tucked those inside the knapsack as well, and grabbed a deadly looking machete to carry along.

Might need this baby for hacking away vines ... or limbs. Yeah, limbs. That's a good one. Sniggering to himself, he hid everything else inside the little tent, then pulled on a warm pair of gloves. Just as the dim shapes of tall pines became faintly visible, he set off through the woods, following the same route he had checked out when he arrived at his hiding place late the day before.

A slow, cold mile later, he could see the faintest hint of dawn through the trees just ahead, and knew he was approaching the clearing. The trick was to get close enough to see without being seen. He found a spot behind some thick but low-growing bushes. It was a perfect place to hunker down and wait. In the gray light of early morning, he pulled out his favorite filleting knife and a small whetstone, spat on the stone, and began to slide the knife back and forth across the surface. Falling into a rhythm, eyes half closed, he continued to hone the knife, metal caressing stone again and again. His excitement rose as he thought about the damage the razor-sharp edge was going to do, slicing deep into tender flesh, and releasing spray after spray of coppery-scented blood into the air. He smiled, already hearing the terrified pleading and the screams that would follow.

The soft noise of blade on stone kept him company as time passed. At last, morning broke in full, and spilled pink and gold daylight into the world, but his thoughts were not on the beauty of the new day opening in front of him. Instead, his hatred morphed into a cold fury as he thought about the full extent of the treachery committed against him, and the bloody revenge he planned to extract.

Lloyd crouched low in the bushes, peering at the little cabin in the clearing. This is what she chose to do with his money? Hide out on a deserted hillside in a stinkin' little wooden shack that looked like it should have belonged to the Beverly Hillbillies, *before* they struck it rich? God, he could kill the bitch. "Oh, that's right," he said. "I'm going to."

Chapter 1
I Don't Have To

"BECKY! IT'S A quarter to five! On Friday!" I stared open-mouthed as the library's intern plopped a foot-high stack of manuscripts down on the corner of my desk.

"Sorry. Mrs. G. said she was sure you wouldn't mind staying late to work on these, Sarah. She said there was a lot of real interesting local history in here, and she knew, just *knew*, you'd love to get your hands on it right away."

"But why does it have to be done tonight? It's Fourth of July weekend. I have things to do."

Becky raised a skeptical eyebrow. "Well, she knows you broke up with what's-his-name, so she probably figures you got no place better to be."

5

"Neil!" I tossed my pencil down. "His name was Neil! And does the whole department know my every move?"

She gave me that look of bored disdain only an eighteen-year-old girl can manage. "God, Sarah. Of course we know. There's only ten of us working here, after all. Who has secrets?" She popped her chewing gum and yawned, as if to prove how uninteresting everything about me was.

I sighed. "Does this mean she wants these done by Tuesday morning?"

"Got it in one, Sare. Want me to pick up a burger from across the street for you?"

"No thanks. I guess I'll take a dinner break later. And don't call me Sare."

"Whatever. I'll be heading home then, if you don't need anything else. Some of us have boyfriends who stick around longer than a month, you know." She snorted in appreciation of her own wit, and headed for the door, calling out over her shoulder, "Don't work too late, *Sare*."

I resisted the urge to throw my paperweight at her. It took all my willpower. Having a snarky, part-time file clerk put me in my place was annoying in the extreme, but I knew she was right. Neil had been the latest in a long line of boyfriends, all of whom had been nice guys, but none of whom had made the earth move for me. I hadn't been interested in a permanent relationship with any man I'd ever dated, so one by one, they moved on, either by their choice or mine. As a result, I'd spent a lot of Friday nights alone.

Once Becky left, I knew I had the building to myself. I sat glaring at my now overflowing Inbox. My sense of frustrated resentment was growing larger with every tick of the clock. Yeah, maybe I didn't have anyone waiting for me, but I liked my time off just as much as everyone else, and I had been anticipating relaxing over the long weekend. Judging by the look of the manuscripts I'd been given, I was

6

going to have to spend most of it here, now. And for what? I doubted there was a thing in this stack that couldn't be read, scanned, and cataloged during regular working hours next week.

Man, I hate this job! And why the hell has it taken me ten years to figure it out?

MY NAME IS Sarah Gray. I'm a thirty-five-year-old library cataloging and research assistant. For the better part of the last decade, I have spent at least forty hours a week in a tiny cubicle, hidden deep within the Leland Walker Historical Library in DeBary, Florida, reading and cataloging old, crumbling manuscripts, diaries, business records, and journals. Most were just the mundane bits and pieces acquired by the library through private donations, and destined to be scanned, then filed away, never to see the light of day again. Once in a great while, something more exciting came along, but not often. Certainly not often enough to prevent the initial pleasure of historical discovery from turning into the stupefying boredom that had become my daily routine.

I thumbed through the first few pages of the top manuscript. It was deadly dull stuff. Itemized packing lists and old warehouse receipts. Crap. This weekend was going to stink! I wanted to go home, take a long, hot soak in the tub, and start on the top novel in my To Be Read basket. That was my idea of bliss, but it sure wasn't going to happen now. Nor would I be making any progress on researching my latest idea for my own novel.

For as long as I can remember, I have been in love with books, which explains how I ended up working for a library. Even as a small child, I dreamed of the day when I would write my own. Lately, I have been less than satisfied with my progress in that direction, which could best be described as none. As I sat at my desk on a Friday night, staring at the pile of work I'd been assigned at the last minute, my frustration with my lot in life reached critical mass. I snarled. I ranted. I pouted. I even teared up pitifully, wailing the eternal cry of losers everywhere, "Why meeee?"

And then the truth dawned—a truth that should have been obvious years ago. Four words popped into my head. Four words that would change my life forever. I don't have to! I. Don't. Have. To.

Wow! A revelation. I didn't have to stay here. Didn't have to keep doing this mind-numbing, soul-sucking job. Didn't have to continue putting my own dreams on hold and living a life I had come to despise. No one was keeping me here. No one was even keeping me in this town. My mother died a few months after I was born, and my father had passed away two years ago, leaving me financially secure enough that I had a certain measure of freedom unavailable to many. I had even, conveniently enough, managed to get rid of my latest boyfriend last week, as Becky so kindly reminded me.

I had no strings to speak of. I could leave. And I knew exactly where I could go—the one place I loved more than anywhere in the world. Oh, man! It would be perfect. There, I could live a simple life surrounded by the beauty of nature, and the peace and quiet of the deep woods. I could write. I could write all day long, every day, if I wished, with no one to worry about but myself. I could quit marking time at a dead-end job, and live the life I was meant to live. I made up my mind on the spot. I would do it! I would move to Wake-Robin Ridge.

SATURDAY, JULY 23, 2011
DEBARY, FLORIDA

THREE WEEKS AFTER my grand epiphany, I walked out of the Leland Walker Historical Library for the last time. I was a free agent, embarking on a whole new life, and I was ecstatic about the changes I had already made. Everything was falling into place just the way I had hoped. My only problem was going to be telling my best friend, and I knew I had put that off long enough. Nervous, I waited for her to show up at the coffee shop. She was late as usual, but that was Jenna. I was so used to it, it didn't even bother me anymore. When I saw her car pull up to the curb outside, I smiled and waved, but my stomach did a little flip. This wasn't going to be easy.

Jenna Munroe had been my best friend since third grade. We pinky-swore eternal loyalty to each other when we were nine, and had pretty much lived by that promise every day since. We went through every one of Life's Big Moments together, from senior prom to college graduation. From my first real job cataloging new books at a small local library to Jenna's lavish wedding. She was there to celebrate every promotion I received, and I was there to lend a hand after the birth of each of her two children. Forever friends. Somehow, it worked, though we were exact opposites in every way. Where she was tiny and blonde, I was tall and brunette. Where she was outgoing and spontaneous, I was far more reserved and thoughtful. Still, we had always been inseparable. Until now.

"North Carolina? Are you crazy?" Jenna's mouth was agape, and she was trying her best to believe I was making a bad joke.

"Umm, perhaps?" I said, afraid to add more until she stopped gasping in shock.

"But why, Sarah? Why would anyone leave Florida for some backwoods cabin in North Carolina? Do you know how far those mountains are from the beach?"

"Yep. And do you know exactly how many days I've spent on the beach in the last two years? If you guess 'None,' you win the prize!"

I was trying to inject a little humor. Judging from the expression on Jenna's face, my efforts were in vain. My guess that this announcement wouldn't go well was right on target.

"But how can you leave the ocean, the walks on the beach collecting shells, the sunshine, the semi-naked Gods of beach volleyball?"

I gave her the single raised eyebrow. The eyebrow almost always worked to lighten the mood. "I think you have me confused with you, Jenna. I don't swim in any body of water that isn't enclosed in turquoise concrete. I collect books, not shells. I get skin problems if I even so much as look at the sun. And I don't give a hoot for ogling those semi-naked Gods of beach volleyball."

She stared.

"Okay, okay, I'll give you that one. But it's not enough."

"Enough for what, for God's sake?" It was obvious the eyebrow and my lame attempts at humor had failed. Her voice went up two octaves, and I think she began hyperventilating a bit. Definitely not good.

I tried to answer in a way that would make sense to her, "Not enough for me. I need more. I need something *else*. Something that's not happening here. Maybe just a change of scenery, or cooler weather, or an autumn you recognize by the color of the leaves, instead of the growing numbers of visitors to Disney World. My life isn't moving forward. I'm not happy, Jenna."

"I don't know. I mean, I knew you didn't like your job any more, but moving to North Carolina by yourself seems pretty drastic, Sarah. Do you think living alone on a mountainside will make you happy?"

"I don't know, either," I said, sighing. "Maybe. Maybe I just need to regroup and find myself. Aw, don't give me the patented Jenna Munroe Eye Roll. I know it sounds lame. But honestly, I do feel lost. I feel directionless. I feel like if I sit in that freakin' cubicle at work and catalog one more stinkin' manuscript, my head will explode! What about all the writing I wanted to do? What about *my* books? I want to go someplace quiet that inspires me. I want to find that girl who graduated college ready to write The Great American Novel."

She went for the low blow, a sure sign she was getting frustrated. "I hate to break this to you, but you aren't that girl any more. You are a thirty-five-year-old woman!"

I was beginning to get frustrated, myself, but I kept my voice level, hoping to sound calm. "Okay, then I want to see if I can be that *woman* who writes The Great American Novel."

"But what about us? Oh, my God, Sarah! We've been friends since third grade. You were my maid of honor. Howie and the kids think you actually are part of the family. What about our friendship, Sarah?"

"Hey, I'm not going to be cut off from the world, you know. This isn't Walden's Pond." Putting my arm around her slender shoulders, I gave her what I hoped was an encouraging hug. "I'll still have access to postal service, and cell phones, and that thing called the Internet. You remember it. Email? Facebook? Skype? I know I won't be having Sunday dinners with you very often, and that will be tough, believe me. But I'll be back for visits, I swear. It's less than two hours away by plane. And I promise to stay in touch. Daily, if it makes you feel better."

The shocking truth began to dawn in her eyes. "So it's a done deal?"

I nodded. "Pretty much. Closed on the cabin last week."

Jenna made a choking sound. "You closed on a cabin already? When did you go up there?"

"I didn't. Oh, Jenna, it all came together so perfectly for me! You wouldn't believe how well it worked out! I took a virtual tour of the cabin online, made all the arrangements via telephone and email, and it's mine now. I feel like I know every square inch of it, and I'm in love with it already. Jenna, there's a stream on the property! A real, burbling, gurgling, water rushing over rocks and boulders, honest-to-God stream! And trees. And a garden. A bit neglected, but it's still there, waiting for me. And the whole thing is surrounded by woods, with deer, and raccoons, and ... " I stopped. Jenna looked stricken, her big blue eyes filled with tears.

"Oh, my God. You're really going. You're moving to the far side of beyond, clear out to some godforsaken, backwoods cabin, and leaving me here. I can't even think what I'll do without you!"

"Well, I don't know about that godforsaken bit. Wake-Robin Ridge has always looked like a piece of heaven to me. But yes, Jenna. I'm moving, and I'm nervous about it, too. I hope you can be happy for me."

She burst into tears and, wailing, flung herself into my arms. So of course, having been her best friend for almost all of my life, I did what any best friend would do. I burst into tears, too.

MONDAY, AUGUST 1, 2011
DEBARY, FLORIDA
JENNA WAS CRYING again. I knew she would be, but I had to give her credit for trying to make it as inconspicuous

as possible. She had a brave smile plastered on her face, and it broke my heart to see how much she wanted me to stay, but everything was in place. My cabin awaited me with electricity turned on, phone and wireless connected, some basic groceries in the fridge, and firewood outside the back door. *Thank you, thank you, Realtor John Inman in Asheville!* All I had to do was get in my car, head north, and walk in the front door to spend my first night in my new home. Assuming, of course, that I could disentangle myself from all the well-wishers assembled on the sidewalk outside my now-empty apartment.

"Are you sure everything is ready for you? Did they send you a key?" Jenna was still fretting over the possibility of me arriving at my cabin in the dark of night.

"Yes and yes," I reassured her. "My realtor took care of getting it all set up for me. I don't even have to unpack until tomorrow. Got an overnight bag with toothbrush and jammies ready to go."

"And we know for a fact the power is on?" Asked one of my former co-workers.

"Yep. Honestly, everybody, I can't think of a thing that hasn't been covered. The realtor's been doing this for a long time, and I have every reason to think he's good at his job. Please don't worry about me. I promise I'll call Jenna as soon as I arrive, and she can update you all!"

More hugs. More pats on the back. More well-wishing and declarations of how much I'd be missed. This was worse than when I left for college as an innocent eighteen-year-old who'd never been away from home.

"Thank you all so much for this send-off. It's so sweet of you, and I will miss every one of you more than you know! I promise I will remember you forever and ever and come see you when I can, and you'll all be mentioned in the foreword of my first book."

Lots of laughing. Even more hugs. And more tears from Jenna.

Giving her one last, huge hug, I whispered into her ear, "I'm going to miss you more than you know."

Jenna replied through her tears, "Just remember, my home will always be your home, if you change your mind."

And with that, I climbed into my brand new, over-packed Jeep, set the GPS for "Deserted Mountainside," and, with a wave, drove off, blowing my horn all the way to the end of the block.

Twelve hours later, shortly after night had stolen the last rays of the sun, I pulled off the two-lane roadway into a narrow break between the tall trees, and drove slowly down a curvy stretch of heavily wooded drive, into a dark clearing. The moon wasn't up yet, but my headlights shone on a small but homey looking cabin with a broad front porch, complete with two rocking chairs on each side of the door. I followed the drive to the turn-around in front of the cabin, where I cut the engine. Rolling down my window, I sat for a moment, transfixed by the thought that I was going to be living in such a place.

A nocturnal concert filled the summer darkness. Insects whirred and chirped, and frogs called from the stream which ran across the back of the property. No traffic sounds rushing by on the country highway, though. No radios blaring or babies crying from neighbors living too close. Just the peaceful sounds of an August evening in the Blue Ridge Mountains. I felt the tension of the long drive ease out of my shoulders, and knew I should get my things and go inside, but I was caught in the spell of the night magic, and the knowledge that I was surrounded by nothing but deep woods on all sides.

Out of nowhere, an eerie but beloved sound came from a tree close to the cabin—a barred owl calling, *"Who cooks for you? Who cooks for YOU-all?"*

I smiled, pretending that the one from the oak tree outside my window in Florida had followed me all the way to North Carolina, just to welcome me to my new home.

Grabbing my overnight bag, I got out of the Jeep and went up the front steps. As I slid my key into the lock, I was conscious of the fact that once I crossed the threshold, it would be official. My new life would begin. A shiver of anticipation slid down my spine. Who knew what the days ahead might bring? I pushed any last minute doubts out of my mind, unlocked the door, flipped on the light, and stepped inside.

Chapter 2

You Aren't Such a Genius After All

BLAST FURNACE HEAT made the asphalt parking lot sticky and almost too hot to walk across. By the time Ruthie reached Lloyd's red Chevy Impala, sweat was running between her breasts and causing her sleeveless white blouse to stick to her back. She loaded the bags of groceries into the car, and glanced at her watch. Nearly 6:00 P.M.

Oh, God, I'm so late! She felt a familiar sinking sensation in the pit of her stomach. *Lloyd's gonna let me have it when I get home.*

Her palms were sweating, leaving damp marks on the steering wheel as she pulled the car out of the parking place and drove away. She cursed the store's long lines and slow cashiers, who meant the difference in whether or not she could get home in time to prevent a major blow up. In recent weeks, Lloyd's temper raged out of control over the smallest things. She could do nothing right, and she paid dearly for every perceived mistake.

Do other women live like this? Am I the only one who's scared to go home after pickin' up the groceries? God, I've screwed up my life so bad.

Ruthie Jane Winn was born in 1932, in the cotton belt of southern Georgia. As the only child of five to survive beyond early childhood, Ruthie had learned to expect nothing from this life but hard work, frequent hunger, and a backhand for anyone who complained about either. By age seventeen, she had grown into a pretty, but not particularly ambitious, young girl, who was easy prey for any of the fast-talking, but going-nowhere men hanging out at the local roadhouse. After a year of looking for love, or even the occasional tender word, any vague thoughts of a happy ending for herself had vanished, and a tired sense of resignation had settled over her.

Still, Ruthie had walked down to the roadhouse most evenings, though her illusions of romance had long disappeared. When Lloyd Carter, a mean-eyed slab of a man with a well-earned reputation for violence and several run-ins with the law, showed up at the bar one night, he took a look at Ruthie's pale, blonde hair and sweet smile, and found something he liked. Maybe she just seemed biddable, a quality a man like Lloyd highly approved of in his women. He soon made sure everyone knew she was his, off-limits to anyone else, and Ruthie figured it was better to belong to someone than to be alone. Lloyd was a chance for something different to happen, and different sounded good. In 1950, just days after her 18th birthday, the pair eloped, and Ruthie went unresisting into a marriage that would bring her nothing but years of physical and emotional abuse.

Twelve years and many small southern towns later, Ruthie was still unresisting, but along the way, she had learned a few coping skills. Following Lloyd's instructions to the letter was one of them. If he said, "Go get me some dinner and cigarettes, and make damn sure you're back here by 5:30," she understood exactly what the consequences would be if she failed to do precisely that.

Now she was almost thirty minutes late. Her hands shook, and her mouth was cotton dry. *He'll likely be sleepin' on the couch. I can get supper goin' before he wakes up, an' he won't even know I was late. Yeah, I bet he'll be sleepin'.* She kept repeating that over and over as she drove, a mantra, a charm to ward off the danger.

The neighborhoods got drearier and dustier as Ruthie neared the latest in a long string of cheap rentals they had called home, in the loosest sense of the word, for the past several years. Each place was dirtier and smaller than the one before. This latest sad little house stank of sweat, and dog pee, and other things it didn't do to think about. Her heart began to race as she approached the rutted driveway that cut through the small dirt yard. It was ten minutes after six.

Please, please let him be asleep.

She pulled the Impala into the yard and parked it in the shade of an ancient pecan tree. She was very careful to put it right where Lloyd always did, out of the broiling sun that he feared would ruin the paint job. If there was one thing Lloyd Carter loved in this life, it was his big, fire-engine red Impala, and she knew he would check every inch of it later, to be sure it hadn't acquired a single scratch while she was out.

Grabbing the groceries, she climbed out of the car, closing the door as silently as possible. She took a deep breath, quietly opened the sagging screen door, and walked across the dim, sweltering living room, toward the tiny kitchen. She never saw the blow coming.

"Bitch!" Lloyd's fist slammed into the middle of her back.

With a harsh cry, Ruthie fell to the floor, skinning both knees, and dropping the bags. Food spilled everywhere. Trying to avoid another blow, she scooted out of range, nauseated by the combination of pain and the smell of rancid sweat and whiskey coming off Lloyd in waves. She began a rapid string of breathless excuses, hoping he wouldn't hit her again.

"I'm sorry, honey, it wasn't my fault. It's Friday, an' them lines were long, an' everyone was gettin' their checks cashed, an' ...."

"Shut your mouth before I shut it for you!" Lloyd's words were slurred but he was steady on his feet, and deadly in his intensity. "Damn stupid cow! When I tell you to be back by 5:30, that's what I mean! I've been sitting here waiting for my beer and dinner, while you're out draggin' your sorry ass around. I'm sick and tired of this crap. Clean this mess up, and get my food ready. I got things to do tonight, an' they damn sure don't include hangin' around here all evenin', lookin' at you!"

Ruthie started scrabbling around for loose potatoes and the package of ground beef, thinking maybe the worst was over.

If I feed him, he'll go. Maybe stay out all night.

She was praying to herself as she gathered up the groceries, then she froze. Where were his cigarettes?

Oh, my God! I left his cigarettes in the basket! Ohmygod, Ohmygod!

As if he could read her mind, Lloyd asked, "Where's my Camels?"

Ruthie stared at the floor. Dread spread through her limbs, turning them to stone.

"Ruthie?" Lloyd spoke very softly, always a bad sign. "You didn't forget my cigarettes did you, Ruthie? Because you know the rules for not bringin' me what I ask for, doncha? How many times we gotta go through this? Rules is rules, Ruthie."

He dragged her name out in a menacing sing-song voice, laughing mean and low. "Ruuuthie ... Ruuuuuthie?"

She felt the sting of desperate tears, and she raised her eyes to him, begging now. "Please, Lloyd? Please? I'll go back an' get 'em, honey. Please don't hurt me!"

Without a single word, Lloyd stepped closer, drawing back his right foot. Ruthie immediately curled into a tight ball, with her arms over her head, screaming as she realized just how much danger she was in. The last thing she saw was Lloyd's size eleven boot coming straight for her.

EVERYTHING IS BLACK at first, then she becomes aware of a soft voice. "Ruthie? Ruthie? Wake up, hon. Ruthie, can you hear me?"

Someone lifts her head, slightly. Something cool touches her face. It hurts. Oh, God. Everything hurts so bad. She tries to open her eyes, but they aren't working right. There's a strange, mewling sound filling her head. Blackness rushes in again.

More voices seep into her mind. Lloyd is shouting, and she cringes, gasping and whimpering. She tries to say she's going to be sick, but the words don't remember how to get out of her mouth. Her side is a flame of agony as she vomits. Dimly, she thinks this should be embarrassing, but she can't remember why. Again, someone wipes her face with something cool.

Time vanishes for a while, then pain pulls her back into the present. She manages to open one eye. The other seems to be glued shut. She's lying with her head in someone's lap, while a man she vaguely recognizes is talking to a policeman.

"He was gonna kill her, I'm tellin' you," the man is saying. The policeman looks her way, then takes the man by the arm and asks him to step outside.

"She's awake," the policeman explains. "She doesn't need to hear this right now."

Ruthie wonders who "she" is, then realizes they are talking about her. She wants to know what has happened, why she's on the floor, but her throat is sore, and talking seems too much of an effort.

Betty. That's who's holding her. Betty's nice, she remembers. She lives next door. It's Betty's husband who's talking to the policeman, she thinks. This is bad. She can't remember why, but she knows it is.

"Ruthie, can you hear me?" Asks Betty.

Faintly, faintly, she hears her own voice whisper, "Yes."

"Honey, the police have arrested Lloyd. We called them when we heard you screaming. Hollis tried to make him stop, but he couldn't get him off of you. He just wouldn't quit, until the police dragged him outside, and even then, he kept on fightin' every step of the way. It was like he'd gone plum crazy. He just kept screamin', 'Where's my Camels?' over and over. 'Where's my damn Camels?' He was just plain crazy, Ruthie."

Betty sounds like she's going to cry. Ruthie moves her head slightly, trying to focus her good eye. She feels a stabbing pain, and a trickle of warmth runs down her cheek.

"Oh, honey, don't move. Please don't move," Betty begged. "There's some people comin' to take care of you. Just lie still now. It's all gonna be okay, sugar."

Ruthie sighs as the darkness comes pouring back over her. The last thing she hears is Betty's tearful voice asking, "Where the hell is that ambulance?"

THAT WAS THE last time Lloyd Ellis Carter ever hit his wife. He was held in jail without bail, awaiting trial for a long list of charges, including assault with intent to kill, resisting arrest, and assaulting an officer of the law. The word around the neighborhood was, when his case came to trial, and the jury got a look at the battered and scarred face of his wife, they'd likely lock him up and throw away the key. And that wasn't even taking into account the considerable damage he did to the arresting officers, before they disarmed him. Lloyd had a wicked way with a knife, especially when he was drinking, and both officers would bear scars for the rest of their lives.

"Yep," folks said. "He's going away for a long, long time."

What "folks" didn't know, however, was that Ruthie had no intention of testifying at Lloyd's trial. Maybe he would still be put away for a long time based on the testimonies of the two policemen who had saved her life, and maybe not, but she was not going to be around to find out. First, she never wanted to lay eyes on Lloyd Carter again. But even more importantly, she didn't trust the legal system to put him away for long enough to keep her safe, whether she testified or not. She knew that he would find some way to get out early—he was very good at manipulating things to his own advantage—and when he did, she also knew he would come looking for vengeance. Ruthie intended to be long gone.

She lay in that hospital bed for nearly a week, ribs bound, face bandaged, fingers on one hand broken and swollen. She lay there in pain, and she plotted. When she finally saw her damaged face, a hard, bright anger grew inside her, pushing the fear she had lived with for twelve years into a dark corner of her mind. Her focus sharpened by anger, she concentrated on what her next move should be.

One thing I know for sure. I'll never let Lloyd Carter hit me again! No matter what I have to do, I will take my life back and live it the way I want. He's not gonna hurt me again.

When she was released from the hospital, and went back to that grimy little rental, the first thing Ruthie did was pack up Lloyd's big red Impala with every bit of clothing she owned, plus every other item in the house she could squeeze into it.

I almost wish I could be around to see his face when he finds out I'm gone, and that I'm not as dumb and blind as he thinks I am.

Ruthie had kept her eyes and ears open as the years had gone by, and Lloyd's secrets were not as safe as he had always imagined. Now was her chance, and she intended to make the best of it, certain it would be the only one she ever got. Going from room to room, she began to search.

She looked in the backs of the closets, through Lloyd's dresser drawers, behind the refrigerator, in the tiny freezer compartment, and in all the hiding places Lloyd liked to use to keep his spending money safe. Finally, she pulled the bed away from the wall, and started checking the baseboard and flooring. She knew at once she had found what she had been looking for—a loose piece of baseboard. In grim determination, she pried it away from the wall one-handed, holding her injured arm to her chest to protect her broken fingers. Behind it was a hole four inches high and two feet long, cut through the wallboard. Resting side by side in that hole were three cloth-wrapped bundles, tied with twine. Ruth smiled. She had found the money Lloyd had been hoarding for years.

Ha! You aren't such a genius, after all, are you, you stupid ass? Let's see just how much we've got in here.

She sat down on the bed, untied the bundles of money, and began counting. Five minutes later, Ruthie sat dumbfounded. After counting the money twice, she knew she wasn't mistaken. There was a total of seventy-five thousand dollars spread out in front of her. Thirty-seven smaller bundles, each containing twenty $100 bills, and one made up of fifties and twenties adding up to another thousand.

Seventy-five thousand dollars! Oh, my God, Lloyd! What did you do?

Ruthie knew she had found a fortune. Seventy-five thousand dollars was enough for her to live on for at least ten years. Maybe fifteen, if she was careful, and if there was one thing Lloyd had taught her, it was how to be careful with his money.

She felt light-headed. She had never imagined seeing that much money in her entire life, much less holding it in her hand all at once. She thought about how they had lived for years, from hand to mouth, on the run, eating ground beef and canned beans. No new dresses. Shoes worn down to nothing before being replaced. And Lloyd blaming her all the while, as if she were spending the little dab of household money he gave her in frivolous, silly ways. The more she thought, the angrier she became. She had no idea where he had gotten that much money, or why he preferred living in near-poverty to spending some of it.

He could have made our lives so much easier! What was he thinking?

She couldn't imagine, but she didn't care anymore, either. Ruthie knew exactly what she was going to do with the money, and that's all that mattered to her. She laid out the packets of bills in a layer across the bottom of her battered suitcase, placed her folded clothes over the top, then closed and locked it. She put the key in her wallet for safekeeping. That money was going to change her life forever, and she was taking no chances on losing it.

This is how I get out of this miserable life and away from that bastard, and I know just where I'm gonna go — a place where I can disappear, and if I'm lucky, Lloyd will never find me. Then I'll be free!

She thought back to one October, a few years into their marriage, when she and Lloyd had been on the run from an angry partner in another of Lloyd's get-rich-quick schemes. They had swung a bit farther north than usual, and ended up in the southern part of the Appalachians, just below Asheville, North Carolina. Lloyd had been in an expansive mood, congratulating himself on scoring $5,000 and getting out of town before his partner-in-crime could come after him. He figured it was time they took a short vacation anyway, and, uncharacteristically, he was in the mood to spend some of his profits. They spent three beautiful fall days driving along the Blue Ridge Parkway, stopping here and there in little towns where the barbecue was good, and the cold beer even better. It was the closest thing to fun they had ever had.

Ruthie had been enchanted by the wide, scenic vistas and the friendly little towns, awash in flaming reds and golds. Never in her sad life had she seen anything as beautiful as those mountains in autumn. She wished the trip would never end. Lloyd, on the other hand, had gotten restless and mean-tempered once more, and antsy to make another score. He circled back around south into Georgia again, and Ruth's life returned to the same grim existence it had been for years.

In her deepest heart, down in the part Lloyd hadn't belittled and demeaned and beaten to death over time, Ruthie had cherished the memory of that trip, and had clung to the idea that someday she would find a way to live in those hills. Providence had put the means right in her hands. When she finished packing up the Impala, she stashed her suitcase full of money in the trunk, and headed north, toward the Blue Ridge Mountains. She never even noticed the dirty gray car that pulled away from the curb two blocks behind her.

Chapter 3
At Least I Think the Dog Liked Me

"THERE," I SAID, stepping back to admire my work. "Now that's more like it!" The last box of books was empty, and every volume had found a home on the built-in shelves along the back wall of my living room. It was a tight squeeze, but I had been determined to bring all of my treasured collection with me, from _Age of Innocence_ to _Zero Hour_. Just seeing them displayed against the mellow warmth of the wooden shelves made my heart happy.

It seemed everything about my new home was making my heart happy, in fact. I found myself wearing a foolish grin pretty much all the time, ever since I arrived on Monday night. Settling in had not been the chore I thought it would be. Unpacking my dishes and clothing, and finding places to hang my few pieces of art, had all been labors of love. Even rearranging the plain but comfortable furniture that came with the cabin had been a satisfying task. I don't believe I had ever felt so at home anywhere in my life. Everything about my cabin and my property seemed to welcome me, as though it had been waiting for my arrival as eagerly as I had been waiting to get here. But nothing made me feel at home as much as seeing my precious books marching across the shelves in neat and orderly rows.

I don't know who I inherited my love of books and writing from. It wasn't from my dad, that's for sure. His medical career had never left him with much free time, and though he did write articles for various journals over the years, I don't think I ever saw him reading a book for pleasure. I guess we arrive in this world carrying at least a few traits that are ours alone.

I lugged the empty boxes out to the front porch to be disposed of later, and decided I had earned a break. Fixing a cup of my favorite Earl Grey tea, I walked out my back door, and began a stroll around my property. It was pretty early yet, and the morning was surprisingly cool, at least by the standards of someone who knew what August in central Florida felt like. Walking down to the edge of the creek, I stopped in the deep green shade of a redbud tree, watching the way the rush of water slowed as it poured into one of the deeper pools. I wondered if there might be trout hiding in there, and for one, insane minute I pictured myself fishing for my dinner. Then I came back to reality.

As if, Sarah! It's all you can do to swat a fly. You'd feel sorry for the fish and turn it loose, apologizing for interrupting its day.

I laughed at my foolishness, and continued to walk around the yard, taking note of how high the late summer grasses were. Might have to get a riding mower to handle the yard. And then there was all the overgrowth along the edge of the creek. Kudzu vines and wild blackberries had run amok. I'd definitely have to hire someone to clear that out at some point. But other than that, it was all perfect, with slow, sleepy bees bumbling among the wildflowers, and the sound of birdsong coming from the woods.

The online photos hadn't lied. The cabin was lovely in its comfortable, solid simplicity, and the yard and garden, with its big, tilled beds, offered a chance to let my famous green thumb run wild. Well, okay, I didn't really have a famous green thumb, having never owned a house with a garden, but I had always loved plants, and on this morning, I felt sure I could develop a garden that would be celebrated far and wide. Visions of sunflowers and roses, carrots and cabbages, and luscious pink and blue hydrangeas danced in my head.

Oh, I felt very lucky, all right. And filled with an optimism I hadn't felt in ten years of cataloging endless mountains of manuscripts and dusty documents. But no more of that for me. Now, I was free to unleash the writer's spirit I was sure had been caged deep within me all this time.

I'm going to put pen to paper—or fingertips to computer keys—and words are going to pour forth. I will send them out into the world to multiply, and become books. My words will be erudite, yet pithy. Evocative, but always grounded. Poetry presented as prose. Or maybe it would be prose presented as poetry. Heck, why not both? Who's to stop me?

I was positively giddy, and I found myself laughing out loud yet again with the sheer joy of it all. Anything was possible, and life was good. Better than good, it was downright perfect.

Deciding I had giggled over my good fortune long enough, I ordered myself back to work. I still had my writing table to set up, and a couple of things to store in the small attic. Taking a last deep breath of delicious mountain air, I was turning to head back to the cabin when I felt, more than saw, a movement in the woods to my left. I held my breath, expecting to see a deer come out of the trees and move off toward the creek that runs along the western border of my land. Instead, a shaggy gray-black creature roughly the size of a horse stepped quietly out of my woods, not twenty feet away, and stood staring at me with brilliant amber eyes.

For a moment, my mind screamed, *"Wolf! Run!"* But before my feet could act on that directive, the animal began to move sedately in my direction, tail wagging slowly.

Almost simultaneously, a voice called from my driveway. "Don't be afraid! She won't hurt you."

Tearing my eyes away from what had to be the biggest freakin' dog on the planet, I saw a man—a really good-looking man—running toward me, empty leash and collar dangling from one hand.

He called to the dog. "Rosheen! Come here, girl!"

She walked a few, slow steps in his direction, then looked back over her shoulder and decided to approach me, instead. Before her owner was halfway across the yard, Rosheen and I were standing nose to nose, for a long moment of species-to-species contemplation. Then the dog, an Irish wolfhound, proceeded to give me a very solemn, but thorough examination, soft breath huffing, as she checked me from head to toe. Apparently satisfied that I was Friend rather than Foe, the scruffy creature sat down by my feet to await the approach of her owner.

He was panting as he neared, and I wondered how long he had been chasing his dog. "She slipped her lead, and was off before I could stop her."

Shaking his head, he continued. "I wasn't expecting her to come this way. She must have figured out that someone was living here now. I know she looks huge and dangerous, but she's really very gentle. You weren't in any danger."

I smiled, wanting to relieve his worries. "It's all right. Honestly. Once I realized it was just a big dog and not a ravenous wolf, I wasn't really scared. Just startled."

He raised an eyebrow in surprise, then bent down without comment to slip Rosheen's collar back over her head, and make sure it was secure. His breathing sounded more normal, for which I was grateful. At least he wasn't likely to collapse in my yard.

"Well, you're braver than most, then," he said, with what might have been a very small smile. It was hard to tell, since he kept his head tilted toward Rosheen while talking. "She's been known to cause strong men to scream like little girls." He scratched her head gently and with obvious affection.

I laughed, and stuck out my hand. "I'm Sarah Gray. I just moved in Monday night, actually. Are you my neighbor from across the road? I've seen the drive heading up the hill, but I didn't know if anyone lived up there or not."

He paused a moment before raising his eyes to mine, then slowly extended his hand. "Yes. I'm MacKenzie Cole," he said in a serious voice, laced with just a hint of old south. "My house is about half a mile up. You can't see it from the road. I heard rumors that someone had bought this place, but I didn't realize anyone had moved in yet."

He glanced away from me, toward my cabin, with a slight frown on his face. I took stock, while he was looking things over. Tall, maybe 6'3", with glossy black hair curling slightly over his ears. Equally dark brows over unusually pale blue eyes, and very fair skin. Overall, he was strikingly good looking, with a sense of quiet strength about him. In his faded jeans and soft blue denim shirt, he looked perfectly at home in these mountains, as though he had been here a long time. He turned back toward me again, and I looked away, embarrassed to be caught staring.

"I'm just getting settled in," I found myself blurting to cover the awkward moment. "Haven't even finished unpacking yet, really. I mean, the place is still a mess, but if you'd like a cup of coffee, I can offer you that much?" As invitations go, it was a bit lame, even to my own ears. He must have thought so, too.

"No, thank you." He paused, still not looking directly at me, then added with an almost formal politeness, "Nice meeting you. Enjoy your new home."

Well. So much for making friends with the neighbors. Way to go, Sarah.

"Another time, then," I replied, feeling somewhat rebuffed. I gave the wolfhound a pat on the head. "Goodbye, Rosheen. Pleasure making your acquaintance. Don't be a stranger, girl."

Rosheen gave my hand a lick, and MacKenzie Cole smiled a goodbye in my general direction, then without another word, turned and headed back the way he had come, big dog in tow. Halfway down my drive, he glanced back over his shoulder, and seeing me still watching, gave a small nod and disappeared around the curve.

All righty, then. At least I think the dog liked me.

BY FOUR O'CLOCK that afternoon, my work station was set up on my small dining room table, and I had already checked in with Jenna to let her know I was settling in just fine. When I told her I had met my nearest neighbor, and he was a very good-looking man, somewhere around my age, she waggled her eyebrows suggestively and made kissy faces at me.

"Forget it, Jenna. I don't think you need to be concocting romantic scenarios with this guy in mind," I said. "He wasn't very friendly at all."

"Don't be ridiculous, Sarah! He was probably completely tongue-tied when he saw how gorgeous his new neighbor was. Next thing you know, he'll be coming around with flowers, and candy, and singing romantic songs under your window in the middle of the night."

Now I was the one making faces, but I laughed and promised to keep her updated on my "Mysterious Mountain Man," as she called him. She was still making those woo-woo eyes at me as I signed off. Skype is a wonderful thing.

I was rocking on the front porch, watching the day sail toward night, when I realized I was hearing faint sounds coming from beneath the floorboards. I stopped rocking for a moment and listened more closely, wondering if I was imagining things. Nope. There was definitely a scritching and rustling, and something that sounded like a faint crying. Getting up, I leaned over the porch railing and waited quietly for a minute, and then heard the crying noise again. I went inside to grab a flashlight, then went down the porch steps, and dropped to my knees. The crawl space under the cabin was black as night, and completely silent by then. I shone the light around for a minute, and was just about to give up when the beam caught the bright silvery-green gleam of two eyes in the darkness.

"Hello, there," I said. "Who are you?"

A very soft mew was my answer.

I ventured a tentative "Kitty, kitty," and the owner of the tiny voice began to creep forward from the inky darkness. Try as I might, saying sweet things did not lure the small cat much closer, so I knew it was time for the oldest trick in the world. Bribery. I went back into the house and returned with a saucer of milk which I pushed under the house as far as I could reach. Then I backed up a bit and waited. Soon, hunger won out over caution, and the dirtiest, raggediest little cat I ever saw came creeping up to lap delicately at my offering. A bit of soft talk and promises of ever so much more yummy milk finally lured the kitten within reach. I was surprised it didn't protest when I gently picked it up, and even more surprised to be rewarded by frantic purring as I cuddled it in my arms.

I've had several cats over the years, and since I currently had no one to share my cabin with, it seemed a stroke of happy good luck that this little waif had showed up.

"Obviously, we need each other," I said, continuing to stroke the kitten as I made my way up my steps. Judging by the accumulation of dirt, and the fact that I could feel its every rib, I was sure this was a pet that had been on his own for a while. Once I washed off all the mud and dirt, I discovered it was a young male, maybe four or five months old. His red and white tabby coloring proved to be very pretty.

"Look at you, Handsome Boy. I bet you'll fill out quite nicely."

For his part, Handsome figured he had found an easy touch, and he was happy to make himself at home in my cozy cabin. He ate some lunch meat, and drank a bit more milk, then proceeded to explore every inch of his new home, before settling down on the old afghan thrown across my sofa.

"Guess I'll be heading into town for some cat food and litter tomorrow," I told him.

Handsome purred.

"It's a good thing I moved in just in time to save your fuzzy backside, huh?"

Handsome purred.

"So that's how it is," I said, rubbing his head and scratching under his chin. "Not much for words, but big on rumbling, huh?"

Handsome purred some more.

It was only after I settled down in bed with my new friend curled up by my side that I began to wonder again about the abrupt behavior of my good-looking neighbor, or as Jenna called him, my Mysterious Mountain Man.

"Mysterious, possibly, but he's not *my* mountain man," I told Handsome. "No matter how much Jenna would like to play matchmaker!" Still, as I was drifting off to sleep, the last thing I remembered was the intensity of those pale, blue eyes watching me from under a tumble of very black hair.

Chapter 4
Trouble with a Capital T

SITTING ON HIS bedroom balcony, looking across the darkening valley, MacKenzie Cole watched as the rising moon bathed the treetops in a wash of silver. Rosheen, his three-year-old Irish wolfhound, sat by his side, leaning against his knee, and seemed to enjoy the transition from evening into night as much as he did.

"It's beautiful, isn't it, girl? Still seems as full of magic as it did when I was a boy."

He fondled Rosheen's ears, and was rewarded by the thump of her tail on the floor. Mac sighed, and the dog turned her head to give him a questioning glance. She was always attuned to his moods, often seeming to know what he was feeling before he did, himself. Tonight, he was decidedly edgy and off-center. His thoughts were a troubling whirl of emotions he did not want to deal with, and he found himself unable to focus on the things that normally brought him a sense of peace at the end of each day.

He tried deep, slow breaths, and letting his mind go blank. Trouble was, it wouldn't stay that way, but instead kept circling back around to what was bothering him. Somewhere in the woods, he heard the call of a whippoorwill, and, for a moment, was transported back to all the summers he had spent camping with his dad, here on this very spot. God, what he wouldn't give to be able to feel like that carefree boy again, when life was marshmallows toasted over the fire, and ghost stories all night long. Or afternoons spent swimming in the cold, deep pool at the foot of his favorite waterfall.

Why did people grow up and lose that sense of joy and wonder? How was it they started out so full of promise and ended up so full of pain?

Thank God he had his refuge now, away from everyone else. He didn't care if he ever left it again, especially on nights like this, when his thoughts would not let go of him.

"I don't know what's the matter with me tonight, Rosheen. You and I, we've got it pretty good up here, don't we? Maybe tomorrow morning, we'll get up early and go for a long walk ... get some exercise. Bet you'd like that, huh? And I could use a few hours away from my desk, too."

MacKenzie and his dog had lived on top of Wake-Robin Ridge for the last year, in a two-story house made of honey-colored logs and soaring walls of glass, and graced with one of the most beautiful views in North Carolina. He built his personal retreat on a twenty-acre piece of prime real estate that had been in his family since 1925. Fifteen years of hard work had made his dream house a reality, and by age 39, he owned a state-of-the-art computer research firm in downtown Charlotte, one of the state's busiest cities. Now, he could afford pretty much whatever he wanted, and what he had wanted most of all was to return to the mountains he had loved all his life, where he could live in peace and quiet, and as far away from the noise, and traffic, and crowds as he could get.

Standing abruptly, Mac stepped to the balcony railing, and leaned his elbows against it. He caught the familiar fragrance of green leaves and wild honeysuckle drifting by on the warm air, but even that failed to work its usual magic on him. After a few minutes, he sighed again, and sat back down in his chair, drumming his fingers on the wooden arm.

Shaking his head, he gave voice to his worries. "I don't feel good about this," he told Rosheen. "I don't feel good about it at all."

Rosheen cocked her head to one side, still focused on his voice.

"You liked her, though, didn't you, girl? Well, too bad, Big Dog. I don't need any complications in my life—even ones that look that good. Especially ones that look that good!"

And Mac had a feeling his new neighbor could end up being a very big complication, if he weren't careful.

There was something about the way she looked and sounded that tugged at him in a manner he hadn't felt in a very long time. Regardless, he was determined he would not let his hard won tranquility be disturbed. He had found a balance that seemed to work for him, and he planned to maintain it. Tonight, however, his restless mind would not leave him alone.

Sarah Gray. You are trouble with a capital T. Where did you come from, and why are you over there, all alone in that cabin? Couldn't you have chosen some other mountain? Why are you here on mine?

He swore under his breath, and got up again, pacing back and forth along the length of the balcony, annoyed with himself. *What difference does it make why she's there? She's no part of my life at all, and that's how it's going to stay!*

Rosheen stood up and paced back and forth, as well, keeping time with Mac's steps. He stopped to scratch her head, and reassured her that everything was fine, though he wasn't so sure about that, himself.

"Don't worry, girl. I'll figure it all out. In the meantime, no more running away, you hear?" He knew she wouldn't like it, but he decided he'd be much more diligent about keeping her on a leash. He did not need her running off to visit his new neighbor again.

Standing, he stretched his long, lean body, and turned his back on the scene below. "What do you say we call it a night? It's getting late, girl."

In bed, Mac tossed and turned for some time, still feeling restless and unsettled; and the last image that crossed his mind before sleep overtook him was that of a tall, slender woman with long, sable brown hair and green eyes, smiling as she held out her hand and said, "I'm Sarah Gray.

THURSDAY, AUGUST 18, 2011
ASHEVILLE, NORTH CAROLINA

BOOKS, BOOKS, AND more books! I was in heaven. The Pathfinder Bookshop was everything I hoped it would be—two stories of shelves and tables, overflowing with books of every kind. Newer best sellers were jammed up against leather-bound volumes from decades ago. Magazines and journals spilled out of boxes, and heaps of what appeared to be vintage diaries were stacked on a coffee table in front of a rump-sprung old sofa. I had the feeling that if you wanted to get down on your knees to explore the dusty bottom shelves, there was a good chance you might find real treasures hidden there.

I had read online that on Thursday evenings, local authors often stopped by the store to sign their latest releases, answer questions, and just talk writing in general. It had sounded like a fun way to meet other writers in the area, so I had made the forty-five minute drive to Asheville to check it out. I was a bit early for the night's guest, but keeping occupied as I waited was going to be very easy. Yep, here I was surrounded by books again, but this was nothing like working at the library. This was an adventure in discovery! I could see myself becoming a regular visitor here, expanding my own little collection with editions not easy to find elsewhere.

The gal behind the counter was friendly but not intrusive. I liked that. "There are a lot more upstairs," she said. "Take a look around and let me know if you have any questions."

I thanked her, and climbed the narrow stairs to the dim upper gallery. It was even better than the lower level. *Man, this place is gonna be dangerous! I'm gonna have to be really careful, or I could blow my budget for the whole month here, in one afternoon.*

I began making my way around the walls, inspecting random titles here and there. When I found myself at the front again, I sat down at a low table beside the balcony. I was paging through an ancient-looking volume of sonnets by Elizabeth Barrett Browning that I just might have to have. Lost in the romance of her beautiful poetry, I barely heard the bell over the front door jingle, but something made me glance below just in time to see my neighbor, MacKenzie

Cole, enter the shop. I was so surprised, I almost dropped poor Elizabeth's sonnets to the floor. I hadn't thought he looked the type to spend much time in dusty old bookstores, but apparently I was wrong.

As I watched, he stepped up to the counter and asked about tonight's guest. Hmm. So he knew about these events and was interested enough to stop by to check on one. Nice. A man who loves books can't be all bad, now can he? The clerk handed him what appeared to be a list of scheduled events, and he was looking it over as I came back down the stairs. He glanced up when he heard my approach, his eyes widening in recognition. To say he looked surprised would have been an understatement, though he tried to disguise his reaction with a polite, somewhat strained smile.

"Oh. Hello ... um ....?"

Ouch. Call me unforgettable. "Sarah," I said. "Hi. Are you here to see tonight's guest?"

He scratched the back of his neck, looking around the shop. "Well, I thought about it, but I ... uh ... see he won't be here until 7:00, and ... I can't stay that late. Rosheen will need to go out."

"Oh, that's too bad." I said, though I had gotten the distinct impression he'd been planning to stay. "This guy sounds like he might be interesting. Have you come before?"

He fiddled with the sheet of paper, glancing this way and that around the shop, before saying, "Yeah, I've stopped in now and then. It's usually worth the wait. You'll enjoy it, I'm sure."

Wow. Three sentences in a row. Progress.

He finally looked directly at me for a moment, and I was struck by the intensity of that pale blue gaze, but his eyes soon skittered off to the side again. He then spent a minute folding his piece of paper into a very small square, which he tucked into his shirt pocket. Clearing his throat, he made a visible effort to soldier on.

"So. Are you ... um ... getting settled in?" he asked, still looking everywhere but at me.

"Oh, yes. I love the cabin. Sometimes I can't believe my good fortune in finding such a beautiful place."

I couldn't remember ever being around a man so bad at making small talk. Or eye contact. He stared at his feet for a moment, then he gave me a sidelong glance and said, "That's good. I'm glad you're doing okay."

He seemed about to say something else, but instead, looked at his watch and frowned. "I really do need to get going now. Sorry to run. Nice seeing you, Sarah. Enjoy the program." And before I could respond, he was out the front door and moving down the sidewalk, hunched slightly forward, with his hands jammed in his pockets.

What the heck? That was just plain awkward.

I had never been as popular with guys as Jenna had always been, but this was the first time I had ever found myself unable to carry on a normal conversation with one. I wasn't sure what MacKenzie Cole's problem was, but in spite of the general weirdness of it all, I found myself torn between being a bit ticked off at his near-rudeness, and wishing I knew more about him.

You're just letting yourself be influenced by that pretty face, is all. Don't go there. The man has issues, girl. Singing songs under my window at night? Really, Jenna? Somehow I don't think so!

I paid for my book, and left, having lost interest in staying for the program. Maybe I'd just go home, curl up with some nice sonnets, and come back another evening.

SUNDAY, SEPTEMBER 4, 2011
CHIMNEY ROCK PARK, NORTH CAROLINA

MAC STOOD LEANING against a tree, tapping his foot and humming along with the group performing Alabama's "Mountain Music" under the tent. He had arrived a bit too late to find a seat, but liked his vantage point outside of the tent just fine. He had a clear view of the entertainers, and of the waterfall behind them, as well, and he was enjoying their mixture of country music, bluegrass, and Appalachian folk songs.

"Wow, that's a really big dog!" Mac turned to see a boy of nine or ten standing in the path, staring at Rosheen with goggled eyes. "Is she dangerous?"

"Only to the bad guys. Would you like to pet her?"

The boy hesitated, then slowly held his hand out. Rosheen sniffed his fingers, then gave them a lick. The boy laughed. "Cool!" He went on his way, stopping now and then to look back at Rosheen, as if to convince himself that he had really seen a dog as tall as he was.

Mac turned back to the performance, just as the first strains of "Aura Lee" began to rise on the warm air, spreading out like the fine mist over the pool at the base of Hickory Nut Falls. *Perfect music for this setting. I'm glad I decided to come by after all.*

As the last notes of the song died away, the lead musician wished everyone a happy Labor Day weekend, and made several announcements as to where they would be playing next. Mac watched as the audience came to their feet and began to disburse. He thought he would wait until everyone had left and then walk down to the rocks at the edge of the pool. He could relax there while the parking area cleared out a bit. People passed him on their way to their cars, laughing and talking, and singing bits of song from the program. Making his way toward the pool, he noticed one or two others had gone that way, as well. He was almost to the edge of the water when he saw her, staring up at the falls with a rapt expression on her face.

Turn around, Mac! Go now, before she sees you. Don't stop. Don't stare. Go!

But of course, he didn't. He both stopped and stared, rooted to the spot. There was just something about her that made interesting things happen inside of him. He didn't want to leave. He wanted to watch the breeze lifting her hair off her shoulders and blowing it around her face, and he liked the way the spray from the falls shone on her bare legs and dampened the edges of her shorts. There was no escaping it. She was beautiful.

Who cares? She's trouble, remember? Leave! Leave right this minute, you idiot!

At that precise moment, Sarah turned her head toward him, and did that damn thing she did every time he saw her. She smiled. And he was caught.

Oh, God. Here it comes. Another episode of her being perfectly nice and neighborly, and me being a tongue-tied jerk. She must think I'm a moron. Why do I even respond to her at all? Why don't I just turn my back and go?

He thought it. But he didn't do it. And Rosheen was no help at all, wagging her tail, and tugging on the leash.

"Hello, neighbor," Sarah said, picking her way across the slippery rocks to reach Rosheen. "Hi, girl. How you doin', big ol' dog?"

She smiled at Mac, all dimples and white teeth, and he realized he was smiling back, in spite of himself. "Hi, Sarah. Enjoy the music today?"

"I did! I'm so glad I came. This day couldn't possibly be any more beautiful, could it?"

He thought maybe not, but he was pretty sure he wasn't looking at the same thing she was. In spite of his intentions, her happy excitement threatened to get through to him. As they started back toward the parking lot, she chatted easily, while he made a valiant effort to maintain his defenses.

"Do you like Appalachian music, then?" She asked.

"I do."

"Me, too, but I'm not an expert. They played a nice selection, though, didn't they? Lots of variety."

"Yes."

With every step along the path, Mac became more aware of the chinks in his armor.

"Have you been here long?" Sarah asked.

"No, I was a bit late."

"I came early so I could climb up to the Chimney before the program," she said. "I haven't been there in years, but it's just like I remembered it. My father and I used to vacation around here every year, and drive the back roads. I thought Wake-Robin Ridge was the prettiest mountain of them all, and I still can't believe I found a cabin on it. How long have you lived up there?"

"Just a year."

"Oh. Somehow I figured you'd been there all your life."

"Only my summers."

"Well, I've really enjoyed being in the park today. They were playing the soundtrack from "The Last of the Mohicans" when I climbed the cliff trail earlier. I felt like I was Cora Munro, following Hawkeye up the mountain, trying to save Alice and Uncas."

"I haven't been up that trail in a long time, I'm afraid. It's nice. At least it is when there aren't so many tourists and visitors swarming all over everything."

The smile slipped off her face. "Oh. I didn't think about it like that. What can I say? I guess some of us just weren't lucky enough to have been born in this part of the country. I'm sorry if we spoil things for you."

"Oh, no. I didn't mean it that way! I just meant, well, sometimes it can be ...."

"It's okay. I get it. I do, really. Well, here's my car. It was nice seeing you again. Goodbye, Rosheen." She climbed into the car, shutting the door at once, but not before he saw that he had hurt her feelings, and that some of the joy was gone from her eyes.

Damn! Why can't I get this right? One minute, I can't complete a single sentence, and the next I say something downright mean. Why can't I have a five-minute conversation without things going totally down the toilet? Just neighbor to neighbor, that's all. What the hell is wrong with me?

He was halfway home before he admitted that his pleasure in the day had taken a hit, too. He sighed, shaking his head. Nothing good was going to come of Sarah moving into the cabin across the road, but he knew in his heart that was more his fault than hers.

MONDAY, SEPTEMBER 12, 2011
WAKE-ROBIN RIDGE, NORTH CAROLINA

DEAR SARAH, PLEASE accept my apologies for being rude to you last week. I spoke without thinking how my remarks were going to sound. It's not an uncommon thing with me, I'm afraid, which probably explains why I spend a lot of time alone. It was a beautiful day in an equally beautiful place, and you were right to be enjoying it.

Sincerely,

MacKenzie Cole

Points in his favor: He apologized. He sent a nice card, with a picture of Hickory Nut Falls on it. He included a hand-written note that sounded genuine and contrite. He didn't email.

Points against: He could have stopped by. Or called. Or just not been so abrupt to start with.

I read through the note for the third time, thinking about my handsome but enigmatic neighbor. I wondered what he did, living up there on top of the mountain like that, apparently by himself—unless you counted Rosheen. No one seemed to know. Yeah, I had made a few discreet inquiries here and there. Not even the gossipy girl at the local convenience store knew anything about MacKenzie Cole, except that he was "hot as hell, and always by himself," though she said she would be glad to rectify that last part. It seems he was always polite and friendly, though very reserved, giving away nothing about himself. I might as well not have asked. I had figured that out already, except for the friendly part, of course. With me, he was heavy on reserved, and a bit light on both polite and friendly.

Still, he had obviously felt guilty about our last meeting and had made an effort, from a distance, to make amends. That ought to count for something, but I guess anything more neighborly than that was out of the question. I sat the card on the mantle, fixed a glass of iced tea, and walked out onto my front porch. Handsome accompanied me, and jumped into my lap as soon as I sat down on my swing. I scratched his head and was rewarded by his usual ecstatic purring.

"What do you think, Handsome? Me, I have no idea what that man's problems are, and I suspect I'm not likely gonna find out, either. But that's fine. I've got a book to write. I don't need any men cluttering up my life right now, even if MacKenzie Cole would make some mighty fine looking clutter. A man that easy on the eyes? Makes you wonder why he's alone, doesn't it? But it's not my problem, and it's not going to be. No, really, boy. I mean it. It's not!"

Chapter 5
You Want A Piece of Me?

SATURDAY, OCTOBER 15, 2011

"OKAY, OKAY," I grumbled. "I'm fixing it as fast as I can, you know." Handsome didn't believe me for a minute. He continued swirling between my legs, rubbing up against me, crying like he was half-starved. I swear, he was a bottomless pit of ravenous hunger, even though he was filling out beautifully. His ribs no longer showed, and his coat was bright and shiny. He was as good-looking as his name implied. I set his bowl on the floor, and thought yet again how remarkable it was that a ball of fluff and meows like this pretty boy could be such pleasant company, especially as the nights began to grow longer. He kept my lap warm every evening while I read in front of the fire.

"Eat up, boy, and we'll go for a walk," I said.

He was the only cat I'd ever had who would stick to my side like glue, whether we were in the yard or taking a short hike through the woods behind my property. He'd follow along like a dog, stopping once in a while to bat at a leaf or check out an interesting beetle. Now and then, he would trot ahead a few feet to scout out the territory before us, but he always came right back, so I figured he liked being with me as much as I liked having him along.

Today was cool and crisp, and Handsome and I stopped to enjoy watching the mist rise off the warmer water of the creek. An early fall morning in the Blue Ridge Mountains has a special quality about it found nowhere else on earth. The air tastes of tart apples and frosted pumpkins, and it seeps into your heart, making you feel that all is right with the world, and you are blessed to be a part of it. I walked along the edge of the creek, admiring the vivid splashes of autumn color that seemed to drip off the trees and onto the shrubs below.

We crossed the small, arched bridge that spanned the creek, and continued down a narrow path winding its way north through the woods. The hush under the trees was deep and peaceful, broken only by bits of birdsong now and then, or the rustle of some small animal in the underbrush. Sometimes the path followed the course of the creek, and other times it swung west for a bit, heading deeper into the woods.

Handsome and I had been going on rambles along the path every couple of days, admiring the continual change of colors, and enjoying the burble of the creek. I often brought home bits and pieces found on our walks—abandoned bird nests, clusters of golden leaves clinging to slender twigs, or smooth, blue-gray stones from the stream. The mantle over my fireplace was filling up with quite an assortment of woodland treasures.

As the days passed, autumn spread like flames across the hills and along all the pathways and roadsides. The air took on an ever-sharper bite each morning, and skeins of honking geese flew overhead in loose, wavy V's. The bittersweet beauty of it made me want to cry at times, though I was never sure why. I wrote furiously, trying to commit every image and sound to paper, as though seeing the words neatly inscribed in the pages of my journal would somehow freeze these scarlet and gold moments forever. I consulted my field guides and studied the names of autumn wildflowers and migrating birds, learning more about these mountains every day.

Sometimes I added small sketches of things that particularly appealed to me. A Blue Jay drinking from a creek-side puddle, or a squirrel scolding Handsome from an overhead perch was fair game for my colored pencils. The October days were so full of tranquil beauty, I had put my writing aside for a while. I was content to let each hour unfold around me, living in the moment and loving it. Moving to Wake-Robin Ridge was the best decision I had ever made. For the first time in years, I was happy.

"SLOW DOWN, HANDSOME! Wait for me!" We had walked along the northbound path a bit farther than usual, perhaps an additional quarter of a mile or more, with my little cat darting ahead now and then to explore on his own.

After curving westward, the trail swung around to the east, until we arrived back at the stream again. It was wider here, filled with large slabs of jutting rock, glinting brightly in the sun. The water rushed by at a noisy pace, foaming and swirling against each stone surface in its mad sweep downstream. I sat on a flat, dry rock close to the edge, a few feet off the path. A damp, earthy smell rose from the mosses and lichens on the ground, and somewhere in the distance, a red-shouldered hawk called with a thin, keening sound.

Handsome began nosing around in the underbrush, leaving nothing but a tall poke of orange and white tail visible from where I sat.

Look at that boy! Such endless curiosity!

I pulled my pad and pencils out of the little backpack I wore. After a quick sketch of Handsome's upright tail, nearly hidden amid the browning ferns, I turned my attention to the creek. I was so absorbed in trying to capture the water's movement and the sparkling sunlight on the surface of the stream that I failed to realize we were no longer alone.

My breath caught as a loud bark disturbed my concentration. MacKenzie Cole was standing on the pathway, with Rosheen straining against her leash in my direction, wagging her tail in greeting. She barked again, but before anyone could say a word, there was a bloodcurdling yowl from the underbrush. Handsome flew out of the shrubs, puffed up to twice his normal size, and launched himself straight at Rosheen's head in a fury of hissing and spitting, just missing the dog's nose.

I was scrambling to my feet, sure that my cat was about to be the wolfhound's lunch, when MacKenzie gave a sharp snap of Rosheen's leash and uttered a quick command. She sat down at once, not moving an inch. Handsome, on the other hand, continued ricocheting around the clearing, hissing and growling, and arching his back to the sky. Eventually, he seemed to realize that he was the only one still making a commotion, and quieted down. He sidled stiff-legged up to Rosheen, and gave her a flat-eared, round-eyed glare that clearly asked, "You want a piece of me?"

Rosheen lowered herself to the ground, and with her great head resting on her front paws, stared at Handsome in bemused silence. After a moment, Handsome gave up the fight, and sauntered off with his tail still held high. He displayed a nonchalant attitude that indicated he had put the dog in her place, and the affair was over, but only because he said so.

MacKenzie and I had watched the whole thirty-second outburst in astonished silence. We looked at each other and burst out laughing at the same time, and just like that, the awkwardness between us seemed to disappear.

"Well, that was exciting," I said.

He was still chuckling as he and Rosheen walked over to the edge of the stream. Dropping down under a tree, he leaned his back against the rough bark, and crossed his long legs in front of him. Rosheen stretched out by his side, and I sat back down on my rock, facing him.

"Quite a production," he said, eyes twinkling with amusement. "Who's your reckless little friend?" He nodded toward my cat, who was now studiously ignoring us all, while he washed imaginary dirt from his face.

"That would be Handsome," I said, grinning. "I found him under my cabin the afternoon Rosheen came to meet me. He was a muddy, half-starved little mess, but he's doing fine now. He's pretty good company, too. Especially in the evenings."

His face clouded then, a hint of embarrassment in his eyes. He studied me for a moment before asking, "Is everything going okay? I mean, with getting settled in and all?"

"Yes, thanks." I wondered why his smile had disappeared. It was such a nice one, I found myself hoping to see more of it.

He looked out over the creek for a moment, then turned back to me with a resigned sigh. "I haven't been very neighborly, have I? I'm sorry. I should have come by to check on you, or see if you needed help with anything." He glanced down at Rosheen, and ruffled her ears while he talked.

"Well, Mr. MacKenzie Cole, I've been living alone for years now, and I'm pretty good at taking care of myself. I don't really need checking up on, you know." I wasn't sure how I should take his comment. Was he one of those men who thought a woman living by herself needed help hanging pictures, fixing the washing machine, or cutting the grass?

"Oh, no! I'm sorry," he stammered, face turning red. "I didn't mean for that to sound like you were helpless. I just meant ... I didn't ... I hadn't really welcomed you, or ... anything." He trailed off, shook his head, and started to stand.

"Oh, for goodness sake! You don't have to leave. I'm not insulted by your offer or anything. I just don't want you to think you have to be keeping an eye on me. Just because we're neighbors doesn't mean I'm your responsibility. Or that I expect anything from you."

For such a capable looking man, he was downright skittish, and once again, I wondered why.

"But thank you, anyway. It was a kind thought."

He leaned back against the tree again, the frown still creasing his brow. Rosheen laid her head in his lap with a contented doggy sigh, and Handsome sat a few feet away, keeping a wary eye on all of us, in case there were any more problems he might have to handle. I watched MacKenzie. The ball was in his court.

"We should start over, shouldn't we?" He asked, after a moment's thought. "I'd like to be a better neighbor. Not because you need me for anything. Just because it's the right way to be."

He was smiling as he spoke, but his eyes still looked concerned. "Neighbors should be friends, and my friends call me Mac."

That line could have sounded cheesy or artificial, but it didn't. There was something sincere about this man, in spite of his hesitant, and often downright awkward, behavior, and he was right. Neighbors should be friends.

"Okay," I said. "Mac, then."

We sat for a moment, just looking at each other in silence. His gaze seemed more contemplative than intrusive, but I was very much aware of him assessing me on some level, and I sensed those remarkable eyes probably didn't miss much. I assessed him right back. He was definitely worth a closer inspection.

Are we setting some kind of ground rules, here? Are we friends now?

Mac looked away first. I studied his profile, enjoying the way the dappled sunlight played across his dark hair. When he glanced back again, he smiled in an easier manner and nodded toward my drawing tablet.

"What were you sketching?"

I handed him the pad, and he seemed interested as he turned the pages, rather than merely polite. He read the detailed descriptions under several of my drawings, a thoughtful expression on his face, then handed it back to me. I waited to see what he would say.

Picking up a yellow-gold leaf, he turned it over and over in a bright spot of sunlight, that small furrow deepening between his brows.

Why's everything so serious with this guy? The most basic conversations seem to be a struggle for him.

"I can tell you enjoy the woods," he said at last, meeting my eyes again. His head was tilted to one side, dark hair falling in a careless tumble over his brow.

"I do," I told him. "'I went to the woods because I wished to live deliberately.'"

He smiled in recognition. "Thoreau," he said.

Okay, I admit it was a bit of a test. I was surprised at how pleased I was that he knew the quote.

"You're a scholar, then?" He asked. He was still meeting my eyes, and the smile held. Baby steps.

"Hardly," I said, trying not to laugh at the idea. "Just a librarian."

After that, the conversation seemed easier, as though we had each passed the other's inspection. I don't remember all that we said, but I know we discovered we shared a passion for books and nature. We had each spent large portions of our summers in these mountains, and we discovered we both planned to spend the rest of our lives here. With his quiet prompting, I found myself telling him about my years in Florida, and why I had finally decided to chuck it all to come here. Talking to him was easier than I ever would have expected. Mac was a very good listener.

WE PARTED WAYS a couple of hours later, after exchanging phone numbers, in case of "emergency," and with Mac volunteering to show me some of the area's best hiking trails soon, perhaps even the following weekend. He headed back the way he had come, and Handsome and I went home to a dinner of leftovers from the previous day's roast chicken.

I Skyped Jenna later and brought her up to date on life in my new home. I may have mentioned Mac once. Or twice. I swear it wasn't often enough for the woo-woo eyes treatment she gave me again.

"Jenna, stop with the eyebrows! Really, it's not like that. He's very reserved, and this is the first time he's ever said more than a handful of words to me. Don't go making it into something it isn't."

"Well, just because it isn't doesn't mean it won't ever be!"

I knew I'd have to watch what I said in future conversations, or I'd never hear the end of it. Jenna's biggest focus in life, besides raising her children, was to see me settled down with her idea of the perfect man, raising children of my own. I, on the other hand, thought my life was looking pretty much perfect as it was. Yeah, I'd definitely have to remember not to mention Mac to Jenna any more.

After our chat, Handsome and I settled down by the fire for the evening. It was amazing how quickly this had become our nightly ritual. I guessed by late spring, I would be tired of hauling in firewood and ready to open all the windows to let in the sounds of warmer evenings, but for now, the flickering light was cozy and comforting. I was looking forward to my first Blue Ridge winter.

I was gazing into the flames remembering the pleasant afternoon, when a thought struck me. I realized that as we sat talking by the creek, Mac had learned a whole lot more about me than I had about him, and I wasn't sure how I felt about that at all.

IT WAS MIDNIGHT. I was lying in bed, still wide awake and feeling pretty embarrassed for having talked so much that afternoon. And I was definitely regretting that I hadn't asked more questions of Mac. What had possessed me to go on and on about my dreams and plans? It wasn't like me to be so open about myself with anyone, really, much less a near stranger. I knew nothing about MacKenzie Cole at all.

I thought about the way he had studied me as I talked, as though everything I said was of the utmost interest. At the time, it had seemed perfectly reasonable to share my thoughts with him, as though we were already fast friends. In retrospect, it just seemed foolish.

"Damn, Handsome! Could I have behaved any more ridiculously, yakking away like some silly twit, without a thought for what he might want to talk about? I didn't even ask him what he does for a living, or where he's from. Or anything else, really. I just talked about myself, on and on. Geeze. I'm an idiot sometimes."

Handsome blinked his sleepy, gold eyes, but offered no feline insights to make me feel better.

For a while, I lay there and worried that Mac thought me silly or stupid. And then I was angry at myself for bothering to worry. Why should I care about what MacKenzie Cole thought of me? I didn't need to impress him, or anyone else, for that matter.

Oh, God, why did I tell him all of that trivial stuff? Because he asked, that's why! It's his own fault if he was bored senseless. Serves him right, being all patient and smiley-faced and nice. I refuse to feel bad about this another minute!

I rolled over onto my side, willed myself to quit thinking about Mac at all, and to go to sleep at once. But another hour passed before I drifted off, and in spite of my resolve, the last thought that slipped through my mind was of Mac, slowly turning a golden leaf over and over in the sunlight.

ACROSS THE ROAD, Mac had given up any pretense of falling asleep. He prowled restlessly around his house for a while, then ended up in his favorite chair on the bedroom balcony, an old blanket thrown over his shoulders. He sat there staring at the moon, another night full of troubled thoughts tumbling through his mind. Rosheen was by his side, as usual. Every few minutes, she would exhale long, exasperated doggy sighs, to remind him that it was well past their standard bedtime, and they should both be inside, snug in their beds. Mac was too deep in thought to notice.

He found himself remembering Sarah as she talked about the new direction she wanted her life to take. She had been so excited about her plans, it was impossible not to feel happy for her. Even talking about the spring garden she wanted to plant had made her eyes sparkle, and her cheeks dimple.

He snorted. *Dimples! Why am I thinking about her dimples? I'm not interested in her dimples. Or her eyes, sparkling or not. So what if she seems smart, or pretty, or loves the woods? You are a disgusting idiot, MacKenzie Cole! An hour and a half of pleasant conversation with a woman you just met, and you can't sleep? Please! What are you, sixteen?*

"And who cares if she's read Thoreau? The hell with Thoreau! That doesn't mean a damn thing. Seems to me you once knew someone else who could quote Thoreau. How'd that work out for you?"

Rosheen stared, but he continued to mutter to himself, ignoring her nervous whines.

"Never again. My life's exactly the way I want it now. Sarah will have to go hiking with someone else. What was I thinking? Being neighborly's one thing. Walking in the woods together is something completely different. I'm not going there. Not. Going. There."

And with that final declaration, Mac rose from the chair and clomped into his bedroom, closing the French doors behind him with a good deal more force than necessary.

He went downstairs to the kitchen, poured and drank a small glass of wine, then went back up to his bedroom. Propping his pillows up against the headboard of his king sized bed, he picked up a half-finished copy of the latest Jack Reacher novel, and started reading. Concentration was impossible. After fifteen minutes, he gave it up as a lost cause, and turned out the lamp.

The moonlight shining through the trees beyond the balcony spread delicate silver lacework across one wall. He stared at the shifting patterns of light and dark for a long time, until sleep pulled him under, and he slid from the day's conflicting emotions into peaceful dreams of woods and waterfalls.

Chapter 6
I Never Liked Him Anyway

"**D**ON'T YOU LET her out of your sight, you hear? I don't give a damn what she does or where she goes, you follow her! I wanna know everything she gets up to!" Lloyd hung up on his cousin, Clete, and was led back to his cell, where he sat staring at the heavy, black bars that prevented him from being the one to take care of Ruthie personally.

Lloyd Carter had sobered up twenty-four hours after his arrest, only to find himself locked in a jail cell. He knew he might not be getting out for a long time, but he wasn't worried about Ruthie's recovery from the beating he had given her. Nor was he worried about what she would do to support herself while he was behind bars. He was only concerned about one thing. His money.

I been buildin' up that stash for more'n five years. No way Ruthie or anybody else is gonna take it from me.

He thought he had hidden the money well enough that it would stay safe until he got out, but it paid to be careful. *Can't take no chances. I gotta be sure she don't find it.*

He wasted his first four days trying to figure out a way to handle the problem himself, before he admitted that he was going to have to find someone on the outside he could trust to check on the situation. Decision made, he called his cousin.

Lloyd's cousin Clete was what would have been referred to as a "two-bit gumshoe" in those old detective movies from the 1940's. He made a living of sorts spying on cheating wives and philandering husbands, and often doubled his profits by selling the sleazy black and white photos he took through dirty motel windows. When Lloyd called, Clete hadn't had a job in three weeks, and was just broke enough to be interested in his cousin's proposition.

BY THAT SUNDAY morning, Clete was parked on a side street in a run-down neighborhood just outside of Macon, watching Lloyd's ratty little house. Within an hour of his arrival, a car pulled into the driveway next door, and a man and two women got out. The man disappeared inside the neighboring house, while the two women walked to the door of the address Lloyd had given him. After a brief conversation, the women hugged each other, and the one with the cast on her hand went inside the house and closed the door, while the other made her way back to her own home.

Clete sat scrunched down in his seat, bored and sleepy, and wondering what Lloyd expected his wife, Ruthie, to do.

He hadn't been very specific, but he offered to pay Clete's full rate, plus expenses.

What the hell. I'll watch for a while. Nothing better to do, anyway.

Within an hour, the front door opened and Ruthie came out, struggling with a heavy-looking shopping bag. She opened the back door of the car and shoved it in, then went back to the house for another one. This was a slow process, since she had to do it all one-handed, but she continued until the car was nearly full. Then Ruthie disappeared into the house and didn't come out for some time. Through his binoculars, Clete could see her moving from room to room, searching through every closet and drawer.

Well, well. So Cousin Lloyd's little woman is runnin'. Wouldn't have figured she'd be brave enough for that, to look at her. What're you huntin' for there, girlie? Money, he guessed. That's the only thing that would put Lloyd in such a panic.

Clete figured Ruthie was about to take off with everything she could find, probably heading for family somewhere. Or maybe a boyfriend. When she came out again carrying a battered old suitcase, he suspected she had cleaned his cousin out. She put the suitcase in the trunk of the car, backed out of the driveway, and drove off.

Now things are beginnin' to get a bit interestin'. Maybe followin' you for ol' Lloyd won't be such a bore after all. Let's just see where you lead me, girlie.

Clete pulled his battered gray coupe away from the curb, and settled in behind Ruthie, staying at least two cars back at all times. He smiled to himself. *Easy money, Cuz. Easy money.*

MONDAY, SEPTEMBER 17, 1962
MACON, GEORGIA

"WHERE THE HELL have you been? It's been over three weeks!" Even over the phone, Clete could tell how furious Lloyd was.

"Easy there, Cuz. I just did what you asked me to do, and I got some very interestin' news for you, too." Clete cleared his throat. "You ready for this? Your wife's in North Carolina."

"*What?* What the hell do you mean?"

"Well, let's see, now. What I mean is, she packed up your car, drove to North Carolina—with only one bathroom break on the whole stinkin' drive, I might add—then got a room outside of Asheville. Started right in visitin' local realtors the next mornin'."

"Goddammit! That miserable bitch!"

"Oh, you ain't heard nothin' yet. Yesterday, it appears she bought herself an honest-to-God log cabin in the boonies, halfway up a damn mountain. I followed her up there, just to be sure I knew which one it was, an' I checked out the lay of the land, to see if there was anybody else livin' close by, or anything, which there ain't, by the way. Then, I went back to the realtor's office, and killed some time there, discussin' property with one of the associates. Figured I might learn somethin' useful. An' I did." He paused for dramatic effect.

Lloyd's breath hissed through his clenched teeth. "Get on with it, Clete. I ain't got all day on this phone, you know."

"Okay, okay. Here's the kicker. It seems she paid cash for it." Clete waited for the explosion, but there was an ominous silence on the line. "Lloyd? You there, Cuz?"

Lloyd's voice came across the wires so low and soft, Clete could barely make out his words.

"Oh, I'm here," Lloyd said. Taking a slow, deliberate breath, he went on in precisely measured phrases, giving away nothing to anyone who wasn't familiar with what his most dangerous rages sounded like. "Thank you very much, Clete. I appreciate your good work. I'll make arrangements to pay you for your trouble."

"Yeah, well, about that," Clete said. "I was thinkin' that you must have had a nice little nest egg socked away for Ruthie to be able to pay cash for the cabin, an' all. So since I went the extra mile for you, bein' as you're my cousin, an' I stayed up there until I had all the answers for you, I figure I'm due for a little bonus — say an extra grand, maybe?"

"I mean, it's only fair," he added, when Lloyd didn't respond right away.

"Just an extra grand, Cousin? Why not two?"

"Aw, well. Family's gotta stick together. An extra grand's plenty. So if that's okay with you, I'll include it on the bill, an' mail it to you, along with my full report on all her activity."

"Tell you what, Clete. You get it all together. Today if you could. Include the address of this cabin she bought, too. But don't mail it. Just go on home an' wait for my boy to pick it up. You'll get exactly what you've got comin', I promise. An' thank you, for helpin' me out." Lloyd hung up the phone, then slammed his fist down on the table in front of him.

You don't know me too well, do you, Cuz? Ain't that just too bad for you!

With Clete knowing about his money, Lloyd had never intended to let him walk away from this unharmed in the first place, but asking for the extra thousand changed Clete's status from the walking wounded to the walking dead.

Lloyd went back to his cell in a cold fury. His anger raged inside him like a living thing, and his hatred of those who had wronged him grew harder and meaner with every shaking breath he took.

So the bitch stole my car and my money, and is living in North Carolina? In a cabin she paid cash for, no less?

He couldn't decide which made him madder—that the stupid cow stole his money and his beautiful Impala, then bought herself a mountain cabin—or that she thought he was too dumb to find her.

And Clete, my own cousin, tryin' to shake me down? Who the hell did these two think they were messin' with?

By the time they called lights out, Lloyd had set the wheels in motion to settle the score with his cousin. He laughed to himself. *Clete won't never be spyin' on any cheatin' wives screwin' their bosses again. Not in this lifetime, that's for sure. Dumb bastard. I never liked him, anyway.*

As for Ruthie, Lloyd planned to take care of her all by himself. He had scored an unexpected $30,000 in an Atlanta burglary five years earlier, and had gotten the idea of starting a little "Retirement Fund," just for himself. He began looking for side jobs that others didn't want to touch. Because he would do just about anything for money, no questions asked, he soon found there were plenty of people willing to pay his price. Lloyd had developed a reputation for getting the job done in a quick, efficient manner. No fuss, no muss. His secret fund had grown faster than he had ever imagined.

Ruthie had always known about his scams, but he made sure she knew nothing of these special jobs. This was his money, and his alone, and he figured there was almost enough now for him to leave both the state of Georgia and Ruthie far behind. His dream was to live like a king, in Mexico, or on some tropical island, maybe. Somewhere with palm trees, Margaritas, and sun-tanned, sweet young things in bikinis. There was no room for a wife in those dreams.

But now I find out that you've stolen everything I worked for? Oh, hell no, Ruthie! If it's the last thing I ever do, I will hunt you down like the bitch you are, and make you sorry you were ever born!

That very night, Lloyd started planning his revenge against Ruthie, and each and every day he spent behind bars, he dreamed up ever-more horrific schemes of torture and retribution. By the time he was paroled more than two years later, Lloyd's desire to kill his wife in the most frightening and painful way possible had become his personal holy quest.

Oh, you will suffer, all right, you back-stabbin', faithless little whore. You'll regret screwin' me over to your last dyin' breath, which I plan to witness personally.

Chapter 7
Let Me Help You with That

RUTHIE COULDN'T BELIEVE six weeks had passed since she had driven Lloyd's big, red Impala Super Sport out of Georgia and into the North Carolina Mountains. Finding a secluded cabin where she could feel safe had taken a few weeks, but it had been worth the time. She had ended up with the perfect spot, and she loved everything about it.

The early October sun was warm on her shoulders as she worked in her yard, prepping beds for spring planting. She was starting with a vegetable garden, and had marked off the boundaries on the south side of her cabin, where it would get the most sun during the growing season.

I'm gonna have a garden of my own, after all these years. A garden, and my sweet little cabin, too, and no more Lloyd Carter, beatin' the stuffin' outta me for no reason other than he feels like it. I'm finally free.

Ruthie was grateful for her second chance, but she was smart enough to know that a $75,000 windfall wasn't likely to come her way again, and that she would have to be clever and careful to make it last as long as possible. Raising some of her own food would be a big help, and it was something she enjoyed. She thought about all the hours she had spent working in her mama's plot, the two of them side by side, tending beds, harvesting produce, then canning tomatoes, okra, and beans.

Come summer, I'll have plenty of food to fill my pantry. I won't be goin' hungry up here, that's for sure. I just need to get through this winter, and then I'll be set.

She wouldn't have homegrown vegetables right away, but it wasn't too late for apples, winter squashes, and other fall produce to be found at the local farmer's market. On Saturday, she planned to head to Darcy's Corner, to find whatever was available for preserving.

She wanted to keep her small freezer filled with meat, too. Thanks to her father, Ruthie also knew how to hunt. She smiled, remembering all the early mornings spent tromping around in those Georgia piney woods. They were some of the few good memories she had of the man.

I wonder how many rabbits and quail Daddy and me shot back then? Hundreds of 'em, I bet.

Of course, she hadn't been around a gun in years, but she knew she would have no trouble adding fresh game to her food stores. She was determined to be as self-sustaining as possible, dipping into her money only when there was no other choice.

And there was protection to consider, too. Ruthie had never told Lloyd she was a good shot. She had been sure he wouldn't take kindly to a wife who knew her way around guns, so she had kept that information to herself. Now she was glad she had done so.

I'm gonna get a shotgun on Saturday, even if I have to drive clear up to Asheville to find what I want. A shotgun is perfect for huntin' and for protection. I'll be ready if anyone comes lookin' around my property. And that goes for that sorry husband of mine, too.

The sharp edge of the spade cut through the soil, releasing the scent of sun-warmed earth. Ruthie knew right away this land would be fertile and productive. She could already picture her pantry shelves loaded with rows of Mason jars, each filled with preserved fruits and vegetables in every color. Food on those shelves would bring her a sense of real security.

As she finished her work and put away the tools, she was grateful for how far she had come, both physically, and mentally. The cast had been removed from her hand, and though she babied it a bit, there had been no permanent damage. Her bruises were finally gone, too, but she had a three-inch scar on her left temple that cut straight through her eyebrow. She knew she had been lucky to escape her husband's abuse with her life, so, for her, the scar became a symbol of survival, and nothing more.

Being a practical woman, Ruth refused to dwell on the past. Instead, she pushed her fears of Lloyd finding her to the far back corners of her mind, and enjoyed every day of her new life to the fullest extent possible. Today, she was free of her abusive husband, and answered to no one. Today, she was planting a garden and planning a future. Today, she was safe in her snug little cabin.

She was happy. It was enough.

SATURDAY, OCTOBER 13, 1962
DARCY'S CORNER, NORTH CAROLINA

SATURDAY DAWNED COOL and clear, with blue skies like watered silk. Ruthie was up at 6:30, eager to get an early start on her shopping. The drive down from the ridge and into Darcy's Corner took her breath away, with every tree along the road vying to be the brightest splash of color on the mountain. A hundred shades of red, russet, and burgundy rubbed leafy shoulders with orange, gold, and amber. The radio played Patsy Cline and Marty Robbins, and Ruthie sang along all the way to the farmer's market.

Darcy's Corner was a tiny mountain village, curving along a mere half mile of Highway 74A, right down the center of Hickory Nut Gorge. There were a few mom-and-pop businesses in the village proper, with Everly's General Store and Farmer's Market being the largest, by far. Six miles away to the east, Lake Lure and Chimney Rock were packed with fall tourists, but the majority of the people shopping at Everly's on this beautiful morning were local residents. Ruthie strolled between tables heaped high with red and green apples, fat orange pumpkins, gaudy bundles of dried corn, and piles of ribbed acorn squash.

Oh, just look at all this! I haven't seen vegetables so fresh an' beautiful since Mama an' me grew our own.

By 9:00 am, she had filled several boxes, paid for her purchases, and was using one of the small market wagons to haul it all to the car. The parking lot was surfaced with loose gravel, and managing the heavily loaded wagon was tricky. Half way across the lot, a wheel caught in the soft gravel, and the unbalanced load caused the wagon to slew sideways. It tipped over, dumping fruit and vegetables everywhere.

Before Ruthie had time to react, a voice behind her said, "Whoops! Let me help you with that."

She turned and saw a smiling, light-haired man, roughly her own age, dressed casually in jeans and a cotton windbreaker.

"Can't have your food scattered all over the place, can we?" He picked up one of the now-empty boxes, and began refilling it as he gathered up the loose apples, squash, and bags of dried beans.

"Thank you," Ruthie said, after a moment of uncertainty. She preferred not to attract anyone's attention, but she appreciated his help, so she set to work beside him.

"Not a problem," the man said, grinning at her. "This is a lot of food for one little gal. You feedin' an army, somewhere?"

"No," she said, giving him a shy smile. "Just doin' some cannin'."

"Oh, my mother used to do a lot of cannin'. Made just about the best peach preserves in North Carolina. You makin' applesauce with some of these Granny Smiths?"

Ruthie admitted she was, and they made small talk as they worked. In less time than she would have thought, they had all the produce back in the boxes, and the boxes back in the wagon.

"I'm Frank Everly," he said, holding out his hand. "Don't even think I'm going to let you try to pull this to your car by yourself. Just lead the way."

Ruthie hadn't planned to be making friends up here. She worried about becoming too visible, but it was too late now, and he smiled at her in such an open, appealing manner that she felt obligated to respond. It would be rude not to, and it would just make him curious about her. So she shook his hand, and said, "Thank you for your help, Frank. I'm ... Ruth. Ruth Winn. My car's over here."

With that one sentence, Ruthie Carter vanished forever, and Ruth Winn began a relationship that would define the rest of her life. And all because of a chance meeting resulting from a twisted wagon wheel.

Chapter 8
You Forgot Freddy Krueger

EVERLY'S WAS UNDER siege. Jack-O-Lanterns of all shapes and sizes filled every available inch of space in front of the general store. They grinned with wicked delight from hay bales, benches, and old, wooden wagons. They lined each side of the wide stairs going up to the front porch. Enormous orange ones sat on every rocking chair. Little white ones perched on the porch railing, from one end to the other. And every one was brightly lit, even at 11:00 in the morning. They glowed fiercely, laughing with snaggle-toothed glee, or scowling from under beetled brows. Some had round mouths opened wide in silent screams, and others snarled with ferocious menace, beastly fangs bared.

It was a sight to behold, and I was delighted by the display. It was the day before Halloween, and Everly's had gone all out! The glowing pumpkins made me feel like a kid again, excited to be going trick or treating soon, and planning my costume. I lingered for some time outside the store taking pictures with my cell phone.

Over the doorway, a white sign with large red letters proclaimed that the store had been in business since 1949. Inside, it smelled deliciously of cinnamon and mulled apple cider, and there were jars of nickel candy on the counter — licorice whips and jujubes and red-and-white-striped peppermints. Pickled eggs floated in briny liquid in another jar, and neat stacks of homemade fudge rested on paper doilies inside the display case. I wandered among the shelves admiring the old-fashioned country displays. Apparently, they took the "general" part of their store name seriously. If you couldn't find what you wanted in here, you probably didn't need it, anyway.

For some reason, I hadn't gotten around to visiting Everly's until today, but I would definitely make it a habit to stop by here more often. It made picking up milk and bread a whole lot more fun than heading all the way over to Lake Lure for a real supermarket. The produce looked wonderful, and the butcher counter at the rear of the store held some very nice looking steaks and chops, so I decided then and there this would be my new favorite market.

As I was trying to make a selection from the meat department, I heard the bell over the door ring, and a moment later, a cheerful voice from behind the front counter called out, "Hi, Mac! What can I get you today?"

I froze for a moment, afraid to even look. Probably not the Mac I know. There have to be plenty of Macs around, after all. *Oh, please don't be the Mac who said we'd go hiking, then never called me!*

I hadn't heard from MacKenzie Cole since our meeting on the path behind my cabin, more than two weeks earlier, and I'll admit it, I was disappointed that he hadn't called. I really did not want to run into him today.

No such luck. I clearly recognized Mac's voice as he replied, "Hi, Brady. Just wondering if you had any scraps for Rosheen?"

"Sure do. Beef and chicken both. Be with you in a minute."

It sounded like Mac was heading straight toward me. I inched my way backward, wondering if I could slip down the next aisle and out the front door, unseen. I felt a twinge of panic, as I tried to figure out which way to go, and then he came into view around the end of the aisle, and my opportunity was lost. He stopped dead in his tracks, frowning.

"Oh. Sarah. Um, how are you?" He sounded embarrassed and uncomfortable, and I felt the same. My mind went blank, and it took me a second to work up a smile and find my voice.

"I'm good, Mac. And you?"

He looked away for a moment, and when he looked back, the corners of his mouth tightened, and there was a flash of irritation in his eyes. He wasn't embarrassed at all. He was annoyed.

I took a step backward in surprise, and then turned and walked away without another word. I wasn't sure what he had to be mad about, but I wasn't going to stand there and feel like I had done something wrong. It just didn't seem worth the trouble. I went out the front door, down the steps and headed for my Jeep. Before I had gotten halfway across the lot, I heard rapid footsteps coming up behind me.

I whirled around in full Defense Mode. "What is your problem?" I asked. "I don't know what I said or did, but could it really have been all that bad? All told, we've talked to each other a total of about two hours. What could I have done in that amount of time for you to be angry?"

"I wasn't angry," he began, but I cut him off.

"Don't," I said, shaking my head. "You were annoyed to have run into me. I could see it and feel it. I just don't understand it."

He sighed, then he looked down, looked up, and looked down a second time. Apparently he came to some sort of decision, finally looking directly at me. "I was going to say, I wasn't angry at you. I was angry at myself." He had the grace to look embarrassed, and he continued in a very small voice, "I was angry because I knew I should have called you. I'm sorry."

"Mac, you weren't obligated to call me. We hadn't made a definite date. And if you changed your mind about hiking, that's fine, too. Just don't look at me like I've done something wrong if you run into me somewhere. I'm not stalking you, you know."

"You haven't done anything wrong, Sarah, and I'm not mad at you about anything. In fact, I was glad to see you, until I realized I should have gotten back with you. I'm sorry if I made you feel bad." He paused then stared at his feet, shaking his head. "I suck at this."

I had no idea what to say to that. This man was so complicated, and he somehow managed to make even the simplest conversations seem complicated as well. Now, he stood there meeting my eyes openly—a change from his usual pattern of looking away every two seconds—and waited for me to reply.

I sighed. "Apology accepted," I said, and was surprised to see a flash of relief on his face. Sheesh. What was the deal with this guy?

He tilted his head to one side and asked, "Any chance we could go get a cup of coffee and try this again? I know you should tell me to get lost, but I hope you won't."

Hot and cold, on and off, here and there. I was totally thrown off track by his behavior, but perversely, I found Mac interesting in spite of it. Or was it because of it? I wondered if maybe it was just that black, black hair, blowing around his face, or those disconcerting eyes, but I couldn't be that shallow, could I? I didn't know. I just knew that whatever conflict had been going on with him earlier seemed to have disappeared. He positively radiated a sincere desire to make up for this morning's run-in, and coffee did sound good, so I threw caution to the winds, and went.

COFFEE TURNED INTO a surprisingly good lunch at the local diner, complete with the always-popular argument over which barbecue sauce was truly the best. I held out for a hickory smoked, tomato-based sauce, while Mac informed me in deadly serious tones that no one who loved pork would ever desecrate it with anything that had tomatoes in it.

"If you are going to make your home here, you'd better learn to love our traditional Carolina barbecue sauces. They're vinegar-based on one side of the state line, mustard-based on the other. Or a combination of both. But never, ever, tomato-based. You'll remain an outsider forever, if you don't accept this basic truth."

I waited for him to smile, but he didn't.

When I eyed the bottle of thin, yellowish sauce dubiously, he egged me on. "Go on. Try it. You know you want to. Tomatoes are for spaghetti. Pork just cries out for vinegar or mustard. Here. Let me help you."

He smiled as he doctored my pulled pork sandwich to his satisfaction. I was already leery of the coleslaw piled high on top of the meat. Now I had this thin, yellowish stuff all over it, too.

He finished messing with my lunch and sat back to watch my reaction. I took a big bite, and nearly swooned. The combination of flavors was out of this world! My rapturous expression gave me away, and he grinned.

"What did I tell you?"

"Oh, Mac," I said, as soon as I swallowed. "It's delicious! I hereby swear to follow your advice on all North Carolina epicurean specialties, without question." I would have said more, but I was too busy scarfing down my barbecue.

Mac just continued the conversation without me. "Good. You should defer to me in these matters. I am, after all, a native of the Tarheel State, and I know these things. Next we'll try you on liver mush."

I paused in mid-bite. The words "liver" and "mush" just didn't sound right in the same sentence.

"I don't think I even want to know what that is," I said, dabbing barbecue sauce off my chin.

"Oh, it's really good. See, they take this stuff kind of like liverwurst, only grayer, and mushier, hence the name. They slice it, dip it in flour, and fry it up all crispy. You'll love it."

I'm sure I looked as appalled as I felt.

"Or not," he said, laughing. "Actually, even I don't like it much, but don't tell anybody I said that. You have to be careful about trash-talking liver mush in this part of the state."

"You North Carolina folk sure take your food seriously," I said, shaking my head in mock bewilderment.

Over a dessert of homemade bread pudding, we talked about this and that for a while, and then I decided it was time for me to learn a bit more about the enigmatic Mr. Cole. I was surprised at how straightforward he was, now that we had gone back to the easy conversation from our afternoon by the stream.

"I'm in computer research," he said, "and I really enjoy it. Plus I can work from home most of the time, which means a lot to me. You already know I spent most of my summers in these mountains when I was a boy, and I love being back here now."

This was easier than I expected.

"Where did you spend the rest of the year when you were a boy?"

"Mostly in Charlotte. My dad was in banking and finance there."

"Was?"

"He's retired now. He and my mother moved to the Florida Keys a few years ago. They love it there."

I smiled. "The Keys are fun, but even though I'm a Florida native, my heart has always felt more at home up here. Do you see them often?"

He looked a bit regretful. "Not as often as I should, I guess. I'm pretty much a homebody. I don't like to go away very often. A few overnight trips to Charlotte to keep an eye on the business, and a week in Florida most winters is about as long as I can handle being gone."

"What do you do with Rosheen when you are out of town?" I asked.

"I board her, but I don't like it any more than she does."

"Don't you have a friend who could watch her for you?"

He looked at me with a rueful expression on his face. "You might have noticed that I don't make friends very easily. And I wouldn't leave Rosheen with just anyone."

I figured I had pumped him about as much as I could at one time. After that, it was just chit-chat until the waitress brought the check. She was a busty woman somewhere in her mid-30's, flaunting an oversized tangle of hair in a flaming red shade that could only have come out of a bottle, and wearing about a pound and a half of heavy, black mascara. She eyed Mac like Handsome eyes his food bowl, and leaned way too far across the table while totaling up the check, giving him a good view of her ample cleavage.

Accentuating her southern drawl, she batted those weighty eyelashes in Mac's direction, and said, "Where y'all been lately, Mac? Haven't seen you around here in a long time, Sugar." She was about ten seconds away from rubbing up against his leg and purring.

I silently scratched her name—Tami according to her embroidered uniform—off the list of possible candidates for dog-sitting Rosheen. I wouldn't have trusted her to take care of a guppy, myself. Mac ignored her simpering and posing, handing her his credit card, and giving me a look that dared me to comment on his picking up the check.

Tami took the card and sashayed back to the register, hips swinging side to side in an exaggerated manner that took up most of the aisle. I think it might have been the first time I ever saw anyone actually sashay. It was an eye-popping performance, I must say.

"Sorry about that," Mac said a few minutes later, as we walked outside.

"No problem," I said sweetly. "I understand how ex-girlfriends can be."

He stopped and stared at me like I'd sprouted another head. "Tami?" He began to sputter. "Are you serious? Tell me you're not serious!"

I started laughing. "Take that, Mr. Livermush," I said, poking him in the arm.

A look of profound relief came over his face, and then he laughed. "Thank God! Give me a minute, though, to get rid of the images now seared into my brain!"

Laughing, we walked back across the street to Everly's, and decided it was too nice a day to go home yet. We took some time picking out a pumpkin for my front porch. I told Mac I could carve a better jack-o-lantern than he could, and he couldn't resist the challenge. He got one for himself, too. Then we took a drive along Hickory Nut Gorge to Chimney Rock, just to admire the scenery there and along Lake Lure. We ended up back at the General Store, just as dusk began to darken the sky. The pumpkins were glowing like things possessed, and we admired them for a bit longer before climbing into our separate vehicles and heading home.

Mac followed me as we drove up the mountain. As I turned into my driveway, he pulled in behind me and waved at me to stop. He got out of his truck and came up to my window. He seemed far more at ease than I'd ever seen him. It made him look a bit younger than the forty years he had admitted to at lunch.

He leaned down and said, "I really had a nice time today."

"Hey, don't sound so surprised! I did, too," I said, smiling up at him.

"Look, um ... I thought maybe ... well ... would you like to come up to my house for a little while? We could have our pumpkin carving contest? We have a bet, after all."

I was astonished. It was so unexpected, I just sat looking at him for a minute, which he instantly interpreted as no.

"I'm sorry. You're probably tired and ready to get home. Maybe another time." He started to straighten up, looking disappointed.

"Yes!"

He stopped.

I nodded at him. "Yes, I'd like that. I was just surprised. I think it would be fun to beat you at pumpkin carving. I need to check on Handsome first, though."

Mac's smile gave me tiny butterflies in my middle, but I knew I'd better be careful about getting any ideas. This guy could barely handle friendship, so I would have to step very lightly, here. But I was getting the feeling that if there was ever a man who needed a friend, it was MacKenzie Cole, and I thought maybe I'd like to be one for him.

"That's fine," he said. "Just drive on up the hill when you're ready. You can't miss it. It's the only thing up there. See you then." He went back to the truck, backed out, and disappeared around the curve toward his driveway.

I got out to check the mailbox, then continued down the drive to my cabin, wondering what the heck had happened today. I ran into the house, loved on Handsome for a few minutes, brushed my teeth and my hair, and zipped back out the door. Fifteen minutes after Mac drove away, I was heading up a very steep driveway that zigged and zagged through a series of switchbacks to climb the hill.

Good Lord. Is his house on the very top of the mountain?

Turns out, it was. As I rounded the last curve, it came into view, and I braked to a stop. Holy Moly.

MAC'S HOUSE WAS beautiful. Every line clean and classic, kind of like him. Elegant, but organic, too, as though it were part of the earth and the rocks it sat upon. The main part of the house was brightly lit, and had a warm, welcoming glow about it.

As I was getting out of the car, I heard the front door open, and Rosheen came bounding down the steps to greet me. She danced around me, hoping for attention, but was far too polite to jump on me. Like many big dogs, I think she knew instinctively she should be gentle with those smaller than she, which would include pretty nearly every human being on the planet. I stopped to give her some scratches and sweet talk, and when I looked up, Mac was standing on his porch watching me, hands in his pockets, and a little smile on his face. I wasn't sure what his expression meant, but then I was finding out it was never easy to understand what Mac was thinking.

He came down the steps to say hello. "Come on inside," he said. "Rosheen, let's go in, girl."

The big dog trotted up the stairs ahead of us, and nudged the door open with her nose. I followed her inside, with Mac right behind me.

High, vaulted ceilings and log walls the color of wild honey greeted us. A huge, stone fireplace took up one whole wall, with a mantle wider than my entire cabin, and a crackling fire bounced golden light around the spacious room. In spite of the overall beauty, the house looked lived in and enjoyed. There were books stacked here and there, and a jacket tossed carelessly over the back of a chair. The desk was obviously used for work, with charts and diagrams spread across part of its surface. While the whole room had a masculine flair to it, there was not a trace of Bachelor Pad anywhere. I realized I was somewhat surprised to see that it looked like a real home, in the best sense of the word.

"It's beautiful," I said, and I meant it. The look of pleasure on his face told me just how much he loved it, too.

"I don't blame you for not wanting to travel. I wouldn't want to leave here, either."

"Thank you, Sarah," he said, reverting to that more formal, genteel tone he used from time to time. "I'm happy here."

Somehow, the way he said that made me feel sure he had come here from a place where he had not been so happy, and I wondered if I would ever find out more about that part of his life.

The entire back of the house seemed to be made of glass, and the view was spectacular. Even this late in the day, the valley was visible under the darkening skies, and the hills appeared to roll on forever.

"Come on out for a minute," he invited. "The pumpkins will wait a bit longer."

He led me through the French doors and onto the wide balcony, where I could appreciate the full splendor spread out in front of me.

"This is my favorite view in the world," Mac confessed. "When I was a boy, we used to come camping on this very spot. What I remember most is waking up early in the morning, before anyone else, and creeping out of my tent to sit on that big rock down there, waiting for the sunrise to spread out over the hills and valleys. It felt like I was watching the whole world wake up."

"No wonder you wanted to build your house here. It's the perfect spot for you."

We stood in silence for a while, elbows on the railing, just enjoying the night sounds. Rosheen wandered out and gave me a gentle nudge, hoping for more scratches. I obliged her.

"She really likes you," Mac said.

"She probably likes everybody."

"No, she's polite to everybody. There's a difference. She is fairly reserved with most people, but much more affectionate with you."

"I'm flattered," I said, feeling ridiculously pleased. Rosheen chose that moment to stand up on her hind legs with her front paws on the railing, looking for all the world like a third person joining in on our star-gazing.

"Get down, girl," Mac said. "Let's go back in. That wind is picking up. We might start getting some colder weather tonight."

The rest of the evening went by almost too quickly. Mac turned out to be a very good host, having laid out wine and cheese before I got there. He offered to grill some steaks if I was hungry, but I declined. I didn't want to overstay my welcome on my first visit. Instead, we set up our pumpkins in the kitchen, on an expansive marble island. After much laughing and general silliness, mostly on my part, we ended up with two halfway decent jack-o-lanterns.

"Mine is definitely the winner. Yours looks like Freddy Krueger," Mac proclaimed.

"Well, better Freddy Krueger than a werewolf that looks like a demented badger," I countered.

We told Rosheen she could be the judge, and she dutifully sniffed both pumpkins thoroughly, wagged her tail, and then left to inspect her doggy bowl. Mac decided that meant it was a tie, and we congratulated ourselves on our prodigious pumpkin carving talents.

At 8:30, I took my leave, but not until I insisted that Mac set up his jack-o-lantern on his porch and light it. He brought out a candle and a big box of matches. As the flame caught, and the pumpkin's spooky face lit up, I turned to him and said, "It was a really fun day, Mac. You know, you are officially my first friend up here."

I toasted him with the last swallow of wine in my glass. "Here's to friendship and good neighbors."

Mac smiled, looking totally at ease. "I'll drink to that," he said, then set both glasses down on the railing, and walked me to my car. He opened the door for me, and as I was getting settled behind the wheel, he leaned over, and looked in.

"If you want to take a short hike next weekend, I know a place you might enjoy."

I gave him a stern look. "Where have I heard that before?"

He smiled, looking guilty. "Yeah, I deserve that, I know. But this time, I promise to call."

"Even if something happens and you want to ask for a rain check?"

"Even then."

"Deal."

I waved at him, and turned my car around to go home. As I headed toward the first curve of his driveway, I glanced in my rear view mirror. Mac was waving and running toward the car.

"You forgot Freddy Krueger!"

I stopped and he put the pumpkin in the back seat, along with another candle and the matches.

"Aw, he could've kept your little were-badger company," I said.

"Nothing doing. You take him home and light him up. You made me light mine, remember."

I promised him I would, and then I drove home. I sat Freddy Krueger on my front steps, and admired how scary he looked with light spilling out of his creepy face. As I watched the candle's flickering glow, I pondered how a trip to pick up a few groceries had turned into so much more than I had expected.

"You just never know where the day will lead," I told Handsome later, as I was getting ready for bed.

Handsome purred.

"That's what you always say, Fuzzy Boy."

I gave him a kiss on the top of the head, and then I turned out the lights.

ACROSS THE ROAD, Mac sat on his bedroom balcony, engaged in an earnest conversation with Rosheen. For her part, Rosheen sat with her head tilted to one side, listening intently to Mac's voice, though not offering much by way of her own opinion, of course.

"I know what you're thinking, Rosheen. I said I wasn't going to get involved. But she's just a friend. There's no law against a man being just friends with a woman, is there? I like her. She makes me laugh, and see things I normally don't even notice. Not to mention she likes doing so many of the same things I do. That's hard to find in a friend, you know. I have a feeling she's not going to take any crap from me, either, and I like that, too."

He scratched the dog's ears while he talked, and as always, she rewarded him with a few thumps of her tail.

"Now don't go thinking I don't know what I'm doing, Big Dog. I am perfectly capable of keeping this a friends-only kind of thing. And no, I don't mean 'friends with benefits,' either," he said, shaking his head. "That would just lead to trouble."

Leaning back in his chair, Mac studied the starry night sky, somehow feeling lighter than he had in a long time. He glanced back down at Rosheen. "Go ahead and look skeptical. I'm telling you, Sarah Gray and I are just going to be friends, period."

Rosheen might have told him differently, if she had really been able to understand what he was saying. Since she didn't, she just wagged her tail and licked his hand, and then the two of them went inside and climbed into their respective beds.

Chapter 9
Turns Out Haunches Are Delicious

THURSDAY, NOVEMBER 24, 2011

THERE IS SOMETHING very sexy about a man who knows his way around a kitchen. I sat at Mac's marble island and watched him preparing a haunch of venison for Thanksgiving dinner, thinking that there were actually a lot of things about Mac that were sexy. Of course, I chastised myself right away for having such thoughts, knowing that Mac's interest in me didn't go beyond friendship.

I told myself that was just fine, since I was really getting into the book I was writing, which was going to consume all of my time for the foreseeable future. I didn't need any distractions right now, even of the thoroughly attractive kind. Still, as I sat sipping my tea, and watching Mac plying his culinary skills, I couldn't help but notice little details about the way he moved with such beautiful and precise efficiency. The sleeves of his flannel shirt were rolled almost to his elbow. I liked the shape of his wrists, and the slight sprinkling of dark hair across his forearms. His hands were especially interesting. Long-fingered and agile, they were almost hypnotic as he cut short, shallow slashes in the roast and inserted garlic cloves. I was totally immersed in watching them when I realized Mac was asking me something.

"Hey! You listening to me, Sarah?"

"Yep." I sat straighter, and banished my errant thoughts to the back of my mind. Bad thoughts! Bad, bad thoughts! "Well, mostly."

He laughed. "No you weren't. You were daydreaming about your book, probably. You literary sorts are always off in some dream world, heads full of clouds."

I made a face, and flicked a small piece of garlic at him.

"Behave," he said, laughing again. "Guilty as charged, aren't you? I asked when you thought the turkey would be ready," he said with exaggerated patience.

After several weeks of meeting now and then for hikes, leaf watching on the Parkway, and even an afternoon trip to The Pathfinder bookstore in Asheville, we had decided it was only logical to share Thanksgiving dinner. Neither of us had family to go to, after all, and we thought it would be fun to put together a joint meal for the occasion.

"I should probably head back over and check on it, though I'm thinking it will be at least another hour. How long will it take to cook your venison?"

I had admitted to Mac that I had never tasted deer, and wasn't sure I wanted to, but he reminded me of my promise to trust him in all things epicurean—as long as they didn't involve liver mush, of course. I knew he went deer hunting now and then, and he promised me that he had cooked venison all his life. He assured me that I hadn't lived until I tasted a garlic-laced haunch, roasted to perfection. I wasn't convinced. Something about the words "Thanksgiving haunch" just didn't sound right to me. But Mac had reminded me that turkey and venison had both been part of the first Thanksgiving, so I reluctantly decided that I would do my best to enjoy his efforts.

"Venison needs to be cooked faster, at a high temperature," he said. "I don't think it will take longer than thirty minutes or so for a haunch this size. Maybe less, so it doesn't dry out. I'll put it on after you bring the turkey over, and by the time we have everything else ready, it should be done to perfection. Then you, Miss Gray, will be in for a treat!"

"Uh-huh. Well, we'll see, Mr. Cole." I was still dubious.

I left him humming to himself, laying a few strips of bacon over the top of the roast, and tying the whole thing up with butcher's twine. Yeah, he definitely looked sexy in "Man in the Kitchen" mode.

As I drove back to my cabin, I was thinking how much I enjoyed Mac's company. He was the perfect hiking companion and always interesting to be around, but I still didn't understand him at all. There were areas of his life that he never mentioned, and when I strayed too close to them, he would steer me away before I knew what was happening.

Sometimes I wondered if I should be concerned about what he might be hiding from me, but I just couldn't bring myself to mistrust him. I have very good instincts about people, and Mac rang no warning bells for me at all, so I figured he'd tell me what he wanted me to know, when he wanted me to know it. But I have to admit, every now and then, it frustrated me, and those occasions seemed to have a direct relationship to the moments when I realized just how attractive Mac really was. I suspect that said a whole lot more about me than it did about Mac.

As I parked in front of my cabin, the mouth-watering aroma of roasting turkey drifted out of my open kitchen window, and pulled me inside. Handsome met me at the door, weaving between my ankles and purring ecstatically in greeting. He was getting big, with oversized front paws that indicated he was going to be a bruiser when full-grown. In spite of his size, he had a tiny little meow that Mac teased him about. Handsome tolerated Mac with restrained good will, but he absolutely adored Rosheen. He would run around her in circles, darting close to slap at her tail, and then racing away to hide behind a chair leg, hoping to ambush her when she wasn't watching. Rosheen put up with it all, showing great patience, and when Handsome grew tired of the romping, the two of them would curl up together in front of the fire while Mac and I planned our next hike or just visited for a few minutes.

The turkey was nearly done, so I removed the lid of the black enameled roasting pan to let it finish browning. Then I made sure everything else was ready to transport back to Mac's house. Mashed potatoes ready to reheat in the microwave? Check. Pumpkin pie and homemade whipped cream? Check and check. Secret family recipe for cream cheese stuffed pears? Already packed in a container, ready to go. As soon as that turkey was crisp and brown, I'd load the Jeep and head back over.

Mac was taking care of a side dish to go with the roast venison, salad, and wine. I thought it sounded like a wonderful feast. Heck, I had even cooked the turkey giblets to split between Rosheen and Handsome, who was going to ride back over with me. I had just enough time to shower and change into something more feast-worthy.

THE FOUR OF us sat on Mac's living room balcony as the afternoon raced towards evening. The feast had been as glorious as I imagined, and Mac's venison had been just as delicious as he had promised me. Dishes had been done and leftovers put away. We were all in that state of sated languor where there was nothing left to do but sprawl and sigh contentedly, complimenting each other on our various contributions to the dinner.

In traditional Southern style, we had eaten our holiday dinner early, and were enjoying a peaceful hour on the balcony before night fell and the temperatures dropped too low for comfort. Mac's head was tilted back on his chair and his eyes were closed, but I knew he wasn't sleeping. A tiny smile played at the corner of his mouth, and then he turned and looked at me with that assessing expression in his eyes.

"That may have been the nicest Thanksgiving dinner I've ever had," he said, turning back to look across the treetops.

"I was thinking the same thing. You have a surprising number of talents, MacKenzie Cole."

"As do you, Sarah Gray."

We relaxed a little while longer, Handsome lying on my lap, and Rosheen sitting by Mac's legs. After a while, Mac sat up straight and stretched, arms flexing over his head. He studied the sky for a moment, then turned toward me.

"I have a feeling we might get some snow tonight. Have you checked out your central heat? Your fireplace might not be enough if it drops down much lower than it has been."

I was reluctant to come back to the real world, but I knew he was right. It was time to wrap up this day and tuck it into that special corner of my mind where I store all my best memories.

"Yep. I think I'm set. I'm actually looking forward to my first winter in the mountains. I like colder weather, and

I've got my emergency supplies handy in case of power outages and so forth."

"Well, we probably aren't having a blizzard tonight, but you certainly won't need groceries for a few days," he said, referring to the neatly packaged leftovers we had split between us.

I stood and put Handsome down, much to his obvious displeasure, and we walked back inside.

"I'd better get going. Thanks again for having us and for sharing your truly astounding culinary skills." I was teasing him, but only halfway. Even his roasted butternut squash had been tasty. "I can't believe I'm saying this," I continued, "but it turns out haunches are delicious! Who knew?"

Mac laughed. "I knew. And once again, I get to say told you so! But it was your turkey and pumpkin pie that made it a real Thanksgiving."

We stretched out the goodbyes, going back over every bite of our shared feast, each of us reluctant to admit it was over. Some days are like that. So picture perfect that you want to stop time and live in that moment forever. Sadly, time just ignores you and plows ruthlessly ahead.

I drove home, my car loaded down with leftovers and one sleepy cat, too worn out from romping with his big, shaggy girlfriend to even complain about the indignity of having to ride in his carrier.

"Now that was a Thanksgiving to remember," I told him later, after all the food was put away, and we were crawling into bed.

Handsome stared at me with those huge, golden eyes of his as I scratched his head and under his chin. He curled into a tight ball and wrapped his paws over his nose, asleep in seconds.

"All seems right in my world tonight. What about yours, Handsome?"

As usual, Handsome just purred.

SKYPING JENNA WAS always an experience like no other. We talked to each other every couple of days, but I still never knew what to expect when I called, either from her tales about her own life, or her questions about mine. The day after Thanksgiving was no exception.

"*Gay?* What? Why would you ... what makes you ... what are you talking about?" I was so surprised, I could only stammer in response.

Jenna shrugged her shoulders, and gave me a patient smile. "Well, Sarah, he's good-looking, apparently rich, and single. He's living alone—at forty. You've been hanging out with him for weeks now, and he hasn't hit on you, even once. I figure he's either gay or married."

I just stared at her, open-mouthed.

"Look, Chickie. It's not necessarily a bad thing. You keep telling me you don't need to be starting any relationships, and let's face it, your track record with men hasn't been so wonderful."

I gave her a glare. "Gee, thanks for the reminder."

She just laughed. "Gay guys make fantastic best friends, Sarah. No complications. Perfect for, oh, let me think. Hiking? Bookstore browsing? Cooking together? Any of this sounding familiar? It's better than finding out he's married, for Pete's sake."

"Jenna," I said with a sigh, "I don't believe Mac's gay. I would've picked up on something by now. And I don't believe he's married. No ring. No womanly things in his house. Hey, more to the point, no actual woman in his house. Ever. Well, as far as I can tell, anyway. Really, Jenna, you're way off on this one."

"Don't think so. It's one or the other. Unless he's a serial killer, of course, and hiding a torture chamber in his basement and trophies in his bedroom. But then, you'd probably be part of his collection by this time."

Now I just laughed at her.

"Well?" She asked with a grin. "Have you been in his basement or his bedroom?"

"No!"

"Oh, my. Is that the sound of disappointment I hear?"

"Absolutely not! Not really. Okay, look. I do find him pretty attractive, but that isn't what our relationship is about. We're friends, Jenna. We both knew that going in. I'm not angling to get into his bedroom, for any reason. Mac and I are friends. Just. Friends."

"Oh, yeah. He's gay." And with that, Jenna said goodbye, and disconnected before I could think of a snappy reply.

I sat at my dining table for a long time, staring out the window and thinking. Damn that girl. Now I found myself unable to stop going over every comment, every look, every gesture. I tried to be totally unbiased, and honestly, I could not find a single moment where anything Mac had ever said or done indicated he might be either married or gay.

Considering Jenna's remarks so carefully forced me to accept two things. One, even if it wasn't any of my business, I wanted to know why Mac was so careful to keep his past life private. And two, I would be heartbroken to find out he was either married or gay. Since I am neither anti-marriage nor anti-gay, that could only mean I had designs on him myself, and they apparently weren't restricted to friendship after all.

Chapter 10

You Just See a Pile of Boards

MONDAY, SEPTEMBER 2, 1963

R UTH CARRIED THE platter of fried chicken to the table and set it down in front of Frank. The potato salad, coleslaw, and sliced watermelon were already in place.

She watched Frank's eyes light up as he admired the food, the sweating pitcher of iced tea, and the fresh-cut flowers in the center of the table. Here was a man who appreciated her. She didn't think she would ever get tired of Frank's open admiration and affection.

"Happy Labor Day, Frank."

"Ruth, you'll spoil me, and make me fat, too," he said. "That chicken smells wonderful, and that potato salad is callin' my name. Come sit down, Hon. You've done enough, now. No need to wait on me hand and foot, you know."

She took a chair across the table from him, and poured the iced tea. They chatted about this and that while they ate, and Ruth was content. To sit with a good man over a shared meal and talk of each other's day—she wondered what else a woman could ask for.

I'm so lucky to have been given a second chance! Frank Everly has to be the nicest man I've ever met, and this has been the best year of my whole life.

Last fall, Frank had made sure to wait on her personally every time she stopped by his family's general store, and had even delivered some of her telephone orders, though his younger brother was supposed to do that. Ruth soon realized he was sweet on her, but it was a couple of months before she felt comfortable enough to let him into her life. He had talked her into lunch at the diner across from Everly's, and bit by bit, his gentle manner had finally won her over. After that, they were always together, and now she understood for the first time in her life what it felt like to be with a man who truly loved her.

"Have some more sliced tomatoes, Frank. This is the last of my fresh picked ones. All the rest've been canned."

Her first garden had been a big success, producing more greens and tomatoes than she could possibly eat by herself. Frank convinced her to set up a table at their Saturday Farmer's Market, so she had taken in baskets filled with produce, and sold everything she brought.

"You did save some jars for yourself, didn't you? I know they been sellin' like crazy at the market."

"Don't you worry, now. I put aside a whole case just for us. We'll be eatin' my tomatoes all winter long, I promise."

Ruth had soon started to include homemade cinnamon rolls, and jars of okra or puckery green pickles at her market table. Those went fast, as well. She earned enough to live on over the whole summer, meaning she hadn't had to touch her "windfall" money in weeks.

"Did you by any chance save us some of your okra, too? I can almost taste it, cooked up with your tomatoes!"

"I saved us some of everything. You know I wouldn't forget about you, Frank. And next year, I'm going to grow twice as much, too. Maybe try some zucchini and summer squash."

Earning an income for the first time in her life was a source of real pride for her, and having a man like Frank offering support and encouragement was the icing on the cake. Ruth was as happy as she could hope to be, but she never let go of the fear that someday her husband would find her. And she never told Frank he even existed.

The summer was winding down. It was a holiday weekend, and Frank had promised to take her to a movie in Asheville, after dinner. When they finished eating, he cleared off the table, and did the dishes. It always amazed Ruth to see him do that, but he insisted she had worked hard enough cooking dinner, and he wanted her to relax while he cleaned things up. She wandered out to the porch, and sat down on the wooden swing that hung at one end.

As she waited for Frank to join her, Ruth's thoughts turned once again to everything that had happened since she had moved into her cabin. She knew she had found something special with Frank Everly, but she was never going to tell Frank what she had been through. The idea of him knowing that she had allowed a man to dominate her so completely was shameful to her, and she knew it would break Frank's heart to find out that Lloyd had beaten her almost to death.

Most of all, though, I can't ever tell Frank I'm already married. He'd be hurt so bad! He wouldn't ever touch a woman he knew was married, neither — not my Frank. He has too much honor for that. And I'll never be able to get a divorce without Lloyd findin' out where I am. If he finds me, he'll kill me. And likely Frank, too.

Ruth understood that making a new life free from the shadow of her old one would not be easy, but she desperately wanted to try.

By the time Frank came out to join her on the swing a few minutes later, she had come to a decision. "Would it be okay if we didn't go to the movies tonight?" Her voice was soft and tentative.

"Well, of course it's okay, Hon. Are you tired, or is there something else you'd rather do?"

Ruth took a deep breath and reached for his hand. "I'd rather stay here with you, Frank."

He smiled, giving her hand a little squeeze. "Whatever makes you happy, Sweetheart. You wanna watch some TV? Or play some Chinese checkers? You name it."

"I just want to be with you." She paused, took another deep breath, and then very quietly asked, "Would you stay with me tonight?"

Frank stopped pushing the swing. He sat frozen for a moment, looking confused. "You mean spend the evenin'?"

"No, Frank. I mean spend the night. I want you to stay with me all night."

Ruth knew the exact moment when her intent became clear to Frank. His eyes widened, and he slid closer to her on the swing, his face lit with hope and wonder. "Are you sure, Ruth? I would never push you to do somethin' you didn't want to do."

"I know you wouldn't. That's why I know you're the right one. Yes, I'm sure."

Frank slowly reached out and cupped the side of Ruth's face. She closed her eyes, his palm warm against her cheek.

"Ruth," he whispered, leaning forward to kiss her. "Oh, Ruth."

When they broke apart again, Ruth smiled at him, and stood. She reached for his hand and led him back inside, then up the stairs to her bedroom.

HOURS LATER, FRANK lay awake beside her, watching her sleep. Making love to Ruth had been the most exquisitely perfect thing that had ever happened to him. He had whispered tender endearments to her in the moonlight, and though she had been shy at first, in the end she had responded with her entire heart and body.

She had loved him back, covering him with kisses and caresses, and whispering over and over, "Frank. My Frank. My sweet Frank."

He couldn't get over the feeling that this was a miracle. This beautiful, warm, perfect woman had come into his life in the most accidental of ways, and now she loved him. His heart felt like it might burst with the magic of it, and he marveled at the gift God had given him.

Love. I am in love. And I am loved in return.

Frank held Ruth all night, dozing from time to time, but mostly just watching her sleep. Once she had cried out as though in pain. He had held her closer then, whispering words of comfort until her trembling subsided, and she turned toward him in sleep, seeking the shelter of his arms. He had never felt such happiness.

From that night on, Frank was a man transformed by love. His whole life centered around Ruth Winn, and he wanted nothing more than to make her as happy as he was. Every hard-earned smile from her was like the springtime sun shining on his face. Ruth still kept her own counsel, and would not talk about her past, but Frank believed it was just a matter of time before she would trust him enough to tell him of her life before moving to Wake-Robin Ridge. And he wanted to know it all, good or bad.

But pushin' her won't work. It's important for her to make her own decisions, with no pressure from me. I don't expect she's ever had that chance before, and it's somethin' I can give her. Freedom to find out for herself who she is, and what she wants to do with her life.

And he was determined to give her just that.

MONDAY, SEPTEMBER 16, 1963

TWO WEEKS AFTER Labor Day, Frank pulled his old pick-up truck into Ruth's driveway. He tapped the horn twice, and climbed out. By the time he closed the driver's door, Ruth was standing on the porch, smiling.

"Frank! I didn't know you were comin' by today. What a nice surprise."

"I didn't know it, either, Hon, but here I am, and I've got a present for you."

Ruth came down the front steps and walked to the truck to give Frank a welcoming hug. "A present for me? What in the world?"

"Yep. Look here in the back of the truck." Frank untied the old tarp covering the load in bed of his truck, and with a proud flourish, sang out, "Ta-daaah!"

"I don't understand? You brought me lumber?"

Laughing at her expression, Frank said, "I expect you just see a pile of boards and the like in here, right?" When Ruth nodded, he continued, "Well, me now—I see your kitchen pantry extended out onto your back porch, with lots more shelf room for your cannin' and stuff. 'Course, you might have to be real sweet to the carpenter who's gonna build it for you, which would be me."

"Oh, Frank!" Ruth fairly danced back to Frank's side, and flung her arms around him. "You sweet man, you! I can't believe how good to me you are!" Then she paused and frowned at him. "But now, Frank, you're not gonna spend your money on a pantry for me. You tell me how much I owe you for these supplies."

"Well, Sweetheart, that's the best part. This is all stuff left over from the addition to the store. It didn't cost me a thing. I've already measured it out and drawn me up a plan, and I can get started over this weekend, if you want."

They went into the cabin, hand in hand, with Frank talking a mile a minute.

"I figure I can remove the back wall of your pantry and extend everything straight out under the porch roof, no problem at all. I've got insulation and wallboard still at the store, and even some exterior siding. That'll make it all weather-proof. Of course, it will look like an add-on. It'll bump out on the north end of your porch."

"Oh, it'll be so useful to me, I won't mind that at all. I can hardly wait for you to get started!"

"Well, then, take a look at these sketches and let me know if you like the way I've planned it."

After getting Ruth's approval, Frank pulled his truck around to the backyard to unload the lumber into the shed at the rear of the property. Its sturdy concrete block structure, cement slab, and heavy tin roof would keep his building supplies secure and dry until he finished the job.

He knew he would need to get busy one of these day, and remove the kudzu that had begun to creep along the creek, and over the back half of the shed. Problem was, there were tangles of blackberry bushes all through it that made it difficult to mow close enough to keep the vines in check. Ruth wanted the blackberries saved, so the cleanup would be a tricky, difficult job, better tackled in the spring.

It's the least I can do for my girl. I'll get this creek bank lookin' so good, she'll be tickled to death! But first I'm gonna get goin' on that pantry.

Pleased with his plans to make things nicer for Ruth, he pulled his truck back to the front, and found her waiting for him on the porch.

"I fixed us some iced tea. Got to take care of my carpenter, now don't I?"

They sat enjoying the late September afternoon, and noting that the edges of the maple leaves had been stitched with red overnight. Cool weather was coming, and soon cups of steaming hot chocolate in front of the fireplace would replace iced tea on the porch.

Frank gave a contented sigh. "What a beautiful afternoon! I love these mountains, especially in the fall. Don't you, Hon?"

"I do, Frank. I know I've only been here a year, but it feels like Wake-Robin Ridge was always meant to be my home. There's somethin' about livin' in the middle of the woods that makes me feel part of every season. I know this is where I belong."

After a while, she leaned over to give Frank a kiss. "You take such good care of me."

Frank pulled her close, kissing the top of her head. "And I always will, Ruth. I always will."

Chapter 11
Is That It?

THE DAYS FOLLOWING Thanksgiving were warmer than usual, with scudding clouds, gray skies, and occasional spatters of rain. Mac had been wrong about the snow, but I had the feeling it was just around the corner. Most of the color was gone from the trees, many having dropped all of their leaves. Branches pointed bare, brown fingers skyward, and the last of the migrating birds, mostly hordes of squabbling grackles, were passing through in noisy flocks. I shivered and pulled my sweater tighter as I walked around my yard, thinking about plans for a spring garden.

I could use the beds that had been established before I bought the cabin. The two largest ones merely needed some weeding and loosening of topsoil, and they would be ready for planting. The beds had been mulched heavily enough to restrict weed growth. I was sure I could do the clean-up work myself.

Clearing along the side of the creek was another matter. Near the bridge, there was one open area which overlooked shallow water racing over the rocks with a happy burble. On either side of this, where there were secretive, dark pools, the banks were overgrown with waist-high weeds, ancient looking blackberry plants, and heaps and mounds of kudzu towering more than fifteen feet high. It was a mess that I knew I couldn't begin to clear by myself. Mac had suggested I let the winter do the bulk of the work for me. It would kill most of the vegetation, and in the spring, I could hire someone with something he called a "bush hog" to get rid of the rest. Then I'd be able to enjoy my view of the entire creek. That plan made sense to me, so I wasn't going to worry about it now.

I walked around to the south side of the cabin, and stood looking over the large rectangular bed there. I figured it used to be the main vegetable garden. It was definitely located in the sunniest part of the yard, so that's what I would have grown there.

I thought it might be fun to add some fresh vegetables to the dinner table. Maybe I could learn how to do some canning. The pantry in the kitchen had been expanded, and I was betting that this bed right in front of me had provided enough vegetables to fill all those extra shelves with jars of tomatoes or beans. I smiled at myself. It was so easy to get caught up in plans like these. Me, canning? Possible, but it wasn't very likely I'd get around to it. It was fun to think about it, though. Maybe I'd just try growing a couple of easy things, and see how it went. A few tomatoes would be nice.

The sound of a truck coming down the drive caught my attention, and I rounded the corner to the front yard just in time to see Mac pulling up. It wasn't like him to drop in unannounced, but I was always glad to see him. I hadn't talked to him in three days, and I wondered what he'd been up to. I watched those long legs of his swing to the ground as he hopped out, and had to make myself quit admiring the way he looked in his faded jeans, as he walked toward me. Don't go there, Sarah, I reminded myself. I aimed for friendly, instead. I was so smilingly friendly it made my teeth hurt.

"Hi, Mac." I gave him a sweetly innocent look designed to say 'I am so not interested in those tight jeans of yours,' and I crossed the rest of the distance between us. "What's up?"

"I have a favor to ask of you, but you have to promise that you won't feel obligated or anything. Really. I know it's a lot, and I don't want to cause any problems for you, and ... "

Oh, boy! Not again with the fidgeting and stammering! I held up my hand. "Mac! Just ask, okay? If I can't help, I'll say so, honest."

He nodded, but I could feel a jittery energy coming off him. There was a tight, pinched look to his mouth, and his eyes had dark circles under them, which made me think he'd had a sleepless night. Or two.

He cleared his throat. "I have to go to Charlotte tonight. I know it's sudden, but I can't help it. I have to go."

He stopped for a moment, looking beyond me to the woods, and then repeated, almost to himself, "I just ... have to go."

He turned back toward me again, but avoided my eyes. "Would you consider watching Rosheen for me for a couple of days? I know it's a lot to ask, but she loves you and it would mean one less thing for me to worry about while I'm gone."

"Is that it? Your big favor?" I smiled at him, wondering where all the angst was coming from. "Of course I'll watch her. I'm happy you trust me to take care of her. Should I come get her now, or do you want to drop her off later?"

He nodded his head, relieved. "Thanks, Sarah. I'll bring her by later, if that's okay. I'm flying out early this evening. So, maybe 3:30 or 4:00?"

"Sure. I'll be home the rest of the day. Just drop her off when you're ready. I promise I'll take good care of her."

He finally looked straight at me. "I know you will, Sarah. There's no one else I'd leave her with. Thank you." He looked so somber, I couldn't help being worried.

"Mac? Is everything all right?"

He sighed, looked away yet again, then forced a very unconvincing smile. "Nothing to worry about. I'll be home Tuesday night. Wednesday at the latest. You can call me if you have any problems. Thanks, again." He turned around, and headed for his truck, driving away without another word.

I stood there staring down the road, thinking that Jenna would surely call this a WTF moment. Sighing, I wondered if I'd ever understand MacKenzie Cole, and if I did, would I be any happier for it?

Mac dropped Rosheen and about a thousand pounds of dog food off around 3:45 that afternoon. He was in a rush, so I just showed him where to stash the food, and wished him a safe trip, and he was gone. He did remember to leave me the phone number for his vet. At least he hadn't let whatever was bothering him distract him from being sure his dog was safe.

As for the big girl, herself, she was more than happy to join me inside the cabin. She and Handsome played until they wore each other out, then fell asleep on the rug by the fire. Rosheen sprawled on her side, long legs sticking straight out, and Handsome curled against her throat, directly under her chin, snug as two bugs.

"ARE YOU KIDDING me? That's not a dog! That's some kind of unnatural wolf-horse hybrid monster!"

Jenna was astonished at the sight of Rosheen, who was staring over my shoulder as we talked. Who could blame her? The giant dog was pretty impressive.

"This is Rosheen, and she's a dog, all right. She's amazing, isn't she?"

"Amazingly huge. You could probably feed a third-world nation with what it costs to keep her in dog food. Tell me again why Mac dumped her on you?"

"Oh, Jenna. He didn't dump her. He stopped by this afternoon and asked me very nicely if I would watch her for a couple of days."

Jenna raised her eyebrows. "This afternoon? That's not much advance warning. What's the big rush about?"

I wondered if I had made a mistake Skyping Jenna while Rosheen was here. I really didn't need to give her any more ammunition to use against Mac, but Sunday was our usual night to chat. She would have called me, anyway.

"I don't really know why he was in such a hurry. He left before I could ask him."

The eyebrows went up another notch.

"Hmm. Interesting."

"Interesting? What's that supposed to mean?"

"Oh, nothing, really. I'm just wondering what Mac has up his sleeve that he has to rush off all mysterious and leave you to take care of his wolf."

"Dog."

"Whatever. What's his story? Someone waiting in Charlotte, maybe? Wife? Partner?"

I didn't answer her, but the look I gave her was enough to make my point. I raise a pretty wicked eyebrow, myself.

"Okay, have it your way. But something about this seems off to me. In fact, a lot seems off about this guy. Am I gonna have to come up there and check him out for myself?"

I grinned. "I dare you! I'd love to see you. But don't come expecting to find out what Mac's story is. He's not talking. And when you meet him, you won't care. You'll like him, anyway."

She didn't believe that for a moment, but she let it drop, and the rest of our chat was pretty much the usual gossip of two friends who have known each other a very long time.

Mac came to get Rosheen late Tuesday night. He looked worn out, and the only conversation we had was just me, reassuring him that Rosheen had been no trouble at all, and was welcome back any time. He was unusually quiet, barely even glancing my way as he loaded the remaining dog food and Rosheen. Mumbling a quick thanks, he climbed behind the wheel, and left. My heart sank. Something was so wrong with this picture, but once again, I had no clue what it was.

Chapter 12
It's Possible I Lied

THREE DAYS LATER, I hadn't heard a word from Mac. I had picked up the phone once or twice each day since his return, thinking I'd just call to touch base, but I hung up every time. I don't know why, but I couldn't work up the nerve to hit that Call button. Whatever the problem was, Mac obviously didn't want to talk to me about it, so I left him alone. But by Friday night, I found I couldn't shake the feeling that something serious might be wrong with him.

"This is ridiculous," I said, grumbling out loud. "We're friends. Why shouldn't I call to see how he is? That's what friends do."

Before I could chicken out again, I grabbed my phone, pulled up his number, and hit Call. Butterflies were doing the samba in my stomach as I listened to the ringing. Just as I was about to disconnect he picked up.

A tired and somehow defeated-sounding voice answered. "What?"

For a moment, I thought I had the wrong number. "Uh, Mac? Is that you?"

He sighed. "What do you want, Sarah?" It still didn't sound like Mac. His voice sounded muffled. Muted, as though he had a cold.

"I, well, um ... I just wanted to be sure you were okay. I didn't mean to bother you." I was confused again, and trying to understand what was going on. Something was definitely off.

Before I could say anything else, Mac ground out, "For the love of God, Sarah, leave me alone!" And he hung up. Just like that.

Stunned, I sank down on the couch, tears stinging my eyes. What had just happened?

I tried to be angry, but all I felt was as miserable as Mac had sounded. Turning off the lights, I lay down in the dim firelight. I could make no sense of it, but a cold lump of dread was growing inside of me. The phone began to ring after a minute or two, but I recognized Mac's ringtone and ignored it. I didn't trust myself to talk to him without losing it. The ringing stopped, then started again. I turned the phone off.

There had been times in my life when men had hurt my feelings, but I couldn't remember anything that had ever made me feel like this. Deliberate cruelty was not part of the Mac I had grown to know. He might be a private man with secrets he wasn't planning to share, but he treated everyone he met with quiet respect and dignity. Our friendship had become something truly special, and I didn't understand what was going on.

I was fighting tears, fearing once I started to cry, I wouldn't be able to stop. We had only known each other four months, but Mac touched my heart in a way no one else ever had. I didn't want to lose that, even if it could never grow into anything more. And I couldn't help feeling that Mac didn't want to lose our friendship, either.

I saw the headlights flare across the back wall before I heard the sound of Mac's truck, and I rose, moving to face the door. My hands were shaking and my stomach was in a knot. He was coming, and I didn't know if that was a good thing, or a very bad one. I heard the truck door slam, and in seconds he was knocking rapidly on my door.

"Sarah? Sarah, please. Open the door. Please, Sarah?"

I stood with my hand on the knob, debating—a mere two inches of wood between us. Jenna's joke about him being a serial killer flashed through my mind. Was he dangerous? Drunk? Mentally unstable?

I heard him make a strangled sound on the other side. "Oh, Sarah, I'm so sorry. Please let me in."

He sounded on the verge of tears. That did it. Whatever the problem was, I couldn't say no to anyone that unhappy, and certainly not to Mac.

I turned the knob and began to open the door, only to have Mac push his way inside, and pull me roughly against him. He buried his face in my hair, his breath hot against my head. "Sarah, Sarah, Sarah. I'm sorry, I'm sorry. I didn't mean it. I'm so sorry." He was trembling all over.

I leaned back to look at him, and the misery in his face was shocking. "Oh, Mac," I whispered. "What is it? What's wrong?"

Instead of answering, he leaned down, and kissed me. Hard. I stood frozen for a moment, then he abruptly let me go, stumbling back with a gasp. He looked almost as shocked as I felt.

"Oh, damn," he choked out, closing his eyes. I took his hand, which was ice-cold, and pulled him into the warmth of the living room, closing the door behind us.

"Sit down, Mac." I led him to the couch, and wrapped my afghan around his shoulders. He huddled there, hunched over with his elbows on his knees, and his face buried in his hands. His breathing was ragged, and he seemed to be struggling to gather control of his emotions. When the worst of his shivering eased, he dropped his hands.

Even by the dim light of the fire, I could see he looked awful. His eyes were bloodshot, and had dark circles underneath them. He hadn't shaved in a day or two, and his hair was tousled every which way.

I felt he wanted to tell me something, but he seemed unable to find the words to begin. When he didn't look at me again, I knelt down in front of him on the floor. I put my palm on his cheek and turned his face toward me. "Mac? It's time. You need to tell me."

"I know," he said, voice barely audible. "I want to, but it's so hard, Sarah." He took a deep, shaky breath. "I don't know how to talk about it. I never have before, not to anyone." His voice broke, and his eyes shone with unshed tears.

I moved up to sit beside him, and took his hand in mine. "Try. Just try, Mac. I can't be here for you if I don't know what's wrong."

He looked at me, searching for something in my eyes. Reassurance, perhaps. Then he turned back to stare into the fire, drawing courage from the warmth of the flames. I waited.

Mac's eyes were focused on something far away, and he held my hand in a death grip. Finally, he took another shuddering breath and began to talk, his voice barely above a whisper. "I went to Charlotte to see my son."

"You have a son?" I asked, after he had been quiet for a long moment.

He started to say something, then stopped. He cleared his throat and tried again, twice, before managing to go on. "Had. I had a son. He died."

It was obvious just saying the words tore him apart. His pain was like a living presence in the room, and I would have done just about anything to ease it for him; but I thought that this was probably a story he needed to tell in his own way, so I waited. He spoke in such a halting manner, it was easy to believe he had never said any of this out loud.

"Monday was his birthday ... he would have been eighteen." He gave a ragged sigh. "Grown up. I still see him small, laughing ... playing in the sandbox with his trucks." He stopped again.

"I always go on his birthday, but I wasn't going to this year. I thought I could stay here ... be with you ... just not think about it, for this one year. I'm good at not thinking about it most of the time. I just pretend everything is all right." Another long pause. "My life is all about pretending."

He was gripping my hand so hard, I thought I would probably have bruises tomorrow. I let him.

He started again, his voice rough with emotion. "I had a dream about him Saturday night. It was so real, Sarah. Like he was right there, at the foot of my bed. He was holding his teddy and crying. It broke my heart all over again."

There was a slight catch in his breath before he could go on. "I got up Sunday, and I knew I had to go. I just had to, Sarah. Mostly, I try to keep it all in one corner of my mind. I couldn't function, if I didn't. But sometimes ... I just ... well, I just have to go. I can't stand it if I don't."

Another shuddering breath. "I hate thinking of him being there, alone and forgotten. No one to visit his grave. No one to tell him how much he is missed."

"Oh, Mac," I whispered, feeling my own tears starting. He turned toward me then, putting his hand on the side of my face.

"Don't cry, Sarah. I don't want you to cry. You are the best thing to come into my life in a long, long time, and all I do is push you away. I don't deserve your friendship, much less your tears."

I blinked the tears back. I was not going to make this harder for him. "I'm all right, Mac, don't worry."

He nodded wearily, took another breath, and started again. The words began to come, slow and halting at first, but then spilling out faster, as he felt the relief of letting go of his secrets. "I got married right out of college to a girl I met there. She was beautiful, and smart. Fun to be with. She came from a wealthy family. Spoiled, I guess. It didn't bother me, really. I indulged her as much as everyone else. Maybe more. I loved her. I thought we would grow old together."

He paused, struggling for control, and then went on, speaking very low. "We had only been married a little over a year when Ben was born."

He turned toward me with a look of love on his face so profound, it took my breath away. "Oh, I wish you could have seen him. He was ... *incredible*! So beautiful, right down to his tiny little fingers and toes! Nothing ever prepared me for what being a father would be like. My dad and I have always been close, but he isn't an outwardly affectionate man. So I didn't know. I didn't understand how it would be.

The first time I held Ben, I felt it. It was beyond anything I could have even imagined. God, I loved him so much!"

His voice was filled with sorrowful longing. "Oh, Sarah! I wanted to give him the whole world, bring him here, teach him to hunt and fish, watch him grow up. Sometimes, even after all these years, I still can't believe that's not going to happen."

He shook his head sadly, staring at the fire, fighting tears. When he turned back toward me, the light had left his eyes.

"Vikki seemed to resent the time I spent with him. After Ben was born, she changed. I thought it was just hard for her to adjust to being a mother at such a young age. She seemed bored and restless. I let her do as she pleased. I wanted her to be as happy as I was, and I thought that after a while, she would want to spend more time together. The three of us. As a family. I was so blind. And of course, I was the last to know what was going on."

He hung his head, staring at the floor, his voice weary, weighed down. "Luncheons with the girls ... tennis dates ... shopping trips. All of it, lies. Everyone knew but me, of course. All of our so-called friends. Talking behind my back. Some of them laughing. Some giving me these pitying looks that I didn't understand."

He stopped, shaking his head in disgust, and taking another deep breath. "I was so stupid. I actually thought forever meant ... *forever*. Can you believe it?"

I believed it. I knew Mac's heart, and I had no doubt he would have taken marriage vows very seriously, indeed.

"You can't imagine what a fool I felt like when I found out. The betrayal was bad enough, but she didn't even care when she realized I knew. She said I was naive and unsophisticated, and that the affairs were nothing unusual in her circles. Why was I making such a big deal of it? It all felt so ... *degrading*. Like my feelings weren't worth worrying about."

He sat remembering for a moment, then took a deep breath, and went on. "She took Ben when she left me. He was only five months old. I felt ... broken. One day I had a beautiful wife I loved and a perfect baby I adored, and the next day, I was alone. I couldn't understand what happened, what I had done wrong. Why hadn't I seen it sooner? Made her happier? Why was I alone, my son and the woman I had loved for three years, gone?" He stopped, then repeated, painfully, "Why was I alone?"

His head dropped lower, and he looked humiliated and ashamed. Ashamed? I hated this woman. I hated how much she had hurt Mac and how deeply she had scarred him, leaving him to think that somehow he had failed her.

I reached over and brushed his hair out of his eyes. He looked at me for a moment with a lost expression on his face, then he turned his face away, and stared at the floor between his feet.

"She got custody of Ben, of course. I never had a chance. I was supposed to have regular visitation, but she managed to find ways to keep me away, as often as not. There were fights and ugly scenes every time I went to get him. I began to hate her, Sarah."

He wrapped his arms tightly around himself, and I could see him beginning to tremble again. I wanted to hold him, but he looked like he might fly apart if I touched him.

"I had never known I was capable of such hatred, but I was. I hated her more than you can imagine! I wanted my son back. I wished for anything that would bring him back. Anything. Some days ... some days, I wished her dead, Sarah. Do you understand?"

His voice had dropped so low, I had to strain to hear. "God help me, I wished her dead so I could have Ben back."

He stopped talking and sat breathing harshly, now staring straight ahead. Somehow I knew what was coming, and I wanted to put both hands over my ears to block it out.

No, no, no. Please don't tell me this.

"I got my wish."

The despair in those four words was utterly heartbreaking.

"I was supposed to have Ben the day before his third birthday. I had planned a party for him, and I was really looking forward to it. He was getting so big, and he was such a happy little boy."

He paused again, taking a shuddering breath, his eyes still glittering with tears. "Vikki called the night before I was to pick him up to tell me he was sick. She said it was a bad cold, and he couldn't come. It was a lie, of course. Instead, she took him sailing near Hatteras, with her latest boyfriend."

There was a hitch in his voice. He paused, took another shaky breath, then started again, almost whispering now. "They never returned to the marina. The boat was discovered capsized the day after his birthday, and they found Ben on the beach, shortly after that. It was another week before Vikki's body was recovered. The boyfriend was just gone."

He was shaking all over again, practically gulping for air. I pulled him to me and wrapped my arms around him. He buried his head in my neck and began to cry. Great, wracking sobs that had been locked inside him all these years.

"I wished it on them, Sarah . . . I wanted her dead, and she died, but she took my son with her!"

I held him a long time, fighting my own tears, and trying to be strong for him. I knew there was nothing I could say to take this pain away from him, but I had to let him know that nothing he had told me would ever change how I felt about him. When the storm was over, I whispered, "Oh, Mac. This is not your fault. You can't wish someone dead. You know that. You can't keep blaming yourself."

He straightened, scrubbing at his eyes, looking shocked at his loss of control. He turned toward the fire, hiding his face from me once again, struggling for composure.

"I know that in my mind," he said in a hoarse whisper, "but in my heart, it feels very different, Sarah. It just hurts. Always."

He shuddered as though the hurt was as strong today as it had been fifteen years ago. "When it happened, I felt like I might as well lie down and die myself. I thought I knew what pain was when Vikki left me, but it was nothing compared to losing Ben. Nothing at all. And the guilt was constantly gnawing at me—the feeling that my own selfishness had cost them both their lives. They say be careful what you wish for, don't they?"

He turned back to look at me. "I never told anyone about it. I was too ashamed. I had no right to wish that on anyone, but I did, and they all died, and I couldn't tell anyone that it felt like my fault. Until you."

I felt a strange sense of responsibility, being the one person he had trusted enough to share his darkest secret with. I only wished I knew what to do to help him deal with it all.

I nodded at him to go on. I had a feeling he wasn't done yet, and I was right.

With another deep breath, he began again, this time with more control, though his voice still sounded rough and thick with emotion.

"I have no idea how I got through the funeral and those first weeks afterward. But when I was finally able to function outwardly like a normal person, I swore to God that I would never again let anyone into my heart. Be damned if I would open myself up to that kind of pain. Not for any woman on earth. For years, I've kept myself apart. I've avoided any sort of relationship at all, except for the most superficial of friendships. I've been very, very good at keeping the promise I made to myself.

"When I moved here, I felt a measure of peace for the first time since I lost Ben. I knew that this was where I was meant to spend the rest of my life. Being here calms something inside of me. I thought I had found everything I needed, and that I had it all under control, at last. And then I met you."

I sat staring at him, not understanding. Had I triggered this painful episode for him? Was he breaking off our friendship? I was heartbroken over what he had been through, yes, but terrified at the thought of saying goodbye to him. He was watching me so closely, I wasn't sure what I was supposed to say.

I heard my voice sounding very small and hesitant. "Did I do something wrong? Make it worse, somehow?"

He gave me an odd little smile. "No, Sarah. You offered me friendship when I didn't think I wanted it. You accepted me, in spite of my pathetic attempts to reject you. You brought laughter into my house before I even knew that's what was missing. You did everything right, Sarah."

I couldn't quite believe what he was saying. After weeks of sticking to a friends-only relationship, was it possible he was thinking about changing the rules? Or was that just wishful thinking on my part?

He tilted his head to the side and exhaled slowly. "Look at you. Sitting here with such patience, letting me unload this on you. Trying to make it easier for me, even after I was such a shit to you earlier. I hung up on you, Sarah! After you called to see if I was okay, I told you to leave me alone, and I hung up! And you ask me if you've done something wrong? God. I'm an ass."

His thumb was stroking the back of my hand as he talked, making me shiver. I wondered if he was even aware he was doing it.

"I thought I was so clever. No one could touch me. I didn't need anyone at all, just me and my dog. Then there you were, sitting by that creek with your goofy cat, and your enthusiasm for all the things you wanted to do. You were so beautiful with the leaves floating down around you. I thought how brave you were, starting your life over, alone."

Brave? And beautiful? Mac thought I was beautiful? My heart missed a beat.

"By the time I got home that afternoon, I was disgusted with myself, and I was afraid of how you made me feel, so I didn't call. I told myself to forget about it. The hiking, you, everything. But when I ran into you at Everly's, I realized how much I wanted to get to know you. I wanted what you had ... the ability to feel something again. Anything. Spending that day with you made me feel ... *hopeful*."

He paused, thinking for a moment, then went on. "You make me see everything with new eyes, Sarah. Even myself."

"Do you think that's a good thing?" I asked in a cautious voice.

"I think it might be." His voice was solemn, but he was looking straight into my eyes. And he was still stroking the back of my hand.

"I think it's probably a thing that has needed to happen for a long time. I just didn't know it. I didn't want to talk about what I had been through. I didn't want to talk about anything at all, really, with anyone. And I thought I was fine just marking time every day."

He looked away for a second, gathering his thoughts, then met my eyes once more.

"I got by like that for years, you know. But from the first day I saw you, I felt something inside me shift. I wanted to resist, and then I thought, why should I? Why can't I have a friend to share things with? It felt good to have someone to laugh with, and to walk in the woods with. But I swore it was not going beyond that. Friends, and no more. I didn't need or want anything more than that."

"Is that still how you feel?" I asked, almost afraid to breathe.

"I'm not so sure," he admitted. "I think I realized I was fighting a hopeless battle on Thanksgiving, when we were sitting on the balcony after dinner. I wanted to hold your hand. It felt so right to be there together, watching the day come to a close. I didn't want you to go home."

My heart was beating even faster. Oh my God. He's really saying this.

"Sarah, this trip to Charlotte was really confusing for me. I felt the same grief I always do when I visit Ben's grave, but Monday, part of me realized it was time to make some changes. Time to start trying to live the rest of my life in a different way. Trouble is, it's hard to bring down walls that have been in place for so long. It's just so *hard*.

"I argued with myself all the way home, wanting to see you as fast as I could one minute, and then never wanting to see you again the next!"

He let go of my hand and rubbed his face, agitated and nervous. "You make me feel all the possibilities out there, but being with you means moving forward. Part of me wants to stay in the past. I've gotten comfortable with solitude. It's a lifestyle I've perfected, and I don't much like change. I don't even know if I can change."

He ran his fingers through his hair, then leaned back on the couch, resting his head, eyes closed. I was determined to let him finish the things he wanted to say, so I sat quietly until he was ready to start talking again.

Finally, he began, voice taut with emotion. "When I stopped to get Rosheen and you came to the door, I couldn't even look at you! I was afraid of what I might do or say. Instead, I went home and hid in my house, and argued with myself for three days, back and forth, until I thought my head would explode.

"I don't want anyone in my life ... I do want someone in my life!

I just want to be friends ... I want to be much more than friends!

I don't need this ... I need this more than words can say!"

I felt tears starting again, and my heart was racing like mad now. I didn't trust myself to say anything at all.

He sat up and took my hand again, holding it in both of his, eyes full of regret. "You caught me in an 'I don't need this' moment when you called. But as soon as I told you to leave me alone, I panicked. What if you did? What if you wanted nothing else to do with me? Who would blame you? Then I couldn't think about anything else but getting to you. I felt desperate to be with you, to be close to you."

He looked back at the fire again, hunched over, shoulders tense, and clinging to my hand like a lifeline. "I needed to tell you everything, no matter how it turned out. I knew it would be hard to say these things out loud, but I thought, if not to Sarah, then who? Who else will ever listen to me, or care? How do I learn to trust anyone, if I can't trust Sarah? Who can ever love me, if she can't?"

I couldn't speak. I couldn't think. I was filled with pain for his loss and what he had put himself through as punishment, and for how he had walled himself off from the world to protect his heart. I was overwhelmed with emotions on every level. My hands were shaking and my heart was pounding, and I was trying as hard as I could not to cry.

I was still having trouble accepting some of the things he was saying to me, but I knew one thing beyond all doubt. I loved this man. I loved him so much! If he just wanted me as a friend, then I would be the best friend he had ever had. If the rules were about to change, all the better, though it would not be an easy path for either of us.

He took a big gulping breath. "I know I've overwhelmed you with all of this, but I was afraid if I stopped, I'd never be able to start again. It's probably more than you ever wanted to know, but I have no more secrets, Sarah. This is who I am. But it's not who I want to be.

"Please forgive me for the times I've been unfair to you. I never meant to hurt you. It's just that I've been set in this pattern for so long, it's hard to be any other way. Letting you into my life scares me. Keeping you out scares me more. Spending time with you has meant more to me than you can imagine. I hope we can still share the things that we both love ... "

My heart sank. I felt a "but" coming.

"But Sarah, I can't promise you that friendship is all I'll ever want. The truth is, what I feel for you is changing. I wake up in the morning, wondering what you are doing with your day, and I go to sleep at night hoping your day made you happy. I know that's not what we agreed on. I know we said no complications, no strings, no messy emotions. But about that 'just friends' thing?" He paused for a moment, "It's possible I lied. To you and to myself."

With a worried—practically terrified—look on his face, he waited for my reaction. He was blotchy-faced and red-eyed from the outpouring of grief. He looked scruffy, exhausted, and miserable. Guilt hung over him like a mantle. Years of unhappiness and self-punishment seemed to have caught up with him all at once.

But there was a deep longing in his eyes, and underneath it all, I saw my Mac. He was a man of honesty and inherent goodness, and he was trying to take a step forward. He had been lost, but he wanted to be found. In short, he was beautiful.

God, I was a goner. I wasn't sure what lay ahead, but I knew I would never turn my back on MacKenzie Cole.

I reached for him, tears spilling from my eyes, and he came to me, with a choked cry. He kissed me over and over, until I was breathless and trembling, myself.

Then he pulled back to look at me, shaking his head in wonder. His long fingers slid down the side of my face, and touched the corner of my mouth. He leaned his forehead against mine, and whispered, "Sarah. Beautiful Sarah. What am I going to do with you?"

I turned my head to kiss the tips of his fingers. "We'll figure it out as we go, Mac."

I wish I could say we ended up making wild, passionate love in front of the fire, but I don't think either of us was ready for that step yet. Mac was emotionally drained. He had trusted me like he had trusted no one else in fifteen years, but telling me this story had left him exhausted.

I was filled with an overwhelming heartache for him, and for his little boy, so long gone, but so loved, still. I didn't imagine Mac's pain would disappear overnight, and the way forward would not likely be easy, but I was willing to go slowly. He was worth it.

We sat on the couch for a long time, watching the fire die down to embers, neither wanting to be the one to let go of the other long enough to add another log. Mac's arms were around me, and my head was resting on his chest. I listened to the steady beating of his heart, and knew I wanted this with all of mine. It was enough for now.

Chapter 13
You Can, You Should, I Should Have

THURSDAY, DECEMBER 24, 1964

FRANK EVERLY WAS as nervous as he had ever been in his life. As his truck climbed the last hill to Ruth's cabin, he kept practicing what to say when he gave her his Christmas presents. Nothing sounded right, and he was getting a jittery feeling in his stomach. He hoped what he had done would go over well, but sometimes Ruth was hard to figure. He knew how she felt about him, though, and he decided to believe that she'd love his gifts because she loved him.

This was their second Christmas together, and though they were both happiest when they were with each other, Frank was worried. Ruth still hadn't said yes to his frequent proposals. He dreamed of them being husband and wife, maybe starting a family someday. He was a patient man,

133

and he knew he'd never love anyone else like he loved Ruth, but he was almost 35, and he longed for a real home. He didn't understand why Ruth still shied away from making that final commitment.

Darn if that's not the exact opposite of how it usually is. He turned his truck into Ruth's drive, and pulled up in front of her cabin. *Well, if she thinks I'm gonna give up, she's got another think comin'!*

Frank killed the engine, opened the door, and hopped out of the truck, with Ruth's Christmas present squirming under his arm.

He climbed the steps to the front porch and knocked, with second thoughts still worrying him. He figured he'd know if he'd made a mistake with gift number one as soon as she opened the door, and he was right. Ruth's delighted squeal put his fears to rest.

"Oh, Frank! He's so adorable!" She grabbed the little dachshund and laughed with delight as the puppy began to lavish kisses all over her face.

"Oh, you are so cute! Look at you with your big red bow! I love him, Frank!" She stopped and turned to Frank, eyes gone wide. "He is mine, isn't he?"

Frank gave her a big hug. "Of course he's yours. Merry Christmas, Sweetheart. This is your new protector for when I can't be here with you."

"He's my new best friend, you mean," Ruth said, resuming her love fest with the puppy. "Come on in, and sit down."

He watched Ruth remove the Christmas bow, and put the puppy down on the floor to play. The little dog scampered around, yapping like crazy, and making them both laugh.

"He's such a pretty little sausage," Ruth said. "I love his red color. He's bright as a new penny. In fact, I think that's what I'll name him. Penny."

"If that's what you like, Hon, but isn't it a bit girly for a boy dog?" Frank asked.

"Not if it's his last name. Look how bossy he is already, plannin' to rule the roost, I bet! He's officially General Penny, my best friend and fierce protector."

"Well, your fierce protector apparently thinks you need savin' from your own fingers," Frank said, as he watched the puppy chewing on Ruth with sharp little baby teeth.

She giggled with delight. "Now Penny, you stop that, silly boy."

Frank looked on, beaming, proud that he had chosen something that made Ruth this happy. If he only knew how, he would wipe away every trace of that deep sadness in her eyes, forever.

"I'm gonna need to get a bowl, and food, and a leash, and a collar ... oh, and lots of toys and blankets for him, too," she said.

"Got most of that in a box in the truck, Hon."

"Aw, Frank! I should have known you'd think of everything," Ruth smiled. Then she grew quiet. "Did you know I've never had a dog before?"

He was amazed, but not really surprised. "I'm sorry to hear that. We always had dogs when I was growin' up. And cats, too. All sorts of pets, really, even some wild ones. It always made the house more fun."

"Well, Penny is my first, ever, and I love you so much for giving him to me."

Frank shook his head, chuckling. "Oh, Sweetheart, please tell me that's not the only reason you're lovin' me?"

Ruth grew still, Penny forgotten, as she gave Frank a serious look. "Oh, no. I love you for more reasons than I can ever explain. I'm so lucky I found you, and I will always love you, Frank. Forever and ever. No matter what happens."

Frank got down on the floor to give Ruth a kiss, and they held hands while they enjoyed the little dog's antics. Finally, General Penny wore himself out, and curled up on the hearth rug to take a nap.

Ruth went back to the kitchen to check on dinner and set the table. Frank stretched out on the sofa, watching little stars of light sparking off the tinsel on Ruth's small Christmas tree, and feeling very happy about how the afternoon had gone.

So far, so good. Of course, there was still the midnight blue velvet box in his pocket, but he wanted to wait until tomorrow to give that to her.

FRANK WOKE AHEAD of Ruth on Christmas morning, and crept downstairs. When Ruth came down later, sleepy-eyed, and wrapped in a cozy flannel robe, he had already turned on the tree and lit the fire. The room was filled with the aroma of fresh-brewed coffee.

Frank hugged her good morning, and led her to the table, where he had laid out sweet rolls and poured coffee. "Merry Christmas, Darlin'."

"Merry Christmas to you, too, Frank."

After they finished their light breakfast, Ruth put the turkey in the oven, and then went back upstairs to get dressed, leaving Frank playing a spirited game of sock tug-of-war with the puppy.

"We should take Penny for a little walk when you come back down," Frank called after her. "He looks like he needs to burn off a bit of energy."

And so, when she returned, they took the pup outside for his first romp in the yard. Penny raced around barking at everything, stubby legs a blur as he ran, and long ears flapping behind him. He was the picture of joyous freedom and happiness, delighting in every sight and smell the yard had to offer.

Back inside, Penny fell asleep in his box, and Ruth went to work at the stove, putting the winter squash in the oven next to the roasting turkey, and doing other mysterious food-related things Frank didn't understand.

He was glad Ruth preferred exchanging gifts on Christmas morning, rather than opening them on Christmas Eve. It had given him a little bit longer to work up his courage. His secret was still snug in his pocket, waiting for her to finish in the kitchen. At last, she took her apron off and joined him in the living room.

"You're as excited as a little kid," he told her, watching from the couch as she got down on her knees and rummaged under the tree. Her eyes were dancing as she pulled out a red and green wrapped box, and handed it to him.

"Aw, Ruth, you shouldn't go spending your money on me," Frank protested, until he realized how happy she was to be giving him a gift. "But, thank you, Hon. It's real sweet of you to get me something." When he opened the box, he found a beautiful pair of warmly lined leather gloves, just his size.

"How did you know how much I needed these?" He asked, grinning with pleasure, surprised by what a perfect gift it was.

"I saw the holes in your old ones last week, and it looked to me like you were goin' to have some pretty cold hands by January. I know they say 'cold hands, warm heart,' but to me cold hands just means cold hands," she said, laughing. "I had to go to Asheville to find some with soft enough leather. I wanted them to feel wonderful, right from the first time you pulled them on."

Frank was already trying them out, and they were perfect. He beamed at her. "This is a wonderful gift, Ruth, and I'll think about you every day when I put them on to go outside." He leaned over to kiss her, and saw that she was blushing with delight.

What kind of life has my Ruth led that she's a stranger to the pleasure of giving a gift to someone she loves? It wasn't the first time he wondered about things like this, and he was pretty sure it wouldn't be the last. Maybe someday he would understand, but for now, he was simply happy to share this beautiful Christmas morning with her.

Her cheeks were still flushed bright pink, and her eyes sparkled as she announced, "I have some more stuff for you, too, but mostly just little things. Oh, and I made you a big batch of your favorite apple butter to take home, so you can have it with your toast in the morning, too."

Her joy and enthusiasm were contagious, and warmed his heart. Then he thought about his real gift for her, and felt jittery all over again.

"Ruth, sweetheart? I have another gift for you, too."

Ruth's brow furrowed. "But, you already gave me Penny, and all that puppy stuff he needs. I can't imagine you have something else."

"Do you trust me?" Frank asked.

"Yes," she answered at once. "I trust you completely."

"Then close your eyes and hold out your hand."

Without hesitation, Ruth did just that. Frank sat the small box in the palm of her hand, and whispered, "Open your eyes."

Ruth froze when she saw the little velvet box. She looked at Frank with a worried frown, but he held up his hand, saying, "You said you trusted me, remember? Just open the box, Hon."

This was the moment he'd been waiting for. He watched as, with trembling fingers, she did just that. She stared, an expression of amazement on her face. Nestled in the box was a heart-shaped aquamarine, her birthstone, set in silver and surrounded by tiny little diamonds. Tears came to her eyes as she looked at him again, and with a sinking feeling, he knew she was going to give it back.

"Sweetheart, listen to me, please? This isn't an engagement ring. I know you don't want to get married now. This is just to remind you every day of how much I love you. It means I'm giving you my heart for now and always. It's a token of how I feel about you. Please wear it for me, Ruth."

She had cried the first time he called her "Sweetheart," explaining later that she had never been anyone's sweetheart before. He meant for her to know every time she looked at the ring that she would always be his. Loved. Cherished. He desperately wanted her to accept it. To him, it proved she loved him back, and made his dreams that much closer to reality.

Now he took her trembling hand, and slowly slid the ring on her finger. It fit perfectly. Ruth seemed too overwhelmed to speak. He held his breath, hoping, praying.

"I don't deserve anything so nice, Frank. I can't ... I shouldn't ... you shouldn't have ... " She stopped even trying to speak when Frank leaned over and kissed her.

"You can, you should, I should have. I love you, and I'm pretty sure you love me. I want to marry you someday, but I know you aren't ready for that. Until that happens, I want everyone who sees you to know what you mean to me. You are my whole life, Ruth Winn. I will never love anyone else the way I love you."

She smiled at him through the last of her tears, and said, "I'll never take it off, Frank. Never. And I will always belong to you, as long as I live."

Frank thought even getting married couldn't top this moment. Ruth had said out loud that she belonged to him. He felt like his heart would burst. Surely, the day couldn't be far off when she would agree to marry him, and they could grow old together, loving each other through all that lay ahead.

It was only a matter of time, and he would be able to call her his wife. Those two magic words. My wife. He could picture himself saying them to strangers. "This is my wife, Ruth." They would look at her sweet face, pale blonde hair framing her big blue eyes, and think he was a lucky man. And he was. He never felt luckier in his life than he did on Christmas morning, 1964.

Chapter 14
Yes, I Said Zany!

I SHIVERED AND pulled the afghan up a bit more, snuggling back against the solid warmth behind me. Then my eyes flew open, and I realized I was lying on my side, with Mac spooned against my back. He had one arm thrown across my body, and his breath was warm against the nape of my neck.

Everything about the night before came rushing back into my mind—the pain, the tears and confessions, the hungry, desperate kisses—and I knew my life was about to move into uncharted waters. It was a sobering, somewhat frightening thought, but I pushed it away for now. I just wanted to revel in the pleasure of waking up in Mac's arms. It felt heavenly. If I could have, I would have purred. It always seemed to work for Handsome.

At some point, we had stretched out on the sofa together and fallen asleep. Now, I lay there looking at Mac's hand cupped over mine, and remembered how I had watched those hands of his when he was cooking Thanksgiving dinner, thinking how beautiful they were. Was that really only a little more than a week ago? How could so much have changed in the space of one night? And how would Mac feel when he woke, and realized what he had said and done? Would there be regret or embarrassment in his eyes? A shutting down of his feelings again?

One after the other, questions rose in my mind, then popped and dissipated like bubbles, to be replaced by new ones. I willed myself to stop worrying about things I had no control over, and sank into the pleasure of the moment.

I knew the minute Mac woke. His breathing shifted out of the deep, regular sound of sleep, and his arm jerked slightly, then relaxed again. I waited for him to say something, but instead, he lay very still against me, as though he wanted the moment to last as much as I did. One by one, he laced his fingers through mine and tightened his grip the tiniest bit. He pulled me back against him, and I felt his soft lips brush the back of my neck.

"Good morning, Sarah Gray," he whispered in my ear.

"Good morning to you, MacKenzie Cole," I whispered back.

We lay in silence for a few more minutes, and then he sat up and stretched. He gave me one of those long, focused looks of his, then apparently decided things were less awkward than they might have been. With a half-smile, he said, "I need to get home. Rosheen will be desperate to go out by now." He leaned over and brushed a feather-soft kiss on my forehead. "I'll call you later, if it's okay?"

"Of course it's okay. Give Rosheen a pat for me."

"Sarah?" He looked down again. God, I hated that he still needed to do that.

"Yes?"

He still didn't raise his eyes to mine, but I knew this was the best he had in him, for now. "Thank you. For listening. For trying to understand. I'm not an easy man to know, but I promise to try to be better."

"Just let yourself be who you really are, Mac. That's all you need to do. Now go let Rosheen out. Talk to you later."

He left then. I stood at the door, watching him walk to his truck and thinking about all that he'd said to me.

Oh, boy. This could either end in a very good way, or a very bad one. Guess I'll just have to have faith that it will turn out to be the good way.

But leave it to me to end up loving a man like MacKenzie Cole, a veritable poster boy for angst and pain. What was I thinking? Of course, the answer was that I wasn't. I was in love, and love does what it damn well pleases, with precious little thinking involved at all.

FRIDAY, DECEMBER 9, 2011

AS GOOD AS his word, Mac was trying hard. A week had gone by, and he had called every night. Our conversations were about day-to-day things, he with his business and I with my book. I didn't expect anything else right away. Getting Mac to step out of his comfort zone would be harder than pulling the proverbial hen's teeth, and I sure wasn't going to rush him. He had years of emotional isolation to work through. Letting go of it, and learning to trust someone again would take time.

I had missed seeing him all week, but I had a suspicion he was trying to come to terms with the fact that I now knew more about his darkest thoughts and bleakest moments than anyone else on earth. I could picture him alternating between profound relief at having finally told someone, and a fervent desire to take it all back. Old habits die hard, and Mac's life, before I came along and poked the sleeping bear, had been nothing but one long, fiercely-guarded habit. I didn't know how he had survived living the way he had. People are social creatures. It's against our nature to wall ourselves off from everyone.

The sound of my phone interrupted my musings. I recognized the opening bars of "Wild Thing," the ringtone I had given Mac weeks ago as my own private joke. I was pretty sure no one could be less wild than he. I glanced at the clock. He was calling earlier than usual. "Hey, Mac. How are you?"

"I'm good. How about you?"

"Me, too." I waited, letting him set the pace, as always.

"Are you doing anything special tonight?" He sounded a bit nervous. Uh-oh.

"Umm, nope. Just working on my book, and getting ready to heat a frozen pot pie for dinner later."

Silence.

"Why do you ask?"

More silence.

"I can hear you breathing, you know."

A nervous gulp that might have been trying to be a chuckle, and then silence again.

I waited. He cleared his throat. I waited a bit longer. Sometimes my patience astounds even me. He cleared his throat again.

Finally, he spoke. "I was just thinking maybe you'd like to go to dinner with me—maybe Asheville might be good, if you wanted to drive that far—but any place is fine with me. Whatever you'd like, I mean."

It came out in a rush, like he was trying to say it before he chickened out and hung up. A sixteen-year-old boy, asking a girl out for the very first time, would have been smoother, and that made my heart hurt. That a man forty years old could be so nervous inviting a possible girlfriend on a dinner date seemed ineffably sad.

"That sounds like fun. I'd love to. Do you have some place in mind? What should I wear?"

Now that he had mustered the courage to ask me out, and I had given him something else to think about, he seemed more at ease. "Casual would be fine. We can decide when we get there. Can I pick you up at six?"

I looked at the clock. Five-fifteen. Close, but doable. "Sure. See you then."

I hung up and raced upstairs to get a shower. Ten minutes later, I was shivering in my bra and panties as I dug through clothes in my closet like a thing possessed. I flung stuff everywhere, rejecting one pair of slacks after another. These were too tight, those the wrong color. Where were my good black ones? Ah-ha. Found 'em.

Then I began fretting over which top would keep me warm on a chilly evening, yet still look nice enough—read "sexy" enough—for a casual dinner date. I wanted him to like how I looked. After all, he'd never seen me in anything but jeans and tees or sweatshirts. I wasn't a particularly clothes-conscious kind of gal, but I wanted to do better than that tonight.

Finally, I settled on an outfit I thought would be flattering without looking like I had tried too hard. The black turtleneck was warm and fit perfectly. I actually felt kind of sexy in it, too. A bit. I tucked it into my best slacks, added a pair of black leather boots and some oversized silver hoops in my ears. Casual and comfortable, and suitable for most restaurants in the area. I raced back to the bathroom to dry my hair, debated putting it into my usual ponytail, and decided against it. I put on a little bit more make-up than I normally would, then took some of it off. When Mac knocked on the door, I was as ready as I was likely to get.

The expression on Mac's face was all I needed to see to know my outfit was a hit. The look in his eyes was so worth the effort. "You look very nice. I like your hair down like that."

I blushed. Can you believe it? I blushed! And here I had thought Mac was going to be the shy one. We were hopeless, the both of us. He leaned down and gave me a sweet kiss. I kissed him back. Then, I locked the door, and we left on our first "official" date, acting like a pair of awkward teenagers. All we needed was a scowling father standing on the porch, and warning us not to be out past curfew.

MAC TOOK ME to a cozy, family-owned Italian restaurant. The lights were soft, the dinner music romantic, but not intrusive, and the food, delicious. It was perfect for what I continued to think of as our First Date.

My beautiful, elegant, and normally unflappable Mac was, well, flapping! Not a lot, but enough to let me know he was nervous. After a glass of very good red wine and some warm, crusty bread, I think he realized things were going fine, and he relaxed a bit. I made small talk, and told him a couple of funny stories about Handsome's antics, giving him time to settle down even more.

"Your cat is crazy, you know. Nice, but crazy," he said, grinning.

"Well, at least he doesn't make people run screaming at first sight, like that hulking, gray beast of yours!"

"Hey! Don't be picking on my dog, now. Rosheen doesn't deserve that!"

"You're right. She's a lovely dog. What does 'Rosheen' mean, anyway?"

Mac grinned. "It's actually Celtic for 'horse.' Fits, right?"

I laughed. "Perfectly!"

We managed to avoid any tricky subjects, and just tried to enjoy each other's company. But there were moments when I caught Mac looking at me with something akin to sheer terror in his eyes, and I remembered the expression on his face when he told me he had sworn he would never let another woman into his life. It was obvious he wanted to open the door he had kept locked for so long, but I could see it was a constant struggle for him.

I wondered how, or even if, I could ever convince him his heart was safe with me. Jenna would tell me Mac was a lost cause, but I believed every small, personal anecdote from him was a step forward. I kept the conversation moving along those lines, and hoped for the best. I took a sip of wine, and as I watched him talking, I realized that everything I had ever really wanted was sitting right across the table from me. There was no way I would give up on him.

As he told a story from a childhood camping trip, Mac was animated and funny. I loved seeing him smile this much. It was distracting, though, that sexy smile, with his white, even teeth, and perfectly shaped lips. Oh, boy. Now I was thinking even his teeth were sexy? I was so hopeless!

Concentrate, Sarah! He's talking, here! Do you want him to think you aren't interested?

That worked for a few seconds, and then I zoned out again, lost in watching the way his hands moved as he picked up his wine glass, or admiring the hollow at the base of his throat, where a pulse beat just below the surface of his skin.

My God, he's beautiful!

His black hair shone in the candlelight, and tonight, those wintry blue eyes seldom left mine, whether he was talking about his unshakeable belief in Santa Claus as a kid, or listening to me tell funny stories about the trouble Jenna would get me into during high school. I had to force myself to stop fantasizing about him like a lovesick schoolgirl.

"Someday, I think I need to have a long talk with your best friend. Maybe you aren't as prim as you'd like me to believe."

"I beg your pardon," I replied. "Why would you say I'm prim? I have my wild side, you know."

He snorted derisively. "Why do I think you could give me a run for my money when it comes to being unwaveringly staid, Sarah?"

"I'm sure I don't know what would make you think that!"

"Well, for one thing, people with wild sides don't usually end up living alone in the woods, like you and I."

"I'll have you know I can be as fun-loving and zany— yes, I said zany—as anybody else," I said, sputtering in indignation. "If I seem all sober and boring to you, it's because I've been working on important stuff. I haven't had time to ... um ... to be all devil-may-care and frivolous about things. I promise you, I can be a lot of fun, MacKenzie Cole! A. Lot."

He tilted his head to one side and gave me a wicked grin. "I never for one minute doubted that you could be a lot of fun, Sarah Gray."

My eyes widened, as I tried to imagine what kind of fun scenario he might be considering. Then he continued, "But zany? Ummm ... nope. Can't see that. Maybe you could give me some visual aids?"

I couldn't help but laugh. "Okay, zany might have been a bit much, but just you wait. One of these days, I'll show you that I'm more than just a stuffy, ex-librarian. You'll see. Staid, my foot!"

I turned to watch a young couple with an adorable baby walk to a nearby table, and when I looked back, Mac was watching me in that intense way he has, but there was a trace of something different in his eyes, this time. I felt a shiver slide down my spine, and my cheeks grew warm.

"I like you just the way you are," he finally said. "Don't go getting all zany on my account." He paused, and with a slow smile, added, "You look beautiful tonight, you know."

My heart did that little flippy thing it does, and for the first time, I was the one to look away.

ON THE RIDE back to our mountain, we were both a bit quiet. I was thankful to have this first hurdle behind us, and I imagined Mac was probably feeling the same. He reached over and took my hand. Lifting it to his lips, he kissed my fingers. "Being with you always feels right, Sarah. It's only when I'm alone that I start to lose my way."

I didn't respond with the obvious. I just held his hand a little tighter, and hoped he would figure it out for himself.

It was nearly midnight when we got back to my cabin, so we parted company at the door. Our goodnight kiss turned into two, and then three. My heart was doing somersaults by the time Mac broke away, breathing a bit rapidly, himself.

"It's late. I think I need to go, Sarah." It was obvious he wanted to stay, but equally obvious that the idea scared the hell out of him. "I wish ... I mean, I want ... "

"Shhh. It's okay, Mac. You don't need to explain. I had a wonderful evening. Go on home, now, and next time, I'll cook dinner for you."

He kissed the palm of my hand, but in spite of my suddenly weak knees, I took a step back and smiled at him. "Goodnight, MacKenzie Cole."

"Goodnight, Sarah Gray."

I shooed him off to his truck, and went inside, locking my door behind me. Then I watched through the curtains until his tail lights disappeared from view, hanging on to his presence as long as possible. I wanted him to stay, too, but not until he was ready.

"Patience is a virtue," I told Handsome as I was getting into bed. "Did you know that, boy?"

Handsome gave me his standard reply, a steady, contented purr as he snuggled into the covers.

Chapter 15
Not Fair At All

THERE IS NOTHING quite like the Troggs waking you from a sound sleep at 7:00 in the morning. I really needed to change Mac's ring tone! After reading until the wee hours, I was in no mood to hear about making anyone's heart sing.

"Hello," I mumbled, barely conscious.

"Get up, Sleepyhead! The day is moving on without you."

"Is it taking anything necessary to my well-being along with it?"

"Come on, Sarah," Mac wheedled. "Throw on some clothes and come over. I want to show you something."

"It can't wait 'til a more reasonable hour? Like noon-ish?"

"Nope. Early is better. We should go now."

I groaned pitifully, but he was not to be swayed.

"I have coffee, you know." He was apparently not above bribery. "Strong, black, steaming hot, and delicious. Coffeeeee. Come on, now. You know you want it. You can practically taste it, can't you?"

I surrendered. "Give me ten minutes. By the way, you cheat."

"When I have to," he said, laughing. "See you in ten."

Twenty minutes turned out to be the best I could do, and even then, I was only half awake. I was sitting at Mac's kitchen counter, drinking what had to be the world's most perfect cup of coffee. Normally, I prefer tea, but Mac has some kind of secret, coffee-making mojo, and whatever goes into the machine comes out smelling and tasting like pure nirvana. I was savoring every swallow, and slowly coming to life.

Mac was busy at the counter, transferring baggies and packages from the fridge into a big, well-used backpack, and tossing the occasional scrap of something to Rosheen, who sat patiently by his feet. It occurred to me again that I could get very used to starting my day with Mac nearby.

"Where are we going, O Man of Mystery?"

"Can't tell you. It's a surprise." He turned around to smile at me, and held up a thermos. "I made you some more coffee, but you'll have to follow me to get it."

"You are a Coffee God, MacKenzie Cole. But you still cheat."

"Whatever works," he said, grinning. "Now get a move on. Time's a-wastin'."

I stared at him. "Did you just say 'time's a-wastin'?' Really? What, you're channeling Jed Clampett today?"

He laughed. "I'm rusty. Sorry. I'll get better." He told Rosheen to stay, shouldered the backpack, and grabbed two walking sticks that were leaning on the cabinet. "Come on. Finish that and let's go."

I wondered what all the rush was about and why Rosheen couldn't come, but I downed the last of the coffee, snagged a doughnut from the box on the counter, then followed him onto the balcony and down the back stairs.

"There better be black gold in them thar hills," I muttered. "Oil, that is ... Texas Tea." I would have whistled a few bars from the Beverly Hillbillies theme, too, but my mouth was too dry from the doughnut, and I figured I'd already gotten as much mileage out of that joke as I was going to.

Mac stopped and waited for me to catch up. He was standing near the woods, by the start of a narrow path hidden behind heavy undergrowth. It appeared to drop straight off, over the edge of the mountain. As I got closer, I could see that there were short sections of logs placed like stair steps, making the descent to the next level easier.

Because Mac's house was perched on the very top of Wake-Robin Ridge, paths from the front of his property all sloped downward to the west. In the back, there was a spectacular drop that seemed to plunge straight down to the valley below. A few feet to either side of that, trees and shrubs interrupted the view. I had never even noticed this trail from his balcony. Now I could see that we would be working our way down the eastern side of the mountain, which was far steeper than the western one. It looked like a more difficult trail than our usual jaunts, but at least he didn't expect me to rappel down the cliff face. Yet.

"Ready?" Mac asked.

"Lead on," I replied, still yawning. He started down the narrow trail, and I followed, enjoying the view, both of the surrounding woods and of Mac's wide, angular shoulders and narrow hips. He made blue-plaid flannel look positively sexy, even with a frayed and worn backpack slung over it.

The path began to angle to the south almost at once, moving away from the cliff, then it swung back eastward and sharply down. Eventually, it paralleled a narrow, tumbling rush of water.

"This is the lower end of the stream that runs along the south edge of my property," Mac explained. "There are a couple of nice, deep pools right on the property line, then it gets narrow and starts flowing over the crest of the hill, heading this way."

The descent of the path was steep, and though we were making good time going down, I wondered how difficult it would be when we began our return trip. I suspected it would take us twice as long to climb back up, but with the clear, blue sky above, and a cool temperature perfect for hiking, I knew we'd enjoy it.

After about thirty minutes, Mac stopped, and turned to face me, putting his finger to his lips. "Shhh ... listen. Do you hear it?" he asked in a hushed voice. I stood still, listening, and realized the sound of the rushing water was getting louder. Much louder. Mac smiled and took my hand. "Come on." We walked around the next curve, and the woods fell away. We were standing on top of the world!

I was speechless with delight. Our path had emptied us out onto a bald, a flattened dome of granite, maybe fifty yards wide and thirty or forty straight ahead to the drop. It was big enough that you could have set my cabin down in the middle of it, with plenty of room all the way around.

The little stream we had been following had grown faster and wider, and now rushed across the surface of the rock, foaming and frothing as it went. It flung itself over the edge of the bald in a frenzied spray of white, then plunged out of sight.

Mac led me over to a large, flat rock, half in the woods, and half on the bald, and we sat down to catch our breath, and to enjoy the view. "Later in the day, it's shady and not as spectacular as it is when it's lit by the morning sun. So, was it worth getting up early for?"

"Oh, definitely! It's amazing, Mac. I've never seen a prettier spot!"

He looked very pleased with himself. "Just wait," he said, eyes twinkling. "There's more."

"Really? I can't imagine anything better than this."

"I don't know that it's better, but it's just as beautiful. You'll see."

After a minute, he turned, pointed up to the northwest, and said, "You can see my house, right up there, just above the cliff face." I looked where he was pointing, and I caught sight of the roofline, with the sun glinting off of his windows.

"Wow. We came a long way. Are we still on your property?"

"No, but I've hunted every inch of this land, and know it as well as I know my own."

"And why can't we see this from your balcony?"

"If you know what you're looking for, you can just see a sliver of the rock between the trees. The falls aren't visible from there, though."

He unscrewed the thermos and poured us both a cup of coffee. We sat side by side on the rock, absorbed in the peaceful beauty of the spot, sipping our coffee in quiet contemplation. A hawk was riding a thermal overhead, and the sun was warm on our faces. A sense of drowsy contentment settled over both of us.

After a while, Mac stretched, stowed our empty cups in his backpack, and stood. He held out his hand and pulled me to my feet. "Are you afraid of heights?" he asked.

"Not particularly. Well, within reason, of course."

We walked closer to the edge of the cliff, being sure to stay away from any wet, slippery areas, and then looked over. The water fell straight down in a snowy plume, for at least a hundred dizzying feet, before pouring into a pool of blue at the bottom of the drop. Watching it fall was mesmerizing.

I started to take another step, but Mac pulled me back against his chest, wrapping both arms around me. "No closer for you," he said, his words warm on the nape of my neck.

"The pool looks like a jewel down there, perfect and untouched." I marveled at the pristine beauty of it.

"It is untouched, pretty much, since I'm the only one who goes there. There's no public access to these falls. Do you want to climb down?"

"Can we? Is it hard?"

"Not much harder than what we've already done. There might be one or two spots where I'll have to help you down, but that's all."

Slinging his backpack over his shoulder, he led me to the far northern edge of the smooth expanse of granite. Sure enough, one step below the bald, the path continued down the mountain. While it was obvious the trail was not used often, the way was clear, but the descent was extremely steep. I could see why Mac had chosen to leave Rosheen at home. It angled abruptly back toward the south, and soon we were scrambling downward over rocks and boulders, with the plunging water of the falls to our immediate right. A fine, rising mist accompanied us all the way to the clearing at the bottom.

The pool was at least twenty-five feet wide and about four feet deep in the center, unspoiled and beautiful. There were still some red and yellow leaves left on the trees around the edge of the clearing, as though time were moving at a slower pace in this hidden spot. Mossy rocks of various sizes surrounded the clear, blue-green water. In a small, open area, there was a fire ring, with seat-sized stones arranged near it. There was no way into the spot other than the path we had just descended, not even a trail following the stream as it continued on the other side of the pond. It was private, secluded, and absolutely perfect.

I turned to Mac, who stood waiting with an expectant look on his face. "I love it! It's a secret world. Magical."

He nodded. "I know. I used to come here all the time as a kid. It was my favorite place to camp, and in the summer, the pool was great for cooling down on hot afternoons. I had a rope swing and everything."

I could picture him, grinning as he swung out across the water, all elbows and shoulder blades and long, skinny legs, black hair falling into his eyes, and his face still unmarked by pain. I wished I could have known him then, grown up alongside him, sharing his childhood memories. I wanted to know every minute of his life, every happiness and every sorrow.

Stepping closer to the edge of the pool, I stood watching silver flashes from small fish darting back and forth along the rocky bottom. I looked over at Mac. He had dropped to the ground in the shade, and was leaning back on his elbows, legs stretched out in front of him, gazing off into the woods with a peaceful expression on his face.

A slight breeze was stirring, and he raked those long fingers of his through his tumble of black hair, pushing it out of his eyes. The movement was so unconsciously beautiful, it made my breath catch in my throat. He had a natural, masculine grace that was a sheer joy to watch, and I wanted to throw myself down beside him, and bury my face in his neck. I longed for that perfect mouth to cover me with

157

hungry kisses again. I just wanted him. Every part of him. And for the first time in my life, I knew I could be happy spending forever with someone — with this someone.

I knew Mac couldn't be rushed into opening his heart, but he told me with every look and gesture that he wanted to let me inside. Would he ever be able to make that last leap of faith? I didn't know, but I did know that I had been waiting for him all my life, and it wouldn't hurt me to wait a little bit longer.

He looked so at ease sitting in the autumn sunshine, I couldn't help thinking how wonderful it would be if I could freeze this moment to revisit whenever I wanted. Oh, to be able to stand beside this clear, blue pond any time I wished, listening to the rush of the falls, and watching Mac with that rare look of utter contentment on his face. What a trick that would be. Sadly, barring a time machine in my future, I knew my only option was to take a photograph or two. I began digging in the various zippered pockets of my jacket, looking for my phone.

"What are you hunting?" Mac asked.

"I wanted to take a picture, but I can't find my phone. I could have sworn I brought it." I looked back the way we had come. "Boy, I hope I didn't drop it on the trail."

Mac pulled his out of his shirt pocket and said, "I'll call you."

Panicked, I tried to tell him no, but it was too late. In the next second, the loud and unmistakable opening bars of "Wild Thing" came twanging out of the hip pocket of my jeans.

Oh, Lord. Just let the ground open up and swallow me, now!

I dug the phone out as quickly as I could, turned it off, then slowly looked back at Mac. He was sitting there, phone still in hand, staring at me with an expression of absolute surprise on his face. I started to stammer. "It was just a ... it seemed ... funny." I gave up.

One eyebrow arched upward in disbelief. "Really, Sarah? 'Wild Thing?'"

I sighed, feeling foolish and embarrassed. "It was a lame joke. It seemed funny at the time, you being sort of, well, totally not wild, and all." I walked back over and flung myself on the ground beside him in abject humiliation, wondering if I could feel any more stupid.

"Ah. I see. Do you prefer men who are wild, then?"

"What? No, of course not!" This was getting worse and worse.

He was quiet for a minute, and when I glanced over at him, I saw he had that wicked gleam in his eye again. "It seems to me," he began, voice low and dangerous, "if my memory serves me correctly, that is, one of the lines in that song indicates the singer loves the wild thing in question."

He paused and I looked away, completely mortified, now. Then, very softly, almost a whisper, he asked, "Do you, Sarah? Do you love me?"

I sat there in tongue-tied silence. I was doomed. Admit how I felt, and I would run the risk of scaring him off forever. Lie badly—and it would be badly—and I risked losing his trust. I stared at my feet for a few seconds, and then in a very small voice, I managed a reply. "Not a fair question, Mac. Not fair at all."

I felt him shift closer. He put his arm around my shoulder and pulled me to him, resting his chin on top of my head. "You're right. It wasn't fair. I'm sorry." He kissed my head, and then sighed, sounding troubled, but not angry. After a minute, he said, "I've never brought anyone here before."

I leaned my head away from him so I could see his face. He was staring off toward the pond, a slight furrow between his eyes. Then he turned back to me, and with a small shrug, he continued. "It's a special place to me. I've never wanted to share it with anyone else."

I managed a bit of a smile, feeling better after hearing that. "Why did you decide to share it with me?"

His cool blue eyes looked straight into mine. "Because you understand. You get it. You see what I see. Because you care."

I kissed him. I couldn't help it. His face was just inches from mine. The shape of his mouth was so perfect, and the sound of his voice pulled me right in, until my lips were against his, and I couldn't help myself. He took my face between his hands and kissed me back.

When he let me go, I asked him, "And how do you feel now that you've brought me here?"

"Like I always feel with you, Sarah. Like it was right."

We ate lunch by the fire ring and headed back to Mac's house. As I suspected, the return climb was a killer, but I didn't care. The day had been well worth it. We reached the house too late for Mac to show me the part of the stream that bordered his property, so we went for Plan B—a glass of wine on the balcony, and pan-fried venison steaks. Did I mention before that there was something sexy about a man in the kitchen? I stand by that.

"I need to go to Charlotte tomorrow," Mac said, as he walked me to my Jeep. I felt a pang of worry, but he reassured me. "Just business this time, honest. I'll be back Tuesday night. You wouldn't want Rosheen's company again, would you?"

"Rosheen is always welcome at my house. Should I take her tonight, or do you want to drop her off in the morning?"

"I can bring her by about 9:00, if that's okay?"

"It's fine. I'll be up. Tomorrow is a work day for me, too. I have to be more disciplined if I ever want to finish this book."

Mac stood facing me with his hands on either side of my waist. He was at war with himself again, and it showed in his troubled eyes. Pulling me close to him, he enfolded me in his arms, then whispered in my ear. "It gets harder and harder to let you go home, you know."

"Part of my devious plan," I whispered back. "Let me know when it becomes impossible for you." For me, that was pretty bold, and it made Mac chuckle.

"Sarah Gray, you are starting to sound like a wanton woman."

"I have my moments, MacKenzie Cole."

I got in my Jeep and he bent down for one last kiss through the window. He looked like he wanted to say something else, but I told him goodnight, and left. A very wise man once said, "Always leave 'em wanting more." I figured it couldn't hurt.

Chapter 16
A Whole Different Kind of Noise

CHRISTMAS EVE DAWNED cold and clear with frost sparkling across the yard, and a lacework of icy crystals in the corners of each window. I shivered as I was waiting for the water to boil for my tea, and went to peek at the thermometer on the front porch. Wow. Thirty-four degrees outside. Not that cold for most mountain folk, I'm sure, but for a Florida gal spending her first winter up here, it seemed pretty nippy. I knew that once I pulled on a warm sweater and some socks, it would feel just fine. I had always liked cold weather better than hot, so I was excited about the coming winter. I threw another log on the fire and plugged in the Christmas tree.

I had thrown myself into decorating my new home with everything bright and pretty I could get my hands on.

Evergreens from all over my property were draped over the doors and along the banisters, and vases filled with holly sat on the mantel and the table. Every swag and wreath was trimmed with vintage mercury glass ornaments I had collected over the years, and my tree was a masterpiece worthy of a magazine spread. It was dripping with garlands and hung with ornaments of every kind. I did it for myself, of course, but the effect was one of a warm Christmas welcome, nonetheless, and it made me happy.

I had shipped my gifts to Jenna and family earlier in the month, and knew they had arrived on time. All I had left to do today was finish wrapping my packages for Mac. A lot of time and thought had gone into his gifts, and I hoped he would be surprised and pleased. I couldn't wait to give them to him in the morning.

We had decided that Mac would cook our Christmas Eve dinner, and I would cook for Christmas day. I don't think either one of us even considered not spending the holiday together, though we hadn't had a lot of time with each other over the last two weeks. Mac had made several trips to Charlotte, and I had been working pretty hard on my book. We had gone to Asheville for dinner again, and Mac took some time the previous weekend to show me the trails he had cleared on his property, which wound through some of the most beautiful woods I'd ever seen. Days would go by, though, with our only contact being our telephone calls each night, which continued even when Mac was in Charlotte. Though he never said as much, I think he wanted to be sure I wasn't worrying about him while he was that close to his son.

I had missed him, and was looking forward to spending Christmas Eve at his house tonight. Talking on the phone definitely was not the same as watching him across the dinner table, or walking through the woods with him at my side. I found myself thinking things like, "I wonder what Mac would have to say about this?" or "I'll bet Mac would love that."

I was becoming a woman obsessed, which was fine with me, except for those times when I wondered if Mac would ever be able to love me without reservation. He still had barriers around him that I couldn't seem to break through, and I tried to warn myself that this might be as good as it would ever get. Myself answered back that I should just enjoy each day as it came. Even a limited relationship with Mac was far better than any I had ever had with a man before.

I hadn't come to Wake-Robin Ridge expecting to fall in love, get married, and live happily ever after. I had expected a secluded life as an author, and imagined myself growing old and eccentric all on my own, with a house full of lazy cats and half-finished manuscripts. And then Mac had come running down my driveway, and nothing had been the same since.

The day passed in a blizzard of shredded tissue paper and snips of ribbon, with me singing along with my favorite Christmas carols. I was feeling full of holiday spirit when the time came to head over to Mac's. I took his packages out to the car, thinking I would leave them under the tree I insisted he put up, and we would open them there when I went back in the morning. I planned to get home early enough to Skype Jenna tonight, then go back tomorrow morning with breakfast rolls. Mac could make his magic coffee, then we could exchange our gifts, and I'd come back to my house to start Christmas dinner.

MAC FOUND HIMSELF watching the clock all afternoon. Never had a day dragged by at such a slow pace.

"This is ridiculous. You'd think she'd never been over for dinner before," he muttered, pacing back and forth in his kitchen. He opened the oven to check on the ham for the third time in the last half hour, and tested the roasting sweet potatoes. Everything was coming along fine, and he had no idea why he was so jittery. Checking the time again, he jogged up the stairs to get a quick shower before Sarah arrived.

Shower finished, he buttoned up a white dress shirt, tucked it into his slacks, and rolled up the cuffs, while his thoughts drifted back over the past five months. He couldn't remember a single day when Sarah hadn't been on his mind. From the first morning he saw her, nose to nose with his dog, he knew there was something different about her. Even his fierce sense of self-protection had made only a half-hearted attempt to push her away. *Yeah, look how well that worked.*

Sarah, with her long, sable brown hair, and her sparkling green eyes, was beautiful to him in so many ways, and not just because she had a perfect, dimpled smile, and creamy, smooth, skin that he found himself making excuses to touch. Nor because her hair smelled like wild honey, and her laugh made his own heart laugh, too. All those things were true, but it was so much more. She accepted him as he was, and never asked anything of him he wasn't ready to give. Sarah was not like any of the women he had known briefly over the years. None of them had ever set foot in his home, much less his heart.

When he sat with her that day by the creek, he realized something long frozen within him was waking up. No one had ever given him hope the way Sarah did, as though somewhere, there was still love and joy in the world. Like it was there even for him, if he would just reach out for it — and he wanted to. He wanted to be happy. To love and be

Marcia Meara

loved in return. With all of his heart, he wanted to reach for Sarah, pull her close to him, and never let her go.

Then why did he still hesitate? He wanted to take the relationship to the next level, and he was pretty sure Sarah felt the same. So why was it that every time he kissed her, fear pulled him back? He knew that Sarah would never hurt him, and yet he would still freeze, scrambling away for some place to continue hiding.

Rosheen padded up the stairs and into Mac's bedroom. Silent, she stood looking at him with her soft, doggy eyes. Mac sat down on the edge of the bed, and she came closer and put her head on his lap.

"You love her, don't you, Rosheen? You see the truth and beauty in her heart, and you aren't afraid to accept it." He leaned forward with a sigh, and laid his cheek on Rosheen's head. Could he not even find the courage of a dog? "Yeah, you love her. And as frightening as it is to admit it, I think I might be able to love her, too. I just don't know if I can be the person she needs.

Rosheen pulled away and looked at Mac, then she turned and padded back down the stairs.

"I don't blame you, girl. I'd be disgusted with me, too."

He shook off the mood as best he could, and went downstairs to finish up dinner. Sarah would be here in half an hour, and he wanted everything perfect. He was not going to let his fears ruin Christmas for either of them. It had been years since he had been with anyone over this holiday, and he was surprised at how much he was looking forward to it. He could worry about anything else later. If there was one thing Mac was good at, it was pushing his feelings to the back of his mind. At least, he had been good at it before the little cabin across the road acquired its new owner.

THE HAM WAS now resting on the stove top, done to perfection. The sweet potatoes were split and buttered, sprinkled with cinnamon and brown sugar. Salad was ready, wine was poured, and Mac was pacing the floor, watching through the front windows for Sarah's headlights.

He frowned, biting his lip as he thought about his Christmas gift for Sarah. What if she didn't like it? He was amazed at how much he wanted her to, and he realized it was another sign of how important she was becoming to him. He might be confused about a lot of things, but there was one thing he knew without a doubt. Sarah was the best thing that had happened to him in a very long time, and he didn't want to think about her not being part of his life.

They were exchanging their gifts in the morning, and he hoped his would make her eyes light up with pleasure. God, he loved that look she got when she was happy, and he loved that she was happy so often. She didn't ask much of life, but she threw herself into the living of it with her heart and soul, and it was beautiful to watch.

He sighed. *There's the difference between us. Sarah has no fear at all, while I'm suffocated by it.*

Before he could dream up any more things to worry about, he saw the lights of her Jeep. His heart began to beat a bit faster, and his mood lifted at once. He felt a sense of pleasure so profound, it shocked him, and a slow smile spread across his face.

Everything is fine now. She's here.

I PULLED UP to Mac's house, and saw the door swing open, and Mac step out. I wondered if he had been watching for me, and the idea made me absurdly happy. He came down the steps, and opened my door, a sweet smile on his face.

"Merry Christmas, Sarah Gray."

"Merry Christmas to you, MacKenzie Cole."

Our little ritual greeting over, he helped me out of the car, and then started to the passenger side where my gifts were resting.

"Oh, no you don't," I called. "I'll carry those, thank you. I'm betting you are the kind who has to shake every box and try to guess what's inside."

He laughed. "How'd you know? That's exactly what I did as a kid. I never really peeked, though. Just listened for clues that might be rattling around."

Inside, I put the boxes under the tree, and stood back to admire how festive it looked. The day we had gone wandering around his woods, we had stopped in a beautiful clearing, ringed with evergreens of varying sizes, and with just enough sky showing in the center to allow sunbeams to play across the ground. I could almost see the springtime bluebells and trillium that would blossom in the open space. It was yet another little magical spot, like so many hidden on Wake-Robin Ridge.

I had cajoled Mac into cutting one of the smaller trees for his house, but only after I promised to help him plant another later to replace it. He had set it up near the big balcony windows, mumbling about how he didn't even have ornaments, but I didn't let a little thing like that stop me. It was Christmas, after all, and I was in the mood to spread the cheer to Mac's house, too. I had some extra sets of white lights that I had been thinking about putting up around my porch, and retrieved them for Mac's tree, instead. Then we had decorated the tree with pine cones and garlands of popcorn and fresh cranberries. When we finished, even Mac admitted it was beautiful, and thanked me for encouraging him—okay, badgering him—to do it.

Now, with the heavenly fragrances of baked ham and cinnamon floating on the air, the tree's sparkling lights reflecting in the tall windows, and a roaring fire casting a warm glow over everything, the whole room was as cheerful as a Hallmark card. And that was without counting Mac, who looked good enough, himself, to be under the tree with a big, red bow on his head. Every time I glanced at him, tall and handsome, with a snowy white shirt setting off that black hair, I felt my heartbeat pick up. I didn't want to get too close to him for fear I would fling my arms round his neck and make a fool of myself.

He just looked delicious. That's all there was to it.

THE FIRE HAD died down to low flickers and glowing embers. Mac gave it a stir, causing showers of sparks to float up the chimney and bright flames to flare up again, then sat back down beside me. He put his arm around my shoulder, and we leaned against each other, warm and content. I knew it was time for me to head home, but I was having trouble convincing myself to leave. His cheek was against mine, and I was aware of the clean, soapy smell of his skin. It made me dizzy with desire, and I had to order my wicked thoughts to behave. They had been defying me all evening.

Mac sat unmoving for a moment, with his cheek still pressed against mine. Then he turned his head very slowly, until the corner of his mouth touched my lips. Shifting slightly, his mouth covered mine. The kiss started feather soft, then gathered momentum as he pulled me into it. Suddenly, it was something altogether different from any other kiss we had shared.

I heard a whimper and wasn't sure which of us it came from. He began covering my whole face with kisses, one after the other, and I knew it had come from me, because Mac was making a whole different kind of noise, somewhere between a low moan and a soft growl. His kisses felt frantic, out of control, as though he wanted to swallow me alive. I

170

could feel his heart beating like a wild thing under my hands, which were pinned against his chest. Both of us were gasping for air.

He slipped his hands under my blouse and up my bare back, sending spasms of delight through me from head to toe. They were hot against my skin as he lowered me down onto the rug, his mouth never losing contact with mine. I tugged my hands free and tangled my fingers in his hair, pulling him closer, and holding him as tightly as he was holding me. His lips moved down my neck, leaving a trail of deliciously hot kisses against my throat and across my collarbone. Somewhere in the back of my mind, I wondered if this was really happening, or if he would realize what he was doing, put on the brakes, and run. But as I felt his hand slide over the satin of my bra to cup my breast, I knew he wasn't stopping this time.

Pushing himself up slightly, Mac looked at me with an expression I've never seen on a man's face before. Eyes filled with desperation and longing and pain and loneliness stared right into my soul. "Sarah," he whispered, his voice breaking with emotion, "stay with me tonight. Please? I want to wake up beside you in the morning. I want it so much." He leaned forward again, burying his head against my neck. begging me, "Please ... please stay with me."

Every emotion he felt had been visible, his face naked and vulnerable with longing. Tears burning my eyes, I held him close again, stroking the hard muscles running down his back, feeling him tremble beneath my hands. Turning him down was not an option. I wanted this just as desperately as he did.

"Yes," I whispered back to him. "Of course I'll stay with you, Mac."

With a strangled sound, he picked me up and carried me up the staircase. By the time we reached his bedroom, he was all but tearing at my clothes, stopping every few seconds to kiss each new place he uncovered. "Wait," I whispered. "I want to take your shirt off. Please? Let me take your shirt off."

He sat me on the bed and knelt on the floor in front of me, holding his arms wide in complete surrender. The sight took my breath away. Slowly, I opened his shirt, one button at a time, watching his chest come into view. I slipped it off his shoulders and down each arm, then ran the tips of my fingers back up over his arms and shoulders, and down the center of his chest. My fingertips followed a slight trail of fine black hair that disappeared into the top of his slacks. I stopped, and bent forward to kiss him directly over his heart. I wanted to claim that for myself.

"Oh, God, Sarah. You're killing me," he groaned, eyes closed, and breath coming in shuddering gasps.

"Shhh," I whispered. "Let me touch you first, just here." I leaned forward again, and kissed that hollow at the base of his throat, feeling his pulse racing under the tip of my tongue. He tasted of salt and desire, and it seemed the very essence of Mac to me.

I could have stayed in that spot forever, drowning in that taste, kissing him there again and again, but his patience ran out. Suddenly, he was on the bed, pulling me to him as clothes flew in every direction. Then his body was pressed against mine, hot and hard, with nothing between us, and I would have done anything he wanted. Anything.

AN HOUR WENT by. Or two. Or maybe it was a year. How do you measure time when the earth stops spinning on its axis and gravity ceases to exist, leaving nothing but heartbeats and gasping breaths and unquenchable fire to anchor you to the face of the planet? I had never known anything could feel like making love to Mac, and it seemed to me that a change in the course of the stars, or the flow of the rivers, or some other cataclysmic reshaping of the universe must have occurred. At least three times.

Mac had fallen asleep with his arms wrapped tightly around me, as though afraid I would disappear during the night. I listened to his breathing and the steady beating of his heart, and thought all the world's music would pale in comparison to those two sweet sounds. Never had I imagined a love like this, and I didn't want to lose it. I said a silent prayer that Mac would still want me when he woke up.

Once, he stirred in his sleep, whispering "Please stay." My heart ached that he worried about being abandoned, even in his dreams.

I turned to face him, whispered "I'll never leave you, Mac," then laid my cheek against his chest, wanting the sound of his heart to be the last thing I heard as I drifted off. It was.

I woke to Mac nuzzling against my neck. "Wake up, Sarah. It's Christmas. Don't you want to know what Santa brought you?"

"I thought Santa gave me my present last night," I answered, giving him a sleepy smile.

"Nope. That was from me alone, and guess what?"

I didn't have to guess. It was obvious that Mac planned to give me another gift. So much for my worries that he would wake up no longer wanting me. We made love again, this time quietly and tenderly, with murmured endearments and astonishing sweetness.

Finally, laughing at his protests, I told him no more, and got dressed. "I have to go check on Handsome and take a quick shower. Then I'll be back with some breakfast. You have to take a shower and get dressed, too."

"Are you sure? I thought maybe we could just make clothing optional now," he said with a slow, sexy smile.

"Yeah, in your dreams, Mac." I kissed him goodbye, headed for the door, then went back and kissed him again. Just because. "I'll be back. Make coffee!"

"Don't be long," he called after me.

Damn. What kind of sleeping dragon had I awakened?

BY THE TIME I got back to Mac's, the aroma of fresh-brewed coffee permeated the entire house. I knocked and walked inside, where Rosheen stood waiting to greet me. She looked around for Handsome, but I hadn't brought him with me. He was sleeping under my afghan and didn't look like he wanted to be disturbed.

"It's just me, girl. Where's Mac?"

I heard him coming down the stairs, and turned. He stopped at the bottom and we just stared at each other, feeling shy for a minute after our night of blissful debauchery. He tilted his head, a tiny line of worry on his brow. "Any regrets?"

I smiled. "Not a one, Mac."

A look of relief crossed his face. "Me, neither."

Christmas Day was everything it should have been. I played elf under the tree and passed out our gifts. Mac was delighted with his new backpack, and vowed we would take a hike as soon as possible, so he could try out all the bells and whistles, and the many, many zippered pockets. His eyes lit up with genuine pleasure when he opened my last gift for him, a hand-tooled leather-bound edition of Thoreau's _Walden_. "It's beautiful, Sarah. Don't think I've forgotten you quoted this to me that day by the stream. Thank you. I'll treasure it."

I was surprised and touched by the thoughtful things Mac had chosen for me, too. A beautiful, warm sweater, in my favorite shade of blue, a hand carved walking stick, and lots of new books by my favorite authors.

"This has been a lovely Christmas, Mac," I said with a happy sigh. I started gathering up torn wrapping paper and bits of ribbon.

"Ah ... it's not quite over." He produced a small, flat package from his pocket and handed it to me, with a nervous smile. I unwrapped the box and found a pair of stunning earrings inside, emerald green tourmaline, wrapped with delicate silver filigree.

I was speechless for a moment. No one had ever given me anything so grand, and tears blurred my vision.

"Don't you dare cry, Sarah! I will *not* be responsible for making you cry on Christmas!" He kissed my forehead, then leaned back to look at me. "Put them on, so I can see if they look as beautiful with your eyes as I imagined." The thought of him imagining whether they would look good with my eyes made me want to cry again, but I swallowed the tears, and fastened the earrings in place.

"They look gorgeous on you," Mac declared, with a huge smile on his face. "I knew they were the right ones. The jeweler tried to talk me into getting opals instead. He said they were more traditional than tourmalines for October birthdays, but they were all so pale. Not nearly vibrant enough for you. Then he showed me these and the green was exactly what I was looking for. Do you really like them?"

I pulled a small mirror out of my bag and admired them. They were spectacular. "I love them, Mac. I've never had anything so beautiful in my life. I don't know what I did to deserve them, but I will treasure them forever and ever."

"I can't begin to list all the things you've done to deserve them," he answered, then added with a charming, devilish grin, "and I'm not even counting last night."

CHRISTMAS DAY ENDED with the two of us snuggled in front of the fire in my living room, dinner dishes done and soft carols playing in the background. We had laughed, and talked, and kissed often and long, and Mac's eyes lost that haunted expression he so often wore, at least for a while. We sat holding hands and staring into the fire, full of turkey and pumpkin pie, drowsy and contented, but not yet willing to let go of the day. I thought about what the future might have in store for us, and how our relationship was changing, but I refused to worry. I knew that for right now, we were both where we wanted to be, and I trusted that everything else would work out just as it should. I figured sometimes you just have to have faith.

After a while, Mac suggested that maybe we should end the holiday in my bed, since we had pretty much started it in his.

Seemed reasonable to me.

Chapter 17
One More Slap in the Face

THURSDAY, JANUARY 21, 1965
MACON, GA

THE NEW YEAR had just gotten underway and major events were unfolding around the world. In London, a fragile Sir Winston Churchill, one of the most influential figures in British history, was near death from a stroke at age 90. In the United States, widespread unrest over the Vietnam War was growing every day. The preceding night, President Lyndon Johnson had been sworn in for his first full term, after having made his famous "Great Society" State of the Union speech on January 4. Turmoil was brewing across the country, and it would get worse before it got better.

If any of these events made an impression on Lloyd Carter, it was so small as to be a mere blip in his consciousness. The only thing on his mind was revenge, pure and simple—and as harrowing and pain-filled as possible.

Lloyd had been out of jail a mere twenty-four hours, after serving almost two and a half years of a five-year sentence. He had walked out of the prison looking to get some money, some decent food, and some sex, not necessarily in that order, and had managed to accomplish all three before his first night was over. Prison had done nothing for him but hone his survival skills, and foster an ever-growing conviction that the world owed him whatever he could take; and being free again did nothing to temper his ever-growing rage, but it did give him more opportunities to express it.

As dawn approached, Lloyd was sitting in the bus station, duffel bag at his feet, and a ticket to Asheville, North Carolina in his pocket. He was smiling to himself as he planned everything he was going to do when he got his chance to teach Ruthie a lesson.

He closed his eyes, picturing her terrified face, begging him not to hurt her. Oh, she was going to hurt, all right. She had betrayed him in the worst way possible, and he hadn't spent month after month planning this trip just to make nice with her. *Oh, yeah ... little Ruthie is gonna pay, over an' over, until there isn't a breath left in her body.*

He shivered, becoming aroused just thinking about it. He was going to make sure she got screwed during the process, too. *After all, hasn't she done a bang-up job of screwin' me?*

After he had his fun with her, he planned to take his big, red Impala and whatever money he could find in her cabin, and disappear. Maybe head west. *Las Vegas sounds good. Plenty of opportunities to get rich there. Might even go clear to California. Or better yet, Hawaii. Oh, yeah. Hawaii would suit me just fine. An' takin' care of Ruthie'll be the first step.*

FRIDAY, JANUARY 22, 1965
WAKE-ROBIN RIDGE, NC

RUTH'S DREAMS WERE never good. She often woke crying out in terror and trying to scramble away from nightmare dangers. Sometimes she remembered what she had been dreaming, other times, she was spared the grim details. In recent weeks, her dreams had become both more frequent and more ominous. She would awaken with Lloyd's voice echoing inside her head, and lie trembling in fear until exhaustion pulled her under again. The most frightening dreams of all ended with Lloyd calling, "Ruuuthie ... Ruuuuthieeee ... " over and over in a terrifying sing-song, and she was glad the dreams were worse when she was alone. She never wanted Frank to witness the effects of a really bad one.

After another violent nightmare jolted her awake, she sat bolt upright in bed, and checked to see if General Penny was still sleeping. He was undisturbed, so she knew they were still alone. Going downstairs, she fixed herself a cup of chamomile tea, hoping to relax enough to get a few more hours of rest.

Ruth told herself she was being foolish to let the dreams scare her so much. After all, she had been here for over two years, and Lloyd hadn't shown up yet. She ought to be feeling safer every day. Instead, her fears seemed to be growing, even spilling over into daylight hours. She tried to ignore them, but a little voice inside her head kept warning her that Lloyd would come. Somehow, some way, he would find her, and each passing day just brought the inevitable closer.

LLOYD CROUCHED LOW in the bushes, peering at the little cabin in the clearing. This is what she chose to do with his money? Hide out on a deserted hillside in a stinkin' little wooden shack that looked like it should have belonged to the Beverly Hillbillies—before they struck it rich? God, he could kill the bitch. "Oh, that's right. I'm going to." He snickered to himself at his own joke, then took another bite of beef jerky, and waited to see if Ruthie came outside.

Hitchhiking down from Asheville the afternoon before had been easy. Finding a detailed map of Wake-Robin Ridge that included hiking trails and logging roads hadn't been much harder. Hiking in along the abandoned logging road, toting his duffel bag full of deadly goodies, was a long, cold walk, but well worth it, in order to keep a low profile.

It was obvious no one had been on the road in months. Maybe years. Lloyd laughed again. Twenty-four hours ago, he had been in Georgia, his grand revenge still a thing of his twisted dreams, but now it was finally happening. Just before dark last night, he had found a sheltered place along the logging road to pitch an inconspicuous pup tent, and leave his sleeping bag and supplies. At daybreak this morning, he left camp and worked his way through the tangled forest for about a mile, until he reached this spot. It was a perfect hiding place, giving him a full view of Ruthie's new home, and the best part? Not one soul knew he was here. He could get in, do whatever he wanted, and drive out in his own car, with no one the wiser.

Eying his Impala parked in the turnaround by Ruthie's front porch made Lloyd's anger sharper and meaner by the second. *After I carve on her a while, maybe I'll tie her up in the driveway an' run over her with it. Real slow like. Unless I think of somethin' better, of course.*

He figured he'd know what he wanted to do when the time came, and dreaming up ever worse scenarios kept him entertained as he settled down to wait.

Thirty minutes later, the front door opened and Ruthie came out, carrying a puppy under her arm. Lloyd's eyes lit up. A puppy? He shivered with excitement, thinking of all the additional ways he could torture Ruthie using a puppy. Tiny little puppy versus long, sharp knives? No contest. This was getting better and better.

The desire to start the games at once was so overwhelming, it was all he could do not to go rushing in right away. But Lloyd was nobody's fool when it came to getting away with violence. He didn't want anyone to interrupt his fun once he got started, and if that meant casing the situation for a day or so first, fine. He had plenty of supplies, and he planned to take his time, leaving no witnesses. Instead of going off half-cocked, he would watch and wait, and then make his move when the moment was perfect.

He watched Ruthie pick up the pup after it had done its business, and go back inside. She was already dressed, even though it was still pretty early in the morning, so he figured she was heading out. He wondered if she had a job, though he couldn't imagine what Ruthie could do, having been a useless drain on him for years. At least he'd have a chance to look around if she left. Lots of information could be gathered that way, and it was always smart to know what you were getting into.

A couple of minutes later, Ruthie came back out with her purse over her shoulder, still carrying the puppy. He watched her start up his Impala and head down her driveway, thinking to himself that she looked better than he'd ever seen her. She looked happy. That the stupid cow had found the nerve to run off with what was his in the first place was bad enough, but to end up looking happy about it was almost more than he could stand.

As soon as the sound of the car faded away in the distance, Lloyd came out of his hiding place and took a closer look around the property. *A garden? Ruthie gardens? Isn't she just full of surprises.*

After circling the house and peering in the windows, he decided no one else was around. The front door was locked, and since he didn't want to break in and leave any evidence for her to find later, he tried the windows. No go. Then he got lucky. The screen door on the back porch was unlocked, and glory be, so was the back door to the cabin.

"Honey, I'm hooome," he sang out, and then he walked inside.

Since he wasn't sure how long he would have to explore, Lloyd went upstairs first, where he thought he'd learn the most. *Might even stumble on my money somewhere. She can't have spent the whole $75,000 already, an' by God, if there's any of it around here, I'll find it.*

He stood in the doorway to Ruthie's bedroom, hating how neat and clean it was, like Ruthie cared—like she took pride in her home. He couldn't remember the last time he had seen Ruthie doing anything that indicated she cared about him, or any of the houses they had lived in. It was just one more slap in the face to Lloyd.

A quick look in the closet revealed no men's clothing, so he was confident she didn't have some new boyfriend living with her. There were no masculine items in the bathroom, either, confirming that she lived alone. He smiled. *Don't tell me that little ol' puppy is the only protection you got, Ruthie. This ain't gonna be no challenge at all.*

He went back to the closet and spent some time digging around on her shelves, but didn't find anything useful, then he headed back downstairs. After another twenty minutes or so, he realized there was nothing of interest in those rooms, either.

Last of all, he swung the pantry door open wide, then stared, open-mouthed. "Cannin'? Ruthie gardens an' cans stuff now? What the ... ?" Lloyd was surprised, but what impressed him the most was that he would have more than beef jerky for dinner tonight. Deciding he'd been in the cabin long enough, he grabbed several jars of vegetables and fruit, rearranging the shelves to hide the theft. Then he grabbed a spoon, and left the way he'd come in. He hid himself in the woods again, and settled down to enjoy Ruthie's canned peaches, while waiting for her to return home.

IT WAS LATE afternoon before Ruth pulled Lloyd's Impala into her drive, stopped to check her mail, and then rumbled down to the turnaround in front of the cabin and parked. Scooping up General Penny, she went inside, cuddling the puppy and fussing over him, as she walked.

"Oh, poor baby! Did that mean ol' vet hurt you, Dumplin'?" Penny went into throes of ecstasy over the baby talk, licking Ruth's nose and wiggling so hard, he almost fell out of her arms. Laughing, she was putting the puppy down when she saw something out of the corner of her eye that caught her attention. The pantry door was standing ajar. A little chill went down her spine as she tried to remember if she had left it open. It wasn't like her. She worried about Penny getting into things stored on the lower shelves, and she had made it a habit to be sure the door was always closed.

A voice in her head yelled, "Get out! Run!" For a moment, her heart rate soared as panic rose within her, but Ruth wasn't the cowering girl she used to be. Taking several deep breaths, she worked up the nerve to approach the pantry. She hesitated for a second, then flung the door wide open. Empty.

Weak with relief, Ruth still didn't want to let down her guard until she had checked the entire cabin. She grabbed a sharp knife from the drying rack on the counter, and began a thorough search of the downstairs area. Over and over, she reassured herself that everything was fine, and she shouldn't let her imagination get away from her, but she had to be certain no one had been in her home.

She knew the front door had definitely been locked, since she just came through it, but she took a close look to see if it had been damaged in any way. That lock seemed fine. Lloyd knew more than one way to get into a house, however. She checked all the downstairs windows next, and found them locked, too. No one had come through the front door or the windows, so Ruth was beginning to believe she must have left the pantry open herself. Then she walked out to the screened porch and checked the back door. It swung open as soon as she turned the handle, and her stomach lurched.

Oh, my God! I left the house unlocked. He could've come right in this door, and I'd never know it.

Moving from room to room again, she did a thorough recheck of each, second guessing herself every step of the way. Had that sofa pillow been moved? Had she really left that glass in the sink this morning? Were those books on the mantel in the proper order? Things seemed just the tiniest bit off everywhere she looked, though nothing other than the pantry door jumped out at her as possible proof that she'd had an uninvited guest while she was away. Still, nothing felt quite right, either.

Holding her knife in front of her, she mustered up every bit of courage she could find, and climbed the stairs. Nothing appeared to be disturbed in her bedroom or closet, and no one was hiding in the bathtub or behind the curtains. She got down on her knees and checked that nothing under the bed had been moved, either. After thirty minutes, she came back downstairs, still unsatisfied and unable to relax, but with nothing concrete to account for her jitters.

I'm just jumpin' at shadows and imaginin' things. I need to stop this right now.

Ruth was sitting at the kitchen table, chastising herself for letting an open pantry door scare her, when she heard Frank's truck coming down her drive. Glancing at the clock, she realized how late it was. Friday was their night for dinner and a movie, but she hadn't even showered yet, and she wasn't sure she felt like going out, any more. She greeted Frank on the porch, hugging him close, and feeling safer right away. She wished she could tell him about what had happened, but that wasn't an option. Instead, she said it had been a long day, and suggested a quiet dinner there.

They ended up having soup and sandwiches by the fire, while Frank updated Ruth on what was happening at the store. Everly's was expanding again, and he was proud of how well the business was doing. They had even cleared and paved a larger area for the farmer's market.

"How's the General feelin' after his trip to the vet today?" Frank asked. "He seems pretty quiet tonight."

"Maybe he's still a bit sleepy from the surgery, gettin' fixed and all."

"Fixed? Heck, seems to me he started out fixed. Now he's broken." Frank gave her a wink.

"Aw, Silly ... you know what I mean. It worked out good, though. They had to keep him for a few hours afterward, so I went shoppin' in Asheville. Got a new pressure cooker to help with my cannin' this spring. I want to add more vegetables than ever."

They talked a bit longer, and then they went upstairs together. At eleven o'clock, Frank told Ruth he needed to head home. He was reluctant to go, and as Ruth walked him out onto the porch, he explained, "I have to open the store tomorrow, so I need to be there earlier'n usual."

"It's okay, Frank. You don't have to stay overnight every time. I know you would if you could."

"You're right, darlin'. I'd stay every night if I could. If you'd just say yes and marry me, we could be together all the time, and I'd be just about the happiest guy in these mountains."

Ruth slid into Frank's arms and kissed him goodnight again, but as he turned to leave, she laid her hand on his arm and said, "Frank? You do know how much I love you, don't you?"

"Yes, Ruth, I know you do."

"Remember that, no matter what happens. Promise me you'll always remember that I love you, and that I've never loved anyone else but you in all my life. Don't ever forget, Frank. My heart will always be yours."

Ruth's eyes filled with tears and she tucked her head against his chest.

"Ruth, honey, what's the matter? Is somethin' wrong? You're not plannin' on runnin' off and leavin' me, are you?"

She blinked her tears away and smiled at him. "I'm not goin' anywhere. I'm bein' foolish, is all. I just want you to know that you mean everything to me, and that you always will, no matter what. There's nothin' I wouldn't do for you, Frank. Nothin' at all."

"I feel the same way about you, hon. I can't wait for us to be together forever, husband and wife. We can fix up my house exactly the way you want, or I'll move here with you. Makes no difference to me. I just want you to be happy, you know. Everything I do, I do for you. For us. For our life together." Standing on the porch, caught in a beam of silvery moonlight, they exchanged more kisses and whispered endearments, with no idea that every move they made was being observed.

LLOYD CARTER SQUATTED behind the thick bushes at the edge of the clearing, watching his wife being kissed by another man. His ragged breath sent plumes of white into the cold night air, as rage, hate, and jealousy consumed him.

You are both so dead. You first, Ruthie, you cheatin', lyin', thievin' whore! And then this hillbilly asshole you've replaced me with. Oh, yeah. Before another day goes by, you two are gonna die!

Chapter 18
I Won't Be Bringing My Paddle

THE NEW YEAR was shaping up pretty well so far. I was spending a lot of time researching my book, and Mac had made a few day trips to his Charlotte office, but we saw each other several times a week, and things had changed between us. Yeah, Mac was still cautious and nervous at times, but not as much, nor as often. I gave him lots of space, and that terrified, deer-caught-in-the-headlights look in his eyes went away. Mostly.

We were in that stage of romance where every moment was filled with an eager, hungry passion, but Mac needed to move forward when he was ready, with no pressure from me. So far, he seemed ready a lot more often than I had expected. He was tender, loving, and generous, and I could not imagine why anyone would have walked out on him. But I was a woman in love, and my days—and nights—were ruled by my heart, and not my mind.

There were still times when Mac was quiet and thoughtful, but I no longer felt he was shutting me out. I loved how his face would light up at the sight of me, and he would hold me so close, it was difficult to breathe. Watching him rediscover love was beautiful to behold.

Now and then, he stopped by my cabin just to kiss me. Jenna thought I was making that up, but it was true. He would knock on the door, and when I opened it, he would pull me into his arms and give me a kiss me that stole my breath and made my knees grow weak. Then he would step back with a grin and a gleam in his eye, saying, "I just wanted to see you before I started my day." He'd hop back in his truck and head home, leaving me walking around all day with a dopey smile on my face.

Of course, we didn't speak of our feelings yet. I don't think Mac understood his well enough to put them into words, and I sure wasn't going to tell him mine. Not at this point, anyway. No way was the "L" word coming out of my mouth first. I hoped that the time would come when I could tell him how much I loved him, but hoping isn't the same as knowing, so I was keeping quiet on that particular subject.

Mac was learning to laugh again, with an exuberance I wouldn't have thought possible a few months ago. I don't think I've ever seen a sight more beautiful than my Mac, white teeth flashing, blue eyes sparkling, and all cares erased from his face. Watching him laugh, and knowing I had helped him find more joy in his life, was the best thing of all.

This morning, I was fixing breakfast for the two of us. Mac had arrived earlier with his chainsaw and was cutting up a large limb that had come down in my yard overnight. Later, he would split the wood for me and stack it on the log rack outside the back porch. The temperature had been dropping each day, and they were predicting possible snow tonight, so I was glad to have it refilled, and for free, as well.

The cabin had been winterized and outfitted with central heat, so it wasn't as much about needing the wood as it was about wanting it. There's nothing like standing with your back to a blazing fire when the shivers hit. It warms both body and soul better than anything I know. Well, almost. I can think of a few nights in recent weeks when both my body and my soul received a pretty thorough warming, and I was nowhere near a fireplace at the time.

I went to the door and waved at Mac to come inside, and in minutes, we were sitting at the table, having pancakes, eggs, and sausage, which he was downing with obvious gusto.

"I'm going to have to come for breakfast at your house more often. I usually just have toast and coffee at home."

"That's all you'd normally get here, too," I said. "But there's something about watching you in full Lumberjack Mode that brings out my inner domestic goddess. I found myself overcome by a desire to produce large quantities of hearty food in your honor. I would have thrown in ham, a frittata, and homemade cheese Danish if you had taken off your shirt while working."

"Really? Hmm. Interesting. A bit chilly outside for that, though. Got any inside chores that could be tackled bare-chested? I'm always happy to encourage your latent domestic goddess to make an appearance."

"Well, there is that leaky fixture in my shower, but I don't know if you'd want to work on that. You'd probably have to take off more than your shirt, to be sure your clothes stayed dry and all."

"Sounds perfect. Hot water, no clothes, and a beautiful plumber's assistant close by. You would assist, right? I mean, if I needed help with a necessary tool, for instance?"

Gulp. The image of helping an unclothed, soaking wet Mac was more than I could handle. I decided I needed to take care of some urgent dish washing. I was standing at the sink, trying to banish naughty thoughts of the two of us playing a rousing game of The Naked Plumber And His Wanton Assistant, when Mac slipped up behind me. He slid his arms around my waist, and I felt his soft, warm lips against the nape of my neck. It felt heavenly, and I leaned back against him, shivering.

"Oh, Sarah. I love it when you get these wicked ideas. Must be that writer's imagination of yours. Tell you what ... let me finish cutting up that wood, and I promise, I'll come take a look at any plumbing problems you might have."

Then he turned me around and gave me a proper kiss. Or perhaps it was an improper kiss. But it was damn well done, whatever you called it.

WE ENDED UP spending the rest of that afternoon together, just enjoying each other's company. Oh, and making sure all of my plumbing was in working order, of course. At 5:30, we drove down to the diner at Darcy's Corner for a burger, and then returned to my cabin. Mac was planning to head home early. He had some work to catch up on before calling it a night, but since he wasn't rushing out the door yet, I put on some coffee.

"So are you working on your book tomorrow?" Mac asked.

"Yep. I'm trying to stick to a firm schedule and get in a few hours every morning. I've been bad about it all week, though, and now I'm behind again."

"Oh? Do you need someone to discipline you, Miss Gray?"

"I most certainly do not, Mr. Cole! You can get that idea out of your head right this minute!"

"Too bad. Guess I won't be bringing my paddle over here on my next visit, then."

I threw a pillow at him, and we spent a few minutes being ridiculously silly, then settled down on the sofa. I knew he would be leaving soon, and it was nice to have a last canoodle, as my father would have called it, before we had to say goodnight.

Mac hugged me to his chest, kissed the top of my head, and grew quiet for a moment. "Sarah?"

"Hmm?"

"When are you going to tell me about your book?"

I leaned back and looked at Mac. He was watching me with a curious smile on his face.

"Oh. Well ... I don't think it's anything you would be interested in," I replied, trying to dismiss the subject with a wave of my hand. He was having none of it.

"Why wouldn't I be interested in what you are writing? I'm interested in everything about you. I find you endlessly fascinating, you know," he said with a teasing grin.

I snorted.

"Seriously, every time I've mentioned it, you've managed to change the subject. Your computer area is always tidied up when I come over, so there are never any intriguing bits and pieces hinting at what you're working on. I'm just curious as to why you aren't as open about it as you are most things in your life. It's not like you. What are you hiding from me, Lady of Mystery?"

I found myself squirming, nervous and embarrassed. I was going to have to come clean.

"Why, Sarah, are you blushing? What can you be writing that would make you look so guilty? Wait! I've got it! It's something X-rated, isn't it? You're a secret porn peddler, writing under some sleazy pseudonym, and probably using me for research. Damn. I knew that whole 'problem with my plumbing' thing was a ruse!"

"What? Porn? No!" I yelped. "Of course not! It's not X-rated. Don't even say that! That's not funny, MacKenzie Cole!" He was laughing at me again. Since I'd already thrown the pillows all over the floor, I had no weapon handy. I settled for giving him a push.

"God, you're easy," he said, fending me off with one hand. "Well, if it's not porn, then what is it? Come on, tell me. You know you want to."

"All right, all right! If you must know, it's a Victorian romance novel." I felt my cheeks flaming again.

"Umm ... is that a bad thing, somehow?"

"No, of course not. I just thought you ... well ... you might think it silly." I trailed off, feeling foolish.

"Or beneath you?" he asked with a quiet smile.

"Yeah, I guess. I thought it would be inconsequential to a man who reads Thoreau and Shakespeare."

"Did you forget that I'm a man who also reads Lee Child and John Grisham?"

"Sort of," I said, sounding as sheepish as I felt.

"Well, just tell me this. Are you writing the best Victorian romance you can? Doing your research, and telling the story in the most compelling way you know how?"

"Well, yes, of course. At least, that's what I'm trying to do."

"Well, then," he said, and pulled me back to his side again. "I'll bet you are doing a fine job of it, and people are going to love reading it. And isn't that the whole point of writing a novel? To give pleasure to those who read it?"

"I certainly think so."

"Ah. That's what I've always thought, too. So why on earth did you think I would judge you for writing something purely entertaining? In fact, I ought to be highly insulted that you thought I'd judge you at all."

"And yet, for some reason, you don't look highly insulted," I said, snuggling against his chest again.

"That's because I've already figured out what you can do to make up for your terrible lack of perception about my character. Would you like to hear my idea?"

"Yes, please. Do tell me how I can atone for the error of my ways."

He leaned down and whispered a suggestion in my ear. Oh, my.

I smiled. "I think I can do that," I whispered back.

Mac didn't go home right away, after all.

Chapter 19
Well, That's Where You're Wrong

THE TEMPERATURE WAS dropping like a stone. Ruth's footsteps crunched across the frosted grass as she walked Penny one last time before bed. Moonlight silvered the ground, and Ruth's breath was a plume of white against the dark woods. She pulled her black chenille robe closer around her, urging Penny to get on with it so they could go back inside.

"Good boy, Penny," Ruth said when he finished. The vet suggested he might need a bit of extra babying after his surgery, so she was even more gentle than usual as she carried him up the porch steps and into the warmth of the cabin

As she was banking the fire and turning off the living room lights, Ruth heard a soft creak from the front porch swing. Hand on the switch, she froze, but everything grew quiet again. "Just the wind," she said, reassuring herself. "It's not like you haven't heard that before, Ruth."

Then a pale streak of movement outside the kitchen window caught her eye. She gasped and spun toward it, her heart racing. Snow. Small eddies of tiny, icy crystals blew by the panes. Sharp relief flooded through her, and she took several deep, shaky breaths, until her heartbeat returned to normal. Lifting the edge of the living room drapes, she peered outside. There was nothing unusual on the porch or in the front yard, but as she watched, the swing stirred again as a gust of icy air hit it.

"Wind and snow," she whispered to herself. "That's all it is. Wind and snow."

Frowning, Ruth paced the room, nibbling on a thumbnail. She still wasn't sure whether or not someone had been in her cabin earlier in the day, but she told herself again that she was being paranoid. Being prepared was one thing, but being scared of her own shadow was not acceptable. She was not going down that particular road again. Ever. Even so, she made sure to double check the locks on all the doors and windows before having a mug of relaxing chamomile tea, then heading upstairs to bed, Penny cradled in her arms.

SATURDAY, JANUARY 23, 1965

RUTH CRIED OUT in her sleep, thrashing in a sweaty tangle of bedding. She was dreaming of fists and boots and terrible pain. Over and over a singsong voice called, "Ruuthiee ... Ruuuthieeee ... "

Her eyes flew open and she lay gasping in terror, waiting for the echoes of Lloyd's voice to fade. It was only 2:00 A.M., but she knew falling asleep again would be impossible. After a moment, she sat up, and reached for her robe. As she pulled it on, she saw that Penny had crawled out from under the quilt and was standing in the center of the bed. His body was rigid, and he was shaking all over as he stared at the window. He whimpered in anxiety, and just like that, Ruth knew it was all over.

Lloyd had found her.

Gripped in a blind panic, she moaned, rocking back and forth in agitation. "Ohmygod, ohmygod, ohmygod. He's here. He found me. Oh my god. He found me." Terror swept through her so hard her teeth began to chatter, and the sudden rush of blood pounding in her ears drowned out everything for a moment.

Ruth had always believed Lloyd would never let her walk away from this alive. He would arrive wanting vengeance, and she would die for her transgressions against him. Compared to the wild fear mounting inside of her, dying almost sounded good. Anything was better than the torture she imagined Lloyd would have in mind.

Oh, God! Where will it start? Is he still outside? Is he pryin' open the front door right this minute? I have to do somethin'. I can't just sit here until he comes up those stairs and kills me. I have to do somethin' now!

Climbing out of bed, she slipped to the window overlooking her driveway, and peered out from behind the lace curtain. *Dear God!*

There in front of her porch steps stood Lloyd Carter, leaning back against the side of his Impala, and grinning up at her window like a madman. She clapped both hands over her mouth to stifle the scream that wanted out, then froze, hoping he didn't see the movement. Lloyd was dressed in a heavy parka, with the hood pulled back slightly. Tiny flurries of snow blew around his head, and the moonlight shone across his face at an angle, leaving his eyes hollowed out and black. Death had come to call.

The window was open a crack for ventilation, and Lloyd's voice was clear on the crisp night air. He began calling her name again, just as he had in her dream.

"Ruuuthieeee ... Ruuuthieeeeeeee. I'm home, Ruthie. Ain't you gonna come down an' welcome your man? Come on down, now. I got a present for you, Ruthie." He held up a long, wicked-looking knife in his right hand, turning it this way and that, and letting the silver light play over the blade. "Come see the pretty thing I've brought you. Soooo shiny, Ruthie. See how pretty?"

Gasping, Ruth turned from the window and scooped up Penny in the quilt. She shut the puppy in the closet, dropped to her knees by the bed, and pulled out a Remington 12-gauge shotgun. Then she sat down in the rocking chair facing the door, racked the gun, and waited in terrified silence. She figured it wouldn't be long before Lloyd kicked in the front door and came hunting for her. This is where she would make her stand.

She tried to focus, taking slow, steadying breaths, but she had never felt such fear in her life. Her hands were trembling so hard, she was afraid it would affect her aim, but she knew at this distance, it wouldn't matter. Ruth had taken to sleeping with her fully loaded 12-gauge under the bed more than two years ago, dreading this day, but sure it would arrive sooner or later. The shotgun was her best bet for a kill shot, and tonight was definitely a matter of kill or be killed.

The sheriff would understand that. He had to. He would see that she had no other choice—that she was defending herself against a man who had come into her home in the middle of the night. She just had to stay calm, and do what was necessary. Lloyd would be caught off guard, having no idea that she knew her way around any kind of gun at all, so that was in her favor.

She could do this. She could. She just had to wait for the bastard to walk through that door, and it would all be over. Then she and Frank would be free to be together. They could build the life Frank dreamed of and be happy. Yes. She could do this.

She aimed at the door and waited.

FIVE MINUTES PASSED. Then ten. Ruth fidgeted in the chair, afraid to take her eyes off the door for even a split second. Her skin crawled with tension, and her shoulders cramped. Lloyd was up to something, but what?

She started to think of all the things he might be doing. He could be trying to get on the roof to find a way in through the attic, where she wouldn't be watching for him. It would be like him to try something unexpected like that. The pull-down door was in the closet where she had just put Penny. The urge to turn toward the closet was almost overwhelming, but she told herself she needed to stay focused. Chances were good he'd come right through the front door of the cabin and straight up the stairs.

But then again, he could be inside already, setting up a trap for her. Maybe he was starting a fire downstairs, planning to burn the cabin down around her. Hell, there was no way to know what Lloyd would do. He was capable of pretty much anything. Trying to second guess him was only making her more afraid, and the longer the silence lasted, the more Ruth's imagination ran away with her.

She couldn't stand it any longer. Easing up from the chair, she crept to the door. She put her ear against the wood, and listened for several minutes. Not a sound reached her. Aiming the shotgun at the door with her right hand, she used her left to turn the knob as quietly as possible. Then, she yanked the door open, and shouldered the shotgun in one quick move. The hall was empty. Exhaling a breath she hadn't even realized she had been holding, Ruth crept out of the bedroom and into the dark hallway.

The foot of the stairs was lit by pale moonlight streaming through the living room windows, and Ruth could see that no one was climbing toward her. Standing at the top, she held her breath and concentrated again. She could hear nothing at all to indicate there was anyone inside the cabin. Holding the shotgun at the ready, she braced for the possibility that Lloyd might leap out in front of her, and began a stealthy descent down each step. By the time she got to the bottom, she was pretty sure Lloyd wasn't inside. Yet.

Stepping down onto the living room floor, Ruth scanned the room. She was alone, unless he was hiding in the pantry. Possible, but it didn't feel right. She was sure she would have heard him moving around inside, opening or closing the pantry door. As she stood peering into every corner, a faint noise wormed its way into her awareness—a soft thumping near her kitchen window.

Whirling to her left, she aimed her shotgun at the window, then froze, her brain slow to comprehend what she was seeing. A shape hanging outside the window jerked feebly in the moonlight. A cat? No, a rabbit. A rabbit spun slowly on a length of twine, hind feet scratching faintly against the glass, leaving black, clotted smears sliding down the pane.

Nausea rolled through her as the full horror of what she was looking at registered. The bastard had slit its belly open and hung it up to bleed out against her window. In a silent agony of black and gray, the rabbit swung back and forth under the silver moon. Her breath caught on a sob, and all hope fled. She knew without a doubt—could see in her mind's eye—that Lloyd was going to gut her just like that rabbit.

This is it. He's gonna to kill me tonight. Oh, God, he's gonna to cut me open and kill me.

Leaning back against the wall, another wave of dizziness hit her so hard her legs buckled. Inch by inch, she slid down until she was sitting on the floor, the shotgun forgotten beside her. "I'm dead," she whispered, wondering how much pain he would put her through before he was done.

Alone in her dark kitchen, Ruth Winn disappeared and Ruthie Carter, terrified abuse victim paralyzed by fear, took her place. Defeated by her own past, she closed her eyes and waited for death with the same blank acceptance she had lived with for twelve years, while under Lloyd's brutal control.

A THUNDERING ROAR shattered the brittle silence of the night. Ruth's eyes flew open, and she gasped in shock. For a moment, she was lost in confusion, still in the grip of her own mindless terror, but then things snapped back into focus.

Lloyd had reclaimed his Impala. He revved the big engine over and over, announcing to the world that he was taking back what was his. Ruth saw the splash of headlights hit the kitchen wall and begin to slide around the circumference of the room. The car was moving. For one foolish moment, she thought perhaps he would just take his Impala and go, but she shook that idea out of her head as fast as it appeared. That was never going to happen. As if to prove her right, Lloyd began a slow circle of the cabin, blowing the horn, and yelling obscenities out the window. He made one complete loop, then stopped in front of the porch, letting the car idle with a menacing growl.

"Ruuuthieeee," he yelled over the rumble. "Come on outside, Ruthie! Let's have some fun. I got us some whiskey here. Come on out an' we'll go dancin' under the moon, Ruthie. Remember how we used to dance when we first met? I got my big car back now. I can take you for a ride, Ruthie. An' then we'll dance. Oh, yeah, baby. We'll dance!" With a wild laugh, Lloyd gunned the engine, and began another circle around her cabin.

The lights appeared and disappeared as the car passed various windows. Lloyd made another loop around the cabin, while Ruth sat numb, once more awaiting whatever he had in mind. He pulled up in front of the porch a second time, and stopped, his anger flaring even brighter when he saw that Ruth hadn't come outside as instructed. She needed to come to him in complete acceptance of his control, cowed and defeated, ready to take her punishment.

He swore under his breath. "Damn whore. Guess you ain't quite scared enough yet." Lloyd began to yell even louder. "Ruthie! Get your ass out here now! Don't make me come in there, you bitch! Come on out now, an' we'll have us some fun. I knooooow ... how about we have us a cookout tonight, Ruthie? Maybe we could roast us some hot dogs, whaddya say? How about a nice *wiener* roast over the fire? You got any *hot dogs* around, Ruthie? Any itty-bitty wieners for us to roast?" He whooped with laughter, as he gunned the engine again, and started the next loop around her cabin.

Shock hit Ruth again, as Lloyd's words began to sink in. He knew about Penny! A sick horror grew inside her. He would make her watch while he killed her puppy. He would throw Penny into the fire without a second thought. Cold sweat dampened her palms, and her heart was thudding so hard she could hear it.

Oh my God. This can't be happenin'. But it is. It is happenin', Ruth. And you are just sittin' here, doin' nothin'.

Shame washed over her, and she willed herself to pick up the shotgun. She had to at least try to fight back, didn't she? She owed it to Penny, if not to herself. Lloyd would kill Penny in the worst way he could dream up, just to hear her scream and beg. She had to do something!

Pulling herself to her feet, Ruth watched the gleam of the headlights move around the room once again. Lloyd came to a stop in front for the third time. He was enjoying the sense of power the big car gave him, and the sense of fear he knew it would put in Ruthie's heart. He banged his palm over and over on the outside of the driver's door, screaming at her this time. "Ruthie, you damn whorin' bitch! You are makin' me mad, now! You are pissin' me off, big time! You make me come in there an' you *will* regret it!"

He paused. Ruth imagined him taking a swig of whiskey out of a bottle. Then he yelled again. "Ruthie! You ignorin' me? You think you can get away with that? I guess you think I don't know what you've been up to. Is that right, Ruthie?"

Lloyd paused again, then continued even louder. "Well let me tell you, you stupid cow, I seen your hillbilly lover boy! You hear me, you piece of trash? I seen him, an' I know who he is, an' if you don't come out here, I swear to you, he's a walkin' dead man! Do you hear me, Ruthie? You better be out here on this porch when I come back around, or Loverboy is *dead*, you stupid bitch!"

This time Lloyd didn't laugh. He just revved the engine, popped the clutch, and took off around the cabin again.

A white-hot rage hit Ruth like a freight train. Frank? Lloyd knew about Frank? Lloyd was going to kill her precious Frank? No way was that son of a bitch going to hurt Frank as long as there was breath in her body. Every trace of her fear disappeared and a cold, calculating fury took over her mind.

As soon as the Impala turned the first corner into her side yard and headed toward the back, Ruth was out the door, and crouching behind the tall shrubs at the corner of her wide front steps. She ducked down low and waited, shotgun primed and ready. Her mind was filled with deadly purpose, clear and steady, and focused on what she knew she had to do. No matter what happened to her, she would never, ever let Lloyd hurt Frank Everly.

She heard the Impala approaching on her right, and pulled even farther into the shadows, hiding her face. The big car rumbled past her, almost close enough to touch, and came to a stop a few feet away, in front of the steps. She peered out from around the shrubs and saw Lloyd's head tilted back as he took another slug of whiskey from the bottle. In three rapid steps, she was next to the driver's door, slightly to the rear of the open window, with her shotgun pressed hard against the back of Lloyd's head, above his left ear.

"Don't move an inch," she yelled, before he could even lower the whiskey bottle. "Don't turn around! Don't even breathe, you sorry bastard!"

She could see the surprise in Lloyd's eyes as he watched her in the side view mirror. He inched the bottle just far enough away from his mouth to be able to speak, his voice now calm, almost friendly. "Well, well. What's that you got there, Ruthie? A gun? Now what're you gonna do with that? You know you ain't gonna shoot me, Ruthie. Is that your boyfriend's? Why don't you just put it down before you get hurt? You don't know nuthin' about guns, anyway."

"Well that's where you're wrong, Lloyd. I know plenty about guns. So happens, I was raised huntin' with a gun just like this one. You aren't nearly as smart as you think you are, and you were never the only one with secrets, either.

"You shouldn't have come after me, Lloyd. You should've just gone on your way and left me alone up here."

"Now Ruthie, you know I couldn't do that. You run off with my car an' my money. What did you expect?"

Ruth sighed. "This," she said in a flat, tired voice. "This is exactly what I expected. I knew you'd come to get it, and I knew you'd kill me for takin' it."

Lloyd smiled, and Ruth recognized the expression. He thought he had her now. He thought she had given up. His left hand dropped from the steering wheel as he started to turn toward her to push the gun barrel away from his head. For once, Lloyd Carter's instincts were wrong on every level, and he was too slow, by far. Ruth pulled the trigger, and with a deafening roar of the gun, Lloyd's head exploded in a spray of blood and bone.

With a disgusted shake of her head, she sighed again. "You should have left me alone, Lloyd. And you *never* should have threatened to hurt Frank."

She lowered the gun, and took several shuddering breaths, as the silence of the cold January night returned. Then she turned around and walked back into the cabin.

SATURDAY, JANUARY 23, 1965

RUTH HAD BEEN sitting at her kitchen table, staring into her cup of tea for an hour, wondering what to do next. She had no remorse that Lloyd was dead, but was sickened that she had been pushed to the point of having to kill him, herself. She knew what she had done would hit her hard later, but she'd have to deal with that when it happened. Right now, she had more immediate problems.

When she first walked back into her cabin, she had planned to call the sheriff and tell him she had just shot her husband in self-defense, but she had realized that story wasn't going to fly. It was pretty obvious Lloyd had been killed sitting in the front seat of the Impala, and not breaking into her cabin to harm her. That wouldn't look like self-defense at all, even once the truth came out about his abusive treatment of her in the past.

Justifiable. That's the term they used on TV. This would not look justifiable, and it didn't matter what she claimed. After all, for two and half years, she had also claimed to be a single woman, living on her own, and free to date Frank Everly. No, her word wouldn't be worth much, and this was going to look like murder, pure and simple. Like she killed Lloyd for her own reasons, maybe even to keep him from finding out about her cheating on him.

She tried out every story she could concoct, but nothing rang true, and the actual events of the night seemed the most unlikely of all, to her mind. Ruth was scared of being charged with murder and sent to jail, or worse, to the electric chair. But almost more awful than her fear of jail was her fear of confessing to Frank that every one of those nights spent loving each other was a lie. Every time she imagined the hurt it would bring to his eyes, her heart broke a little bit more. She was determined not to do that to him. He deserved so much better than to find out he had been committing adultery for over two years, and that the woman he loved was a liar and a cheat.

Frank was a church-going man. He had a strong sense of honor, and of right and wrong. He would have every right to hate her for leading him on, and she had. She had let him dream he could have a life together with her. A home and children. Love and happiness and lifelong commitment. She had longed for it herself, so she had let him build on that dream, knowing all the while it could never happen. His hurt would turn to anger and the anger to disgust, and she deserved it. But she just couldn't bear it. And then there was the matter of what she had done tonight.

Oh, my god. Frank can't ever know I've murdered a man.

The longer she thought about the mess she was in, the more certain she was that she had to hide her crime. There were just so many ways this could go bad, otherwise, and most of them would end up hurting Frank, or even endangering him. After all, everyone knew she was Frank's girl. What if they thought she shot her husband so they'd be free to marry? Worse than that, what if they thought Frank was involved? That the two of them plotted to kill Lloyd, and tried to pass it off as self-defense? He could be questioned, or even arrested.

She'd shoot her own self before she'd put Frank under that kind of suspicion. Even if he was never charged, people wouldn't forget. They would always wonder if he had taken part in the crime, and his good name would be ruined. No, calling the sheriff would be trouble all the way around. She would have to take care of this mess herself.

Glancing out her window, she saw it wouldn't be long before the sun came up. She had a car with a dead body in it right outside her front door. If she wasn't going to report the murder, she'd better come up with another plan, fast. Of course, she could bury Lloyd out back somewhere, and no one would ever know. Trouble was, she couldn't dig a hole deep enough for his damn Impala, and it had to disappear, too. There was no way to clean up the mess inside that car. It could never be driven again.

Ruth sighed, chewing her bottom lip. No doubt about it. She was going to have to get rid of the car and Lloyd together. After a few more minutes, an idea began to gather shape. It was probably crazy. No, it was *definitely* crazy. But it might work. She needed to hurry, though. This had to be done before daylight arrived. Frank might be opening the store this morning, but that didn't mean he wouldn't show up later to surprise her.

After turning her idea over in her head a few more times, and looking at it from every angle, Ruth made her decision. She wasn't happy about it, but it was all she could think of. Going to the coat rack, she put on her vinyl raincoat and an old pair of gloves, and walked outside carrying her flashlight, a long butcher knife, and her house keys.

The Impala had stalled out as soon as Lloyd was shot, and his nearly decapitated body was now slumped half way across the front seat, with his legs still under the steering wheel. There was no room for Ruth to get in. Shuddering, she walked around the car, opened the passenger door and yanked Lloyd's ice-cold body as far over as she could manage, refusing to look down at what she was doing. Then she went back to the driver's side, shoved his legs and feet out of her way, and climbed behind the wheel.

Gore covered the seat, splattered the dashboard, and obliterated the windshield with a mixture of blood, brain matter, and shards of bone. The smell of death was already building, and the seat was slippery with blood and bodily fluids she didn't want to dwell on, but the raincoat served as protection from the worst of it.

Lloyd's key was still in the ignition, but the car didn't spring to life when she turned it. Instead it cranked slowly, barely turning over. With shaking hands, she tried again, with no better luck. The headlights had been left on for the last hour, and the battery was low. Her entire plan hinged on getting the car started. She couldn't afford to panic now and flood the engine. Saying a prayer, she tried once more.

The third time was the proverbial charm, and, thank God, the engine caught. She let it run for a minute to be sure it wouldn't stall again, then put the car in first gear and started to move forward. Seeing through the windshield was impossible, so she had to drive leaning out the open door.

Tiny, hard flakes of snow stung Ruth's face as she inched the car around the side of the cabin, following the path Lloyd had taken earlier. When she got to the backyard, she turned away from the house, and drove straight to the old shed near the creek. Using the headlights to see by, she got out of the car and dug through her keys for the one to the padlock. The metal was freezing cold, but the lock worked fine, and she swung the doors wide. The shed was empty and there was plenty of room for her purposes. Getting back into the Impala, she pulled it all the way inside, cut the engine, and scrambled out of the car.

This will work, at least for now. She knew the building was watertight and well sealed around the roof, and that the concrete floor would keep out unwanted animal visitors. Nothing would get in unless she wanted it to.

Leaving the shed open, she walked back across the yard to her kitchen window and used the butcher knife to cut down the dead rabbit. She hurried back, opened the rear door of the Impala, and threw the rabbit's body onto the seat. Then she removed the bloody raincoat and gloves, and threw them inside the car, as well. That was everything she could think of, except for cleaning the kitchen window, which she would do after daylight.

In less than ten minutes, it was done. Ruth secured the padlock and walked away. Halfway back to the cabin, she stopped and turned around. The shed crouched in the moonlight like a slumbering beast—a concrete block sphinx, holding the answer to a riddle she hoped no one would ever ask. The entire back half was covered in kudzu vines, bare of leaves for the winter, but the dry, brown vines were still so thick you couldn't see through them to the building underneath. If left uncontrolled, the kudzu would swallow the rest of the shed in another year or two, leaving no trace of the building visible at all. No one would be able to tell it had ever existed. All she had to do was wait. And learn to live with the fact that her dead husband was lying inside.

Chapter 20
Far Too Polite To Question A Lady

SATURDAY, JANUARY 23, 1965

FAT, LAZY SNOWFLAKES floated this way and that outside the window. Ruth watched them drifting down, relieved to see that they were slowing, but not before they had done a good job of hiding the incriminating car tracks that encircled her cabin and led down to the shed. That was a trail Frank did not need to see. The snowfall hadn't been very heavy once dawn had arrived, but at 9:30, she used it as an excuse to call him and postpone their dinner date. She knew Frank's truck needed new tires, so she asked him not to risk the roads up the mountain, wanting to have some time alone to go over her plans.

"You worried about me, Ruth? Aw, that's sweet, hon. See, this is why we need to be married and livin' together."

Frank's gentle scolding made her feel guilty, and she longed for his comfort and strength, but it wasn't time for that, yet.

"If we were married, you'd be down here with me, safe and snug in my house," he said, "and we could be enjoyin' dinner together tonight. And the whole rest of the evenin', too. All our evenings, for that matter." Since Frank had no way of knowing how much snow was actually falling up on the mountain, he took Ruth at her word that it would be safer to wait another day or two before driving up.

"You're right, hon. Even though it would be nice to be with you, I can't risk getting stranded up there. I'd miss church in the morning, and I have to open the store tomorrow afternoon, too." With reluctance, he promised just to call Ruth later, and make new plans then.

Knowing Frank wasn't coming by before she got things sorted out gave Ruth one less thing to worry about. "On to the next," she said to General Penny, surprised that she felt so detached from the horror of the last eight hours. "I'll worry about what I've done later, I guess. I have other things to deal with first."

Her next problem was going to be how to explain the missing Impala. She would need to replace the car as soon as possible, and that presented several problems. First, she would have to come up with a plausible story about where it went. Then she had to figure out a way to get a new vehicle delivered to her. Tricky, but not impossible. She just needed to think everything through to be certain she got her stories straight. Ruth pondered her next move for a while, sipped her tea, and pondered some more. She couldn't afford to make any mistakes.

By the time she had eaten lunch and cleaned up the dishes, she had a plan worked out to her satisfaction. Picking up the telephone, she called Bosley's, a garage between Bat Cave and Lake Lure, where she had taken the Impala for oil changes and tune-ups a time or two. She had told Frank a week ago that she was thinking about getting a truck this spring to make it easier to haul her produce and tables to the Farmer's Market. Of course, she had planned to buy the truck as a second vehicle, rather than to replace the Impala, but Frank didn't know that.

The last time she had taken her car in to Bosley's Garage, Ruth had noticed two or three decent looking used trucks for sale, sitting in his parking lot. When he answered his phone today, Ruth explained to Willis Bosley that she had sold her Impala on the spur of the moment, and needed his advice on where in the world she could find a good deal on a truck as soon as possible, since she was totally without transportation now.

"I'm afraid I was a bit impulsive, Mr. Bosley, but he had cash, and I didn't want to let him get away. Now I'm stuck." She tried to sound helpless and uncertain. "I thought you might know somewhere I could get a good deal."

"Well, Miss Winn, you are in luck for sure. I'm happy to say, I happen to have a couple of trucks for sale right here, any one of which would be perfect for what you need."

When Willis found out Ruth intended to pay cash too, he recommended a 1964 Ford pickup that he thought she would like, and volunteered to deliver it right to her doorstep. "No, it's no problem at all, Miss Winn. I'll have Willis Junior follow me up so you won't even need to drive me back. Don't you worry your head a bit."

She hung up the phone, sighing with relief. Frank had been right to steer her business to Bosley's Garage. Mr. Bosley was well-known as an honest mechanic, and he had a gentleman's soft spot in his heart for a lady in need of a bit of help. Of course, he had no idea just how much help he was being in this case, and she said a little prayer that he never found out what really happened to her car.

In less than an hour, Willis Senior pulled a shiny blue Ford pickup truck into her driveway, followed by Willis Junior in a big, white tow truck, with "Bosley's Garage" written in fancy red script on both sides. Ruth agreed the Ford was the perfect answer for her needs. The Bosleys came inside to complete the paperwork, and Ruth handed over the cash, promising to bring the truck to their garage any time it needed servicing.

Father and son were all smiles when they left, and asked no questions at all about her sudden decision to sell her Impala. Large sums of cash will do that to people, but Ruth suspected Mr. Bosley was far too polite to question a lady, anyway.

When she was certain the skies had cleared and no more snow was on the way, Ruth drove her new truck down to Darcy's Corner, and headed straight for Everly's.

"YOU DID IT! You bought a pick-up truck. Good for you, Hon. It will be a lot easier for you now on market day. You keepin' the Impala, too?"

Ruth was not a natural liar, but having lived with a con man for years, she knew a good lie should have some element of truth in it. People hear something they already know to be fact, and they tend to believe what comes next. And, the closer to the truth a lie is, the easier it is to remember.

"Nope. It's already gone!" She smiled at the look of surprise on Frank's face. "When we talked about me gettin' a truck last week, there was already someone comin' for the Impala, but I wanted to surprise you. He took it earlier today, and I called Bosley's right away, because you told me how honest they were and all, and now I got me that pickup truck I needed."

She was rattling on, hoping Frank wouldn't press too hard for details.

"Worked out perfectly, didn't it?" She asked. "And isn't it nice? Nearly new, too. Since the roads didn't get bad after all, I wanted to test drive it, so here I am. And now at least one of us has a truck we can drive in snowy weather. The tires are brand new."

They walked outside and admired the truck from all angles, Frank commenting on how nice it was and what a good deal Ruth had gotten. "Who'd you sell the Impala to? Anybody I know?"

Ruth climbed into the truck, talking over her shoulder in an offhanded manner. "No, he was just here on some personal business, I think. Some guy named Carter. He really loved that big car, though." She shivered, thinking that it was a good thing that he *had* loved it, since Lloyd and his Impala would likely be together a long, long time.

She turned the conversation right back to her new pickup. "Look here, Frank. See what a nice radio my truck's got, and the heater works like a champ, too. I can already tell how much easier it's gonna be for me on market day." She gave him her biggest smile. "I did good, didn't I?"

"Looks to me like you sure did, Sweetheart. I'm proud of you, and pleased as can be that you have yourself a good truck now. It's goin' to be much more practical for you in lots of ways."

Ruth wandered the aisles in Everly's, doing some shopping while Frank closed out the register for the day, and then they stopped by the diner for a quick burger. They made a dinner date for the next evening, and Ruth drove home not long after dark. She had been awakened at 2:00 A.M. by her deranged husband, blown his head off and hidden his body, bought a new vehicle, and set things up to go on as if nothing had happened. Extreme stress, fear, rage, and exhaustion had taken a toll on her. After building up the fire and taking care of General Penny, she sat down on the couch and—all alone in the darkened room with no one to see or hear—Ruth Winn had a complete and total breakdown.

BY 10:00 P.M., Ruth felt like an empty shell. She had cried, both for herself and for the perverse stupidity and cruelty of her husband, which cost him his very existence. She had raged at Life and Fate and even God for every injustice that had come her way for the last thirty years. She screamed at the world, asking what she had ever done so terrible that her one chance of ever being happy was now hanging by a thread. Why had she been beaten and terrorized for years, and then put in the position of having to kill one human being in order to protect another? And when the enormity of that murder finally struck her with its full force, she collapsed under the weight of it, tearing at her hair in anguish and guilt.

A dull, emptiness had begun to seep into Ruth's heart and soul. She had no tears left, and her voice was almost gone from three hours of screaming and sobbing into the couch cushions. She sat staring blankly at the low flames in the fireplace, too exhausted to move. Penny crawled out from under the couch, where he had hidden during her wildest moments, and now stood in front of her, whimpering in distress. It took a minute for the sound to register. When it did, Ruth picked up her little dog and held his velvety, warm body close, kissing him on the top of his head as he snuggled against her, and licked the drying tears from her cheeks.

A moment later, she stood in the open door and watched as Penny took care of business, too worn out to walk down the steps with him. When he scampered back in, she scooped him up and lay back down on the couch, not even willing to attempt the stairs. Dragging an afghan over them both, Ruth fell into an exhausted slumber.

SUNDAY, JANUARY 24, 1965

AT EXACTLY 2:00 A.M., Ruth's eyes flew open and she sat up with a gasp, momentarily confused at finding herself on the couch with General Penny snuggled against her. Shivering, she noticed the dying embers glowing faintly from the cooling hearth, but the only sound she heard was the thudding of her own heartbeat. She wondered what had awakened her, but a glance at Penny showed the little dog was still sound asleep, so she told herself one of her bad dreams must have roused her, and nothing more.

Huddled under the afghan, she was trying to muster the energy to grab Penny and head upstairs to her bedroom, when a wash of light spread over the back wall of the living room. For a split second, she thought it might be from Frank's headlights, but she discounted that idea, knowing Frank would never come up here, unannounced, in the middle of the night. She stared in growing horror and shock as the light began a slow crawl around the room, sliding in oily silence from wall to wall. Hand at her throat, Ruth rose from the couch to watch the pale, greasy-looking light disappear toward the back of the cabin, then reappear on the other side of the room seconds later.

I'm still dreamin'. This isn't real. It isn't real. It can't be!

She watched, dry-mouthed and trembling as the light came to a stop. It remained smeared on the back wall in a nasty, sickly stain, only vaguely resembling the clean, sharp gleam of real headlights.

The faint rumble of an engine insinuated its way into the quiet of the night, a low throb, barely loud enough to be heard. She spun to face the front door, eyes wide with disbelief. Growing in volume, the sound projected a sense of bone-chilling menace that brought Penny scrambling to his feet, growling in fear. Ruth stood frozen, unable to make sense of what she was hearing, but too afraid to look out the window. The muted snick of a car door opening sent Penny into a frenzy of shrill barking, yet Ruth stood in the center of the room, paralyzed, fear rising thick and clotted within her.

The rumbling vibration of the engine faded away, and was replaced by another noise coming from right outside the living room window. Creak-creak. Pause. Creak-creak. Pause.

Ruth gasped. It was unmistakably the sound of the porch swing moving back and forth in a deliberate, steady rhythm, slowly and softly at first, then growing louder and faster.

Creak-creak. Pause. Creak-creak. Pause. Creak-creak. Creak-Creak. *Creak-Creak-Creak-Creak-Creak.*

Louder and louder, the harsh sound of metal grating on metal grew more shrill and horrifying every second, until it became a mind-shattering shriek that rent the night. Penny's barking took on an insane pitch, and Ruth clapped her hands over her ears, screaming in mindless terror.

And then—nothing. Silence, complete and absolute. A dead hush settled over the room, muting even the sounds of Penny's miserable whimpers and Ruth's ragged breathing.

Shaking from head to toe, and filled with a nauseating horror she'd never imagined existed, Ruth wanted to believe whatever had just happened was finished. The sickly, greenish light began to fade from her wall, and she whispered a frantic prayer. "Oh dear God, please let it be over! Please, please let it be over, let it be over." She choked back a sob as she turned to comfort Penny, and then she heard it—an answering whisper as cold and evil as damnation itself.

"Ruuuthie … I'm hoo-oome".
Ruth Winn dropped to the floor in a dead faint.

Chapter 21

See It, Believe In It, Then Make It So

MAC FINALLY LEFT for home at 10:00 P.M., and I realized I'd only talked to Jenna once since Christmas. I made a cup of Earl Grey and sat down to Skype her. After our usual "how are you's" and "what's going on's" were taken care of, we got down to serious girl talk. Jenna has never been one to beat around the bush, especially where I'm concerned, so she asked for a detailed accounting of my love life, right off the bat.

I brought her up to date, skipping the more intimate bits, of course. She was thoughtful for a moment, then, looking a bit incredulous, asked, "Is Mac really *The One*, Sarah? Are you truly, for sure, in love this time?"

I didn't hesitate. "I think I am, Jenna. I've never felt this way about anyone before. Oh, God. Did I just say that? I sound like every corny Chick Lit book in the world. But Jenna, it's true. No wonder I kept pushing my old boyfriends out the door. Somewhere in the deepest part of my heart, I think I suspected a man like Mac was out there somewhere, waiting for me."

"Um-hmm." She tilted her head and studied me with a gleam in her eye. "You mean a man with a tortured and tormented soul, carrying a train car full of baggage, which renders him so insecure, he takes three steps backward for every one forward?"

"Well, sure, it doesn't sound very good when you put it like that," I said with a laugh, "but I was thinking more along the lines of someone so honorable and honest that he can't accept the duplicity of others. Someone with an inborn love and respect for nature, who is as at home in the woods by a campfire as he is in his own house, and who loves sharing it all with me."

I thought of everything I loved about Mac. "He's also someone who enjoys books and reading almost as much as I do, quotes Thoreau as easily as he quotes Jack Reacher, and who believes in me and my writing. That's something I treasure. He makes me laugh and he gets my corny jokes, and when he kisses me, my knees get weak and my heart rate soars, and, well, you know." I trailed off, embarrassed at such an outpouring, but realizing just how much I meant it all.

Jenna sat looking at me for a moment, and then her expression changed from skeptical to a look of cautious optimism. "Are we talking the M-word here, Sarah?"

"Oh, Jenna! I honestly don't know what I'm talking about. It's just so damn complicated!"

She grinned. "Let me help you. Do you find yourself writing 'Mrs. MacKenzie Cole' or 'Sarah Cole' on scraps of paper, just to see how it looks? Are you trying it on out loud? Have you been thinking about what you'd like to do with the living room decor at Mac's house? Does even the thought of washing his dirty socks for the next fifty years make you hot? If you answered yes to any of the above, you are in a Marriage State of Mind, Chickie."

I laughed, but she had a point. I had, in fact, done at least two of those things in recent weeks. Gulp. I changed the subject.

"I don't believe it matters how I feel right now. Whether I love him or not, what matters is how Mac feels. I know he's happy when he's with me, but like I told you, he's a complicated man. It's not my story to tell, so you'll just have to take my word for it. He has things to deal with, yet."

"Yeah, I get it. Honest I do, Sarah. Something happened, and he has issues. I believe you when you say they're serious and understandable. But Sarah, are you going to be happy with things where they are right now, if that's all he wants? Is this going to work for you, like, forever?"

"Yeah, that's the big question, isn't it?"

I sighed, but Jenna made encouraging noises, so I continued. "Okay, I admit that sometimes I'm frustrated, and I feel like it's nowhere near enough. But other times, I think I'll take Mac any way I can have him, under any circumstances. I'm happy for a while, then the next thing you know, I find myself wanting more, all over again.

"When Mac isn't with me, I feel incomplete. It's not that I can't function without him. It's that I don't *want* to function without him. I like the sound and scent of him in the room with me. We don't even have to be doing the same thing, but there's something so comforting about knowing he's near. So if I say his name, he'll look up at me, and smile. Oh, Jenna! That smile! His face lights up with this look of wonder when he smiles at me, and it takes my breath away."

Jenna shook her head, a small frown furrowing her brow. "I don't know how you let him go home at night, if you feel like that. How do you make yourself leave his place and drive back to your cabin alone?"

"It's harder than you can imagine. I don't want to, believe me. I want him to hold me all night, every night, and wake up next to me every morning. Just watching him sleep makes me feel like all is right in the world. No one has ever, ever, made me feel like he does, Jenna.

"But even though I can see how much he cares for me, he still has some boundaries up, some places I can't reach. There is something about taking the next step that scares him deeply. I can't push him, Jenna. Forcing him would never work. I'd lose him for sure. And I wouldn't want any man I had to force, anyway."

"You are a stronger woman than I, Sarah. I can tell you love him. It's written all over you, you know. Talk about a face that lights up! I've never seen you like this. In the summer, I'm going to come up there, myself, and meet this man who has stolen your heart. I was beginning to think it would never happen."

I gave a rueful laugh. "I had given up on it, myself. This wasn't in my Big Plan at all, when I moved up here. But I do love him, Jenna. I love him more than I ever dreamed possible. I can't even imagine life without him, and I don't want to."

"Then don't, Chickie. Don't imagine that. See it in your mind as you want it to be, you and Mac together always. See it, believe in it, then make it so."

Later, as Handsome and I headed upstairs, I was still thinking about what Jenna said. It might have been the best advice she had ever given me.

In my heart, I did believe Mac and I belonged together. I think I had believed it almost from the start. At the very least, from that day by the creek, when he had studied my sketches so intently, and then studied me the same way. I think I knew even then that meeting him had changed my life forever. Now if only Mac would let himself believe in us, too. I was not going to say that to him, though. He'd have to find his way there, himself.

"Life would be perfect if that happened, wouldn't it, Handsome?" Handsome thought life was pretty much perfect as it was, if his loud, rumbling purr was anything to go by.

I turned off the lamp and imagined Mac lying beside me, holding me close. I drifted to sleep with the memory of his warm heart beating next to mine.

MAC SAT AT his desk, staring at nothing, unable to concentrate on the papers spread in front of him. Rosheen was sprawled on the nearby sofa, long legs dangling clear to the floor. Her soft snoring had been keeping him company for the last hour, as he shuffled documents around and pretended he was accomplishing something.

Exasperated, he turned off his computer, got up, and began to pace the room, wishing it were just a bit warmer so he could sit out on the balcony in comfort. He did his best thinking out there, feet up on the railing, watching the moon pour quicksilver over the trees.

Instead, he walked back and forth in his living room, feeling more and more discontented and unhappy by the minute. He was annoyed and frustrated to realize that after all these years of seeking comfort in solitude, he now found himself lonely. Night after night, when he was here by himself, he was lonely for Sarah. Intensely so.

He had been thinking about her ever since he got home. *This is making me crazy! Why can't I get her out of my mind? We just said goodnight two hours ago!*

What should have been a soothing and peaceful silence in his house now bothered him. It didn't feel right, and it made him edgy.

Why can't I just enjoy the time I spend with Sarah and come home to enjoy my time alone equally as much? I like being alone. I do! I've perfected it. Made it an art form, for God's sake!

But there she was, drifting around in his head, distracting him when he wanted to work, keeping him awake when he wanted to sleep, and leaving him lonely and discontented in his own home. It was maddening.

It's ridiculous! I see her several times a week, and we spend the night together on a regular basis. I talk to her on the phone every day. I'm surrounded by Sarah. It should be enough.

But somehow it wasn't, any more.

Back and forth, he walked, still annoyed with himself, still frustrated and edgy, but most of all, still missing Sarah. Still lonely without her. Not that he needed to be doing anything specific with her, though there were some specific things he liked doing with her very much. But that was beside the point. Tonight, he just wanted her here, near him. Or he wanted to be there, near her.

He liked watching her when she didn't know he was paying attention. Just watching the way she moved, the way her hair shone in the firelight, the way she smiled to herself as she read. When he looked up from his work, and she wasn't there, the house didn't feel right, or sound right, or smell right. It simply *wasn't* right. So what was he going to do about it?

"Yeah, that *is* the big question, isn't it?" he muttered.

Rosheen stretched and got up to join him as he walked back and forth across his living room. After his third loop around the room with her walking step by step at his side, he had to laugh at his big dog. He leaned over to give her some attention, and as he scritched and scratched under her chin and around her ears, he felt his tension ease a little.

"You wanna go out, girl?" He asked, as he stood back up. She waited by the front door while Mac grabbed his jacket and her leash. They went out into the cold air, and crunched across the frozen yard, making their way to the back of the house.

Mac let Rosheen off the leash for a few minutes, deciding she wasn't likely to go running away tonight, given how fast the temperature was dropping. While she sniffed around the edge of the trees, he leaned against a large boulder and stared out over the drop-off to the valley below. Yeah, this was what he needed. Cold, clear air, and his favorite view spread out in front of him.

As always, it calmed him down, settling his thoughts and centering his emotions. But it didn't change the fact that there was a Sarah-shaped hole in his house tonight, and he had to decide what he wanted to do about it.

As he stood there staring into the night, he thought about how miserable his life would be if Sarah weren't part of it any more. Did that mean he loved her? He had loved Vicki, too, and she had broken his heart. If what he felt for Sarah was love—if he actually admitted that out loud— wasn't he setting himself up for the same thing?

And why would he think that just because he was feeling this way, she was, too? She seemed to be happy with their relationship as it was, never asking him for more. He tried to picture her wandering around her house, miserable without him there. He couldn't see it. What if he told her he loved her? Say he worked up his nerve, and told her, and she pulled away from him? It hurt just to think about that possibility.

Mac didn't count himself as much of a prize. His finances were in pretty good shape, sure, but that wouldn't carry much weight with Sarah. Take the money out of the equation, and he knew he was a man with too much baggage and a definite need for privacy.

He thought he was difficult and moody, used to doing things his own way. He knew he resisted change, liked a quiet, uneventful lifestyle, and hated leaving his woods for any length of time. He'd be both annoying and boring as hell to live with.

Surely Sarah sees me for what I am, and knows I'm not a wise investment. Why would she ever give up her independence for a man like me?

He was certain she enjoyed his company, and the chemistry between them was breathtakingly intense. God, he couldn't get enough of making love to her! But sooner or later she was bound to lose interest, and she'd go back to wanting to be just friends. He had no reason to think otherwise, and feared she would reject him outright if he told her he wanted more.

No, it was better not to rock the boat. He'd be smarter to just accept what they had, for as long as it lasted, and put off thinking about the inevitable conclusion of their romance. Being rejected by Sarah would kill something in his soul that had only just started waking up again. He wouldn't chance it.

Calling Rosheen, Mac went back inside, more determined than ever to keep his feelings hidden so deeply he wouldn't even have to acknowledge them to himself. The decision left him less edgy, but much sadder, and he went upstairs to a cold and lonely bed, longing for the sweet warmth of Sarah curled up next to him in the dark. Sleep was a long time coming.

Chapter 22

Why Would You Ever Think Anything Else?

SUNDAY, JANUARY 22, 2012

SUNLIGHT FLOODED THE bedroom. I opened my eyes, realizing with dismay that I had overslept. I didn't have to be anywhere this morning, but I'd been making a conscious effort to get up early enough to watch the day wake around me. I discovered I loved sitting on my back porch, bundled in my warm robe, and sipping my first cup of tea while the mist rose from the icy surface of the creek. My creek. My woods. Both awaiting me every day, in a visible validation of this choice I've made.

I crawled out of bed, moving slowly, and feeling disgruntled that I'd lost those moments of grateful solitude. As I brushed my teeth, I thought about the dreams that had troubled me through the night. Only bits remained in my waking mind, but those were unpleasant, and threaded throughout with frightening echoes of a chilling voice calling someone's name, over and over. I shivered. No wonder I'd overslept, having my rest disturbed like that.

"Come on, Handsome," I mumbled, pulling the covers off my cat. Handsome hissed and swatted my hand, his ears flattened, and eyes flashing.

"Ouch!" I pulled back in surprise, frowning as Handsome leapt off the bed and raced downstairs, tail puffed to twice its normal size.

"I guess I'm not the only one who had a bad night," I called after him.

By the time I got to the kitchen, Handsome was sitting by his bowl, calm and collected, and with a sweet as cream expression on his face. He gave me a pitiful mew, and wound back and forth through my legs as I fixed his breakfast. While he was eating, I made my long overdue cup of tea, and wandered to the living room to peer out the frosted window. It looked cold outside, and the sun that had awakened me was fast disappearing behind low, gray clouds. I sighed, disappointed, figuring snow was on the way. Going for a morning walk was no longer very tempting.

"So. It's going to be that kind of day, huh? Well, have at it," I said. "I'm ready to kick butt and take names this morning. Do your worst, Day."

Fate loves it when we say things like that.

ACROSS THE HIGHWAY, Mac had been lying awake for hours, lethargic, and staring at the ceiling. He just couldn't seem to make himself get out of bed and get busy. He had expected to wake feeling full of pep and ready to go, having made his decision to avoid any and all actions regarding the status of his relationship with Sarah. He thought his mind would be free to think about other things for a change, like his business, and ... well ... whatever other things he wanted to think about.

"Damn, and damn again!" He thumped his pillow around and ordered himself to relax and enjoy a lazy Sunday morning at home. "I had a life before I met her, and I still have a life, and I don't need any more of this endless, soul-searching misery. What did I used to do on a sleepy Sunday morning, before I found out how nice it was to share one with Sarah? I did stuff. I know I did! I hiked, and ... sat on my balcony, and ... relaxed! Yeah. I did whatever I damn well wanted to, that's what I did! And it was good, too!"

Bolstered by that thought, he finally got up, put on his jeans and a warm sweater, and headed downstairs to feed Rosheen, and pack himself a lunch. He was going to take his dog for a long walk, cold weather or no cold weather, and he was going to enjoy it, by God.

Three hours later, a cold and dispirited Mac headed back to his house with his big dog plodding behind him. Both were shivering in the damp, chill wind, and ready to call it a day, though Mac wasn't quite ready to admit total defeat.

"There," he said to Rosheen, as he stamped leaves and mud off his boots, and hung his jacket in the closet. "I can still do fun things by myself, can't I? I don't have to have Sarah along for every single outing. We had a good time, didn't we, girl?" Rosheen ignored him, walking off without a backwards glance, to lie by the cold hearth in hopes that a fire would soon be forthcoming.

Mac did build a fire, much to Rosheen's delight, and then he settled down to try to get some work done. He managed to forget about his personal life for a few hours, and actually felt pretty good about what he had accomplished by the time he turned off his computer at 7:30. He fixed dinner, and afterward began a debate with himself about whether to call Sarah before it got too late. Finally, he decided against it, in a perverse desire to see if he could manage to go a whole day without any contact with her.

As soon as he decided he wasn't going to call, he thought of a dozen important things he wanted to tell her. Then he thought of some other things he ought to ask her. He simply couldn't keep her out of his mind.

At 10:00 P.M., he gave in, reached for his phone, and hit the Call button.

"Hi, Mac. How's everything?"

The minute he heard Sarah's voice, the band that had been steadily tightening around his heart since he left her the previous night, loosened. Everything that had felt so wrong with his day felt right again. He closed his eyes, breathed out a long, deep sigh, and knew his whole world had returned to normal.

"I'm fine. How about you? Get any writing done?"

After their conversation was over, Mac sat staring into the fire, marveling that all it had taken to make everything okay was the sound of Sarah's voice. A simple truth worked its way into his heart, like a song long forgotten, but instantly recognized when heard again. There was no hiding from this. Not any longer.

"I love her," he said in bewildered astonishment. "Oh my God, I really do love her."

With shaking hands, he poured himself a small glass of Scotch and drank it in one gulp, then walked to the balcony doors and stared out at the night. "You're an ass, MacKenzie Cole," he told the reflection in the glass. "You've been sleepwalking through life for fifteen years, being oh, so careful to avoid feeling anything at all, and along comes this perfect, beautiful, intelligent, delicious woman, who never asks you for more than you are in the mood to give her, and what do you do? Everything in your power to keep her out of your heart, that's what!"

He leaned his forehead against the cool glass of the door.

"Are you too stupid to recognize a second chance when it's right in front of your face? Right across the road? You love her, and you know you do, in spite of all your denials and protestations. *You love her.* Tell her, for God's sake, before she decides she's done with your sorry ass. Tell her, and pray that she might love you back."

Mac grabbed his phone. He would call Sarah at once, to tell her he loved her, and that he wanted her with him all the time, and he'd wait as long as it took, until she felt the same way. Words tumbled over each other in his head, as he realized how many things he had to say.

He glanced at the clock. Almost midnight. Sighing, he put the phone down. It was too late to call her again tonight. He'd wait until tomorrow, and go over around lunchtime, when she would be taking a break from her writing. He could tell her then. It was too important to say over the phone, anyway. It would be better if he could hold her hands and look into her eyes, so he could declare his feelings openly. He would beg her to love him, too. And she would. She had to. He would do whatever it took to win her heart.

There was no excuse for why he had been too afraid to even try, but he was done with that kind of fear. He swore tomorrow would be the day he left his old life behind, and found his way to a new one.

MONDAY, JANUARY 23, 2012

A PHONE RINGING at 2:00 A.M. never means anything good. No one calls at 2:00 A.M. to ask how your day went. No one calls at 2:00 A.M. to complain about their job, ask what good books you've read lately, or see if you want to have dinner on Friday. Calls at 2:00 A.M. are bad news. Someone has died. Someone is hurt. Or, someone needs help.

Mac struggled into an upright position on his sofa, where he had drifted off to sleep fully clothed, while thinking of all the things he wanted to tell Sarah. He blinked, sleep-befuddled and groggy. Grabbing his cell, he saw Sarah's picture on the screen, and fear lanced through him immediately.

"Sarah? What's wrong?"

She answered with a frantic whisper. "Mac! There's someone here! There's someone in my yard!"

"*What?*" He was across the room in an instant, unlocking his gun cabinet and pulling out his shotgun and a rifle, all thoughts of sleep forgotten. "Where are you?"

"I'm in the kitchen." She sounded terrified. "He's yelling again, but I can't see anyone from my windows."

He interrupted her. "Sarah! Get away from the windows, and stay low where he can't see you. Hide! I'm on the way. Don't hang up, okay?"

"Okay. Hurry, please."

He pulled on his jacket as he headed to the door, talking softly to Sarah all the while. Rosheen was hard on his heels as he left the house.

"I'm getting in the truck, right now. I'll be there in a minute. Don't be scared. I won't let anything happen to you, I promise."

Sarah's voice was low and shaky. "Okay. I'm in the pantry, now. Mac? I can't help it. I'm scared."

"I know. It's okay. It'll be okay. I'm coming. Just stay real quiet so he won't hear you."

"Do you have a gun with you?" She asked softly. "Because I think he might be dangerous. He's ranting and yelling crazy stuff."

"I have guns with me," he reassured her. "I won't let him hurt you, I swear, Sarah. *I won't!*"

"Mac?"

"Yes?"

"Please be careful."

He could hear the tears in her voice, and anger rose inside him at the very thought of someone scaring his Sarah this badly. "I'll be careful. Can you still hear him?"

"No. It's quiet now." She sounded surprised. "Maybe he's gone?"

He could hear the hope in her voice. "I'm pulling into your drive. I don't see any cars or anything."

"I can hear your truck. Oh, God, be careful, Mac. Maybe he's just hiding."

"I will. I'm in front of the house now. I'm just going to sit here a minute and look around. Be very quiet for me, okay, so I can hear."

He rolled his window down an inch and listened carefully. Nothing greeted him but silence, and the sound of Rosheen's soft panting from the passenger seat. He studied the shadows next to the cabin, and along the dark edges of the woods, and saw nothing at all.

"Sarah?" He whispered into the phone. "I don't see anyone, and Rosheen doesn't act like there's anyone here now, but I'm going to take a closer look around the property to be sure he's gone." He spoke calmly and very quietly. "When it's safe, I'll knock on the door and you can let me in, okay?"

"Yes. God, I'm so scared. Please don't get hurt."

"I promise I won't get hurt."

A pause. "Sarah?"

"Yes?"

"I love you."

He clicked off the phone, and dropped it on the passenger seat. After reassuring himself that there was nobody close by, he climbed out of the truck. He slung the rifle strap over his left shoulder, and held the shotgun at his side, in his right hand. Rosheen scrambled out, and waited next to him, looking interested but completely calm. He racked the shotgun, and quietly stepped away from his truck, with Rosheen following closely—a lean, gray shadow—as silent, and as deadly as either of his guns.

MAC MOVED CAUTIOUSLY around the perimeter of Sarah's property, sharp eyes alert for any evidence of the person who had terrorized Sarah. The moonlight washed over her yard brightly enough to throw shadows across the frosty, white ground. He had made the loop around her cabin, and had seen nothing suspicious whatsoever. In fact, it was what he didn't see that worried him most of all. It made no sense, and left him wondering what the hell was going on here.

Rosheen turned around and went back to Sarah's front porch as soon as he headed toward the rear of the property. He signaled her to come twice, but she ignored him, and stayed put. She could be stubborn, but it wasn't like her to ignore a command. He decided to let her go, figuring it wouldn't hurt if she were guarding the front entry, anyway.

Where was this guy? How could he have disappeared so quickly? Just as he decided the intruder wasn't anywhere in the yard, it hit Mac that maybe he had found some way to get inside the cabin. Maybe he already had Sarah. Fear rose within him, adrenalin-laced and bitter, as Mac pictured some psychotic killer in there with her.

He spun away from the edge of the creek and began to run back toward the cabin, sure now that she was in danger. He tried to move as quickly and quietly over the slippery frost as possible. If Sarah was in the hands of some lunatic, he didn't want to advertise that he was coming. Ugly images of her being hurt flashed unbidden through his mind as he came around the side of the cabin.

To his surprise, Rosheen was no longer on the porch. In fact, she was nowhere to be seen, which was not good at all. As he neared the steps, there was a loud crash from inside, followed by a strangled scream, cut short. His fear spiraled into overdrive.

Terrified he might already be too late, he hit the porch running, skidding on the icy steps. The door was still locked, and for a split second he hesitated, but the sound of glass breaking somewhere within spurred him on. The sturdy door was not going to give, so he slammed the butt of the shotgun into the living room window, knocking out as much glass as possible. He clambered through, and came to a halt. The room was empty. He listened for a moment, but had no sense of anything amiss. Instinct told him there was no intruder inside, but there had been a crash, and something had made Sarah scream.

"Sarah! Where are you?"

"Mac? I'm here!" Her voice was muffled, but near. There were more crashing noises, and in two long steps, he was at the pantry, pulling open the door. Sarah was on the floor, with broken jars and boxes of food on top of her, and collapsed shelves everywhere.

"Oh, God! Are you hurt? What happened?" He laid the shotgun to one side, and started moving away shelves, cans of vegetables, and a lot of shattered jars.

Sarah scrambled to her feet and flung herself into his arms. "Oh, my God, Mac! You're alive!" She was shaking all over and crying uncontrollably.

He made a quick assessment, checking for blood or visible injuries, but other than some ugly scrapes along one arm, and tiny shards of glass clinging to her wet nightgown and hair, she seemed to be unhurt. He pulled her close to him, feeling nearly sick with relief.

"God, Sarah! I thought I'd lost you. I thought he was in here with you, hurting you." His voice caught, and he had to take a deep, shuddering breath to continue. "What happened?"

She was babbling through her tears. "I heard a noise on the porch, and then I heard Rosheen growling, and then a sort of yelp, and I thought he was out there, but it got really quiet again, and then I heard another noise, and I was so scared, I jumped to the back of the pantry and crashed into the shelves and they all fell down! There were jars and bottles and groceries on top of me!"

Sobbing with fear, she clung to him. "Then I heard the window breaking, and I thought he was coming in! Oh, God, I thought you were dead, Mac! I thought he killed you, and he was coming to get me next, and I was so scared. I needed to find you, but I was trapped in the pantry, and I had broken glass on my face, and a crazy man coming to kill me, and you were dead, and ... and ... " She broke down completely, burying her face against his chest.

He held her tightly for a minute while she cried, then carefully put his hands on each side of her face and looked into her eyes. "Shhh, shhhhh. Don't cry, Sarah. Don't cry," he murmured. "I'm right here. I'm not dead. And you aren't dead. And whoever he was, he's gone now. I looked everywhere. He's not outside and he's not in here. He's gone. We're okay, both of us. We're okay. I'm here, and I'm not going to let anyone hurt you. Not ever. I promise. I'll never let anything happen to you! Don't cry. It's all right now." And then he kissed her. She had bits of glass in her hair, and she reeked of dill pickles, and he kissed her anyway, with a frightened desperation that stunned them both.

When he finally stopped and let her catch her breath, she tilted her head back, and looked at him in teary-eyed amazement. "You said you loved me."

His heart lurched. "I did say that, didn't I?"

"Did you mean it?"

"I try not to say anything I don't mean, Sarah."

"So ... you love me?"

"I do. I love you so much, I couldn't even think about it. Not for weeks and weeks. It terrified me."

"But you're not scared now?"

"Not of loving you. I'm only scared about whether or not you can learn to love me back."

She shook her head, and his heart plummeted.

"I can't *learn* something I've known how to do from the first day I met you. I already love you, Mac. Why would you ever think anything else?"

A FEW MINUTES later, Mac stood watching as Sarah came down the stairs. After having checked the upstairs very carefully, in what was probably an excess of caution, he had waited below, keeping an eye on the front door and broken window, while she changed from her soaked nightgown to a pair of jeans and a sweater. Bits of glass still clung to her hair and the reek of pickle brine accompanied her approach, but he just wanted to get her out of here as quickly as possible. Back to his house where it was safe, and she could take a long, hot shower, and he could hold her the rest of the night. He never wanted to feel as afraid as he had earlier, when he thought she was being attacked.

As she loaded Handsome into his carrier, he went to the door and called Rosheen again, with no more luck than he'd had the first time he tried. He finally closed the door and turned back to Sarah. "I'll go looking for her as soon as I get you settled at my house. You have everything you need for tonight?"

She nodded, but he could tell from the expression in her eyes that she was not likely to stay behind while he hunted Rosheen. That was okay by him. He really didn't want to let her out of his sight, anyway.

"I can get anything else I need tomorrow," she told him. "In the daylight." Her face had a frightened, pinched look about it, and it hurt him to see the joy gone from her eyes. For that alone, he hated whoever had done this to her. She had loved her cabin so much, and had been so happy, but it was obvious now that she was shaken to the core, and just needed to get out of here.

"Do you have some sheeting or a tarp I can put over the window before we go, to help keep the weather out? I'm sorry I had to break it, but I didn't want to waste ammunition on blowing the lock off the door. I was afraid I might need it when I got inside."

"Don't even think about apologizing for a stupid window. You came for me. You thought there was a madman in here, and you came to get me, anyway!"

"I'll always come to get you, Sarah."

She gave him a shaky smile, but added, "I don't want to stay here long enough to make even temporary repairs, Mac." She shivered. "What if he comes back?"

He sighed. This wasn't likely to go well, but he had to say it. "Well, about that. I couldn't find any sign of him out there, anywhere."

She shrugged. "I guess he must have left through the woods or something, maybe when he heard you coming?"

"No, that's not what I mean, Sarah. There were no *signs*. No footprints, no car tracks. Nothing disturbed anywhere. I couldn't find anything that indicated anyone had been here at all."

She frowned, looking confused. "I don't understand. He would have to have left footprints by the windows and in the yard, wouldn't he?" Mac nodded, waiting for her thoughts to catch up with his. She stared at him, then dropped her bag, and walked to the door. "Show me."

They went outside together, Mac keeping his shotgun at the ready, just in case. Moonlight bounced brightly off the thin layer of snow covering the frozen yard. Even from the porch, Sarah could see the tire tracks Mac's truck had left in the driveway. They were the only set visible. She stepped down and walked to the side yard. There was a single line of footprints leading from the truck to her kitchen window, then disappearing around the back of the cabin. Rosheen's prints ran from the truck to the area in front of the porch. Nothing else disturbed the icy snow.

Mac took her hand, and they followed his earlier tracks all the way around her cabin, adding their own double set beside his. When they were back to the porch, Sarah went inside without a word, and sat down in the dining area. He followed and stood leaning on the table, watching her closely. The confusion in her eyes was all the confirmation he needed. Whatever had happened tonight, Sarah knew nothing about it.

She stared at the table for a long time, working it over in her mind, then looked at him with sudden dread in her eyes. "Do you think I made it up?"

He didn't hesitate. "No. Of course not."

Her relief was obvious. "Well, then, what *do* you think? It couldn't have been a dream, could it? I clearly remember waking, and coming downstairs to try to see who was out there. All the screaming and swearing scared me. And I had to get my cell phone to call you. I left it by the computer. I even checked to be sure the doors were locked. I knew it would take forever for the sheriff to get someone here, so I called you. I *talked* to you. I wasn't dreaming, Mac. I wasn't!"

"I know you weren't. You were definitely awake when you talked to me."

"Oh my God, am I crazy, then? Could I have hallucinated it? Imagined it?"

She looked even more afraid. And what was clear to Mac was that she was trying hard to explain to *herself* what had happened, rather than trying to convince him of anything. To his mind, that was even more proof that his faith in her wasn't misplaced. She was as much in the dark as he was, and by God, he was going to find out how this was done, and who had gotten such a twisted kick out of scaring her so badly. Who could ever hate Sarah that much? And why? It made no sense at all.

"Am I having a breakdown? Some kind of psychotic separation from reality?"

He pulled out a chair, sat down facing her, and took her hands in his. "Sarah," he chided gently, "I don't know anyone more sane than you. Listen to me. I don't believe you made it up. I don't believe you were dreaming. And I don't believe you're crazy." He stood, pulled her to her feet and put his arms around her, holding her against his chest.

"Well, how do you explain it?" Her muffled voice was so small and frightened, it made his heart ache.

"I can't explain it. Not yet. I don't know how it was done. But I believe in you absolutely and completely, Sarah. And we'll figure it out together, you and I."

She looked up at him doubtfully, and started to say something else, but he gently shushed her, putting his fingertip against her lips.

"We *will*. No one will ever do something like this to you again! Not ever!"

"You promise?"

"I do. I promise you, Sarah Gray."

She smiled at him then. "I believe you, MacKenzie Cole."

And he knew she did. She had faith in him, and he realized that she always had. It was a revelation that touched something deep inside him, and he swore to himself he would keep his promise to her, no matter what. He would keep it for the rest of his days, if she would let him.

"That's better." He smiled down at her. "We'll report this to the sheriff's office first thing in the morning. Now let's get out of here. We can deal with everything else tomorrow, okay?"

"Yes. I'm ready."

He slipped the strap of his rifle over his left shoulder and grabbed her overnight bag. Holding his shotgun in his right hand, he was moving toward the door when the silence of the winter night was shattered by a series of blood-curdling wails, one after the other in an ear-splitting wall of sound. Mac dropped the bag and pushed Sarah behind him, then raised his shotgun to cover the front door and the open window next to it. He recognized that sound, and he knew things were about to get bad.

As quickly as it had begun, the unearthly noise stopped.

"What in God's name was that?" Cried Sarah.

"That," answered Mac, "was *Rosheen*."

Chapter 23

She Knows Something We Don't

MAC STOOD BETWEEN me and the front door, shotgun at the ready. I didn't think it was possible to be more terrified than I had been in the pantry, when I heard someone smash through my front window. I was wrong. Something truly bad was about to happen. Mac knew it, I knew it, and Rosheen seemed to know it, as well. I had never heard any animal make a sound filled with so much primal fear and rage.

Almost worse than being afraid was the total confusion I was feeling. Who had been in my yard, yelling obscenities outside my windows? Where had he gone? And most of all, why were there no footprints or tracks of any kind? If I hadn't seen it with my own eyes, I would never have believed it. Mac's footprints circling my cabin and the perimeter of my property were clearly visible, but there was no sign that anyone else at all had been in the yard. I was amazed that Mac didn't think I was completely delusional. Maybe love really is blind.

And speaking of love, I hadn't had time yet to process all that Mac had told me. I was going to revisit that topic with him as soon as we made it to his house, assuming we survived whatever the hell was outside, of course. All of that would have to wait, though. Right now, the two of us stood in my living room, watching the occasional scattered snowflake blow through the smashed window, while we waited for ... *something*.

Mac wasn't moving a muscle. He held the shotgun in front of him, head cocked to one side, as he listened intently for anyone who might be approaching. His calm, quiet voice belied the tension I knew he had to be feeling. "Sarah, you should go upstairs now."

I'm ashamed to admit, I considered it for a second. Going upstairs and hiding under the bed seemed like a sensible plan to my screaming Inner Coward, but I had calmed down enough from the earlier drama that my sense of outrage was beginning to make an appearance. The longer I stood there wondering what kind of danger we were in, the angrier I was getting.

Someone had done a first-rate job of scaring me senseless, and I could definitely feel the menace behind the episode. It still hung so heavily on the cold air, I could almost taste it. And now Mac, who had thrown himself through my window like Indiana Jones to the rescue, was in danger, too.

My Mac! Oh, hell no! I wasn't hiding in any more pitch-black pantries or under any beds, waiting for what might come. That just turns you into a gibbering idiot covered in broken glass and pickle juice! I was not going to be that helpless female from all those old movies, screaming in the corner while her man gets beat up. If there was a battle to be fought, I would stand with Mac, and do my best.

"I'm not leaving you down here to deal with some crazy person alone, Mac. Don't even think it. Is the rifle loaded and ready to go?"

"Yeah, but ... do you know how to use it?"

"Yep. And I'm not afraid to shoot, if I have to."

He glanced over his shoulder at me, hesitating only a second, then held out his left arm so I could slide the rifle strap off. I took the gun, and gave him a half smile. "I've got your back, MacKenzie Cole."

A slight smile curved his mouth as he watched me release the safety, then his head whipped back around as a heavy thud hit the porch, followed by the sound of paws scrabbling frantically at the door. Mac leaned to the right, and looked out the window.

"I don't see anyone following her," he said, and opened the door. The big dog shot into the room, mud and ice clinging to her wet fur. She whirled around to stand with her feet planted firmly on the threshold of the open door, hackles raised and teeth bared. Gone was the gentle giant that tolerated Handsome's silly games, and in her place was an enormous beast nearly five feet tall, with murder burning in her eyes. Mac let her cover that spot, while he knelt down near the window.

I moved to Rosheen's left, where I was partly hidden by the open door. It had been a long time since I fired a rifle, and I had never shot at a living target, but anger laced with righteous indignation was pouring through me. I had no doubt I could do it if the circumstances were right. My anger fueled my determination, and I put all thoughts of being afraid out of my mind. I was ready.

"Do you see anyone?" I whispered to Mac.

"No, but Rosheen is in full defense mode. She knows something we don't. Someone is out there, and I'm assuming they mean trouble, until they show me otherwise."

I shivered. Being ready to fight, and wanting to, were two different things. I was praying this was someone's sick idea of a prank. "You'll yell 'Who goes there?' or something before you start shooting, right?"

"Don't worry. I usually make an effort not to gun people down without reason, but Sarah? I think this would be a good time to dial 911. I know it will take them a long time to get here, but we might be needing some help."

I backed up to the open pantry door and looked in. Protruding from under a fallen shelf was my cell phone, smashed flat.

"Phone's a goner," I said. "Where's yours?"

"In my truck," he said, mouth tightening. "Stupid move on my part."

No help coming, then. Mac and I were on our own.

"I could make a run to the truck for it," he added, weighing the risk.

"No! Don't go out there, please, Mac. You'd be an easy target. Oh, this is wrong! This whole thing is just so wrong!" I stopped. Rosheen had started a low, rumbling growl, deep in her chest. Every hair on the back of my neck stood up, and I had a feeling we had just run out of time. Listening hard, I realized I was hearing another growl, as well. Low, but louder than Rosheen's.

"Mac? I hear ... I think I hear ... is that a car coming?"

"I hear it, too, but I can't see it anywhere." He was almost leaning out the window, trying to pinpoint the direction of the sound. "Where is it? Where the hell is it?" The noise gradually grew louder, until the rumbling vibrations filled the whole cabin.

"What the hell?" Mac scrambled back from the window, and stood staring outside, with a look of profound shock on his face.

"*What?* What is it?" In a split second, I was by his side, looking out, too. There, in front of my porch steps, sat a big, red car, rumbling ominously, and there was no one in it!

"Mac?"

"It just ... appeared," he said, in stunned confusion. "There was nothing there, and then, there was! I swear, Sarah. It didn't come down the drive or anything. It just *appeared!*"

For some reason, that didn't surprise me as much as it should have. This night seemed to have slipped into Twilight Zone territory from the moment I had been awakened by that madman shouting under my window.

We stood staring at the car, unable to take our eyes off it. I guess we were just trying to process the idea of what looked to be a decades old Chevy Impala materializing out of thin air. As we stood staring, the sound of the engine began to fade away, becoming fainter and fainter, until once again, Rosheen's steady growl was the loudest sound in the night. She glared out the door, trembling from head to toe, her lips pulled so far back from her sharp, white teeth, it looked like it would hurt.

"Sarah?" Mac was paler than I would have imagined possible. "Tell me I'm not seeing this," he said, nodding at the window.

I looked back outside, and froze. "What's happening to it? It's ... it's disappearing!"

And it was! Right in front of our eyes, it was slowly fading away, just like the sound of the engine had. First, the edges grew blurry, then the colors became watery, and in seconds, it was totally transparent. Finally, only a vaguely car-shaped red smear remained.

My mouth went dry. "What the hell, Mac? It's almost gone."

Rosheen was getting more and more agitated by the minute. She was now alternating between deep, throaty growls and high-pitched, anxious whines, shifting restlessly from foot to foot. Nervous energy rolled off her in waves, and she looked as confused as Mac and I, but her fierce protective stance never wavered.

As if things weren't bad enough, Handsome chose the next moment to add his voice to the mix. He started to yowl, hissing and spitting, and thrashing around in his carrier so hard, it rocked its way across the surface of the table, and tumbled off the edge, the door popping open upon impact with the floor. Handsome streaked across the room, between Rosheen's legs, and into the night. I didn't have time to react, before I realized that Mac was talking.

"Get your car keys, Sarah. Your Jeep is closer than the truck. I don't know what the hell is going on, but we're getting out of here!"

"*What?*" I was practically shrieking. "We'd have to go right by ... *that*," I said, nodding my head at what was left of the car. "I don't want to go anywhere near it, whatever the hell it is."

"Yeah, neither do I, but we can't stay here, either. We're like fish in a barrel."

I reluctantly put the rifle down on the kitchen table, and started to dig through my purse, but before I could locate the keys, all hell broke loose.

OUTSIDE THE FRONT door, the big, red Impala roared to life again. The noise was astonishingly loud, and coupled with Rosheen's anguished howls, it felt like enough decibels to make my ears bleed.

"The car is back!" Mac yelled from the window. Looking out the door, over the top of Rosheen's head, I could see that in addition to having regained its loud, rumbling growl, it had solidified into that bright red, disturbingly solid-looking vehicle again. The headlights threw twin beams of a sick, greenish color into the cold night.

My mind was grappling with the impossibility of it all, when I heard a heavy thumping from behind me. I whirled toward the kitchen, and opened my mouth to scream, but the only thing that came out was a horrified whimper. Hanging outside my kitchen window was some sort of dead animal, all bones and tattered, rotted fur. It swung slowly back and forth, while one gore-encrusted, skeletal foot scratched feebly against the glass. With both hands clamped over my mouth, I backed toward the living room, unable to turn away.

The Impala's engine was revving over and over, unimaginably loud, and I tore my eyes away from the thing in my window just in time to see the car move forward — still without a visible driver. Mac was staring out the door with a stunned look on his face, as it turned left and headed toward the back of the cabin.

"I don't believe any of this," he yelled over the bedlam. He turned to me. "Did you find your keys? We need to get out of here, *now!*"

But before we could move, the noise stopped. Just stopped, as though a switch had been turned off. Even Rosheen was silent, though she was still in the doorway, braced for attack. We stood for a moment looking at each other in glassy-eyed disbelief, stunned by the sudden quiet. The car had now disappeared from view, and when I looked back into the kitchen, nothing hung in bloody tatters outside my window.

"Let's go before it gets back," Mac said, slinging the rifle I had put down over his left shoulder, and grabbing my overnight bag, while I dug my keys out of my purse. He put one arm around my shoulder and we started for the door, but a screaming tirade from somewhere behind the cabin stopped us in our tracks.

"Ruthie! Do you hear me? Dammit, you bitch! Stop ignoring me!" Wild laughter echoed through the night, then changed to a lower-pitched wheedling that chilled me to the bone.

"*Ruuuthieeee* ... come on outside. Aw, now, Ruthie. You know you want to. Let's have some fun. Come on, baby, ain't you gonna welcome your husband home? I got a pretty present for you, Ruthie. *Ruuuuthieeeeeeee?*" The voice paused, and then bellowed, "*Ruthie!*"

I gasped. "Oh, my God! That's him, Mac. He's back! We can't go out there now. He might have a gun, too."

Mac stood thinking over our options. Go or stay? He looked at me, and I could almost hear him thinking, *no way I'm taking her out there*. Frustrated, he turned and yelled out the living room window. "Who are you? What do you want?"

This time the voice was right outside the kitchen, growing louder again, in a slithery, singsong sort of way that made my skin crawl and my teeth hurt, like a thousand fingernails on a blackboard.

"Come on out and we'll go *daaaaancin'* under the moon, Ruthie. I got us some *whiiiiskey* here! Oh yeah, baby. We'll have us some fun!"

Mac yelled out the broken window again, "There's no Ruthie here. Get off this property, *now!* The sheriff is on the way, and I've got a gun. This is your only warning! *Get out of here!*"

If anything, the yelling grew louder yet. Now, it was coming from closer to the front of the cabin.

"I got my big car back now. I can take you for a *riiiiiide,* Ruthie. And then we'll dance. Oh yeah, baby! We'll *daaaance!*"

Mac slipped into the dining area, keeping to one side of the window, and glanced out. He had a clear view of the entire side yard, but if he hoped to get a look at whoever was out there, he was disappointed. He shook his head at me. "Nothing," he mouthed.

I could hear the sound of the car once more. It seemed to be approaching along the south wall, near the living room windows, but before Mac could cross the room again, it roared around the corner and back into place in front of the cabin.

I thought I saw the dark, indistinct shape of a man behind the wheel, gesturing wildly. He gunned the engine and disappeared once again, sliding on the icy ground as he rounded the side of the cabin. No matter how quickly Mac moved from window to window, he was always too late, and the car would be somewhere else. And now, to make matters worse, the sound seemed to be coming from everywhere at once—both the constant rumble of the Impala's engine, and the lunatic screaming—giving him no clue which way to turn.

"Mac!" I yelled. He turned toward me, shaken and confused, desperate to make some sense of this onslaught. "I think I saw him in the car this time," I shouted over the noise.

"He's in the car, now?"

I nodded.

Mac moved to stand behind Rosheen to wait for the car to appear again, shotgun pointed out the open door. His eyes held mine for a long moment, in a wordless promise that he would not let anything happen to me. To us.

"I believe you, MacKenzie Cole," I reminded him, and I did. I knew my Mac would never be beaten by this insanity outside. I think he wanted to tell me again that he loved me, but we could both hear the car returning. He took a deep, steadying breath, and swung back to the door, waiting. The rumbling growl of the engine grew louder and louder, until it reached an impossible pitch. Even with my hands over my ears, the din was deafening—a freight train of noise causing the whole cabin to vibrate. Floors, walls, and furniture shook with such force dishes slid off the counters and smashed on the floor, lamps were knocked over, and books toppled from the mantel.

Mac stood braced and ready, ignoring the chaos in the room, focused instead on what was about to happen outside. An unnaturally cold and foul-smelling wind rose, blowing fiercely through the door. He leaned slightly into it, looking like an avenging angel, ready to fight to the death, if need be. I prayed that wouldn't be the case. Then Rosheen threw her head back, wailing like a thing possessed.

Hell was arriving, and it was riding in a fire-engine red Chevy Impala.

The car came barreling around the corner of the cabin, sliding to a stop in front of the steps. The man behind the wheel was screaming like a banshee, but before Mac could do a thing, Rosheen gave a hideous, raw-throated howl, and launched 115 pounds of pure fury across the front porch and into the air—in a full-on kill-or-be-killed attack—and flew straight through the car, driver and all, as though it weren't even there!

She landed on the ground on the other side, and Mac and I stared in shock. Just when you think things can't be any more screwed up, you find out how wrong you are. We could see her through the car, as she attacked again and again. She spun in a furious circle, snarling, snapping, and biting in a frenzy, foam flying from her mouth as she tried in vain to sink her teeth into ... well ... into *anything*.

"Oh, my God! A ghost?" Mac gave voice to what we had both been thinking. "What the hell? Is it a ghost, Sarah? Are we dealing with somebody's damned, godforsaken *ghost*, here?"

"I don't believe in ghosts," I said, automatically.

"Yeah, me neither," Mac replied, "but someone forgot to tell Rosheen."

Mac tried calling her back to the safety of the cabin. "Rosheen! Come here, girl!!" The big dog continued biting and snapping at the air around her, reluctant to admit defeat. Mac yelled again, and this time, she stopped. Wheeling, she ran straight back through the car, and onto the porch. She slunk by us, shivering in fright and confusion, but turned to keep her eyes on the apparition outside.

"I don't think we are going to make any headway against ... *that* ... with guns," I said to Mac. He was silent, breathing heavily, and looking more frustrated and angry by the minute. The three of us stood there, side by side, and knew we were not equipped to fight this battle. We didn't believe in it. It couldn't be happening. And yet, it was, and we had no idea what to do.

The car's engines rumbled softly, and the man behind the wheel appeared to be drinking something from a bottle—maybe the whiskey he kept yelling about. Then he screamed again, and we knew everything else had just been a preview. This was the main feature, oozing pure, saturated evil, and there we stood, waiting like sacrificial lambs.

"You damn, whorin', lyin' bitch! You get out here right now! You're coming with *meeeee!*"

I took an involuntary step backward, as he climbed out of the car, keeping his head tucked low. Then he looked at me, and I screamed in horror. The moonlight was bright enough to show us what we hadn't been able to see before. Most of his head was gone, and what was still there was a ruined mass of pulp and bone.

He paused by the car, staring straight at me with what was left of one eye, his low laughter more chilling than any of his screams had been. That foul wind blew even harder, lifting snow off the ground in brittle white eddies, and bringing the smell of the grave with it. It howled through the front door, whipping my hair into my eyes, and turning my blood to ice.

Still staring straight at me, the ... *thing* ... opened its ruined mouth and bellowed into the night, "You belong to me, you piece of trash! You think you can get away with ignoring me? Get your ass out here *nooooow*, or I will come up there an' get you!"

A look came over Mac's face that I had never imagined seeing on him. He was like a man possessed, eyes blazing with rage. "*You son of a bitch!*" He roared. "You can't have her!"

Then he raised his shotgun, and walked out the front door, into a wind so strong, it threatened to rip his jacket off. With his black hair flying around his face, he crossed the porch like an invincible warrior god, firing the shotgun as he went.

Empty, the gun was flung aside, and Mac pulled the rifle off his shoulder, still yelling as he started down the stairs. "I said ... you can't *have* her!" He punctuated every few words with a blast from the gun. "Go *back* ... to whatever *pit* ... of *hell* ... you crawled out of! You will *not* ... take *Sarah* ... with you!"

When the rifle was empty, too, he turned it around and waded straight into the middle of the apparition, swinging the gun like a baseball bat, and punctuating each swing with another angry roar. Under his furious onslaught, the very fabric of both car and driver seemed to tear apart like wet tissue, with filaments of sickly color floating away in the air.

Mac's attack focused on our tormentor, tearing him to shreds in front of my eyes. In the end, he was using the butt of the rifle to pound the final, fading remnants into the ground. The nasty-smelling wind stopped abruptly, and the last tiny bits and pieces of torn, smeary color shimmered in the moonlight for a second, then, with a faint pop, disappeared.

It was over.

Mac was bent double, chest heaving, as he gasped for air. Dazed, he looked around him, realizing it was finished, and flung the rifle down in disgust. He climbed the steps, pulling me into his arms. For a moment, we stood holding each other tightly, afraid to believe we had made it through the ordeal. Then, without a single word, he grabbed my things, and we headed for my Jeep. Rosheen climbed in behind us, and we drove across the road to his house in total silence, Mac holding my hand all the way.

The headlights hit his front porch, where a pair of watchful eyes glowed green in the dark. We climbed out, trudged to the door, and I scooped up Handsome from the welcome mat. The four of us went inside, and Mac locked the door behind us.

Chapter 24
What Took You So Long To Get Here?

MONDAY, JANUARY 23, 2012

ROSHEEN HEADED STRAIGHT for the couch, with Handsome hot on her heels. Within seconds, they were asleep together on Rosheen's blanket, obviously wanting nothing more than to forget this night ever happened. I knew just how they felt.

Mac and I were standing in the middle of the living room, looking like two weary refugees from a war zone. The adrenalin that had carried us through the whole ordeal seemed to be wearing off, and I felt myself shivering. I took a step toward Mac on legs gone wobbly, and he was by my side in a split second, arms around me in support. We stood that way in silence for another minute, neither of us having a clue what to say, where to begin. Yeah, I was definitely shell-shocked and shaky. Mac seemed fairly collected, all things considered.

After a moment, he released me and took my hand. "Come on," he urged softly. "Let's go upstairs. You still have glass in your hair."

I followed him mutely, feeling numb and distant, my shivering growing worse with every step. He led me straight into his bathroom, where I stood in trembling silence while he turned the shower on and adjusted the water temperature.

With tender care, he pulled my sweater over my head, murmuring to me all the while. "It's okay, Sarah. It's all going to be okay. It's over now."

He slipped my shoes off, unzipped my jeans, and pulled them down my legs. In a few seconds, he had everything else off, as well, and then, he was out of his own clothes, too. Stepping into the shower, he took my hand and pulled me in with him.

I faced him, wrapped in his gentle arms while the hot water streamed down my back. The sensation of warmth spreading through me was heavenly, and my shivering eased. I leaned my cheek against his bare chest, and knew we were safe, that the horror was gone.

I didn't want to cry. Crying, now that it was all over, seemed like a silly waste of time. I told myself not to do it, but I didn't listen. I cried. And Mac held me until I hiccupped my way to a stop, all the while whispering quiet words of comfort and love.

His hands were opened wide, sliding up and down my back, and his calm, quiet voice was so soothing that I found myself breathing normally again, and accepting the fact that no matter what had happened, we were going to be all right. He made me believe it, because he did.

"Lean your head back for me," he whispered, cradling the back of my neck with the palm of his hand. With gentle fingers, he worked the warm water through my hair, loosening up the sticky strands and rinsing out the little bits of glass.

I watched his face as he worked. He wore the most tender, loving expression I had ever seen, as he made sure he rinsed my hair carefully. His brow was furrowed in concentration, and his lower lip was caught between his teeth as he worked out a difficult tangle. A feeling of love so profound it was almost overwhelming poured through me. I couldn't imagine how I had ever lived a single day of my life before I met Mac.

Satisfied that he had gotten all the pieces of glass removed, he reached for the shampoo, and worked it into my hair. His long fingers massaged my scalp slowly and gently, easing my tension even more. It was unbelievably sensual. He smiled down at me as he was rinsing away the shampoo. "There. No more glass. Or pickle juice."

I put the palm of my hand against his cheek. "Don't ever leave me, Mac," I whispered. "I don't think I could stand it if you did."

He shook his head, and pulled me closer. "Oh, Sarah. I'll never leave you. I've waited for you for years." His kiss was feather-soft, then he leaned his forehead against mine, and gave me a look of mock reproach. "What took you so long to get here?"

"I didn't know where you were, Mac. I'd have been here much sooner, if I had," I said, kissing him back. "But I've found you now."

"Umm," he murmured, still kissing me. "You have, indeed."

"Finders, keepers?" Another kiss.

"Finders, keepers. I'm yours, Sarah."

I'm not sure if I got any cleaner after that point, but the rest of the shower certainly took my mind off what we had just been through, at least for a while. I needed to feel safe, protected, and loved, and I felt all three of those things. Especially that last one.

I THINK BOTH of us knew sleep would be impossible, so we didn't even try. The sky was still dark when I finished drying my hair, but the stars were winking out one by one. Mac was sitting in bed with pillows piled high behind him. "I like you wearing my robe," he smiled, holding his arms out to me.

"I like it, too," I said, climbing into bed beside him. "It smells of you."

"Really? What do I smell like?"

"Like more, please." I replied, snuggling into his arms, and laying my head against his chest.

He gave a soft, sexy chuckle. "That can be arranged." Then he was quiet for a minute, running his fingers slowly up and down my arm.

"Brave Sarah," he finally said. "I'll never forget the sight of you holding that rifle and telling me you had my back." He kissed the top of my head.

"Me, brave?" I was astonished. "Never in my life could I have imagined anyone facing down what you did tonight. You were unbelievable, Mac. What made you think you could win against that ... *thing* ... with just a gun? What made you even try?"

"You, of course. Did you think I would let you go without a fight, after only just realizing what you mean to me?"

He smiled and ran his fingers through my hair, tilting my face so he could look down at me. "No stinking, two-bit, cheesy-assed ghost-with-no-head is going to take you away from me! I'd never let him have you. Besides, I promised you." He cupped my cheek with his palm, and looked me straight in the eyes. "And I swear to you, I will keep my promises to you, Sarah."

"I'm going to hold you to that, O Mighty Warrior God." I pulled his head down to me and kissed the corner of his mouth, his cheek, his eyelids, the pulse near his temple, and back down along his jawline, stubble and all.

We slid down a little lower in the bed, and Mac turned toward me, burying his face in my neck. I felt a shiver go through him, and when he spoke again, his voice was husky and tight with emotion. "I was so afraid, Sarah. You rescued me, you know. Without you, I'd have stayed broken forever. You're like a shining light, so full of joy and love. Everything about you is a miracle to me."

Taking a deep, shaky breath, he went on. "All I could think of was that I just couldn't lose you. I *couldn't*! It made me so damn angry that this monstrous thing was trying to take you. I wanted to rip it to pieces. I didn't stop to think about whether I could or not. I just wanted to destroy it."

He took another shaky breath, and then whispered, "I love you, Sarah. God, I love you so much."

He pushed my borrowed robe apart and kissed my shoulder, his tongue tracing back along my collarbone and down the V between my breasts. Untying the belt, he opened the robe the rest of the way, and slid his hand along my waist and down, fingers stroking like feathers over the curve of my hip.

"I just can't get enough of you. I don't ever want to leave this bed again. Tell me we can stay here making love forever."

I smiled, but I knew how he felt. I wanted him again, too. It seemed being frightened half out of our wits had made us both insatiable. "I'm not sure about forever, but right now would be good."

That was all the invitation he needed. He rolled over on top of me, his body pressed the whole length of mine, and what he did next made me forget everything we had been through. We didn't talk any more for a while.

THE SOFT GLOW of an iridescent, mother-of-pearl sky shone through Mac's bedroom window. I sat at a small table that had been positioned for watching the day awaken, and sipped hot cocoa, which Mac had brought me before taking Rosheen out. Snug and warm in his robe again, I felt comforted, and much less fragile than I had an hour before. I guess it's true we frail human beings reassure ourselves that we have survived the unthinkable by seeking the most life-affirming thing we can. It had worked for me.

I watched the sky growing a tiny bit lighter as this as the new day approached. *How many mornings did Mac sit here with his coffee, watching the whole world come awake, as he had imagined as a boy, sitting on the rocks below?*

The rolling hills becoming visible in the distance were as old as time, and something about them made me feel connected to the earth in a way I never had before. No wonder this was the place he had come to when he couldn't stand the constant abrasion of city life any longer. It was a place that promised healing, and it made me feel a part of something much larger than I. Between that sense of strength, and the love that was growing between Mac and I, I knew I was going to be fine, in spite of what we had been through. But there were so many questions bouncing around in my head. We had a lot to talk about when he came back.

I heard the front door open and close, the sound of Rosheen galloping across the living room, and Mac calling out, "It's just me. Be right there!"

I smiled. He was letting me know I didn't need to worry about who had entered the house. He did these things automatically, and I wondered where he had learned to be so thoughtful and loving. Certainly not from his late wife. I still could not imagine what she had found in all those other men that could have been better than a single day with Mac.

I heard him climbing the stairs, and knew it was time. Tempting as it was, we couldn't go on making love over and over, pretending nothing had happened last night. I was sure Mac knew that, too. He had just wanted to give us some breathing room—a bit of grounding—before we had to face the truth.

He came into the room, cheeks flushed from walking Rosheen in the cold morning air, and his hair once again a black tumble across his forehead. At forty, he still had a boyishly elegant look to him that always made me smile. He would probably look that way at sixty, too. Even wearing a hastily donned pair of plaid pajama bottoms and a gray sweatshirt, he looked good.

"I brought some more," he said, balancing a steaming pot of cocoa and a plate of doughnuts on a tray.

I smiled at him. "Chocolate. Lots of it. It always makes everything better, doesn't it?"

"I thought you might feel that way." He sat down across from me, and poured a cup for himself. "It's pretty cold out there. Even Rosheen wasn't in the mood to linger. I lit the fire, and those two are snuggled in front of it again."

We sat in silence for a moment, sipping our cocoa and lost in our individual thoughts. When Mac put his cup down, he gave me a sweet smile, and asked, "So are you ready to talk now?"

"Yes. I just don't know what to say. What we saw, what happened, how is that possible? Was it really a ghost? Is there no other explanation?"

"I don't think so. I think that's it. We were visited by an apparition of some sort. We saw a ghost."

"Okay. Say I admit that. Say we were menaced by some malevolent ghost who threatened to haul me away to God knows where. What do we tell people, Mac?"

"Why do we need to tell anyone anything? Do you think they would believe us? And what difference would it make if they did or not? We know what we saw, what we felt. It doesn't matter to me if anyone else believes us or not. Does it to you?"

"It just seems like we should tell someone. How do we not? It means that nothing is as most of us have always thought it is. It *changes* things."

I tried to picture explaining it all to Jenna, or to anyone, for that matter. I sighed. "You're right. They wouldn't believe us. They'd think we were crazy or looking for attention, wouldn't they?"

I ate a bite of doughnut, still thinking about what we ought to do. "But shouldn't people know that it's true, that it can happen, that ghosts are apparently real?"

"A lot of people have already beaten us to this conclusion. They have been reporting ghost sightings for centuries, from every part of the world."

He stared out the window for a moment, sipping his chocolate, then continued. "Sometimes it only happens once in a person's life. Other times, spirits are said to haunt a particular location and anyone who goes there might see them, just like in any ghost story. Some say the visions aren't dangerous and can't touch anyone. That they're sort of like images from the past, projected onto the fabric of reality."

He frowned as he looked at me. "Other people think they are connected to evil, in some way. After last night, I'm inclined to give that view some credibility, myself. But there seem to be as many theories as there are stories."

I watched him for a minute. "You sound like you've done some research on this."

He gave me a rueful little smile, and took my hand. "I have. A lot, actually. After Ben died, I was so desperate, Sarah. I wanted to believe I'd see him again. I wanted to understand what others had seen, so I read a lot about it. I thought maybe if that many people claimed to have had these experiences, at least some of them might have been telling the truth."

"Did you find anything to convince you?"

"Not really. I never found anything that felt like proof. And nothing ever happened to me personally. But other people have experienced things that they do believe in, and some of them have found comfort from it. I just ... hoped ... is all. Last night was the first time I've ever seen anything supernatural in my life, and I could have lived out the rest of my years without going through that, frankly."

I shivered, remembering how frightening it had been. "You seem pretty calm about it, today."

"I don't know that I'm calm, but I have accepted that it happened, and to me, that means at least some of those claims made by others could be true, too."

We sat in silence for a few minutes. I sipped my cocoa and thought about what Mac had said.

"Are you hoping to see Ben someday?"

"I can always hope, but if you're asking me if I believe it will ever happen, no. Not any more. Not in this world, anyway. I gave up on that a long time ago. I do dream about him fairly often, though, even after all these years. And the dreams seem very real, more concrete or tangible than my normal dreams. Sometimes when I open my eyes, I almost — *almost* — feel his presence in the room. I know it's left over from the dream, but it makes me feel like part of him is still with me."

"Part of him is still with you, Mac, and it always will be. As long as you are here to remember him, he'll never really be gone. Your love is like a bridge from this world to that one, and after what we saw last night, I guess you could be right. Who knows?"

He sighed, running his thumb across the back of my hand. "If Hate can come calling from beyond, why not Love, huh? I guess we've found out that nothing is impossible, anyway. Somehow, it helps."

He sat looking out the window for a while, then he smiled. "Look, Sarah. The sun is hitting the mountain peaks. The day is waking up."

He pulled me to my feet, and we stood at his window, arms around each other, and watched the world turn to gold in front of our eyes. It was a miracle we could both understand, and it would do for now.

MONDAY, JANUARY 23, 2012

AS MAC TURNED the Jeep into my driveway that afternoon, I felt a knot of fear in my stomach. I was almost afraid to look as we approached the cabin, as though there would be visible scars of last night's mayhem all over my property. There weren't, of course. The sun had been shining all day, and the frost and snow that had been on the ground last night had disappeared. Even the tracks from Mac's truck no longer marked my driveway.

He stopped in front of the porch, and turned to me. "Are you sure you want to go in? I could just grab your clothes for you, if you tell me what you want."

After much discussion off and on throughout the day, I had agreed to stay with Mac for a while, until we figured out a plan of some sort. Translation—no way in hell was Mac going to be able to deal with me being alone in my cabin right now. Not as long as there was any possibility of any more ghostly episodes. And I have to confess, I didn't argue with him very long. The thought of staying here by myself was terrifying, though I had hopes it wouldn't always be that way. I wanted my cabin back.

"I'm sure. It will be easier for me to find the stuff I need. Besides, I'm not afraid to go in there with you along for protection, O Mighty Warrior God. No ghost would have the nerve to mess with us after last night. You'd just smite him about the head and shoulders, and send him running home to his ghostly mama."

He smiled, but both of us knew this was just whistling past the graveyard. Neither of us relished going back inside so soon. If I hadn't needed my clothes and my computer, I wouldn't even consider it, but I did, so I tried to sound a lot less scared than I was.

"Honestly, Mac. I lived here for months with no problems at all. And it's daylight out. No self-respecting ghost would show his creepy face in the daylight, right? I'm okay. Let's hurry, though. I don't think I want to hang around."

And with that, we climbed out, crossed the pristine yard, and went inside. If the sight of everything looking so normal outside the cabin was unsettling, what was waiting for us inside was even more so. Smashed dishes and lamps, scattered papers and magazines, and yard debris blown through the broken window left no doubt that what we had been through really did happen. Things were a mess. It was hard to look around my lovely little home without crying, but I did my best.

We had brought Rosheen along with us, thinking she would sense trouble before we would, and if she exhibited any signs of nervousness, we would leave right away. So far, Rosheen seemed just fine. Dogs have a way of living in the moment. They don't worry about the what-if's. They take a

271

look around, sniff the air a few times, and if things seem okay, they get on with their lives.

As far as Rosheen was concerned, we had banished the bad guy, and everything was cool again. She was now lying on the porch, looking lazy and relaxed, so Mac and I both were feeling confident that there was nothing lurking about to harm us. There was a sense of peace inside the cabin that even we could feel, and there was no hint of evil on the premises at all.

I packed what I thought I would need for an indefinite stay with Mac, while he boarded up my broken window, then we went back to his house, planning to have an early dinner and get to bed at a reasonable hour. Even though we had both napped during the day, I felt decidedly sleep-deprived, and Mac looked exhausted, as well. When Tuesday morning dawned, we were both well-rested and felt a bit more in control.

After breakfast, Mac had some work to do on a project for his company, and I spent some time arranging my clothes and cosmetics so that they wouldn't be in his way, and then I took Rosheen for a walk. He had cleared several pretty trails through his woods, and Rosheen was good company as we strolled along together.

I had a lot of questions I wanted answers to, and I did realize that the sooner I understood what had happened at my cabin, the sooner I would know if I could ever go back there again, but I just couldn't make myself start digging yet. Wandering through the woods on this crisp, sunny day seemed like a better idea, at least for now, and I felt my spirits lift with every step we took.

Chapter 25
Money For Nothing

TWO WEEKS HAD passed since I abandoned my cabin and moved in with Mac, and as I sat at his little bedroom table, working on my book, I stopped for a moment, and looked out across the mountaintops. I realized that I was ridiculously happy being here with him. What on earth had happened to that girl who couldn't stand for a guy to start talking about living together? It had always seemed like such a sacrifice of personal freedom to *her*. Funny, nothing about living with Mac felt like a sacrifice. I loved everything about sharing my days with him. I did miss my cabin, and I knew that problem would have to be addressed soon, but for the moment, I was content to let the days drift by.

As for Mac, he hadn't said as much, but every gesture made me feel welcome in his home. He seemed more relaxed each day, and even exhibited a goofy, off-the-wall sense of humor I would never have suspected of him. He had always been funny in a wry, cerebral sort of way, of course, but this was different. It was a quirky streak that seemed to be so natural, I suspected he was rediscovering a side of himself long hidden away.

Turns out, Mac is also a man whose extraordinary passion has long been denied, and I was reaping the benefits of his self-imposed exile every night. I smiled, thinking about the way Mac made love to me with total abandonment, and an exquisite commitment to pleasing me. And I loved making him feel good, as well.

Just as I was getting some interesting ideas along those lines, my thoughts were interrupted by Mac sticking his head in the bedroom door to ask if I was hungry. I felt my cheeks burning, and I was glad he didn't know what I had been thinking about. He would never have let me live it down, and probably would have demanded I demonstrate for him right away.

"I made sandwiches, and there's leftover chili from last night. Want me to heat a bowl for you?"

I loved that Mac enjoyed cooking so much, and I tended to let him do most of it. I was the designated washer-upper, and that was fine by me. "I guess I am hungry, now that you mention it, and that sounds good. I'll be right down."

I closed my laptop, and went downstairs to join him at the kitchen island.

After lunch, we grabbed our sweaters, called Rosheen and Handsome, and went for a walk. We had gotten into the habit of working in the mornings and spending the afternoons together, either walking the trails on Mac's property, or packing a lunch and going on a longer hike, weather permitting. The winter had been mild enough for us to spend a lot of time outdoors, but on bad days, we visited local bookshops and antique stores.

Today, we ambled across Mac's property, arm in arm, to the stream and pools that made up the south border. Often we walked in companionable silence, just enjoying being together, but today, we were chatting about this and that, and laughing at Rosheen and Handsome as we reached the bench overlooking the larger pool. We sat down and Mac put his arm around my shoulder and pulled me close to him.

He grew serious for a moment. "My life is better with you in it, Sarah. I'm so grateful to have you to walk beside me, and to share this world with me every day. I've always loved this little pool, but it never looked as beautiful as it does when I see it through your eyes. You make me more aware of all that's around me." He leaned down and kissed me. "I love you," he whispered.

"I love you, too, Mac, and I feel the same way. I never knew just how much I was missing until I met you. I think about you running up my driveway, chasing Rosheen, and I wonder why no one told me I was moving into a cabin across the road from this ... umm ... this ...." I faltered.

"This Wild Thing?"

"I was going to say this Hunka-Hunka Burnin' Love, but Wild Thing will do."

He grinned. "Well, when I came across your yard and saw you standing there, face to face with my dog, I remember thinking two things almost at once. 'She's beautiful,' followed immediately by, 'She's trouble.'"

"Were you right?"

"Only about one of them, and don't ask which."

We settled back against the bench to watch the water come burbling across the stones into the deeper pool, before exiting on the other side and heading down the eastern slope of the mountain. It was a peaceful spot, and I was looking forward to watching the winter slide into spring over the weeks ahead, and seeing the trees budding out in fresh green and chartreuse.

I decided it was a good place to have a more serious conversation, too—one I had been thinking of for a while—so I took a deep breath and plunged in, hoping I wasn't going to spoil the day. "You had another bad dream last night, Mac."

"Did I? I don't really remember."

I looked at him, brows raised in challenge. He shrugged. "Okay, I do remember. I just don't like remembering."

"Could that be part of the problem?"

He frowned. "What do you mean?"

"That you don't like remembering? Maybe, deep down, you really *want* to remember Ben. Maybe part of you is sad that you try so hard not to think about him."

"I think about him all the time, Sarah. More than I should after so long."

I hoped I could say this next part right. I didn't want to hurt Mac or make him angry. Taking his hand in mine, I kissed his palm. Then I took a deep breath and went on.

"Mac, I can't know what's going on in your head all the time, it's true, but it seems to me that what you are remembering about Ben is how you lost him. How bad it hurt. How guilty you felt."

His brow furrowed, but he was listening.

"I'm not saying those aren't natural feelings. I'm just saying that maybe you could try remembering them *less*, and remembering the time you got to spend with him *more*. Remembering his life, and how much joy he brought you, and all the good things you did with him. Remembering

276

who he was, what he liked, how he played, what his laugh sounded like. Maybe those are exactly the things you should be remembering, and not the rest. Is that possible, do you think?"

He sat very still, his gaze traveling over my shoulder, remote and turned within. He swallowed once, and then again, then looked back at me. When he spoke, his voice was quiet, and his eyes were filled with pain. "It hurts to go there, Sarah. It reminds me of all the things he didn't get to do."

"I know. But maybe it's okay if it hurts at first. Maybe you have to walk through that pain in order to put it behind you, so you are able to celebrate Ben's life, even if it was shorter than it ever should have been. He was here. He was part of you. He was loved by you and loved you in return. He deserves to be remembered for those things, and not just for the sad way he died. If you keep the memories of who he was close, maybe you can release some of the others, now.

He was giving my words careful consideration. He didn't seem angry, but I could tell he wasn't sure he could do what I was suggesting. His troubled gaze was filled with doubt, but the door was open, and I wanted to encourage him.

"Tell me about him, Mac. Just a little bit? Did he look like you?"

He was quiet for a moment, then nodded. "He did. He looked like my father, too. He was a Cole, through and through." He struggled to stay composed. "He had my hair and eyes, definitely."

"Do you have pictures of him?"

"Well, yeah, sure. I just ... keep them in some albums."

"Will you show them to me when we get back? I want to see him. I want to know everything that was special about him."

He looked down at my hand in his, tracing over my fingers with his thumb, then raised his head and nodded again. "Yes. I'll show you." He took a deep breath and continued. "I'll make us some coffee and get the albums down, and tell you about him."

And he did.

MAC AND I spent the rest of that afternoon going through his photo albums. I don't think he had looked at the pictures in several years, too afraid of the emotional impact. And make no mistake. It *was* emotional, and tears were shed by both of us.

Mac was unhappy to see me crying. "Oh, Sarah. I hate that this makes you sad, too."

"Of course I'm sad, Mac. I'll never experience the pain you've been through, but I love him, too, because he was part of you. And look at him. So beautiful. I'd know he was your son anywhere."

As we pored over the pictures, with me asking questions about when this or that one was taken, and who the other people in some of the photos were, I could see Max's tension easing up. He was talking more, a slight smile showing now and then, as he remembered a trip to the zoo, or a day at the beach.

By the time we stopped to eat, I could see that some of Mac's fear of opening up about Ben was easing. I felt like we had made a lot of progress, and when I asked Mac if he would leave the albums out so we could look at them again another time, he did. I pulled out a sweet picture of Mac and Ben together, and asked if I could frame that one. He looked at the photo, a wistful smile on his face. "His second birthday. His Puppy took the picture."

"His puppy?"

He gave a small, quiet laugh. "That's what he called my dad. It was supposed to be Poppy, but he couldn't quite say it. It always came out Puppy."

My heart felt so sad for the little boy who wouldn't live long enough to learn how to say Poppy, but I was more determined than ever to keep alive the memory of who he had been, rather than the one of what had happened to him. It seemed a more fitting way to remember Ben, and I hoped it would be the right thing for Mac, too.

After dinner, Mac disappeared upstairs for a few minutes, and when he came back down, he handed me a small silver frame. "Will this work for the picture?"

I put my arms around him and held him tight, then slipped the picture into the frame. "Where should we put it?" I asked him, hoping he wouldn't hide it away where he didn't have to see it.

His brows drew together as he thought it over, then he shrugged and smiled. "You choose, Sarah. But don't think I don't know what you're up to. You are going to force me to face the things I've been hiding from, even if you have to drag me kicking and screaming the whole way." He leaned down and gave me a soft, sweet kiss. "Thank you."

We put the picture on the bedroom mantel. It was a spot where he could see it every morning, before heading downstairs to work, but it wouldn't be in front of him all day long. That was enough for now. Mac was trying so hard, and I loved him all the more for the fact that he was doing so, even though it wasn't easy for him. I hoped it would help his heart heal, and I had some thoughts about how to make the rest of him feel better, too. He'd earned it.

SUNDAY, FEBRUARY 19, 2012

I PARKED MY Jeep in front of Mac's porch and hopped out, grabbing the eggs and milk from the passenger seat. I was heading toward the steps when I realized there was very loud music coming from inside the house. Very loud rock and roll music. What the heck? This was new. My curiosity kicked in immediately, and I quietly crossed the porch and opened the front door. Dire Straits was blasting from the radio, and Mac was in the middle of the living room, with his back to me—playing air guitar!

Oh. My. God. Mac! Playing air guitar!

And better yet, he was dancing around in wild abandon, and singing along with Mark Knopfler, too. Oh, this was too good to be true!

Being very quiet, I set the groceries on the floor, and took my cell phone out of my purse, praying he wouldn't spot me. My luck held. He was so into the music, he never even glanced my way. I managed to get at least five good pictures, before he leaned over backwards, playing his guitar to his imaginary fans in the balcony, and saw me out of the corner of his eye. He nearly broke his neck trying to straighten up without falling over. I was jubilant. At last! Something to make up for my Wild Thing fiasco—in spades!

While Mac scrambled to turn off the music and tried to gather any shreds of dignity he could get his hands on, I collapsed on the sofa, unable to stop laughing. He stuttered and stammered, and made all kinds of noise about not expecting me back so soon. I just continued to laugh, barely able to find enough breath to talk.

"Oh, my God, Mac! 'Money For Nothing'?"

It was too perfect. I was in heaven! "Am I supposed to be yer chick for free? Cuz I'm not cheap, Mister."

Mac's face turned the approximate shade of a boiled lobster, and he sat down on the other end of the sofa, looking thoroughly mortified. "I like that song," he said. "It was popular when I was young. I *was* young once, you know."

I took pity on him, and scooted over beside him, trying to be as serious as I could. I looked him dead in the eye, and sang the next line in my best Mark Knopfler voice, then asked, "Tell me, is that the way I do it?"

His mouth twitched.

"No MTV camera here," I said, still straight-faced, "but you could play your *git-tar* on your *bal-con-eeeeee.*

His mouth twitched again.

I was relentless. "Lemme see your little finger, and how about that thumb?" I examined his hands. "Air guitars can cause painful wounds, I've heard."

He tried but failed to hide his sheepish smile—and then he broke. We fell all over the place, laughing together in full-on hysteria. My sides hurt, and tears were pouring from my eyes before I could catch my breath. Mac was gasping for air, too. Finally, we calmed down enough that speech was possible.

"Come here, you," I said, holding out my arms. He did. I held him close to me and whispered in his ear, "I have never loved you more than I do right now, you know."

He leaned back and looked at me with a small, lop-sided grin. "Really? Just for playing bad air guitar and dancing around?"

"And singing. Don't forget the singing."

"I can sing lots of things. You should have told me that was the way to your heart. I have other songs in my repertoire, you know."

"Like what?"

"Like lots."

"Sing one for me."

He cleared his throat. Oh, boy. This was going to be good.

In a surprisingly gruff and sexy voice, he sang the first verse of "Bad to the Bone." George Thorogood, move over. This man can be just as baa-aad as you, any day!

My Mac. Would he never stop surprising me?

ROSHEEN CAME SLINKING back down the stairs when all the noise came to a stop. Apparently, she wasn't a fan of 80's rock and roll. Nor of people going into hysterics all over her normally quiet living room. Handsome was following right behind her, having decided if it was safe enough for Rosheen to come back down, it was safe enough for him. The two had become inseparable, and it was cute to see my kitty trotting behind the big dog, everywhere she went.

I decided to make some scrambled eggs for our breakfast, figuring Mac deserved a break from cooking after my unmerciful teasing. Afterward, I asked Mac if he would go with me while I sorted out the mess in my cabin. Cleaning up was long overdue, though we had taken care of the worst stuff, like the dill pickles, when we had been there last, almost a month ago.

"Of course I will. I was just waiting for you to be ready."

I felt a small twinge of worry. Did he mean he was waiting for me to be ready to move back, or just ready to face another trip over? My doubt must have shown on my face, because he got up and put his arms around me. "You aren't planning to stay there tonight, are you?" Now he sounded worried.

I sighed, relieved. At least he wasn't trying to get rid of me right away, though I knew that sooner or later, he would want his privacy back. "No, I'd like some answers before I can think about that. I just want to get it cleaned out, and grab a couple more things of mine. As long as it's okay with you for me to be here a while longer, of course."

"Take as long as you need, Sarah. I like the company."

I wasn't sure I was happy being relegated to the status of company, but it would have to do for right now.

We cleared away the dishes, then headed down to my cabin, and whatever might await us on that side of the road. Once again, I felt nervous as we wound down my drive and approached the front of the cabin. Mac parked his truck, and I sat for a moment, thinking my little home looked sad and abandoned. There was an emptiness about it I would have felt, even if I didn't know the owner wasn't in residence. I sighed.

Mac took my hand and gave it a squeeze. "Ready?"

"As I'll ever be, I guess." And with that, we got out.

As with our last trip, Rosheen came along for the ride, and was sniffing around outside in her typical, laid back style. Nothing seemed amiss with her, and when we unlocked the door and went inside, things seemed fine, as well. Except for the big mess, of course, and the fact that the room was dark, with the main window covered in plywood.

I stood there surveying the damages that wretched night had wrought in my little sanctuary, and felt angrier by the second. "Why did this asshole have to come back from beyond the grave just to smash all my good dishes and scare the crap out of us? What the hell was the goddamn point?"

Mac stared at me, open-mouthed.

"What?" I demanded.

"I've never heard you use language like that before."

"Oh." I may have blushed a bit. "Well, I've never had a reason quite like this one before. I know how to swear when I need to. Mostly I don't need to."

He put his arm around my shoulder, and we stood there in silence for a moment, thinking about that whole horrible night. "I think you're entitled this time," he said. And then we went to work, picking through rubble to see what could be salvaged, and throwing away the rest.

Shards of glass and ceramic were everywhere in the kitchen, where my dishes had exploded upon impact with the floor. Some of the ceramic bits were even embedded in the doors of the kitchen cabinets and the legs of my table. It's a wonder we hadn't been badly injured from flying glass when it happened.

We swept most of the debris from the kitchen floor into a couple of sturdy cardboard boxes, and then Mac sat down with some needle-nose pliers to see if he could remove the shards from the lower cabinets. I decided to tackle the mess in the pantry.

I opened the door and stood for a moment, remembering how terrified I had been, hiding there in the dark. I shivered, but pushed the thought out of my mind, and started pulling sections of fallen shelving out of the pantry and into the kitchen. Most of the boards themselves had survived the big collapse, but a few were broken in half, and there were pieces of drywall everywhere. I created separate piles for broken boards, whole boards, trash, and salvageable food items, working my way through the pantry from front to back.

The little room was quite deep, and had been expanded at some point, so that it jutted out onto the back porch. Wide, twelve-inch shelving had lined three walls, and when I had slammed into the back wall, knocking the first shelves down, it had started a domino effect, ripping out chunks of drywall as the shelving collapsed. When I looked at what had come down on top of me, I couldn't believe I had escaped with nothing more than a few bruises and scrapes.

Mac had finished with the cabinets, and was busy carrying out trash, and setting the salvageable lumber to one side for use later, when he would help me rebuild the shelving. A gaping hole in the drywall along the inside wall made me wonder if I could break off what remained with my bare hands, or if I needed a heavy tool of some sort to knock it down. I figured it might as well go out with the rest of the debris, but I wasn't having much luck pulling it down by myself.

When I gave one last big tug, a chunk of it broke away in my hands. I peered into the hole between the studs to see if there was any wiring that I'd have to be careful about. I couldn't see all the way to the bottom of the dark hole, so I got a flashlight and checked again. The space was about four feet deep, and at the very bottom, something metallic gleamed in the beam of light. Whatever it was had a handle, and it didn't look like it belonged sealed inside my pantry wall.

I was about to go ask Mac for a sledgehammer or crowbar so I could demolish the rest of the drywall to reach it, when I noticed that a section of the baseboard the width of the studs looked loose.

Far too curious to ignore this mystery, I found a screwdriver and pried the board away from the wall. Tucked between the wooden uprights was a metal box, roughly five inches high, four inches deep, and eighteen inches long. It had a folding handle on top, and the latch had a small brass padlock in it.

I pulled it out of its hiding place, wondering who had hidden it away, and when. Someone had gone to a lot of trouble to make sure no one found it. If the drywall hadn't been damaged when the shelves came down, it might never have seen the light of day again.

Pantry cleaning forgotten, I carried my discovery to the kitchen table, and sat down. It looked like a small toolbox, perhaps intended to hold screwdrivers or drill bits, or something else long and narrow. I could tell there was something inside, but when I shook it, it didn't sound at all like tools.

My curiosity was running wild. We already had a mystery to unravel, and a ghost to explain. This probably had nothing to do with any of that, but I wouldn't know until I looked, so I called Mac to come in and open it for me. He brought a bolt-cutter, made short work of the little padlock, and stood looking over my shoulder, as curious as I was. I hesitated a moment, still thinking about what might be in a box hidden away so carefully, and hoping it wouldn't turn out to be something I'd rather not know about.

I looked at Mac. "Should I?" When he nodded, I shrugged, and mumbled, "Okay ... in for a penny, in for a pound."

I slowly opened the lid, and we both stared in surprise.

Chapter 26
You Held Me Up High

DEAR FRANK,
PLEASE FORGIVE ME. I did it because I love you. You aren't safe here with me. Not from man nor monster, either. I watched you drive away tonight and I knew how bad I hurt you and I felt like I might die myself it was hurting me so much too. But dying would be too easy.

It should be me paying for this and not you. So I reckon I need to accept whatever is coming. I'm writing this letter because it makes me feel some better, and because I miss you already. I won't call you no matter how much I want to.

But I really want to.

Love Always,

Your Ruth

SUNDAY, JANUARY 31, 1965

DEAR FRANK,

IT HAS BEEN a whole week since I sent you away and every day with you gone leaves my heart all broken and lonely and sad. I never thought I could miss someone so much. All the days are just plain empty. I feel like I used up all of my smiles when we were together. I don't know how I'll ever find another one in this life.

I know you don't understand what happened and I'm so sorry for not telling you the whys of it all but I just can't. I hope you won't hate me forever for doing this to you but I'd rather you hate me than for something bad to happen to you.

I'm so scared, Frank. I did something awful bad. A terrible thing. I didn't have a choice and I'm not sorry about it except that I'm scared it could ruin your life too.

You held me up high Frank and made me feel good but I didn't deserve it. I wanted to deserve you and be the person you thought I was but I didn't and I wasn't. I wanted to say yes and marry you and live the rest of my life loving you Frank. I swear you are the only man I've ever loved and the only one I ever will. But I couldn't never marry you no matter how much I wanted to. I can hardly stand to tell you this even in a letter you likely won't ever read but the reason I couldn't marry you was because I was already married. I ran away from him and I just couldn't make myself tell you about him. I'm so sorry Frank.

I lied to you Frank. I lied by never telling you the truth and I lied by hiding things from you that you had a right to know. Someday I hope you will understand and forgive me and someday, I hope you can see that no matter what bad things I ended up doing I always loved you with all my heart.

You will probably never read this, but it gives me a feeling kind of like I'm talking to you so I'm going to keep writing you when I can. Maybe someday after enough time has gone by it will be safe for me to send you these letters. I never expect you could forgive me or anything but I want you to know that you were the best thing that ever happened to me in all my whole life. My sweet Frank. If I live to be a hundred I'll never forget that you loved me once but I can't live with putting you in danger because of what I did here so I have to let you go.

I said a prayer tonight that you find someone else who really deserves you and that can make you happy better than me. Someone who will treasure you and be proud to be your wife and who will never lie to you and maybe give you that family you want so much. I wish it could have worked between us but now it can't and maybe it never could have. This mess is all my fault and none of your doing.

I'll probably spend all eternity in hell paying for this awful thing I done. I think one piece of hell already came looking for me last week. But even if hell is all I have to look forward to at least I'll know that you are safe. I'll think of you every single day for the rest of my life.

Oh, Frank. It's so lonesome without you.

Yours Forever,

Ruth

SUNDAY, FEBRUARY 19, 2012

I'M NOT SURE what I expected to find when I lifted the lid of the metal box, but it wasn't this. Mac whistled under his breath, and I was speechless. The box appeared to be filled to the brim with papers, but lying right on top was a small, clear plastic box. Inside the box, nestled in a bed of cotton, was the prettiest ring I had ever seen.

"Whoa. You found a treasure chest, Sarah!"

I shook my head in confusion. "I don't get it. Why would someone have hidden this inside the wall and left it there?"

"Well, they did have access to it through that cut baseboard, so maybe it was just hidden there to keep it safe from prying eyes or thieves or something?"

"I suppose so, but why did they leave it there?" I opened the little plastic box and took the ring out. It was beautiful. The main stone was heart-shaped, and looked like it might be an aquamarine. It was surrounded by what appeared to be small diamonds. The setting was silver or platinum, I couldn't tell which, with a vintage feel to it.

The ring hung from a tarnished silver chain, as though someone had worn it around their neck, before hiding it in my wall. I turned it over and over, watching the light from the kitchen window play across the stones. I suspected someone had paid a pretty penny for something this elegant, and I wanted to know the story behind it.

"It's so beautiful, Mac! We need to find out who hid it there, and why." I set the ring aside, and lifted out a thick stack of papers, folded and tied together with a piece of pink ribbon. They looked like letters to me, and I could hardly wait to delve into them. I put them on the table next to the ring. Underneath the letters was a faded photo. My heart did a little skip and jump.

The photo appeared to have been taken on my front porch, and showed a nice looking man around my age, sitting on the swing. He was smiling at the photographer, eyes sparkling with affection. The back of the photo said "Frank, 1964" in a dainty, penciled script.

Under that picture was a second one. This time it was a young woman sitting by a Christmas tree in what looked like my living room. Her sweet smile looked very shy, but her eyes brimmed with love. She was holding up her left hand to the camera, showing off the ring I had just found. Her wavy blonde hair was worn a bit shorter than shoulder length, in a simple but sweet style. There was nothing written on the back of the young woman's picture, but even if the pictures hadn't been faded to a warm sepia tone, I would have been able to tell that they had been taken decades ago.

I felt pulled in by the faces of this couple, and I just knew they *were* a couple. They looked like newlyweds, or lovers still shy with each other. I stared at the photos a long time, before laying them aside.

"Look at her face, Mac. You just know he gave her that ring for Christmas."

Turning to the last item in the box, I took out an old, manila envelope that had been folded in half twice to make it fit inside. It contained a stack of $100 bills. I counted them and turned to Mac.

"Six thousand dollars. You were right. This is a treasure chest. Money, jewels, photos, and what looks like letters. It's amazing!"

Mac had been watching in silence as I explored the contents of the box. He pulled out a chair and sat down beside me, leaning over to tuck a strand of hair behind my ear. He smiled at me. "You're entranced, aren't you? I can see it all over your face."

I smiled back, nodding, and feeling my excitement growing by the minute. "Oh, yes! This is wonderful. It's like a time capsule and buried treasure in one. Can we go back home so I can go through the letters?"

He laughed. "Might as well. I don't think we're going to get anything else done here, today."

We were halfway back when I realized I had just referred to Mac's house as "home." I wondered if he had noticed.

MONDAY, FEBRUARY 20, 2012

I WAS SITTING at Mac's bedroom table again, laptop open and a cup of his fabled coffee growing cold beside it. We had speculated about the contents of the metal box all through dinner last night, and decided we were going to approach the mystery of the letters and the former owner of my cabin in an organized and efficient manner, starting this morning. I was all for starting last night, at first, but watching Mac working in the kitchen always distracts me, and somehow, I managed to distract him back. By the time we were undistracted again, it was too late for any serious research, so we went to bed. And distracted each other some more.

This morning, I had gone through all of my computer files dealing with the purchase of my cabin. The sale of the cabin had been handled by Inman Realty on behalf of a Davis Ledlow. The name meant nothing to me, but I jotted it down on my notepad, along with the telephone number and email address of John Inman, who had been my only contact during the purchasing transaction. I decided to give him a call after lunch to see what information he might be able to give me.

I had also decided to put off reading the letters until after lunch, as well. I figured I'd find out as much about the sale of the cabin as I could first, in case it would help me understand more about who the letters referred to. Also, Mac was almost as curious as I was, and wanted to read them with me, so I would wait until he took care of some work, and we could go over them together.

Mac had also volunteered his services as a fellow researcher, and I knew that would come in pretty handy as we gathered information on who had lived in my cabin, and tried to learn more about the events of the night that had made me leave it. Mac had access to resources far beyond mine. He made his living doing computer research, after all, and legal documents would pose no challenge for him. When you threw in my experience with old books and personal papers, I was certain we would get all the answers we needed.

Stretching, I rose and headed downstairs to see if Mac was ready to take a break. He was. We fixed some sandwiches, and made small talk while we ate, then I got on the phone, while Mac sent off some final instructions for some projects his staff in Charlotte was working on. At about 1:30, we sat down at his kitchen island and began to think about the mystery in front of us.

"I talked to John Inman," I said, bringing Mac up to date. "He told me the previous owner of the cabin was a man named Davis Ledlow, who lives outside of Raleigh, and is in Medical Research & Development at Duke University. He said Ledlow mentioned something about inheriting the cabin, but he doesn't remember any details. Just that Ledlow didn't have any interest in living there. I've found him online, and think I should give him a call. Hopefully, he'll be able to give us a bit more information."

Mac frowned, thinking for a moment. "The cabin was already empty when I built my house, and the only thing I remember hearing anyone say about it was someone at the diner asking me if I was building across the road from 'Miz Winn's old place.' We need to find out who this Ledlow is in relationship to the mysterious Miz Winn, I guess."

I took off for a quick grocery run to Everly's, leaving Mac behind to get online and do some digging on Davis Ledlow while I was gone. Everly's was quiet, with Brady taking advantage of the lull in customers to replace last week's Valentine displays with St. Patrick's Day items.

I found the few things I needed, and wandered back to the register, admiring all the displays as I waited for Brady to finish what he was doing and ring me up. I found myself looking over a collection of old photos on one wall, depicting an earlier, smaller version of Everly's, and coming up through the years, showing additions and expansions. Several pictures had men standing in front of the steps or on the porch, which apparently hadn't changed since Everly's was built in 1949. As I studied the photos, a face caught my eye. I leaned closer, and I felt a small thrill of discovery go through me.

Brady joined me. "Been here a long time, haven't we?"

"Yes, you have, and no wonder. It's a fine store. Brady, do you know who this man is?" I asked, pointing out a smiling face on the front row.

"Well, sure. That's my step dad, Frank Everly."

Oh my. I had found Frank. There was no doubt that he was the man in the photo from the box, even if that one had not had "Frank" written on back. This was an exciting discovery. "Frank Everly was your step dad?"

"Is," he corrected me. "He's still with us, thankfully, though he's in an assisted living situation, due to his health."

I thought for a minute. "Is your last name Ledlow, by any chance?"

"Yep. I'm sorry, I forget that not everyone in Darcy's Corner knows my whole family."

"And do you have a brother, perhaps, named Davis?"

"Sure do. How do you know Davis?"

"I bought my cabin from him last August."

Brady frowned, looking confused. "Davis sold you Ms. Winn's cabin? I'm not sure I understand. We don't see each other often, Davis being all big-city now, and me stayin' here to keep the store when Daddy Frank couldn't run it any more. But I sure didn't know he owned that cabin. Ms. Winn lived there as long as I can remember, and kept to herself. I can't imagine her selling it to Davis, or even how it would have come about."

I was even more intrigued now, and determined to get to the bottom of this story.

"Well, I have come across some papers that I'm researching, and I would really love to ask your brother some questions. I looked him up online and got his email and phone number, and was thinking about calling him this afternoon. Do you suppose he would talk to me?"

"I can't imagine why not. We're a pretty easy-goin' bunch. Shame, really. We kinda grew apart after he went off to college, but he's a nice guy. Real smart, an' all. He took good care of Daddy Frank when his health started to go, and I think he's payin' for the home, too. If you got his information online, it's probably his office number. I'll give you his cell phone, and you can tell him I suggested you call."

I couldn't wait to get home. Wow! Who would have thought a simple trip to buy groceries would have netted me so much information. And who would have guessed "our" Frank was connected with Everly's at all? I thanked Brady for his help and left right away.

Mac met me at the front door, eyes dancing and teeth flashing. We both spoke at once.

"Guess what I found when—"

"I discovered who—"

We laughed. "You first," Mac said.

"I know who Frank is!" I squealed.

"Me, too!" he laughed. "I found more records online. How did you figure it out?"

"I saw his picture on the wall at Everly's! He's Brady's stepfather!"

"No kidding? Then Davis would be Brady's brother?"

"Bingo!"

We went in and sat down at the island to compare notes, heads together like co-conspirators planning a heist. Mac had found the paperwork transferring the deed for the cabin from Frank Everly to Davis Ledlow. It didn't give any information on what the connection was between the two, but Brady had answered that for us.

"Now the biggest question is, how and when did 'Miz Winn' deed the cabin to Frank? There is there no mention of him ever living there. And why didn't Brady know anything about his stepdad owning it, or his brother inheriting it, and selling it?" I shivered in excitement. "Ooooh! Secrets, secrets! This just keeps getting more and more interesting."

Mac grinned. "It does, indeed. The plot thickens."

"Frank is still alive, by the way," I told him. "He's in a home of some sort. Surely he would know the whole story, wouldn't he? Oh, and Brady gave me Davis's cell number. I'll call him shortly and see what information he might be willing to share."

I made an outline of what we knew so far, starting with me buying the cabin, and working backward from there. Between the point at which Ms. Winn lived in the cabin and I acquired it, all I had was a few names with question marks beside them.

Mac did a another search through land records using Frank Everly's name, and found out that the cabin's ownership transferred from an R. J. Carter to Frank Everly on March 17, 2010. Another new name. Who was R. J. Carter? And where did Ms. Winn fit into all of this? And the biggest question of all still loomed unanswered. Who was the man whose wretched ghost assaulted us last month?

After dinner, I placed a call to Davis Ledlow, feeling apprehensive for some reason. As I soon found out, Mr. Ledlow was a perfect southern gentleman, and happy to talk to me for a few minutes. Unfortunately, he couldn't give me a great deal of information beyond what I already knew. His "Daddy Frank" had told him one day that he had deeded a cabin over to him, and said to do with it as he wished. Frank apparently didn't want to talk about it, but felt Davis should have it as a sort of repayment, and he had specifically asked Davis not to tell anyone about the cabin, though he never said why. Curiouser and curiouser.

"Honestly, Miss Gray, I had no desire to live in the mountains again, nor to be a long-distance landlord, so I decided I would just sell the cabin and put the money in the bank for anything my stepdad might need. He's had some health problems for a few years, and it was looking like he was going to need round the clock nursing care soon. I thought it was the best thing to do with the proceeds from the sale, so I set it up through Inman Realty out of Asheville. I just didn't have the time to take care of it, myself. I do confess, though, I've always wondered how he came by the cabin and why he was so reluctant to talk about it."

When I explained in more detail what we had found in my pantry wall, Davis sounded as curious as Mac and I were. He asked us if we'd like to meet Frank and talk to him ourselves, saying his step dad loved company and would enjoy a visit from us, he was sure. By the end of the conversation, we had set a date for a trip to Raleigh to meet Davis Ledlow, who would take us to visit Frank Everly. I felt we had made great progress towards solving our mystery by the time I ended the call.

At last, Mac and I curled up side by side on the sofa in front of a lovely fire, untied the pink ribbon, and began to read the letters inside. The first one in the stack was dated Sunday, January 24, 1965, and was written by someone named Ruth, who had apparently just broken up with Frank Everly, and was distraught over it. At the sight of her signature, Mac and I looked at each other, both remembering the sound of our crazed phantom screaming, *"Ruuuthie,"* over and over outside my cabin door.

"Oh my God, Mac. Ruthie is the girl in the photo. Frank's girlfriend!"

"So it would seem. Now who is the miserable wretch I had to beat to smithereens to protect my ladylove?" I knew he was trying to keep the tone light so that the sense of all-pervading evil from that night wouldn't filter into the room with us.

"That remains to be seen, but I'm betting the answer is right here in this stack of letters somewhere."

As we read the second letter, we both recognized a likely candidate at once. The husband Ruth had run away from.

"Even the phrase 'I ran away from him,' rather than 'I left him,' makes him seem like someone to be feared, perhaps violent in some way," I murmured. "And she sounds so sad without her Frank. It's heartbreaking, isn't it?"

Mac's arm was around my shoulder, and he pulled me closer as we read. The third letter was dated Valentine's Day, 1965, and Ruth's own words painted a pretty clear picture of what her life was becoming, alone in my cabin almost fifty years ago.

Chapter 27
Crying Don't Fix Anything

SUNDAY, FEBRUARY 14, 1965

DEAR FRANK,
TODAY IS VALENTINE'S Day and I'm remembering being with you last year and missing you more than I even know how to say. I cooked us pot roast last year and made you a chocolate layer cake for dessert and I remember how much you loved it so I made it again today. Eating it by myself made me awful sad so I gave most of it to General Penny. At least one of us was happy anyway.

I heard you weren't getting out any more and that people were worried about you and that made it all feel even more terrible. I don't want you to keep feeling so bad. I'm still praying for you to find someone who deserves you and then you will be happy again. I know you won't forget me because that's not how you are but I hope you can love someone else and just keep me in a little place in

299

your heart. My sweet Frank. I'll always think of you as mine even though you been gone for nearly a month now and I can't let you come back here again. In my heart you are mine and always will be so forgive me for calling you that.

This morning I drove into Darcy's Corner and parked on a side street where I could see the church and watched for you. When I saw you walking down the sidewalk by yourself and looking all sad and everything I wished I would have stayed home but I wanted to see your face again even from far away. You have to move on now Frank. I don't want to have ruined two lives because of what I did here.

I remember everything about last Valentine's Day you know. Every single thing. Your eyes were all happy at dinner and you gave me roses which I never had before and you told me you loved me and always would. I wonder if you still do or if you hate me now. I remember later how you made love to me so sweet and gentle and I can still feel every single place you touched me.

Sometimes I think about those nights with you on purpose so I won't forget that I have been loved in this life and by a good man too. The nights are hardest because I know I'll never feel you holding me again and whispering sweet words to me in the dark. Now it seems like it's always dark but not the warm safe kind. Now the dark is cold and I'm scared a lot. I heard that old hoot owl calling last night and he sounded just like I felt.

Here's a picture of General Penny for you. I wish you could see how he's all grown up. I'm so happy you gave him to me. He's my only friend and company now and he keeps me going on the days that aren't so good.

I love you with all my heart and I always will and I'm sorry every day of my life that it had to end.

Your Ruth

PS I remember how you called me darlin and hon and sweetheart, and how much I loved hearing you say those words because I knew you meant them. I miss you.

MONDAY, FEBRUARY 20, 2012

THE THIRD LETTER in the stack had a surprise tucked inside. A photo of a little red dachshund fell out when I unfolded it. The letter explained that the dog was named General Penny, and he had been a gift to Ruth from Frank Everly.

Reading about Ruth's first month alone after breaking up with Frank was heartbreaking. There was no doubt that this woman had loved him with all of her being. I could hear her pain in every word, and Mac and I were both feeling melancholy after we finished reading it.

"I know how hard it is to get used to being alone when you've been part of a couple," he said, staring at the fire. "You don't feel like the same person any more."

Suddenly he pulled me to him and kissed me with a fierce intensity that took my breath away, then whispered, "Don't ever, ever leave me, Sarah. Without you ... " I stopped him with a finger on his lips.

"Don't even *think* about that, Mac. I will never leave you. Not. Ever. I am yours, heart and soul." I stood and held out my hand to him. "Why don't we take a break and have some dinner? We can read more later, or tomorrow."

We spent the next hour in the kitchen. I decided we needed a celebration of life, so I set the big table with candles and Mac opened a bottle of wine, and we dined, as opposed to merely eating. It was exactly what we needed to remind ourselves how lucky we were to have each other, and how long we had each waited to find this relationship.

"We have so much to be grateful for, Mac. I don't want to let a single day slip by without being aware of how precious life is. Let's always remember to celebrate the ordinary!"

Mac smiled at me, candlelight making his pale eyes shine. "There *is* no ordinary, you know. Only miracles."

TUESDAY, AUGUST 31, 1965
DEAR FRANK,

MY FIRST MOUNTAIN summer without you is over. I haven't seen you in months even from a distance and I try so hard to hold on to your face and your voice in my mind. Sometimes I think I hear your truck coming down my drive and I want to run to the door to greet you but of course it isn't you at all. No one comes down my drive any more. It wouldn't be a good idea to have visitors anyway most especially not you. Too many secrets hiding here. This is not a good place any more Frank and I am having a gate put across the drive just to be sure no one even tries to come here.

I started taking my vegetables and canned things to a farmer's market outside of Asheville last April since I couldn't come to Everly's any more. I miss the days when I could be outside Everly's selling things and knowing you were right inside and would come home with me afterward. It will never be the same at this new place but the money is real good and I haven't had to touch my windfall money in a long time. Not since I bought the truck. So that's a good thing Frank because it has got to last.

I never told you I had it I know but that was part of my past and I didn't want you to know anything about that. Especially not the part where I stole all that money from my husband but it wasn't as bad as it sounds because he stole it from someone else to begin with. He wasn't a good man like you Frank. He was evil and mean and that's why I ran away but if I wouldn't have run away I never would have met you so I'm glad I did.

I don't know why Lloyd was so mean. I been thinking on it a lot lately. He never talked about his family at all except to say that his daddy was dead and good riddance. He had some old scars across his shoulders and back and I always wondered if his daddy had beat him but whatever happened to him I think Lloyd figured out that the best way for him to get by was to be the biggest and the meanest person around. He practiced that plenty believe me. His sweet talking went away pretty soon after we got married and it never came back.

I figure I was lucky to get away from him when I did and like I say it brought me to you. I would never have known a man could be so good if I had gone anywhere else on this earth when I ran away. Wasn't I lucky Frank? Wasn't I lucky to have found you?

It will soon be fall again with cool nights and warm fires that should feel cozy but there's only me and Penny to enjoy them so I think it will be hard. Long nights are nicer when you are with someone you love. I did hear some gossip last week that you were doing some better and were getting out a lot more and it made me feel good Frank. I want you to be happy and live a good life or I did it all for nothing and that would be the saddest thing of all.

My pantry you built me is full to the brim with stuff I canned this year so I will have plenty to eat over winter. One person doesn't use up much even when they give a lot of it to the dog. Penny is fat and happy though and truly my boon companion.

I'm still saying prayers for you Frank and I just know they will be answered. You deserve the best and that is what I think is waiting for you.

You will always be my love.
Your Ruth

SATURDAY, DECEMBER 25, 1965
DEAR FRANK,

TODAY IS CHRISTMAS. I wonder where you are. I hope you are spending the day with people you love and eating lots of turkey and having fun. That's how I'm picturing you Frank and how I want it to be for you because then it will all have been worth it and if I never do another good thing in all my whole life at least I set you free to find real happiness somewhere.

I set up a little tree but only got halfway through putting the lights on it and then I took it back down because it hurt too much to think of last Christmas and how happy we were. I reckon that was one of the last times I let myself believe we could stay together and be happy before I found out I was lying to myself almost as much as I was lying to you.

Oh my sweet Frank. You deserved so much better than I gave you and I hope you are finding it now. It doesn't matter much what happens to me because sometimes I think my life was over the day I married Lloyd but then I remember the time I spent with you and know that those are the only days that really count. I would go through everything all over again even being beaten half to death just so I wouldn't lose those. I know what real love feels like now because of you so in the end it was all worth it.

Oh Frank sometimes I wake up at night so scared I can't breathe and I always reach for you but you aren't there of course so I just hug Penny to me and wait for the terrible feelings to pass. Sometimes I dream there is knocking at my door and the police are here and then I'm so glad you aren't lying next to me but safe somewhere else. And sometimes when I wake up I think I hear Lloyd yelling at me again how he's going to kill you and I start to shake so hard it about makes my teeth chatter but I'm still glad you aren't here where he might find you.

I dream a lot now but none of them are good ones. Maybe my good dreams are all over. It makes it hard to get up in the morning. Of course I don't have much to do this time of year with it being too cold to garden yet but still I got to take care of the cabin and Penny and pay my bills and things like that so I try to keep busy. But mostly I just try not to think too much.

It seems so long since I have seen you but I remember a year ago today how you gave me my precious General Penny and this beautiful ring which you should have taken back when I sent you away but I'm glad you didn't because it means so much to me. I know I promised you I would never take it off remember but I couldn't go around with it on my finger in public anymore because that would make people talk. The sooner they forget we were going steady with each other the safer you will be.

Now I wear the ring on a chain around my neck right over my heart and I can feel it there all day long and remember you giving it to me and telling me it meant you had given me your heart. I'm pretty sure that was the happiest moment of my whole life Frank and sometimes when I remember it I want to cry from knowing what I have lost. But crying don't fix anything so I am trying to smile a little bit when I think of all the things you did for me and gave me while we were together. I was a very lucky girl for more than two years and some people go through this life without even that much so I try to feel happy for what I had.

Merry Christmas my Sweet Frank. I love you.

Your Ruth

MONDAY, JANUARY 23, 1966

DEAR FRANK,

OH MY GOD he came again last night Frank. I just knew sending you away was the only safe thing to do and I was right. I feel sick at my stomach when I think on what might have happened if you had been here. Every night for this whole year I been expecting him to come back and now he has and it was so horrible I don't even know how to tell you about it. It doesn't matter I guess because you would surely not believe me and would think I've gone crazy out here by myself. But I know I'm not crazy because there is stuff broke up all over the place in my kitchen.

Near about everything I had sitting on my counters is on the floor now, and lots of it is smashed to pieces. If you had been here I think he would have smashed us both too if he could have gotten inside. But even with him outside the whole house was shaking like it was about to come apart and I could hear things breaking and he was yelling that he would kill me and calling me things you would have hated to hear him say. And just like when he was really here last year he kept telling me he would kill you if I didn't go out there to him.

Penny like to have had a seizure barking and growling and crying like he was but I sat on the bed and held him with the blankets over both of us and I just waited because what else could I do? You can't kill what's already dead can you? I thought I was scared the first time he came but this was even worse because it was just all kinds of wrong that he could even be here and I don't know how to explain it but he was Frank. He was here.

After it all stopped and the sun come up, I came downstairs and started trying to clean up this mess and I realized it was exactly a year ago that he was here last so now I'm wondering if he will come back every year. Maybe some people are too mean to ever really die. Maybe he's so mean even Hell doesn't want him so they keep sending him back?

What am I going to do now Frank? I got nowhere else to go and no one to go to, and I don't want to go anywhere else neither. I want to stay here where you spent so many happy hours with me and where I learned what love really is. I don't want him to drive me away from here. This is my home Frank and I don't want to leave.

I pray he doesn't come back tonight. Oh why won't he just stay dead?

Your Ruth

TUESDAY, FEBRUARY 21, 2012

THREE MORE READ this morning, and many more to go. I found myself getting hooked on Ruth's letters. There was something wildly sad and lonely about them, and my heart just ached for her. I had finished the last three in rapid succession, reading them aloud to Mac as he made coffee. He was almost as fascinated by her story as I was, and boy, these last three had certainly answered a lot of questions for us.

I had added the new information to my outline as I read each letter. We now knew that Ruth had done something "awful" that no one knew about, that she had stolen money from her husband who was apparently a thief, as well, and that Frank had built the pantry extension. But the most important fact we had learned was that Ruth's husband, Lloyd, was dead, which led us to the question, did Ruth kill him? Is this the secret she's hiding? And if Ruth did kill him, where is he buried? Is this why she doesn't want anyone on her property?

Oh, my God, is there a body buried in my yard or woods?

So much learned, and yet so many questions still unanswered.

"I think maybe she killed him, Mac. It's the only thing I can think of that would cause her to break up with Frank, and try so hard to keep people off her property."

"That would make sense, but I just don't know. She just seems so unselfish and loving. It's hard to imagine."

"It wouldn't be the first time an abused woman has turned on her abuser. And it sounds like he threatened 'her Frank.' I think she might have been capable of taking extreme action to protect him, maybe more than she would have resorted to in order to protect herself."

One thing Mac and I both agreed on. Frank should have a chance to read the letters, if he wanted to. It was possible that he never knew why Ruth had sent him away, and we both felt he deserved to understand what had happened to the woman he had loved so much.

We planned to go to Raleigh on Saturday to meet Davis Ledlow and visit Frank, and I wanted to be sure we had read all of the letters before we left. There were dozens of them left, and maybe there would be more answers revealed.

After breakfast, Mac had company work to do, so I settled down on the sofa, not far away, ready to immerse myself in Ruth's story. She was just begging for someone to understand what she had been through, and I wanted to know as much as possible about her. Her story was riveting, and it was impacting my life, all these years later. Strange to imagine, but it seemed our ghost was Ruth's husband, Lloyd, and I wanted to know if he had really been haunting my cabin since 1966.

Maybe Ruth was right. Maybe he was so mean even Hell didn't want him.

Chapter 28
You Do Good Work, Research Boy

DEAR FRANK,
HAPPY BIRTHDAY! I baked you a cake today like I do every year, and General Penny and I ate every bit of it and drank ice tea and toasted to your happiness. Well I drank ice tea and toasted you because Penny doesn't much like it but you know what I mean. It's been more than three years since you drove off down my driveway and took my whole heart with you but I still know it was the right thing to do Frank and I am so happy that you aren't here to see some of the things I have seen. It makes me feel like I can put up with most anything as long as I know this evil will never touch you and no one will ever wonder if you were part of what I did.

I don't talk to many people from Darcy's Corners any more because it always makes me feel bad and I don't think many of them care to see me anyway so I shop in Lake Lure now or sometimes near Asheville. I still hear things from time to time though because in this itty bitty part of the world you can't help but know nearly everybody's business.

But I heard you were dating Anne Ledlow now and for a little bit I was so jealous and wanted to hate her for having you when I don't but then I got over it pretty much. I know you are finally moving on with your life like I wanted you to do and that's good Frank. I remember Anne from when I had my table at Everly's and she always seemed like a really nice person to me and her little boys was always dressed clean and nice and behaved like little gentlemen. I'm wishing the best for you and hope this might be a chance for you to finally have that home and family you wanted so much. I'm praying she sees what a good man you are and she treats you right like you deserve.

I still can't keep Lloyd dead no matter what I do. He's been back two more times and he's worse every time and I think I might be worse too just from being so afraid. I figured out last year to take all the dishes and things off the shelves the day before I thought he would show up which is January 23 since that is the date he was supposed to take his miserable self out of this world and never come back. I sure wish it had worked that way but it didn't.

Penny and I just hide in the closet and wait for daylight to chase him and his big red car away. If you was to build you a house in the middle of an airport it wouldn't be as loud as it gets when he starts going round and round this cabin Frank. I can feel his evil like cold hands on my shoulders which is what I'm afraid I might really feel one of these times if he ever gets in the cabin. It seems he stays longer and gets louder every year and I'm afraid someday he'll just come right on in the door and then I don't know what might happen to me and Penny.

I thought about going away for the days when he might come but something in me just says no I won't let that bastard drive me out of my home. Sorry for the bad word but that's how I think of him Frank because he is the meanest man in the world. Even dead. I just hide and wait for him to go back to wherever he stays the rest of the year and then I try to forget about him.

You go on and be happy now. You have a chance for a wonderful life and I hope you take it. I'm doing mostly okay when Lloyd isn't here. Me and Penny talk about you a lot. Well I talk and Penny listens but I always think he knows when I'm telling him things about you so it's like sharing with a friend almost.

I hope you got some chocolate cake tonight. I know how much you like it.

I still love you and I always will.
Your Ruth

SUNDAY, APRIL 12, 1970
DEAR FRANK,

I STOOD ON the sidewalk across from the church again this morning. I was really careful so you wouldn't see me and nobody else did either. They were all too busy throwing rice and yelling and hollering when you and Anne came out of the church. I wish I could have thrown some too but it wouldn't have been right.

You looked so handsome and happy and Anne looked just beautiful and those little boys of hers are getting so grown up. Yes I cried some for what we might have had since I never, ever forget that you wanted to marry me once but I try not to think about that too much because a lot of things have changed in five years. Now you are safe and have a real chance to be happy and you are getting a head start on a family plus you are only forty so you might even have more babies. Your life will be a good one I just know it. I haven't never heard a bad thing said about Anne and from looking at her face I think she must love you near about as much as I do so it will all be fine.

I know you will still remember me in a little part of your heart and of course I will never ever forget you Frank Everly but I

don't regret letting you go since certain things just keep getting
worse and worse here and you are well out of it. I will be watching
from a distance though to be sure you are all right but I just know
I will see you living a good and happy life.

God bless you and your new family and keep you safe always.
I love you.
Your Ruth

TUESDAY, FEBRUARY 21, 2102

MAC LOOKED UP from his computer and smiled at
the sight of Sarah curled up on his couch, feet tucked under
her, and head cocked to one side as she read. He still
couldn't believe that she was here. In his home, and in his
heart. It amazed him every time he looked at her.

She was absorbed in Ruth's letters, which she had been
reading all morning, and her face reflected deep sadness as
she turned each page. Her hair fell in loose waves over one
shoulder, and he thought about how silken it felt cascading
over him at night. He could get lost in that honey-scented
sable cloud and those green, green eyes. Everything about
her made him feel that way. He never dreamed he would
find himself in love at his age, but he knew in his heart that
this woman was his true purpose in life. She always had
been, even though the journey to her side had taken so long.

What if today is the day she moves back to her cabin? How
will I stand it around here when she does?

Every morning, he found himself nervous and unable
to relax until he was sure she wasn't leaving yet. He didn't
want her to go. Ever. But he knew it wouldn't be fair to try
to influence her, so he had decided not to say anything. She
would be free to stay or go, as she chose, and if she left, he
would try to deal with it the best he could. As though she
knew he was thinking about her, she slowly turned her head
toward him and smiled.

There. That look right there. The one that says she loves me the same way I love her. I would die for that one look!

A silent message passed between them, and without a word, he stood and walked toward her at the same moment she rose and came toward him. They faced each other, inches apart. Mac threaded his fingers into her hair on each side of her face and pulled her closer to him, until his lips were barely brushing hers. He closed his eyes, drinking in the scent of her, holding her head still as he nuzzled her cheeks and eyelids and down the side of her neck.

She stood unmoving, eyes closed as well, and he could feel her breath coming faster as his mouth moved along the hollow at the base of her throat and worked its way back to her lips, claiming them in a kiss so sweet it left them both dizzy.

When he released her, she stroked his cheek with her fingertips and smiled again. "What did I do to deserve that?"

"You saved me. You love me. You made me love you. You belong to me. You have stolen my heart and my soul, and I belong to you, too. Do you need to hear more?"

"No," she whispered. "Just kiss me like that again."

So he did.

TUESDAY, FEBRUARY 21, 2012

SOMETIMES WHEN I'M watching Mac, I am astounded at having found the man I was always meant to be with. It seems so random. What if I hadn't bought my cabin? What if I had chosen a cabin one mountaintop over? What if I had gone to Maine or Alaska or Fiji, instead? Would I ever have met him if Rosheen hadn't run away that morning, and Mac had never come down my drive chasing her?

It's frightening to contemplate how even the slightest change in my plans or subsequent events could have meant the difference in being with Mac or being alone. I don't think I would ever have met another man that completes me in the way Mac does.

After lunch, I settled down to read some more of Ruth's letters. Mac put on his Research Assistant hat, and between us, we started unraveling a bit more. My job was to look for clues in Ruth's writing, though I was far more interested in how she was coping on the lonely path she had chosen.

Mac's job was to find out the identity of R. J. Carter, and see what he could learn about Ruth's husband, Lloyd. We figured the more we knew about him, the sooner we could lay his ghost to rest, which was our ultimate goal. I mean, the thing had been hanging around since 1966, for Pete's sake. That's forty-six years! Surely even *he* is getting tired of all the yelling and revving of engines and terrorizing of women. Not to mention that Ruth Winn is gone. Didn't he get the memo?

Funny thing is, it didn't even seem weird any more that we were talking about ghosts and hauntings as though everyone had to deal with them at one point in their lives or another, like car trouble or taxes. If someone had told me about this a year ago, I would have thought they were crazy. Now, I just shrug and go see what else I can find out.

Sitting on Mac's sofa with a cup of Earl Grey tea close by, I pulled the next letter from the stack.

SATURDAY, MAY 12, 1973

DEAR FRANK,

OH MY GOD I'm so sorry Frank! I never meant for you to see me! I usually just stand in a dark corner by the bleachers and I only watch for a little while because it makes me feel good to see your sons in Little League and you there cheering for them.

I guess you were getting drinks when I slipped in tonight and I didn't know you would be walking right by me or I would never have been there Frank honest. When I saw you staring at me I wanted to crawl into a hole but had to settle for running off real quick instead. I'm sorry you dropped the cokes too. You looked awful shocked and I don't blame you it's been so long.

I am surprised that you even recognize me any more as I know I've changed a lot in the last eight years but you haven't. You still look as handsome and sweet to me as you ever did and I guess you always will but I really really wish I had stayed home tonight because you didn't deserve a shock like that and I promise it will never happen again. You don't have to worry about me showing up and embarrassing you in front of your family or anything because I swear I won't ever spy on you again. I feel so bad that I did this time only lately I been a bit more lonely than usual and it was just that I wanted to be a part of your life in a tiny way for just a few minutes but I know that doesn't make it right and I'm ashamed of myself for upsetting you. I wish you could know how sorry I am.

I will find ways to keep up with your life without spying on you any more honest Frank. I wouldn't hurt you for anything in all the world and I'm so proud of you for loving your family so much and making such a good home for them. People never say a single unkind word about you or them so I know you are living that good life I wanted for you and that makes everything that has happened worthwhile even the horrible stuff. None of it matters as long as you are safe and happy.

I'm so sorry for tonight and I love you as much as always.
Your Ruth

SUNDAY, FEBRUARY 3, 1980
DEAR FRANK,
HAPPY BIRTHDAY TO you. I baked you another chocolate cake and shared it with Bobby who thinks I should be baking cakes

a lot more often. I have not told you about Bobby though since it's been such a long time since I wrote you. I lost General Penny two years ago and it was a sad sad day for me because not only was he my best friend but he was a gift from you so it about broke my heart when he died. He was fourteen and the vet said his heart just gave out but he was playful and full of fun right up until his very last day so I like to think he never felt bad at all.

I thought I would never get another dog but I got too lonely here without someone to talk to and plus I was afraid to be here by myself when January rolled around again so I got Bobby who is a Jack Russell terrier and a fine and brave little dog. He was already a year old when I got him and needed a home so I took him in and me and him get along just fine and he hates when Lloyd comes near as much as I do and would like to bite him and shake him like a rat I think. Wouldn't that be funny to see my little dog trying to kill my ghost?

Well Frank you are fifty years old today and I am not far behind at 48 and I wonder if you feel like me and can't believe you are so old. Some days I think it was only a few weeks ago that you were coming to see me after work and we would sit on the porch and swing and drink iced tea and talk. Other days I feel like I've been here in this cabin by myself for my whole life and the time I had with you seems like a dream I can barely remember. I hope that having a loving family around you has filled your heart with so much joy you wonder how the time could have passed so fast and that you've been happy every day of it too.

You been married ten years come this April and your boys are near grown up now and I read in the local news that Brady will graduate high school this year and that he works with you at Everly's. They talked about him being "the next generation" to run the store and I guess that means he plans to follow in his daddy's footsteps which is a real good thing for a son to do. I wonder what Davis will decide to do when his time comes to move on with his life. I heard he is a straight A student and real smart and likes science.

You've done good Frank but I hope it will be a long time before anybody besides you is running Everly's so you take special care of yourself and I hope Anne is doing fine too since she seems to have been good to you and that makes her okay in my book too.

I'm still doing all right with my gardens and selling my canned goods but sometimes it gets to be a lot of work and I wonder why I bother. Then I tell myself that everybody has bad days and I should stop complaining and keep on going because it is not really so bad and at least I don't have anybody beating me half to death any more. It could be worse than just me being here all by myself. And I have Bobby now. Bobby is a Jack Russell terrier that I got after Penny died and he's a good boy did I tell you that already? Oh, I see I did. I better quit now. Sometimes I just plain lose track of what I'm talking about.

Happy birthday Frank and many many more. Please take good care of yourself. You are a special man and everyone loves you especially me.

Your Ruth

TUESDAY, FEBRUARY 21, 2012

FIFTEEN YEARS! FIFTEEN long, sad, lonely years had passed for Ruth between the first letter she wrote Frank, and the one I just put down. I found I could only read one or two letters at a time before I had to walk away. Ruth touched something in my heart, and it made me cry to think of her having lost so much.

It still wasn't totally clear if she had murdered Lloyd, but I didn't even care very much, because if that's what had happened, she had paid for it ten times over in her self-imposed prison. And if he had tormented her the way his ghost tormented Mac and I, I believed it would have been self-defense. Why hadn't she simply called the sheriff, I wondered? I hoped her thoughts about that would be made clearer as I worked my way through the rest of the letters.

I picked up the two photographs and studied them again. Those two youthful faces brimming with love made me want to cry, too. All those possibilities that had been there for them, gone. Once again, I sent a silent prayer of thanks to the powers that be for leading me to Mac, and I also prayed that nothing would ever come between us, now that we had found each other.

My train of thought was interrupted when Mac burst out with a resounding "Yes!" I looked over just in time to see him talking to his monitor with a big grin on his face. "Gotcha!"

He made a couple of notes on a sheet of paper, keyed in a few more strokes on the computer, then stood, stretching. He grinned as he walked to the couch and plopped down, pulling me to him and giving me a smacking big kiss. "How much do you love me?" he teased. "I have information you might be interested in."

"Are you trying to extract payment from me, MacKenzie Cole?"

"Most definitely, Sarah Gray. I have answers about certain names we discussed earlier. What's it worth to you?"

I offered him a few suggestions for things he might be willing to take in exchange for said information, and he gave me a wicked grin. "Oh, yeah! Either of those would definitely be acceptable to me! How about I collect tonight, right after dinner? Deal?"

"Deal. Now tell me what you found."

He handed over a printout with a few hand scribbled notes on the bottom, then, unable to wait long enough for me to read it, he began reciting. "Ruth was born Ruthie Jane Winn in 1932, in Clay County, Georgia. In March of 1950, she got married to ... ready? ... Lloyd Ellis Carter. Carter! Ruthie Jane! *R. J. Carter*. Voila!

"Ruth Winn Carter dies March 1, 2010. The title of your cabin is deeded to Frank on March 5, the afternoon of her funeral, and there you go, Sarah. That's how Frank came to own it. She left it to him in her will."

"Wow! You do good work, Research Boy. I'm impressed."

"You ain't heard nuthin' yet, Writer Girl. Let's talk about our ghost."

"Oh, yes! Let's. What *is* his problem?"

"Well, we'll have to do some reading between the lines, unless you find out more from Ruth's letters, but here is what I do know. On August 18, 1962, Macon, Georgia police department responded to a domestic violence call at the residence of Lloyd Ellis Carter and his wife, Ruthie. Ruthie was beaten badly, and Lloyd apparently went after the arresting officers with a knife. She spent a week in the hospital, and Lloyd ended up being convicted of a whole host of things and was sentenced to five years in jail.

"Ruthie Carter disappeared shortly after being released from the hospital, and reappears in Asheville, where she paid cash for your cabin, and settled in. While her name was never changed legally, it appears folks in Darcy's Corner knew her as Ruth Winn, and I'm guessing she kept a pretty low profile, not wanting Lloyd to find her. Since there is not a single record of her ever having been employed or paying taxes, I'm also guessing she was totally dependent on Lloyd, and yet she paid cash for the cabin."

I thought for a moment. "She admits in her first letters that she stole his money. You know, I'll bet the big Impala was his, too. If he was as mean as she says, taking his money and his car would be reason enough for him to hunt her down, don't you think?"

"I do. And I suspect that's what happened. He finally found her, and she was forced to defend herself."

"She killed him, didn't she?"

"Probably. He drops totally off the grid from the moment he walks out of prison. It's like he ceased to exist, and the most logical explanation is that he actually did. My people are pretty good, and I'm not bad at this stuff, either. Between us, we would have found him in the system somewhere, if he was alive."

"If she killed him in self-defense, why didn't she report it to the sheriff? I know she is protecting Frank, but why would she even worry about him coming under suspicion? And what did she do with the body? Do you think he's buried in my yard?"

Visions of Lloyd Carter being buried in one of the vegetable beds made me feel faintly ill. Could she have done that? And lived that close to the body for another forty-five years?

Mac shrugged and shook his head. "I don't know. At this point, I think our best shot for figuring it all out is in her letters. If she got away with murder, that means it isn't on the records anywhere, so there's no way for me to find it. We just have to hope she tells us. Are you doing okay reading them? They're truly sad, aren't they?"

"Yes, they really are, but I'm fine. I just have to know what happened. I feel like finding the box means I've been charged with uncovering the truth she kept secret for so long, and what's more, I want to. I want to do it for her. For the two of them, really. And I'm hoping Frank can fill in some of the gaps."

I sat lost in thought for a few minutes, remembering the night Lloyd's ghost came after Mac and me. As much as I would have preferred not to recall any of that night in detail again, I couldn't help but think about the moment when that *thing* stepped out of the Impala and looked up at me, exposing its ruined head. I was pretty sure someone had used a gun to blow Lloyd's head half off his shoulders, and it seemed to me that someone was probably Ruth Winn.

Chapter 29

The Kind of Mean That Just Don't Quit

AFTER BREAKFAST AND a half a pot of Mac's most divine and heavenly coffee, I was ready for another journey into the past. I was determined to finish Ruth's letters today, and hoping she would provide the rest of the answers we were looking for. Did she really kill Lloyd, and if so, what did she do with the body? It was that second part that still had me worried.

It was funny, but my cabin no longer frightened me. Apparently, the miserable wretch that was Lloyd Carter's ghost only dropped by to terrorize Ruth in January, the same time every year. The rest of the year, she seemed perfectly comfortable in her little home, and when Mac and I were last at the cabin, neither of us had felt anything threatening or dangerous, either. My cabin had seemed as warm and welcoming as it had the day I moved in, except for the boarded up window and the mess in the kitchen, but that was just harmless debris that we had almost finished clearing out.

I knew that the time was coming for me to move back in, but I wasn't sure any more how I felt about that. Mac was keeping his feelings to himself, which made me feel like I should plan on leaving soon. I glanced over at him as he talked on a conference call to Charlotte, and tried to imagine not waking up next to him every morning. It wasn't a happy thought, so I pushed it to the back of my mind, and got busy with the task at hand.

I read through the next few letters in just a few minutes. They were short, scribbled notes, commenting on day-to-day events, like how well Ruth did at the market that Saturday, or what was ready to harvest from her garden.

It seemed she had stuck to her word not to spy on Frank any more, and I felt her sense of loss coming through in each letter. She missed seeing him, but she was still keeping track of him and his family through the local grapevines, gleaning every little bit of information she could, and clinging to it in sad desperation. Birthdays and the various accomplishments of his sons were noted with genuine pride, and a total lack of resentment over not being a part of it all. She was amazing in her unselfish and generous love for Frank Everly. I was looking forward to meeting the man who had inspired this deep devotion.

As I worked my way through these forlorn little letters, I realized that Ruth's thoughts were becoming more and more scattered, and her sentences less cohesive. I wondered if, in addition to everything else she had to cope with every day, she might be succumbing to dementia or Alzheimer's. It wasn't there yet, but something different seemed to be slipping into her words. It wasn't until I finished reading her last four letters, however, that the final heartbreaking pieces of Ruth's life came together for me.

SATURDAY, FEBRUARY 3, 1990

DEAR FRANK,

IT'S YOUR BIRTHDAY once again and Lord, don't it seem like I've written you about a hundred happy birthday letters now. Of course I haven't because you are only sixty. Sixty and I can hardly believe it because it just does not seem possible that nearly 30 years have gone by since you helped me pick up my spilled vegetables in the Everly's parking lot. I can remember the way you smiled at me that day just like it was yesterday and that's pretty strange since I can barely remember what I did yesterday at all.

Remembering is a funny thing isn't it because when I want to remember something special it blows away right out of my head like dandelion fluff but when I am not even thinking about a certain thing it will pop into my mind clear as a painted picture. And if I'm trying really hard to just plain forget about something awful well I can't get it out of my head at all because it will just play over and over like a stuck record. And sometimes when I'm remembering something I am not even sure if it really happened or if it is just something I wanted to happen. Is this just from growing old I wonder or am I getting crazy out here by myself.

Well I might be getting a bit absent minded now but I am still doing pretty good with my vegetable garden and I am still taking stuff to market and it sells good so my windfall money is hidden away safe for now. I have been pretty careful with it over the years so it is lasting longer than I ever thought it would though I had to have some work done on my central heat last winter and that ate up a chunk of it but I got a pretty good emergency nest egg hidden in my special place.

My market customers always catch me talking to myself and probably think I'm crazy but Bobby usually goes with me and I tell them I'm talking to him. Bobby has been a good boy but sometimes

I forget and call him Penny and he doesn't like that very much but I give him extra treats when I do so his feelings won't be too hurt.

I saw you last week Frank and I couldn't believe my eyes because your hair is all silver now but it looks really nice and you are just as handsome as ever and you walk straight and tall so a woman would be proud to call you her man. I hope Anne still loves you as much as the day she met you and she should because I know I do.

I heard your youngest boy went away to college and graduated top of his class and that does not surprise me one bit but I was sorry to hear he was not moving back to Darcy's Corner because you probably miss him really bad. I know that boy's name but I can't think of it right now so forgive me for that. It will come to me later I'm sure.

Anyway I saw you and Brady coming out of a little shop in Chimney Rock as I was sitting at a stop sign and it's a good thing I was not moving or I might have run off the road I was so surprised. You were laughing and looked so happy and it made me know all over again that I made the right decision to let you go Frank even if I have missed you so much and always wonder what kind of life we might have had if we had gotten the chance.

Oh how I wish I could kill Lloyd Carter all over again but this time I don't think a shotgun would work and I don't want to get close enough to find out. He never should have said he was going to kill you Frank because I would have given him back the rest of his money and his car and he could have driven away happy as you please. But he was too mean to do that and now he's dead and no one knows but me and that's how it will stay because I can't let them think you helped me kill him. You have to stay safe.

I've thought about it over and over and over through these years and I just can't see that there was ever any other choice for me. No one would have believed I killed Lloyd in self-defense because he was sitting behind the wheel of his car and it would have looked for all the world like he was ready to drive away when he was shot.

I tried and tried to think of a way to explain it but evidence is evidence and I knew I would probably get charged with murder. I was so scared of going to jail and maybe getting a death sentence even but most of all I was really scared they might think you had helped me since I was cheating on Lloyd with you and all.

It wasn't worth the risk that you would have been pulled into something so ugly and maybe be charged with taking part in getting rid of him. I have seen stories like that and it never turns out good and I figured the best thing that would happen to you is that your good name would be ruined forever and the worst thing was that you might actually be convicted of something and that was not something I could take a chance on. You have a good name in this town and that is how it should always be and I'm happy I was smart enough to know that even then.

Of course I thought once I killed him he couldn't bother us any more but I should have known better than that because Lloyd was the kind of mean that just don't quit no matter if he is dead or not. And of course I couldn't have you here any more because what if you found him which you surely would have and then knew I killed him. You could not have lied and lived with the secret for years and made yourself a part of the crime by covering it up. You wouldn't be the man I fell in love with if you could have done that and I would never have asked you to.

So you see I had to kill Lloyd to save you from him and then I had to let you go to save you from what I had done and there it is. That's the mess I made of my life and I wasn't going to pull you into the muck and the fear with me.

Well this is not a very happy birthday letter is it but sometimes I get these thoughts piled up in my head and they have to come out somewhere and I can only tell Bobby so much. He's pretty smart but I really do know that he doesn't understand me when I talk to him.

I am going to picture you having a beautiful birthday dinner with your family tonight and everyone singing to you and giving you gifts. I can see you now all smiles as you open up every package and tell the person who gave it to you how much you like it. They are so lucky to have you Frank and I am so lucky that I had you once, too, and I try to hold that thought in my heart no matter what else happens.

You were the brightest thing in my life and I love you still.

Your Ruth

PS Your other son's name is Davis. I told you I knew it. I just had to shove things in my mind around a bit until I uncovered it.

WEDNESDAY, FEBRUARY 22, 2012

I GASPED AND sat bolt upright on the couch. Mac stopped working and came to sit beside me.

"What is it? What does she say?"

"She says she killed him, Mac! She says she wishes she could do it again. Oh my God, I really didn't think she would admit it, but she did." I handed him the letter.

"And not only does she admit to shooting him, but she as much as says he's buried on my property somewhere!" I pointed out the paragraph. "See, right here where she says she couldn't have Frank there any more because he would surely have found him. I have a dead body on my property!"

Mac scanned the letter and nodded. "Well, she definitely admits to killing him. As for the body, maybe it was there immediately afterward, but it's been a long time, Sarah. She could have gotten rid of it later on. Moved it somewhere else. It could be anywhere, even out in your woods, where you would probably never find it."

"Okay, this is just majorly creepy, if you ask me. I will never be able to look at anything on my property again without wondering if Lloyd Carter is under it. But I've been all over the cabin and garden area, and I can't imagine anywhere a body could be, except buried in one of the big beds. And you're right. She could have moved it farther away eventually." I shuddered. "Not knowing is kind of awful. There's got to be some way of figuring it out."

"Maybe when you have read the last of the letters, you'll have a better idea. How many more are there?"

"Three. Three more letters and then that might be all we'll ever know about Ruth Winn's sad story." I sighed, and Mac gave me a hug.

"Read on, Sarah, and when we go see Frank, maybe he can give us some insight, too."

Mac went back to his desk to finish his work for the morning, and I eyed the next letter, wondering what other surprises might be in store. I was almost afraid to open it and start reading.

THURSDAY, FEBRUARY 3, 2000

DEAR FRANK,

HAPPY BIRTHDAY AGAIN. Another ten years gone in a flash and it does not seem possible at all but it is true. You are 70, and today I found myself staring at the back of my hand and wondering who it belonged to because it looked like some old lady's hand and then I remembered that I am that old lady. Can you imagine?

I haven't seen you in years and years but I still think of you tall and handsome with silver hair now but mostly the same as you looked when we were together. I don't look so much the same any more because I have spent too much time working in the sun and dirt and not taking the best care of myself I guess but no one is here to see so it doesn't really make any difference. Since I wrote you last I lost my little dog Bobby but then I got another red dachshund that looks just like General Penny only smaller and I named him Pocket Change but I called him Penny because it made me feel good to have a Penny in the house again.

Frank do you know if ghosts can sometimes touch you I mean like really touch you like a real solid person can? Because something bad happened when Lloyd came last month that I never seen before and I am still not sure of exactly how it happened.

I wish I could ask you this for real and not just in my letters because I sure would like an answer but I know even if I could I probably wouldn't because you would think I am crazy. I been going through this hell every January for so many years sometimes I forget that the rest of the world is full of people who do not believe in ghosts at all because they have never been so unlucky as to have one coming around and raising the devil every year over and over like clockwork.

I think he wants to put me in that car and drive me back to hell with him and sometimes I'm so scared and want it to end so much I think about walking right outside and letting him have me but then I don't do it because I don't want to die yet. I don't want to say goodbye to you yet Frank because I just need to be sure that you stay safe and happy for every day of your life so I don't give in. I just hide inside and cry a lot when he is here.

Do you know if ghosts can sometimes touch you Frank? Like really touch you and hurt you. I want to know this because this time when Lloyd came he made so much noise that Penny got away from me and went running downstairs to try to get to him because Penny wanted to protect me but something awful happened instead.

I tried to catch Penny but he was fast and I am not fast any more and I just made it to the top of the stairs in time to see him barking at the front door and then it crashed open with nasty cold wind blowing so hard it flung Penny clear across the room and into the bricks around the fireplace. I could see the ugly mess that's left of Lloyd on my porch screaming and reaching towards me and

I was so scared I ran back upstairs to the closet and hid and when it got quiet again I came back down and little Penny was dead.

I think he died when he hit those bricks but I don't know Frank and I feel horrible about it because maybe if I had been brave enough to come down and get him he would still be alive but then maybe not. Maybe we would just both be dead or riding off in that car that I hate so much and going back to hell beside Lloyd Carter where we'd never get away from him again. In hell he'd probably beat me over and over for all eternity so I don't much want to get in that car with him.

Do you know if ghosts can sometimes touch you Frank like a real person can touch you or hurt you like a real person can? I really wish I knew if this can happen because I think Lloyd killed my little Penny but I just don't know if it is possible and I'm too tired to tell you what happened right now. I'll tell you later. I just wanted to wish you a happy birthday Frank and tell you I love you as much today as I did all those years ago when I had to send you away.

Did I tell you Penny died? I think Lloyd did it. Do you know if ghosts can touch you like real people touch you? I wish I knew.

I love you, Frank. That's one thing I know for sure.

Your Ruth

WEDNESDAY, FEBRUARY 3, 2010

DEAR FRANK,

HAPPY BIRTHDAY TO you once again. Imagine. You are turning 80 and next month, I will be 78 if I make it that far.

Frank Frank Frank. Three times Frank. A hundred times Frank. My whole life has been about you but without you. Are you still happy Frank? I think you are but it is hard to tell any more because I don't get out much or hear much about you or your son who took over running Everly's. I quit going to the farmers market because it was just getting too hard for me so I don't run into people who know you there either.

I've been living off my hidden money for a while now but it is okay because it doesn't have to last me too much longer so they tell me. I don't even have a dog to talk to any more because I am afraid I will forget to feed it and it would not be fair to have an animal I can't care for any more.

Yesterday I was making my dinner and I was telling you about my plan to add more vegetables to my garden and buy a truck to help me set up my stand at Everly's and when I turned around to see what you thought you weren't there at all. I was scared at first but then I remembered I was thinking about a day longlonglong ago and I don't even have anything at all planted in my garden this year because I am just too tired to work in it.

The doctor told me that was how it would be and that I should not be out here by myself any more but I told him if anyone came to get me they would have to talk to my shotgun so he did not say any more about that.

Oh yes about the doctor I saw last month right after new years eve well wasn't that an experience Frank. Lots of tests and stuff and then bad news and I had to pay for it. I hate paying for bad news don't you Frank. Frank. Frank. Sometimes I hear your name in my head just like that FrankFrankFrank and I know it is because you have been the one and only really true and good thing that ever happened to me so it is okay with me to hear your name over and over and I hope it will be the last thing I ever think about.

Don't be mad at me Frank but I told the doctor no when he wanted to do more stuff to me because I'm too old and tired for them to be cutting in my head and putting me through a long long treatment and stuff. I don't care what's growing there I don't want to do it. Don't don't don't. I only wanted to live long enough to be sure you were safe Frank and I am sorry I have to go before you but I think you will be safe now surely because it has been so so so long. Long and long. And still nobody ever found out none of the secrets did they?

You should know one thing while I can still remember it though and that is that I have left you this cabin for your own because maybe you will want to come out sometime and remember when we were young and in love or maybe it would just be bad memories but it is yours to do whatever you want. This cabin has been my home for almost all of my life and everything I love is here and everything I hate is here but I think Lloyd will probably go when I do so it should be fine for whoever comes next.

My head is scrambled like those things I made for you for breakfast sometimes. Eggs. Eggs. Eggs. If I say it three times it might stay in my mind a little while.

FrankFrankFrank I will keep saying that as long as I can and I hope it will always mean you when I say it and that I won't forget because if I forget who you are I will not know who I am either.

Frank. My Frank. How I have loved you.
Your Ruth.

FEBRUARY 14, 2010
DEAR FRANK
I THINK THIS may be the last time I will be writing you. I am not feeling so good this morning and I have called 911 but it takes them long long and I wanted to say I love you one more time because I remember you Frank even though I don't always remember me I still remember you. You are my Frank my sweet Frank and I hold on to that tight as I can

I will put this goodbye into my box with the ring you gave me and hide it in my special place and call my lawyer to tell him to get it after I go so you will know that I never stopped loving you Frank

I'm so tired and I need to end now so I don't forget what to do forgive me frank for everything

I feel so sick frank and I need to lie down soon so I will just say I love you

and love you and love you
you are my frank
always my frank
*

MONDAY, MARCH 1, 2010

RUTHIE JANE WINN CARTER died at 10:15 A.M. on March 1, 2010, as she lay in an Asheville hospital, aware of almost nothing since the paramedics had picked her up at her cabin on Valentine's Day. At the end, she had a brief moment of clarity, realizing she had forgotten to call her attorney, but it didn't seem very important any more.

Smiling, she whispered "Frank," one last time, then slipped out of this life, remembering her beloved Frank Everly exactly as he had been the day she met him, forty-eight years earlier.

Chapter 30

A Definite Air of City Boy

WEDNESDAY, FEBRUARY 22, 2012

I FOLDED RUTH'S last letter, tied the pink ribbon around the stack, and put it back in the box, laying her ring on top, and closing the lid. I sat staring into the fire, my heart heavy with overwhelming sadness. After a moment, I wrapped the afghan from the back of the sofa around my shoulders, and went out to the balcony, sliding the door closed behind me.

Mac didn't follow. I think he knew I needed a few minutes to myself to process all the emotions running through me. My heart was aching for Ruth and all she had been through, and I truly hoped Frank was the kind of man who deserved that type of love and sacrifice. I made a useless swipe at my tears and pulled a rocker closer to the railing, where I could sit and look out over the hills. That amazing sense of timelessness washed over me as I huddled there, watching them roll in miles and miles of gentle curves, all the way to the horizon. There is nothing like a view spreading clear to the end of the world to put things into perspective, and after spending the morning reading the last of Ruth's letters, I needed just that.

After a few minutes, my throat felt less tight and my breath stopped hitching. I sniffled a few more times, and then made a promise to myself that I would never forget Ruth Winn as long as I lived, and I swore that I would make sure Frank got the letters she had always meant for him to read one day. He needed to know the reasons behind everything she had done, but most of all, he needed to know how much she had loved him.

When I felt calm enough to go back in, I found Mac sitting on the couch waiting for me. He patted the cushion next to him and I went straight to his arms.

"Are you all right?" he asked, wiping away the last traces of my tears.

"Yes. I'm fine now. But her letters just break my heart, Mac." I took a shaky breath. "Do you want to read the rest of them?"

"Yes, but I'll read them later." He kissed the palm of my hand and pulled me to my feet. "Why don't we go for a short walk before we have lunch?"

It sounded like a good way to finish clearing my head, so we grabbed sweaters, called the animals, and set off down one of Mac's pathways.

There is nothing as restorative to the soul as nature in all its glory. We walked along the quiet trail, taking note of tiny green leaf buds on the dogwoods and the tight purple-pink bumps marching along the redbud stems. A few wildflowers were beginning to peek through the leaf litter here and there. It wouldn't be long before spring would announce its arrival in an exuberant celebration of new beginnings throughout the mountains. Life goes on, and seeing clear evidence of that lifted my spirits considerably.

This would be my first spring since moving to Wake-Robin Ridge. I was ready to put winter to rest for another year and to greet the wild plums and bluebells and trillium, including the one known as the wake-robin, which the ridge was named for. By the time we got back to the house, my melancholy was almost gone, as Mac knew it would be, and I volunteered to make soup and sandwiches for lunch.

As we ate, Mac was quiet and thoughtful, and I wondered where his mind had gone. I trusted that he would tell me what he was thinking about when he was ready, and sure enough, he finally pushed his empty plate away and cleared his throat.

"Sarah, would you mind if we stop in Charlotte on our way back from Raleigh? I like to check in with my office now and then, just to touch base with everyone and make sure things are running smoothly, and I'm overdue."

He was staring at the plate, brows drawn together. There would be more coming, I was sure, but I merely addressed what he had said so far. "I wouldn't mind at all, in fact, I would really enjoy seeing your offices and meeting some of the folks who work for you."

He nodded, and sat fiddling with his crumpled napkin and pushing the silverware around aimlessly. I waited.

"Okay," he said, still fidgeting. "We'll go by there for sure. We can stay overnight, and I'll take you to dinner. There are some pretty nice places to eat in Charlotte."

He paused, still not looking directly at me, then took a nervous breath and continued. "I haven't gone to see Ben in a long time, either. I was thinking ... well ... maybe I could take you there? To visit him with me? I mean, if that would be okay?"

I couldn't say a word for a minute. This was enormous for Mac. I knew he had never gone to visit Ben's grave with anyone else before, and I had never even imagined he would ask me to accompany him. I was very happy that he trusted me enough to invite me. It couldn't have been an easy decision to include someone after all these years of solitary visits and lonely grief.

"Yes, Mac. I'd like that very much."

He nodded again, exhaling, and I sensed his relief came more from having worked up the courage to ask me than from my answer, which he had to know would be yes. I pulled my stool closer to his, and brushed his tousled hair out of his eyes. "Do you have any idea how much I love you?"

He gave me a sweet smile, and ran one finger down my cheek and along my neck. "I'd like to think you love me as much as I love you."

I'm pretty sure I convinced him that I did.

SATURDAY, FEBRUARY 25, 2012

DRIVING DOWN OUT of the mountains was like watching winter fast forward into spring. The lower elevations were much warmer than Wake-Robin Ridge, and brown branches morphed into pale green right before my eyes, as tiny new leaves emerged along awakening stems.

Low, dead grasses by the roadside gave way to a faint pink haze as wildflowers burst upward, reaching for the sun. After a few miles, the vivid yellow-green and lime of newly leafed out maples and sweetgums took over the woods, and entire fields were blanketed in the pink, white, and purple blooms of annual phlox. The riot of color made my heart sing, and I wished I had brought my sketchbook along. I snapped a few pictures out the window for future reference, and decided that when spring isn't ready to come to you, the answer is simple. Go to it.

The air grew softer and warmer as we headed eastward to Raleigh, and I was lost in the beauty that is North Carolina. Only one thing was missing. Or two. I turned to watch Mac, and I could tell he felt it, as well. He was humming to himself, but every now and then, he would glance into the rear view mirror as though looking for something, then catch himself and go back to his humming.

"You aren't used to leaving Rosheen behind, are you?"

He laughed, looking guilty. "Nope. It's always hard, but for this trip, boarding her was the right thing to do. She and Handsome will both be fine at the vet until we get back."

I knew he was right, but it's surprising what a hole in my life those two animals left when they were elsewhere. We had hit the road at 8:00 a.m., a few minutes after dropping them off. Davis had suggested we meet at his house around 11:30, have lunch together at a nearby restaurant, and then head over to meet Frank.

I found myself fidgeting a little more with every mile we traveled, glancing often at the metal box holding Ruth's letters, which rested on the seat between us. I hoped we were doing the right thing, but I had no idea of how Frank would react to this reminder of his past, nor how it might make Davis feel, as his stepson. I just knew I had to make the effort, for Ruth's sake.

SATURDAY, FEBRUARY 25, 2012
RALEIGH, NORTH CAROLINA

DAVIS LEDLOW SAT picking at his salad, his friendly demeanor of an hour ago replaced by a suspicious frown. He was a stocky, balding man in his mid-to-late forties who, with a few more wrinkles and a lot more hair, could have been the twin of his brother, Brady. The resemblance ended there, though.

He had a definite air of "city boy" about him that Brady would never acquire, and he had polished the corners off his country accent until it bore little resemblance to the way his brother spoke. Maybe it was easier to be taken seriously in the medical research and development field if you didn't sound like you were raised in the hills. For myself, though, I preferred Brady's easy country charm.

"Mr. Ledlow," I said, offering him a reassuring smile, "I know this must all come as a surprise to you, but please don't get the wrong idea. I promise you that any relationship your stepfather had with Ruth Winn was over long before he and your mother fell in love. There was never anything between them from that point forward, and I think that the reason Ruth left her cabin to Frank was simply because she never forgot how good he was to her when they were dating."

His shoulders lowered as he released some of the tension that had been building. "I thank you for clarifying that, Ms. Gray. I would never believe it if you claimed anything else, and wouldn't even want you to talk to him. My stepfather is the most honorable man I've ever known in my life. In all the ways that count, he is my father, and I wouldn't let anyone hurt him."

"Please call me Sarah, and based on the things that Ruth Winn said in her letters, I believe your description of your dad completely. She was totally committed to making sure nothing ever happened to hurt Frank, and her fondest dream was that he find happiness with your mother and you boys. She lived the rest of her life accordingly, praying for that every day."

He nodded, relaxing a bit more. "I have to say, this explains why Daddy Frank didn't want to talk about how he came to own the cabin. I'm sure he wouldn't have wanted to explain to me who R. J. Carter was, for fear I would jump to conclusions. You know, he was forty before he married my mama, so even though we kids never gave a thought to his life before us, it's only natural he would have had other girlfriends. He was a popular, friendly guy, well thought of in Darcy's Corner. It would have been weird if he hadn't had earlier relationships. Mama had already been married and divorced by the time they met."

Then Davis frowned again. "Is there anything in the letters that will upset him?"

"Well, Mr. Ledlow ... "

"Call me Davis, please."

"Thank you, Davis. I don't know Frank, so I'm guessing here, but I would say that most people his age might get a bit emotional when going through things from their past, especially unexpected things. So, I think it is possible he might be taken by surprise, but I would try to ease into what we found in a way that would let him decide for himself if he wanted to read the letters. I just think he deserves the chance to understand events that happened to him in 1965, which I believe would have left him hurt and confused."

"So he and Ms. Winn were a couple?" He said, shaking his head in amazement. "Huh. Imagine that. And what? She broke up with him?"

I nodded.

"And he never knew why. Is that what you are saying?"

I nodded again, and watched as he ate a few more bites of salad, pondering this information. Finally he put down his fork, took a drink of iced tea and carefully set the glass down on the coaster, then looked at me and said, "The first girl I was ever serious about broke up with me. I never knew why. Seems to me when you care about someone, knowing why it didn't work out would be a good thing."

This was taking a turn for the better, here. "I think so, too. I think there are things in these letters that will answer a lot of questions for Frank and may make him feel much better about that part of his life. I can't promise some of it won't be painful, though. You have to be the judge of whether it would be too much for him, as far as his health is concerned."

"Oh, Daddy Frank is in real good shape, mentally, and he's got a good, strong heart. It's his kidneys that are the problem. He needs medical care and regular dialysis, and it had gotten too difficult to arrange while he was living with us. Mama died several years ago, so there was no one home with him during the day, and no one to drive him to the clinic when he started to need more care. It was so much easier on him to go into the assisted living facility. He has his own efficiency apartment and makes his own meals and everything, but the medical team is right there and he doesn't have to leave the building for treatment.

"You know, it was your buying the cabin that enabled us to afford placing him there, so you have already been a blessing to him. And if you think this is something that might bring him peace of mind, then I'm okay letting you ask him if he wants to read the letters."

Mac had been silent through this exchange, but he spoke up then. "Mr. Ledlow ... Davis ... I have a feeling that reading these letters will be a pretty emotional experience. It was for Sarah and I, and we didn't even know Ruth and Frank. But I think Frank would be happier in the long run for learning what Ruth wished she could tell him. You can trust Sarah to let him make his own choice, and if he decides not to read them, we will put them away for him, in case he changes his mind later. We both would still like to meet the man who inspired the kind of deep and abiding love Ruth Winn felt for him. He must be a pretty special guy."

Davis nodded his head. "He is that. Okay, it's settled then. I'll take you guys over to the home. My boy has a Little League game today, though, so I can't stay very long. Would it be okay if you followed me over so I can leave without having to rush you? I mean, assuming it all goes well?"

We made small talk about his experiences playing in Little League as a boy, and now coaching his own son, and then we headed out to our vehicles, ready to leave. I could barely believe it. Finally! We were on our way to meet Frank Everly in person. He had achieved near celebrity status in my mind by that point, and little tickles of anticipation danced along my spine.

Frank Everly. Please, please, please be everything Ruth thought you were. I wasn't sure I could stand it if he turned out to be something less than she had been remembering all those long years by herself.

Chapter 31
Like A Little Injured Bird

I'M NOT SURE why I was so worried. Frank Everly had one of those open, cheerful, boy-next-door faces that just radiated kindness and generosity. I knew within minutes of our arrival that everything Ruth had believed him to be was exactly who he was.

The moment we walked into his apartment, his face lit up with delight at seeing Davis and meeting new people. He welcomed us all into his home with the easy hospitality and friendliness of a down-home country boy who enjoyed having visitors. Mac and I sat on the sofa in his sunny living room area, watching him put on a pot of coffee and set his small table with mugs, creamer and sugar. I felt all my reservations disappear, and I enjoyed watching him laugh and chat with Davis as he worked, asking about his grandsons and their Little League performances.

Mac's friendly smile made it clear he was charmed by the man, as well. Leaning over, he whispered, "He looks like the real deal, to me."

I agreed. And I was surprised at how spry and energetic Frank looked, too, for an 82-year-old man with a serious health problem. No complaining about aches and pains, here.

His hair was the silver color that Ruth had last commented on, but there was still plenty of it, and he had incredible bright blue eyes that seemed to miss nothing. But most of all, it was his wide, sincere smile that seemed to let his real character shine through. I liked him instantly.

When we all sat down at the table to enjoy the coffee, Davis told Frank that I was the new owner of the cabin, not mentioning the fact that Davis now knew who it had belonged to. Frank paused for a moment, the faintest shadow clouding his eyes, and then he smiled. "Well, I hope you're enjoyin' livin' on Wake-Robin Ridge, Sarah."

We had already dispensed with formalities, so my response was in kind. "Thank you, Frank. I love the cabin and the property. It's everything I was looking for." *And some things I wasn't.*

"Daddy Frank, Sarah has something she wants to show you," Davis said.

Frank looked curious but guarded when he turned to me with a questioning lift of his eyebrows. I reached into my tote bag and removed the metal box, setting it on the table between us.

His eyes opened wide in instant recognition. "Why that's one of my old toolboxes," he said, looking confused. "I used to keep files and drill bits in it. Where on earth did you come by that?"

"I found it hidden inside the wall of the pantry. There are some things in here that we thought you might want to know about, Frank."

For the first time, his smile faltered. My heart sped up and I took a deep breath, praying this was the right thing to do. "We believe Ruth wanted you to have this after she died."

To his credit, the first thing Frank did was look at his son in a protective way. Davis gave him a pat on the arm. "It's okay, Dad. I know you used to date Ms. Winn before you and Mama got married. I'm all right about that."

"Son, nothin' that happened way back then changes the way I felt about your mama one bit. Anne was a wonderful wife and I loved her very much, and miss her every day. Don't you ever doubt that."

"I know, Daddy. But I imagine you'll probably want to see what's in this box, and I think you'd be more comfortable about it if I weren't here, so I'm going to head back over to the ball field now, and let you folks talk about these things privately. I'll tell the boys you send your love, and we'll be back to see you for dinner tomorrow, okay?"

They walked to the door, Frank looking grateful to his son, and a bit relieved, as well. After exchanging goodbyes, he sat back down at the table, staring apprehensively at the box. We waited for him to collect his thoughts, and after a moment, he took a deep breath and said, "Okay. Tell me what's in there, please."

My mouth went dry. After all, who were we to barge into Frank's life after all these years and stir up memories of things he had long since moved beyond? Talk about second thoughts. I was working on third, fourth, and fifth thoughts, but it was a little too late to turn back now. Mac squeezed my hand encouragingly, and, mentally crossing my fingers for luck, I took a deep breath and plunged in.

"Letters, Frank. A whole stack of them. All written to you, starting the night Ruth broke up with you, and continuing right up until just before she died."

I watched his face run the gamut of an entire range of expressions as he processed that information, ending with a look of astonished wonder. "Letters? Ruth wrote me letters?"

"She did. She wrote you everything she felt, everything she had wished for, and why she felt things could never happen that way. But mostly, she wrote about how much she loved you, and that never, ever changed, for the rest of her life."

A little, strangled sound escaped him, and his eyes filled with tears. He put his face in his hands and his breathing was harsh for a moment as he tried to regain his composure. Mac went to the sink and filled a glass of water for him, then we both walked to the balcony doors to look outside, giving him a moment to himself.

A few seconds passed, then Frank cleared his throat. "I'm okay now, thanks." His voice was subdued, but he sounded calm, and gave us an embarrassed smile as we came back to the table.

"I know this must be very emotional for you," I told him, "but we wanted to be sure you had a chance to understand what Ruth went through, and how she really felt about you. It's all here, if you want to read it, and some of it is very sad. But it all had such a profound effect on your life at the time, it wouldn't have been right not to let you know what we found."

He nodded. "I appreciate that. And you're right. I want to read it all, hard or not. I always knew there was somethin' she wasn't tellin' me. I couldn't believe she didn't love me, no matter what she said to get me to leave. I knew her heart better than that. I think that's why I waited so long for her to change her mind before I finally moved on. These letters ... they'll explain that?"

"Pretty much. It isn't hard to read between the lines," I said, "once you find out what the main problem was."

He sighed. "She was married, wasn't she?"

I nodded, and he continued. "That's where the R. J. Carter came from, isn't it? I knew Jane was her middle name, but I never saw the name Carter before I was notified about the cabin bein' left to me. That was all I could come up with—that she was married."

I was glad he had already figured a few things out. "Yes, she was. But she had run away from him and was afraid he would find her. She never meant to hurt you, Frank."

He sighed again, swallowed hard, then started to talk in a quiet voice. "I thought that might be it. Even back then, it crossed my mind. I wasn't totally naive about the world. But I didn't want to believe it. I wanted to think she could be mine for always and that I could protect her."

His voice broke. "Someone had hurt her, you know. She would never talk about it, but she had a pretty bad scar right here." He indicated his left temple. "Ran right down through her eyebrow. I figured someone had hit her awful hard to bust her up like that. I couldn't imagine what kind of man could do that to any woman, much less a tiny little thing like Ruth. She was fragile and shy, like a little injured bird. And so sweet." He shook his head, looking down for a moment. "No wonder she ran away from him."

I nodded. "She was lucky to escape alive. And there's something else you should see, as well, Frank." I opened the box and took out the ring, still on the silver chain, and laid it in the palm of his hand.

His gasped, and his eyes filled with tears again. "Oh, Ruth. You did keep it!"

For a moment, he struggled to speak. "She tried to give it back to me, but I didn't want it. I told her I'd given her my heart for all time, and I wasn't goin' to take it back. I was still hopin' she'd change her mind in a few days. Then after a while, I heard she wasn't wearin' it any more, and I thought she'd sold it or somethin'. I didn't mind if she needed the money, you know, but then I thought maybe it was because it wasn't important to her any more."

I shook my head. "She always wore it—every day—just under her clothes so no one would see it."

He turned it over and over, watching the light play across the gems. "I remember the day I gave it to her, like it was yesterday. Christmas, 1964. I think it might have been the happiest day of my life. And then, a month later, well ... that was the saddest day of my life. I just couldn't understand what happened."

He closed his eyes for a minute, buying time until his voice was steady again, then turned to me, puzzled. "Why did she have to hide it? It was hers, and I would never have tried to get it back from her. It wasn't an engagement ring. It was a Christmas present. She could have worn it if she'd wanted to."

"All of the answers are in her letters, Frank, and I think you would understand it better if you read her own words. There are a lot of letters in the stack, so reading them all will take you a while, but I pulled out the first letter, the last one, and five or six in between. They're the ones that tell most of the story. And there's an envelope in the bottom with $6,000 in it. I'm guessing she wanted you to have that, too."

He shook his head, a look of bewilderment on his face. It was a lot for him to take in.

"There was no one else in her life, Frank. I think whatever she had when she died was supposed to go to you."

Brow furrowed, he was very quiet as he thought about what I had told him. "I thought she forgot me. After three years went by, I just gave up. After five, I was ready to start over again. I had been seein' Anne, who was a good woman, with two fine young sons, and I cared very much for her."

He gave me a smile that radiated a gentle sweetness. "There's no limit on how much a heart can love, you know. I loved Anne and we made a good life together. But I never, ever forgot my Ruth. She was ... special." Another sigh slipped from him. "Should I read the letters now?"

"There are some things that Ruth talks about that may startle you," I told him. "It might be best if you read the ones I pulled out while we're still here, in case you have any questions. How would it be if we took a walk and gave you some privacy? We can come back in a little while and talk to you about some of the things she says, if you like? Or you can read them later after we're gone, whichever you prefer."

"No, if you think I might have questions, I'll go ahead and read the ones you're talkin' about. But I thank you for the offer of some privacy. We have a nice pond on the east lawn, with a walkin' path around it, and some benches. Maybe you might take a walk down that way?"

I handed him the smaller stack of letters. "They're in order, and I'm really glad you want to read them, even though some of it might be difficult for you. We'll take that walk now, but we'll be back in a bit."

FRANK GREETED US at the door, looking a bit shell-shocked, but I thought he seemed to be doing pretty darn well for someone who had just read that the woman he loved decades ago had murdered her husband to protect him, and then claimed to have been haunted for years by the ghost of her victim. His face was splotchy, and his eyes were red-rimmed, but he escorted us back to the table, where he had fresh coffee waiting.

"I don't know what to say, Sarah." He paused, taking a deep, steadying breath, then went on. "I'm so grateful that you brought the letters to me. You were right that I needed to read them to understand what had happened. They sure are sad, though. My poor Ruth. It breaks my heart to think of her there alone all those years, tryin' to protect me. Me! And I thought I was goin' to protect her. She was stronger than I ever knew, and braver, too."

Mac and I both nodded our agreement with that, waiting for the questions we knew would be coming.

"She says she killed her husband ... Lloyd. Do you think she really did?"

"Yes, I do. Mac, could you tell Frank what you found out about Lloyd?"

Mac pulled a folded printout from the inside pocket of his jacket, and handed it to Frank. "I did some research on Ruth shortly after we found the letters. You understand we didn't even know who you were at first, and we were just trying to unravel the mystery of this box, and why it was hidden in Sarah's pantry wall."

Frank nodded, and Mac went on. "Well, it's all in here for you, but to sum it up, Ruth married Lloyd Carter in 1950, and in 1962, he beat her up pretty badly, and went to jail. While he was locked up, she disappeared from Macon, Georgia, and reappeared in Asheville, where she bought her cabin.

"Putting together what she said in her letters and what we found online, we think she stole a large sum of money from Lloyd, took his car, and ran away. Lloyd was released from jail in 1965 and almost immediately drops off the grid. He's never been heard from again. It seems logical that he found Ruth, and that she killed him, just like she says in her letters."

Considering this for a minute, Frank agreed. "I think you're probably right, then. If you found nothin' sayin' otherwise, I'm inclined to believe she did it, too."

He gave a small shrug of his shoulders. "I should be more upset over her killin' him than I am, I reckon, especially since she may have done it to protect me, but I swear, there are some people that this world is better off without. And if that sorry so-and-so came after her, it probably wasn't for any sweet talk."

He took a swallow of his water, then went on. "Maybe she would have been charged with murder, and maybe not, but it wouldn't have been a pretty process. And she sure thought she would, so I guess I can see why she hid what she had done. But, there are still so many questions, like, well, what the heck did she do with him? You have any idea about that?"

I shook my head. "Nothing for sure, but I'm afraid he's buried somewhere on the property. There was some reason she didn't want you to come out there any more. She thought you might find him."

We were all quiet for a few minutes, thinking about Ruth trying to decide where to hide a body. This was something I was going to have to sort out when we got back. I really needed to know what she had done with Lloyd if I was ever going to be able to live in my cabin again.

Frank was tapping his fingers on the table, brow furrowed in thought. Then he looked up, eyes wide. "Oh my God! The car! The day before Ruth broke up with me, she bought a truck. Had it delivered to her cabin. She came to the store to show me, and told me that she'd sold the Impala to someone from out of town."

I shook my head, confused. "Would that be important?"

Frank raised his eyebrows at me, then looked at Mac, who said, "Well, yeah. Think about it. She says she killed him in the car. It's why she was afraid of not being believed about the self-defense thing."

I was still not connecting the dots. Frank smiled at me. "You've never used a shotgun, have you?"

And then I got it. "Oh, God. If she killed him in the car, it would be a mess, wouldn't it?"

Mac grimaced. "Oh, yeah. It wouldn't have been in any condition to sell to anyone. Probably ever."

I shuddered, trying not to picture the scene. "So now we don't just have a missing body, we have a missing car. Oh, my. Maybe you were right, Mac, when you said that she had might have moved the body somewhere else. Maybe Lloyd and his car are in a reservoir or on the bottom of a river somewhere? I mean, the car and body could even have been in the backyard when you were there last, Frank, and after she sent you away, she could have driven it somewhere to get rid of it. That's possible, isn't it?"

As awful as it sounded, it was better to me than a body buried in my backyard.

We all thought about it for a few minutes. Frank sighed, again. "Lord. I can't even imagine Ruth havin' to go through all of that. Bad enough he found her, and she had to defend herself and maybe me, but then she's got to handle everything all by herself afterward? It doesn't seem fair, does it?"

"No, it doesn't. A lot of what Ruth went through wasn't fair, but she made her choices and she never complained about them. And as you read, she never regretted letting you move on with your life. She was incredible."

"That was my Ruth." A wistful smile appeared for a moment. "Just the sweetest thing you ever saw. And there she was, watchin' me all those years, to be sure I was doin' okay. Can you imagine? She watched me get married, and came to the ball games, and I never knew."

He was unable to continue for a moment, but then looked at us, eyes glittering. "I saw her that night at the game, though. I remember walkin' back to our seats and lookin' up, and there she was by the bleachers. I just froze. She was so beautiful, it was like seein' a ghost ... or an angel. She looked shocked to see me, too, and she took off across the parkin' lot."

He paused, lost in the memory again, then went on. "I wanted to run after her, but I had no idea what I could have said to her. It had been ... just ... so *many* years! I went back to get more drinks, and joined Anne in the stands, but I didn't see much of that game, I can tell you. I kept wonderin' why she was there, and why she ran. When I read it in her letter, it hit me pretty hard."

It was hitting him pretty hard right now, and I reached over and patted his hand until he was composed again. He looked at me with such sadness, it broke my heart. "All she wanted was to be a little part of my life, just for a few minutes, and I never knew. *I never knew.*"

Shaking his head, Frank went on. "It makes it even worse that she was startin' to imagine things so early on. Do you think it was from bein' alone all the time, or could it have been the tumor she mentions? I mean, seein' ghosts and all? Could it have started causin' her to have hallucinations like that for all those years, before it got worse?"

Mac and I looked at each other. He raised his eyebrows in question, and I nodded, hoping we weren't about to be summarily dismissed as lunatics.

"Well," Mac began, "about that ... "

FIFTEEN MINUTES LATER, Frank had finally quit staring at us in open-mouthed dismay, and was staring instead at the tabletop, in total silence. Mac and I glanced at each other in concern. Frank had looked pretty skeptical when we told him of our experience with Lloyd's ghostly attack, but when he realized we were serious, he had asked three very pertinent questions.

"So, you *both* saw this happen?"

"There was actual physical damage left behind in the cabin after it was over?"

"Neither of you knew anything about Ruth's experiences before this happened?"

We answered yes, yes, and no.

Now he had been quiet for so long, neither of us knew what was coming next. I was afraid he might ask us to leave, thinking we were at best, crazy, and at worst, downright dangerous. But when he raised his head and looked at us, he was definitely not wearing the incredulous expression I expected to see. Instead, he was smiling!

"Well, isn't that somethin'!" He breathed in wonder.

I looked at Mac in confusion, then asked, "You mean you believe us ... and Ruth? And you're okay with it all?"

"Oh, yes. I don't believe either of you is the hysterical type, and now that I know that you experienced the same thing years after Ruth, without any knowledge of her, or her story, well, how could you possibly have made it up?"

I felt relieved, but it still didn't explain his smile. "I must say, I'm curious. The whole thing scared me within an inch of my life. Why does it make you happy, Frank?"

His gentle smile grew wider. "Don't you see? If there are such things as ghosts, then there are surely such things as angels."

Mac smiled, and nodded in agreement, having once said something similar to me.

Frank chose his next words with care. "I'm a simple man, Sarah. I've been a churchgoer all my life, and believe in the mercy and kindness of a loving God, and the possibility of heaven in the afterlife. But I'd be lyin' if I said I haven't had my doubts now and then over the years. The world we live in is always puttin' faith to the test, you know.

"Your story strengthens everything I've ever believed in. To me, if evil can linger after death, why not good? If there's a hell, then there must be a heaven."

His smile grew wider. "It seems to me that I've been blessed with two wonderful and lovin' women in my life, and if I've done my part well enough to make it to heaven myself, I may just have the chance to see them both again. At the very least, I believe they could actually be watchin' over me. Now when I sense them with me, it might not be just wishful thinkin'."

He stood and held his arms open to me. I rose and stepped into his embrace. He gave me a gentle hug, and whispered in my ear, "You've given me more than you can ever know. I thank you with all my heart."

He stepped around the table as Mac stood, and held out his hand. They shook, and then he embraced Mac, too, in one of those hearty man-hugs with much back thumping. "Thank you for comin' all this way, and for bringin' me Ruth's letters," he said, growing solemn again. "I'll treasure them, and I will never forget what you two have done."

"It was our pleasure, Frank. Sarah and I both believed from the start that this box held things that belonged to you, and that it was important that you be able to choose whether or not you wanted to know what had really happened with Ruth. I'm glad I got to be part of this."

It was getting late and we still had the drive to Charlotte to make, so we said our goodbyes. As we were moving toward the door, Frank was going back over the afternoon's discoveries.

"I'm still surprised that Ruth had my old toolbox. I must have left it in her shed. I did a few things for her, you know, like the pantry addition, and I used to leave my stuff in it, so it wouldn't be in Ruth's way in the cabin. Wonder if that's all I left there?"

"I'll keep an eye out, but I haven't seen anything in the cabin," I told him, "and there's no shed on the property."

"Oh. Well, it was a long time ago. Things change. That's a shame, though. It was a real nice one. Anyway, I do hope you're able to get back to enjoyin' your cabin soon, Sarah. It's a special place, and I'm glad it belongs to someone like you, now. Ruth would be happy. She would love you."

I was touched, and felt my eyes filling with tears as we hugged goodbye a second time. We exchanged phone numbers and Frank told us he hoped we would visit him again. I assured him I would call and set a date when we could take him to lunch. I liked Frank, and knew I would enjoy getting to know him better.

"Oh, no!" he said. "You let me know when you're comin' and I'll cook for us. I like cookin', and I don't get much chance to do it any more. It would be a pleasure for me to make lunch for you."

His smile faltered a bit and he gave a deep sigh. "Well, I guess I got me some more readin' to do. I'm real happy to have these letters, but they sure are sad, aren't they? I wish I had known back then what she was going through, but I don't reckon she would have let me help her."

"No, I think not. She wanted you to be safe and to have a wonderful life with someone she thought deserved to be with you. I don't think she ever regretted her decision. She was completely unselfish in her love for you, Frank. You may be right, though. Even though she always thought she would go to hell, Ruth Winn just might be an angel."

Chapter 32
Bagel Man Is Here

SATURDAY, FEBRUARY 25, 2012
CHARLOTTE, NC

DINNER AT THE beautiful and elegant McNinch house was everything Mac said it would be. Ridiculously expensive, wildly romantic, and absolutely delicious, beyond any culinary experience I'd ever had. The turn of the century Victorian home in Charlotte's historic Fourth Ward was the kind of restaurant where guests are treated like royalty—and some of them just might be.

With true southern hospitality, we had been escorted to our table in a small room that might once have been a formal parlor. The fireplace crackled, giving off a warm glow that caused the abundant crystal and silver to sparkle like jewels, and the soft strains of classical music added to the sense of having gone back in time to a far more elegant era. It was a scene right out of Edith Wharton's *Age of Innocence*, and I was impressed by how well Mac fit into these surroundings. He was impeccably turned out in a beautifully made suit, which I thought might be Armani, and he looked as at home amid all this finery as he did while hiking mountain trails in faded jeans and plaid flannel. My Mac. A man for all seasons, and drop-dead sexy in every one of them.

"Do you like it here?" He asked, pale eyes sparkling in the firelight. He poured me a glass of wine so fine it probably cost more than my car.

"Oh, yes! How could I not? It's absolutely lovely. But tell me, MacKenzie Cole, what are we celebrating, dining in such an impressive establishment?"

"We're celebrating *us*, Sarah Gray. Aren't we worth it?"

He reached across the table and took my hand in his, brow furrowing as he thought about what he wanted to say. "Spending the afternoon with Frank has made me even more aware of how important it is to cherish every minute you're given with the people you love. I don't want to end up thinking of all the things I wish I'd done or said, and I never want to throw away another day, especially not one I can spend with you."

He bedazzled me with his gorgeous, megawatt smile. "So why not celebrate being together tonight in the finest restaurant in Charlotte? Let's drink the best wine and eat the most sumptuous dishes, and finish off with some sinfully rich and decadent desserts. Then we will always have this memory, even when we're eating grilled venison on the balcony."

"Never think that grilled venison on your balcony is a step down from anything," I assured him, "but for tonight, I'm delighted to be sharing a meal with you here in the famous McNinch House. And we *will* remember this night, always."

He lifted my hand to his lips and kissed my fingertips, only stopping when he heard our waiter discreetly clear his throat, and ask, "Are you ready to place your order, Sir?"

Oh, what a meal we had! From pear and arugula salad to juniper-brined duck breast and pulled confit leg, accompanied by vanilla parsnip risotto, maple bacon Brussels sprouts and orange crème. These were all things I had never even heard of before, much less eaten, but trust me, they were all deliciously swoon-worthy. "Sinful and decadent" were pretty much on the money for our desserts, too. The buttermilk blue cheese cream puffs, with pickled dried cherries and wildflower honey were divine. Far better than any dessert with the word "pickled" in it ought to be.

"Now that was a dinner worth remembering," Mac said, savoring a last glass of wine.

"Absolutely," I agreed. "The best pulled confit leg I ever ate."

Mac gave me a sardonic look and raised one eyebrow in challenge.

"Okay," I said, "so it was the only pulled confit leg I ever ate. It was still heavenly. Everything was."

"True. But the most delicious-looking thing in this restaurant is you."

Amazing. He could still make me blush like a schoolgirl.

WHEN WE ARRIVED back at Mac's apartment, I placed the single red rose McNinch House traditionally gives their female guests in a small vase, and set it on the table. "If I tied a black ribbon around it, I could pretend it came from the Phantom of the Opera," I told him.

"Do you want me to put on my mask, and take you to my lair?"

"Skip the mask." I gave him my best come-hither look.

It must have worked because he pulled me close to him, and placed his hands on each side of my face. He stood very still for a moment, just looking into my eyes, and then he gave me a slow, sweet kiss. He leaned back, and studied me again. "You *are* mine, aren't you, Sarah? Really mine?"

"Yes, Mac. I'm yours."

"And this isn't just a temporary thing? You *will* be mine forever?"

"As long as I breathe."

"And we'll never grow old apart from each other, alone and forgotten, and not knowing what happened between us?"

"No, Mac. That will never happen to you and me. Not ever. Not for any reason. I'll always be yours, and I'll never leave you, I promise you. As long as you want me, I'll be here." I repeated slowly, with emphasis, "I will *never* leave you."

Satisfied, he leaned his forehead against mine, and whispered, "Sarah. My Sarah. I love you more than you can possibly imagine."

His fingers traced along the neckline of my slinky, low-cut dinner dress. "You look beautiful, tonight, you know. You are gorgeous in black. Very sexy."

"It's the stunning green earrings someone gave me for Christmas."

"Well, they are beautiful. Maybe that *is* all it is." He removed them, and looked me over again. "No. That wasn't it. Still beautiful."

"Well then surely it's the dress?"

He slid his hand behind my back and slowly pulled the zipper down, the sound making me shiver. Then he slipped the narrow straps off my shoulders, and let the dress fall to the floor. "Hmmm. No dress, now. Still beautiful, though.

Maybe more so. Of course, it could be that lacy black lingerie. Follow me, and we'll see if that's all it is."

Taking my hand, Mac pulled me into the bedroom, where he paused beside the bed, and reached for me.

I stopped his hand. "Turnabout is fair play, you know. I think I should also get a chance to see if clothes really make the man, or if you're equally gorgeous without them."

He had taken his jacket off when we first came into the apartment, so I removed his tie and silk shirt, then stood admiring his smooth chest for a moment.

"Well?" He asked.

"So far, so good," I said. "Still looking pretty damn gorgeous." I couldn't help but notice I was sounding a bit on the breathless side. Seeing Mac shirtless always had that effect on me.

He slid his hands up my back, the warmth of his touch making me breathe even faster. Bending forward, he kissed the swell of my breast above the lace cups of my bra, and then, my bra joined his shirt on the floor. After that, it was a matter of mere seconds before we were both naked and lying on the bed.

"Hold still, Sarah," he murmured. "Hold very still and let me love you."

His fingertips slid over my body, caressing me with exquisite tenderness ... just the barest of touches skimming along the surface of my skin. Everywhere his fingers stroked, his lips followed ... my neck, my collarbone, my shoulders. Stroking and kissing, taking his time as he moved down my arms, stopping to kiss inside the bend of each. He lingered over the sensitive skin on the underside of one wrist, then the other, his tongue tasting the pulse points. I was shivering with desire, holding still almost impossible.

Shifting down the bed, he kissed the arch of my right foot, then began working upward again, stopping to kiss behind my knee and continuing up my leg. His tongue was warm and erotic against my hipbone, and as he tasted that little hollow just beside it. He worked his way across my tummy to my other hip, then continued kissing his way down the outside of my left leg.

When he reached that knee, he changed course, and began to work upward along my inner thigh, his tiny kisses and licks leaving me gasping. A sound somewhere between a whimper and a sob escaped me, and Mac gave a low growl in response, though his progress never slowed down. I let him love me exactly as he wanted to, and soon felt my whole body go up in flames, as I cried out his name again and again.

In an instant, he was poised above me, looking directly into my eyes as our bodies joined together. Moving very slowly and deliberately, he made love to me in a way he never had before, gazing straight into my soul the entire time. He held back nothing of himself and never looked away, until he gasped, shuddering, and collapsed against me, murmuring my name over and over into the hollow between my neck and shoulder.

Afterward, Mac pulled me to him, face to face, and stroked my hair as his heartbeat slowed down to a steady pace. "You're everything I've ever wanted in this world," he whispered. "You *are* my world."

We fell asleep like that, wrapped around each other, face to face, complete in our love.

SUNDAY, FEBRUARY 26, 2012

"WAKE UP, SLEEPYHEAD! Bagel Man is here!"

I opened one eye and smiled lazily. "Bagel Man? You moonlighting these days? Will I have to tip you?" Then both eyes opened wide. "Is that coffee I smell?"

Mac grinned. "Yep. It's on the table waiting for you."

"Your coffee? Or the bagel shop's?"

"Mine, of course. I might lose my mysterious power over you if I gave you anything else."

Two minutes later, I was sitting at the dining room table, eating bagels with cream cheese and drinking Mac's Magic Mojo coffee.

"I swear, I don't know how you do this. I've been a confirmed tea drinker all my life, but your coffee is divine. Heavenly. Nectar of the gods! What do you do that makes it so much better than anyone else's?"

"It's my secret. No one can ever know. Not even you, Sarah Gray."

"Okay, but you can never stop making it for me, MacKenzie Cole."

"Deal."

I looked around his apartment, admiring the clean, masculine way it was furnished, in neutral grays and soft creams. "So this is where you lived before you built your house?"

"Uh-huh. For nearly ten years. I was going to sell it when I moved to the Ridge, but then I thought about how often I come to town, and I decided I'd rather stay here than at a hotel. Now it doubles as a guest unit for anyone at my office who has out-of-town company coming. Miranda, my bookkeeper, handles it, and it gets used several times a year by various family members of my staff. It's a nice perk for them, and I maintain access to it, as well."

"You are good to your employees."

"I have really good people working for me. Most of them have been with my company since the beginning. I treat them well, and they stay happy and productive. It works out all the way around."

"When are we going by your office, so I can meet everybody?"

"I thought maybe we'd go in tomorrow around ten or so, and then we can get lunch before we hit the road for home. Sound good?"

"Sounds good."

Mac had gotten a bit restless as we were talking. Now he was pacing around the room, idly picking up books and bits of pottery, then putting them down again. He wandered over to the front balcony and stood looking out for a minute, then walked back to the couch and sat down. Two minutes later, he was on his feet again and walking around with his hands in his pockets.

I couldn't stand it any longer. "Mac? Come sit down with me a minute."

He came back to the table and perched on a chair, but kept glancing off toward the windows. I took his hand, and he turned back to me, still looking distracted.

"Would you feel better going to see Ben alone?" I asked.

"What? No. Unless you don't want to go, that is. I mean, I'd understand if you didn't."

"I would like to go very much, but only if you are ready to take me with you. It doesn't have to be today. If you've changed your mind, I can wait here."

He smiled at me and shook his head. "No, I'd like to take you. I'm sorry I'm jittery. It's not because of you. Not really. I usually feel unsettled when I'm going. Some trips are harder than others, but I want you with me, if you want to go. It feels strange, is all. I've never been to his grave with another person before, not even my parents, so it just ... feels strange."

"Okay, then we'll go together. When would you like to head over?"

"I was thinking right after lunch, but maybe it would be better to just get ready and leave now? Would that be all right? I haven't been in so long, I feel guilty, and that's probably making me edgy as well."

"I think going sooner is better than later. I can be ready in thirty minutes. Can you?"

He smiled, relaxing a bit. "I can, as long as you don't distract me. I won't be held responsible for any delays if you go parading around in those lacy bits from last night."

I was *so* tempted. But I didn't.

I SAT ON A wrought iron bench in the shade of a towering magnolia, and watched Mac as he stood at his son's grave, a few feet away. I felt he should have a moment or two alone with Ben before I joined him. He stood there, head bowed, speaking in a low, quiet voice.

After a few minutes, Mac turned toward me and held out his hand. Carrying a bouquet of tulips and daffodils, I joined him by the grave. He put his arm around me, pulling me to his side, and turned back to face the small angel that knelt at the head of Ben's resting place.

His voice was rough with emotion. "I talk to him, you know."

"Of course."

I felt him relax a bit, and then, just loud enough to be heard, he said, "I love you and I always will." I knew he was talking to Ben, so I stood waiting as he continued. "This is Sarah. I love her, too. She's very special, and she's brought you flowers today."

He let go of me and I stepped forward to put the flowers on the grave. "To remind you of spring," I whispered, and returned to Mac's side.

We stood there in silence a few more minutes, and then we went back to the bench and sat down. Mac was holding my hand tightly, lost in thought. Every now and then he would take a deep, shaky breath, and I knew he was struggling to stay composed. Being deeply moved by visiting his son's grave was understandable, but letting it chase him back into an emotional hole was not a good thing. If being with me helped him face this without going over that cliff again, I was happy to hold his hand for as long as it took.

When he could breathe evenly again, and his grip on my hand relaxed, I thought maybe it was time to talk to him about an idea I had gotten a few weeks ago. I crossed my mental fingers that it was something that would help Mac reach some measure of peace, if not that indefinable thing called closure.

"Mac?" He turned toward me, and I went on. "I was wondering ... what is the hardest part about coming to visit Ben's grave?"

He didn't hesitate. "Leaving. Knowing he's here by himself, all alone, day after day. I can't even think about it."

I paused a moment, wanting to get this just right. "Why do you have to leave him here?"

He stared at me, confused.

I continued. "Well, think about this. You have twenty beautiful acres in the part of the world you most wanted to share with Ben. You could bring him home with you. The little glade where we cut your Christmas tree would be a perfect resting spot for him, and you could visit him any time you wanted. Every day, if you wanted. He'd be right there, close to you, and you'd never have to think about him being alone again."

It was as if time had come to a halt, and Mac was frozen in place. Not a muscle moved. Not a hint of expression showed on his face. I was terrified I'd gone too far, and touched on his personal grief in a way I had no right to do. Then he turned and looked at Ben's grave, and when he looked back at me, I saw a cautious hope in his eyes. "Can you even do that? Is it legal?"

"Yes it is. I did some research, and there is no state law that prohibits burial on private property. I checked with the county, and as long as you follow a few basic restrictions, there's no problem."

"I could bring him home?" He whispered, as much to himself as to me. "Oh, my God. I never thought ... I didn't know. Oh, my God, Sarah. He could be with me and not alone here where no one even knows who he is?"

I nodded.

It seemed almost too much for him to process. He reached for me and buried his face on my shoulder. I put my arms around him and held him for a few minutes, then he pulled away, looking at Ben's grave once more.

"People walk right by that kneeling angel every day, and no one knows a thing about the little boy resting there. It has always hurt me, especially after I left Charlotte, but I never once thought about moving him. Why is that? You've only been in my life a few months, and you thought of it. Why did it never even cross my mind?"

"Well, maybe you were too close to the pain and grief. Maybe you just couldn't think beyond how much it hurt. But be fair to yourself. It's not something people do every day. And Ben has been here a long time. I don't think it's surprising that you never thought of it. As for why I did, well that's simple. I was watching *you*."

I reached over and brushed his hair back, just wanting to touch him. "I could see how having him so far away made you sad. I wanted to know if there was a way to resolve that, so I looked. And there is, if you want to do it."

"Oh, yes. I want to do it. I want to start the process as soon as we get back. I want to bring Ben home."

He pulled me to him in a hug so fierce, it was hard to breathe, and I knew Mac would never have to feel heartbroken about Ben being far away and alone again. "If it's what you want, then you definitely should start making some calls and getting the wheels in motion. It will involve getting permits and paying fees, and hiring someone to prepare the site. But once that's done, it shouldn't take very long, and then he can be right there, near you."

Shaking his head with an expression of wonder on his face, Mac leaned over and kissed me. "You give me back pieces of myself every day." He kissed me again. "You are a miracle, Sarah Gray. *My* miracle."

He walked back to Ben's grave, and I could see him talking again. I knew he was saying goodbye, and sharing the plan to bring Ben home to Wake-Robin Ridge. Everything about Mac's body language was different than it had been during his earlier graveside conversation, and when he walked back to me, there was also a profound difference in the expression on his face. Even his step was lighter, as though a bit more of the weight he carried on his shoulders had been lifted.

MONDAY, FEBRUARY 27, 2012
CHARLOTTE, NC

MAC'S SUITE OF offices was very impressive. All sleek glass and chrome, with state of the art electronics everywhere, yet with a warm and inviting reception area for clients who chose to drop by in person. It was larger than I had imagined, and there were at least twenty people at various workstations, all busy tracking down information and processing data.

We walked in unannounced, and it was nice to see all the surprised smiles throughout the office. Mac gave a quick wave to everyone, saying we'd be back after checking in with Miranda, then steered me down a carpeted hallway, past a large and inviting break room, to a door marked Accounting. The name Miranda Phillips was lettered in gold beneath that. He stuck his head in the open door. "Are you busy, Miranda? I have someone I'd like you to meet."

"Mac! I didn't know you were coming by." The woman rising to greet us was a very trim sixty-something, with beautiful silver hair in a stylish, shaggy cut. She was all smiles at the sight of Mac, and gave him a big hug in greeting.

When she let him go, she turned to me before Mac could say a word, and held out her hand. "I'm Miranda Phillips. Please have a seat."

I returned her handshake and said, "I'm Sarah Gray, Mac's neighbor."

Mac laughed, and said, "She's so much more than that, Miranda." He put his arm around me and gave me a quick squeeze. "I wanted you to meet her before anyone else, but we had to run the gauntlet to get back here. I didn't do introductions, though. I didn't want to deprive you of the pleasure. I expect the whole office is abuzz by now."

The look on Miranda's face was one of complete astonishment, which gradually morphed into delight. She took both of my hands in hers. "Oh, my, my, my. I never thought I'd live long enough to see Mac with a girlfriend. This is wonderful! Why haven't you said anything, Mac?"

He gave her a crafty smile. "I have to have some secrets, you know, even from you. Besides, I wanted you to meet her before I told you about us."

"Well, you certainly succeeded in keeping this secret quiet. I'm delighted with the news. It's about time you found someone to keep you on the straight and narrow."

I laughed. "I'm not sure how I'm doing with that, Miranda. Mac pretty much chooses his own path, without much help from me."

There was a knock at the door, and one of the staffers stuck his head in and asked Mac if he wanted to see the reports on the Bratton case, and Mac excused himself and disappeared with the young man, leaving us to "get acquainted," as he put it.

Miranda sat in one of the chairs across from her desk, and indicated I take the other one. She wasted no time at all. "Do you love him?" she asked in a voice that indicated lying to her wouldn't be tolerated.

"I love him very much," I said, looking her straight in the eyes without flinching, which wasn't as easy as it might sound. I had a feeling she'd take me out in a heartbeat if my answer wasn't convincing. It must have done the job, because she relaxed and sat back in the chair, her smile friendly again.

"Sorry if I sounded blunt, but Mac is like a second son to me. I couldn't stand it if anyone were to hurt him again. I am assuming you know about his ex-wife and the loss of his son?"

"Yes," I nodded. "Mac has told me a lot about what he went through."

Her face clouded for a moment. "You can't imagine how bad it was for him. And then he just walled himself off. I had pretty much given up hope that he would ever let anyone into his life again, though it sure wasn't for a lack of women chasing around after him, I can tell you that. He was determined to keep them all at arm's length, though, and he did. The rest of us, too, for a very long time. He's still cautious, even with friendships, so you can imagine how surprising this news is."

"Yes, I can understand why you would be concerned about any woman entering his life. All I can tell you is, I don't take Mac for granted, and I treasure every moment we're together. I will never, ever lie to him or betray him, and I trust him to treat me the same way."

"Good to know. Mac doesn't do flings, you know. He never does anything by halves." She rose to her feet. "Come on. Let's go introduce you to everyone else before they implode from curiosity. I've been waiting a long time for this! Can't wait to see the expressions on their faces."

She linked her arm through mine, and walked me back out to the main office. I could see Mac inside a glass cubicle, he and the young man who had whisked him away studying some printouts spread across a table.

Miranda took me around to every desk and introduced me as Mac's girlfriend. I admit, it gave me a little shiver of pure pleasure, every time she said it, and I could see why she was having fun with this.

One by one, their looks of stunned disbelief changed into delighted grins. It seemed that everyone was happy for Mac, and they all, at one point or another, made sure to tell me he was a wonderful boss, and a decent guy.

At one point, I looked at Mac just in time to see him raise his head and take in the scene. He knew exactly what was happening. He shrugged his shoulders and gave me a sheepish grin, and I realized he had planned things just this way, knowing Miranda would take over and save him from having to tell people over and over that yes, he had finally found a girlfriend.

"Devious," I mouthed at him.

He nodded in agreement, happy to see his plan had worked.

When Mac came back out, he was inundated with wolf whistles and all sorts of congratulatory remarks, largely consisting of things like, "How did you get so lucky as to find a girl like Sarah? She looks far too good for you, Mac." He took the ribbing with good humor, and I could see that he enjoyed having surprised them all.

When we left, he whispered something in Miranda's ear that made her laugh, then hugged her goodbye. When I asked him what he had said, he grinned. "I asked her to let me know who won the pool."

When I frowned, he explained, "They've had a pool going for a long time about whether or not I'd ever meet someone and settle down. I'm not supposed to know about it. I think the choices range from "Stranger things have happened" to "When Hell freezes over." Miranda tells me the wagers are always changing. I imagine they started a whole new round of bets when I walked in with you."

I laughed. "I'd love to be a fly on the wall right now. I'll bet they're all talking at once."

"Oh, yeah. I'm sure they think my having a girlfriend means it's The End Of Days."

And on that thought, we grabbed some lunch and headed home. I found I couldn't wait to get back to Wake-Robin Ridge. Visiting Frank had been a moving experience, and Charlotte had been filled with emotion—and passion as well—but my heart was in those mountains, and I was ready to go back. I had a cabin to reclaim, ghost or no ghost, a book to finish, and I was missing Handsome and Rosheen. My life was there on Wake-Robin Ridge, and that was just fine by me.

Chapter 33
Possible Doesn't Mean It's a Fact

"HANDSOME! GET DOWN from there, you wicked boy!" I shooed my kitty off my dining room table, where he had been busy scattering pages of my manuscript all over the floor. "I guess that's what I get for daring to take a bathroom break and leaving my work unguarded for three whole minutes."

I gathered all the loose sheets of paper, put them back in order, and tucked them in the big folder labeled "First Draft." Sighing, I slapped the folder down beside my laptop, and went to make myself a cup of tea. This day was not going well at all. Maybe Earl Grey would help. It certainly couldn't hurt. I could go back across the way and see if Mac would make me a cup of his fabulous coffee, but that would mean giving in, and I wasn't ready to admit defeat yet. Bad day or no bad day, I was supposed to be getting some work done.

Outside my dining room window, a cardinal was singing in the dogwood tree, which was becoming an absolute storm of white blossoms. Inside, the storm was much darker. Oh, the cabin was ship-shape again, thank goodness. I had been coming down for a few hours every day since we got back from Charlotte, cleaning up the last of the mess from our personal Fright Night, and doing all the dusting and sweeping that a house needs when it's been empty for more than a month.

The living room window had been repaired, and I frowned, remembering how hard Mac had worked, spending two afternoons patching my pantry drywall and replacing the shelves. I nibbled at my thumbnail, wondering if it had been part of a need to ease me back out of his house and regain his privacy. Love me or not, he was a man who had lived by himself for many years. He had to be feeling a bit cramped since I moved in.

I sighed. Now I was craving chocolate, in addition to the tea. *Chocolate helps everything, right?* I settled for some stale, broken bits of Oreo cookies I found lurking in a canister. It would have to do until I went shopping, and restocked my shelves.

I wandered aimlessly around the living room, munching on the dry cookies. I knew the cabin was pretty much ready for me to move back into, and I wasn't really afraid of any ghostly visits at this time of year, yet I still hesitated to bring all my things back down here. I wasn't ready to return to living without Mac, even though I sensed it would be coming to that soon. But right now, I had something else on my mind.

It appears that a five-week break in the middle of writing a book is fatal to my personal creative process. I'm talking about total Kiss Of Death stuff, here. I had lost it. Gone. The few mornings I had even toyed with writing while staying with Mac didn't count. I was far too distracted by his presence to lose myself in my work.

"What was I thinking, going that long without working on this story?" Yeah, okay, I wasn't so much thinking as just enjoying being with Mac all the time, but now I was paying for it. Obviously, too much good lovin' makes me stupid.

It wasn't just temporary writer's block, oh no. It was more like a sudden sense that this book wasn't even worth pursuing. I had to restrain myself from grabbing all of the pages and burning them in the fireplace, which would, of course be a futile and symbolic gesture, since the document is saved on my laptop. But the bottom line was, I hated it. Hated. It. And after several days of fruitless attempts to write a single worthwhile paragraph, I was in a definite stall.

Maybe I really don't have a decent book in me, after all. Maybe after all these years of thinking of myself as a writer, I'm going to have to face the possibility that I'm not.

"Who's gonna fill your cat bowl then, Handsome?"

Handsome looked at me from the sofa, purring, then continued to wash his face in a nonchalant manner that clearly said, "You'll figure it out. Not my concern."

"Ah, the hell with it!" I muttered, closing my laptop. I wandered onto my back porch, and stared at the stream, my thoughts drifting back to all the discoveries of the past few weeks. I made a mental note to call Frank Everly later on, and make plans to go see him. There was still so much I wanted to know about Ruth and her life here in my cabin. She was on my mind more and more, every day.

The creek was running high this time of year, water rushing by in a mad frenzy of white foam. It was a beautiful sight, swirling along under the trees, and after a few minutes, I felt the knots of tension in my neck and shoulders loosen. I smiled, picturing how nice it was going to look with all the overgrowth along the banks cleared out. I could take my laptop out to the chairs down there and write. How inspirational would that be? Of course, clearing it all away was going to be a heck of a job, but Mac had told me he'd help.

A tangled jungle of wild blackberry bushes reached as high as my head, and the kudzu was totally out of control. The blasted stuff had consumed a whole corner of the yard, reaching fifteen or twenty feet high, and so thick that I figured it would take heavy equipment to get rid of all of it. I shook my head, sighing. It was sure to be a hefty expense, even if it was worth it in the long run. I wasn't in desperate shape for money, but I would be, if I didn't start adding to my coffers soon. I needed to produce something I could sell, or I was going to have to think about getting a job.

"Damn, stupid kudzu, eating half my property! Heck, Handsome, we're lucky the blasted stuff is confined to the yard!" He was standing beside me, staring out the door, too. I let him out, thinking about pictures I'd seen where kudzu had swallowed up entire buildings.

I was heading back into the house to be sure there were no more Oreos anywhere when a sickening thought slithered through my mind. I stopped in my tracks, then turned and stared at the big, ugly snarl of vines and new green leaves. A shiver went through me as I remembered some of the photos I'd seen. Kudzu could swallow whole buildings, all right. Buildings like ... sheds!

Bits of conversation from last Saturday tumbled through my mind. " ... my old toolbox ... must have left it in her shed ... Oh, my God, the car ... we don't just have a missing body, we have a missing car ... she's got to handle everything all by herself afterward ... it was a real nice shed ... "

The hair on the back of my neck stood up, and my mouth went dry as dust. I felt rooted to the spot.

Oh, good Lord! Surely not. Surely there's not anything under that tangled mess? And even if there is, well, that doesn't mean it's anything awful, does it?

Even as I denied the possibility, something inside me already knew better. It made perfect sense. My heart pounded, and I ran back into the kitchen and grabbed my phone. With shaking fingers, I hit Mac's number.

"Hello, Sarah Gray," he drawled in a slow, sexy voice. "Missing me already?"

I swallowed twice before I could speak, and still my voice was strained. "Mac? Can you come down here? Please?"

His tone changed in an instant. "What's wrong? Are you all right?" I heard him push his chair back, already on the move.

"Just come, please. And Mac? Bring a chain saw."

MAC FROWNED AND cleared his throat. "Well, I guess it's possible. But don't go getting alarmed yet, Sarah. *Possible* doesn't mean it's a fact."

He had been standing on my back porch for several minutes, staring intently at the offending mound of kudzu. The look of doubtful skepticism he had worn when I first explained my theory slowly faded away, as he studied the size and density of that tangled hill of vines. He took a deep breath. "Okay, then. Might as well find out, if just to put your mind at rest. Grab a broom, and we'll take a closer look. Unless you'd rather wait here?"

"No, I'll go with you." I followed him out the back door, bringing the broom, and wondering what he planned to do with it. We crossed the yard and stopped in front of the largest mountain of leaves. Mac took the broom and pushed the handle into the middle of the greenery. He poked and prodded around for a few minutes, trying several places, with no results.

"I'm not feeling anything in there. It's likely just leaves and vines all the way through," he reassured me. He kept poking, though. "Maybe if I had something longer." He stopped to survey the wall of glossy green leaves and thick, twisted vines.

"Would some old conduit do? There are a couple of pieces of some kind of pipe under the back steps, left behind from some old project, I guess."

"Worth a try. We can push them in a bit deeper and see if we feel anything solid in there."

Five minutes later, we were each pushing a length of metal pipe as far into the dense, tangled vines as we could, checking out random spots. I was developing a rhythm. Poke. Nothing. Move over a bit. Poke. Nothing. Move over again. Poke. Nothing.

I was starting to feel a bit silly, and was about to tell Mac to forget about the whole idea, when I moved another foot to my left and shoved the pipe in almost the full length.

Thunk.

I gasped and dropped the pipe, scrambling backward so fast, I plopped down on the ground. Maybe I didn't need to know what was under there, after all.

Mac came over to where my piece of pipe was protruding from the vines. He pushed his in a foot farther away, hard.

THUNK!

Breath I didn't realize I was holding whooshed out of me.

He moved four feet farther along and tried again. Another solid thunk. Another poke, another *thunk*. He dropped the pipe and turned to me. "I think it's time for me to fire up the chainsaw."

AN HOUR LATER, Mac had carved a rough, door-shaped tunnel into the kudzu. It extended about 4 feet deep, and the back wall of the tunnel was a solid mass of dead, brown vines, way too thick to see through at all. By jamming one of the pipes into it, we could tell we were still at least 5 feet shy of exposing whatever structure was hidden inside.

Slicing through the new growth and then the ropy, dead tangle underneath was hard work. Mac had bits of leaves and vine stuck in his hair and all over his clothes, and was sweating, despite the fairly cool day.

While he ran the chainsaw, I piled the debris into a large stack in the middle of one of my empty garden beds. I figured we would have to burn it later, so I was trying to mound it in a spot where a fire wouldn't be a hazard. At least, that's what I told myself. Mostly, I was just trying to give myself something to do, so I wouldn't keep thinking about what I was afraid we were going to discover. I continued to pretend there was nothing awful hidden under the kudzu at all, but I wasn't fooling myself, and I could tell by the look of grim determination on Mac's face that he had a bad feeling about this, as well.

After another thirty minutes, Mac shut the chain saw off, and turned to me. I dropped my bundle of vines and walked over to his side. He still had a way to go, but had cleared enough vines that we no longer needed to use the pipes to feel what was inside. We could now see a section of dirty white concrete block dead ahead, with what looked to be a portion of a gray metal door showing to the left.

I sighed, and turned to Mac. "It's a shed, isn't it?"

"I think so, Sarah. Looks like I'm just a couple of feet too far to the right to be able to access the door, but I'll start cutting in that direction—unless you want me to call the sheriff and have them send somebody to help clear it away?"

"Oh, do we have to yet? Maybe it will just be an empty shed. Or a shed full of old tools and stuff. Maybe I'm totally wrong. I'd hate to get the sheriff involved at this point. I don't want to tell them about Ruth's letters unless we have no choice. Do you?"

"No, not really. It doesn't seem fair to expose her when we don't even know what we're dealing with here. I say let's have some lunch first, then I'll start shifting the direction a bit and see if I can uncover the whole door."

So that's what we did. After we ate, Mac went back to work carving his way, bit by bit, through the nearly impenetrable wall of kudzu, and I worked clean-up detail, loppers at the ready when needed. Between us, we made better progress than I would have imagined, but it was still slow, hard work.

I was raking up another pile of debris when the chainsaw went silent. Turning, I watched Mac emerge from the middle of the mound. He put the saw on the ground and looked at me, eyebrows raised. Dread weighed down my movements, my feet heavy and slow as I walked toward him. He opened his arms, and I went straight to them, thinking how lucky I was to have such a warm haven.

Together, we turned back toward the mound, Mac's arms still around me. I was astonished at how much more vine he had cut away while I had been raking. The entire door to the shed—and there was no getting around that it was a shed—was exposed. The wide, gray metal door was secured by a large padlock and rusted around the edges. I knew it was the last barrier between us and the truth. For a moment, I wished I could cover it all back up again.

Mac pulled me closer, and kissed the top of my head. "You are one smart lady, you know that?"

I sighed. "Right now, I wish I had never thought of this. I'd like to go back to yesterday."

Mac shook his head. "No, you don't. Not really. You needed to know, one way or the other, so you can put this behind you. It'll be all right, no matter what. Let me go get my bolt cutters and flashlight from the truck. Be right back."

"Hey! I'm not staying out here by myself." I trotted after him. "I may never be able to stay out here in this back yard by myself again!"

A few minutes later, Mac had cut through the padlock and removed it from the door. He turned to me. "Ready?"

"As I'll ever be." My heart thudded loudly in my chest, and I shivered, wrapping my arms around myself.

He took a deep breath and pulled hard on the door, dragging it across the stubble of vines and dirt on the ground an inch at a time. I stood to one side, peering into the widening crack. Within seconds, pale sunlight leaked into the shed, revealing a dusty glimmer of red metal and a bit of dirty chrome. There was no doubt about it. Our ghostly Impala was inside.

"I'll be damned," breathed Mac.

I think I may have whimpered.

When the door was wide enough, Mac stepped inside with the flashlight. With both hands clamped over my mouth, I watched as he leaned over and shone it through the front window of the car. He straightened to look at me, and I had my answer.

Crap. This is really happening. Crap, crap, crap!

"I want to see for myself." I entered the shed to stand beside Mac.

"Are you sure? It's not pretty."

"It can't be worse than how his ghost looked—as though he had just been shot that day."

Mac handed me the flashlight and stepped back. I forced myself to bend down and peer into the front seat.

"Oh, my God!" I breathed. There was no more denying it. Lloyd Carter had been killed in his big, red Impala, and locked in Ruth's shed. He had been waiting the better part of fifty years for us to open that door and find him.

I took it all in, trying to make sense of the mess in the car. The body had been reduced to bones, for the most part, and not all of them were still connected together. Rotted denim encased his lower body, though foot bones and part of one leg appeared to have fallen onto the floor of the car, where it was stuck in some sort of dried glop that I didn't want to look at too closely. His torso was jammed against the passenger door in a totally unnatural way, as though Ruth had shoved him there, maybe in order to drive the car back here. My stomach did a slow roll at the thought.

Geeze, Ruth. Where did you ever find the nerve to do that?

The windshield of the car was covered with dried gore and bits of matter that could only have been bone and brain. Most of his head was gone, after all, and I suspected that was what had sprayed all over the dash and window. I straightened, feeling a wave of nausea pass over me.

Mac stepped back to my side, putting an arm around me. "Okay?"

"I will be as soon as I get out of here."

Though the smell of death was not overwhelming inside the shed, since all the windows and doors on the car were closed, it was still there. Old blood and rot did not encourage lingering. But as I turned to follow Mac back outside, something in the back seat caught my eye.

"Wait, Mac." I shone the flashlight in the rear window. "What's that? Is that ... oh God, are there more bones in the back?" A chill ran down my spine.

Please, please don't let there be any other bodies.

Leaning closer, I could see remnants of another garment on the back seat. It looked like brittle pieces of vinyl, and there was a hood of some sort showing. Maybe a raincoat? I could also see what looked like an old glove, and yes, there were definitely some smaller bones protruding from underneath that. A rounded piece, like part of a tiny skull, and what looked like arm bones!

Mac stood beside me, staring into the car with a perplexed expression on his face. "What the hell?"

No, no, no!

I wanted to cover my ears and run away. Instead, I put my hand on his arm, and braced for the worst.

"Mac, please tell me that's not ... a *baby*?" It was all I could do to get the words out.

He turned to me at once. "Oh, no, Sarah! No, don't worry. It's not a baby, I promise. I'm pretty sure it's a rabbit. But I just can't imagine what it's doing there."

Not a baby. A rabbit!

I could breathe again. But I couldn't wait to get out of the shed, and apparently Mac felt the same way. He closed the door behind us, and we walked back to my house in silence. I washed my hands and put on a pot of coffee.

Mac splashed cold water on his face and arms, and dried off with paper towels, lost in thought. Then he turned to me with an apologetic shrug. "Unfortunately, it's time to call the sheriff. I think it's fair to say we have found Lloyd Carter. What the rabbit has to do with anything, I have no idea."

Chapter 34
Yesterday's News

SATURDAY, MARCH 10, 2012

"IS THAT THE last of them?" I asked Mac, as we stood on my front porch and watched the big truck disappearing down my driveway.

"I think so," he replied with a tired sigh. "God, what a week!"

And it had been. We had spent two hours with the Sheriff late last Saturday afternoon, showing him what we found in the shed, and answering questions.

"Well now, I knew ol' Miz Winn for years," he had said, shaking his head in disbelief. "Never woulda suspected her of anything like this! And you say y'all have letters from her admittin' to havin' killed this person?"

"Yes, we do," I had responded. "The man in the car is undoubtedly her husband, Lloyd Carter. Mac has records that indicate he had beaten her severely enough to put her in the hospital for a week, and when she got out, she took his car and ran away from him. We think he found her and she shot him when he threatened to kill her and her boyfriend at the time, Frank Everly. And here he is, car and all, so I don't think there will be much doubt as to what happened here."

"I don't reckon there will be. The M.E. said the body has been here for decades, so I think that speaks for itself. Sure never seen nothin' like that rabbit in the back seat before. Course, this is the first time I ever saw a corpse in a car, hidden in a shed for decades, too. The whole thing's just weird."

I glanced at Mac, but neither of us said a word. I had told him earlier what I had seen hanging in my kitchen window on the night of the haunting, and we both thought killing a rabbit sounded like something Lloyd would dream up to terrorize Ruth. There was no way to explain our theory about the remains without discussing what Mac and I had seen ourselves, and we weren't prepared to do that.

Taking off his hat, the sheriff scratched his balding head. "We'll have to have an investigation, you understand, for the record. I don't know if you'll be asked to testify to anything, but since you've only been here a few months, I doubt it. Still, we'll need to cover all the bases before we close it out."

"Sheriff, what'll happen to the body?" I asked.

"Well, after the M.E.'s office determines the cause of death, it'll be released, and the county will bury it, unless they can find next of kin somewhere who wants to claim it. Don't you worry none, Miss Gray. It'll all be taken care of."

We had promised to be as helpful as we could, and the sheriff and his crew went on about their business, stringing crime scene tape everywhere, and taking all sorts of photographs.

I had called Frank the next morning to tell him what we had found. He was even more astonished than the sheriff had been. I asked him to have his son send us copies of the letters where Ruth talks about having killed Lloyd, without any of the bits referring to Lloyd's after-death shenanigans, of course. Everything was dutifully turned over to the authorities, and once the medical examiner had cleared the shed, removing both Lloyd's remains and the Impala, we were allowed to clean up.

We had hired a crew with heavy machinery to clear out everything else—kudzu, shed, and all. It took them several more days to finish the job. As the last truck rumbled down my driveway, filled to capacity with vines, broken block, and chunks of concrete, I felt nothing but weary relief, and a strange sense of melancholy.

We walked back inside together, hand in hand, and sat down next to each other on the couch. "How are you feeling, Sarah?" I saw real concern in Mac's eyes as he studied me.

I managed a tired smile for him, and leaned against his shoulder. "Glad it's over. Glad every trace of Lloyd Carter is gone from my property. And hopeful that whatever hold he's had on this cabin is gone now that his body's been taken away. I want that sense of peace back—that *rightness* that I felt the first day I moved in here—so that being here feels good again."

Mac looked away, not saying anything for a moment. Then he gave a slight nod. "I'll help you move back in whenever you are ready." He stood and walked to the back porch to look out over the now cleared banks of my creek.

Well. So much for him asking me to stay at his house permanently, or anything. I had been thinking about what I wanted to say when he mentioned it, but apparently that would not be an issue. Okay. I could deal with that. I loved my little home, and he was right across the street. We would still be seeing each other, I was sure, so it was okay. Really. I told myself that twice, but I was still disappointed that he hadn't at least asked me to stay.

Oh, suck it up. It doesn't mean he loves you any less. You know that.

He'd shown me over and over how he felt. I believed him. He just wanted his own space, that's all. I reminded myself that living with him was never meant to be permanent. I needed a certain amount of privacy, myself. I probably would have insisted on moving back, even if he had invited me to stay.

Yeah, probably.

I joined him on the back porch. "Do you want some coffee?"

He shook his head. "No, thanks. I should get a little bit of work done this afternoon. I still have time to finish a project or two. You coming back over now?"

Things had turned awkward between us, and I wasn't sure if I should go back with him. I decided against it. "No, I think I'll stay a bit longer. Get a few things ready before moving back in. Meet you there for dinner?"

"Sure." He leaned down and gave me a quick kiss, and then he was out the door and gone, just like that.

DINNER WAS VERY quiet. We were both tired and subdued, and decided to call it an early night. I woke at 2:30 to find myself alone in bed. Worried, I was about to go looking for Mac when I saw him sitting on the bedroom balcony with Rosheen by his side. He was staring off over the hills, absently rubbing her head, and I could tell by the set of his shoulders, he wasn't a happy camper.

I debated going out there to ask him what was wrong, but decided it might be better to let him work his way through it himself, with no interference from me. Another hour passed before he crept back into bed and curled up against my back. He lay perfectly still, but I could tell he was awake for a long time. So was I. Somewhere around daylight, I fell finally asleep. When I woke around 10:00 A.M., I was alone, and my head was muzzy from a poor night's rest.

I showered and went downstairs to find Mac bringing in boxes from his truck. He gave me a blindingly bright smile. "Good morning, Sarah. There's coffee if you want it."

I went to the kitchen to fix a cup, but also to keep Mac from seeing my expression, which I'm sure must have given away my feelings of confusion. Why was he in such a hurry to get me out? Had I been so difficult to live with as that? When I calmed myself down, I walked back to the living room and thanked him for fetching the boxes.

"No problem," he said, still being breezy. "I thought it would save you some work if I made a quick run into Everly's and got a few for you. Do you need help packing?"

My heart felt tight and sad, but I wasn't going to let it show. It would just make him feel bad, and he had done so much for me already, that would have been unfair. "Oh, no, thanks. It's mostly just clothes and cosmetic stuff. I can do it myself."

"Okay." He turned back toward his desk. "I'll just get a few things done for the folks in Charlotte, and you can let me know when you're ready to haul it back across the street. We can use the truck, and probably get it all done in one trip."

For some absurd reason, tears stung my eyes as I went upstairs to gather my belongings. I know I said it was a temporary arrangement, and I had missed my cabin a great deal, but damn. Now I felt like yesterday's news—useless and uninteresting.

I tried to think about how many times Mac had told me he loved me, and all of those long, warm nights we had spent together in recent weeks. Somewhere inside, I knew he wasn't pretending about those things. But it hurt that he didn't want me to stay here with him any more. As I packed, I told myself things would go back like they were before the night Lloyd Carter had come calling, and that I had been happy with our relationship then, hadn't I? Mostly. I could be happy with it again. Maybe.

I went halfway down the stairs and asked Mac if he could help me carry the boxes from his bedroom to the porch. He jumped to his feet and scooted past me on the stairs, whistling softly to himself. I felt almost dizzy watching him zip back and forth. In mere minutes, everything was on his porch, and from there, loaded into his truck. Wow.

I grabbed Handsome and we drove across the road to my cabin. Mac unloaded the truck almost as fast as he had loaded it, and before I knew what was happening, he was ready to leave. "Do you want to come back over for dinner tonight, or would you rather celebrate reclaiming your cabin on your own? I think there's still food in the freezer, if you'd rather do that."

I didn't know what to say. This wasn't going like I pictured it at all. In keeping with my usual approach of giving Mac plenty of freedom, I decided maybe dinner apart was something he needed. "You know, that sounds like a good plan," I answered, forcing a big smile. "I'm sure I'll be unpacking late, and a quick bite here is all I'll need."

"Okay then," he said, eyes darting around the room as though he were trying to make sure he hadn't forgotten anything. "Well. You'll call me if you need me, right? And we'll see each other soon?"

My throat was so tight, I could barely squeak out a reply. "Of course. Don't worry about me. See you soon."

He hugged me awkwardly, and then went down the steps to his truck, turning once to say, "I'll call you," before driving away.

I walked inside and sat down at the table, staring out my front window, and wondering what the hell had gone wrong, here. The cabin was filled with a silence so thick even the birds outside the window sounded muffled.

Sighing, I stood and went upstairs to begin sorting through my boxes. I was done in an hour.

I made some lunch, then walked down to the creek and enjoyed my unfettered view of the entire bank. I moved the old Adirondack chairs to a spot under a red bud tree that I remembered as being nice and shady in the summer, and I took a small table off the back porch and set it between the chairs. Perfect for both writing and relaxing.

That done, I wandered back inside, and organized my work space on the table. I sharpened pencils and found bookends for my dictionary and thesaurus, and tidied my Inbox and my little dish of paperclips and pushpins. I crossed to the living room and stood staring around.

"Now what, Handsome?" I scratched his chin.

He purred. Business as usual.

Except that it wasn't. Nothing felt right at all. My "as usual" wasn't the same as it once was, and a sense of discontent continued to grow with every passing minute.

"Oh, this is ridiculous," I muttered. "You are never satisfied, Sarah Gray! Get your act together and start writing. That's what you moved here for, after all. Just sit down at the desk, turn on your laptop, and start!"

Two hours later, I was still staring at my document, having written nothing new whatsoever. I closed the laptop and went out to the front porch swing with a cup of Earl

Grey. I sat there, moving slowly back and forth, and thought about the picture of Frank Everly taken so many years ago in this very spot.

How young and hopeful and in love he had been. And how beautiful and happy Ruth had been in her Christmas picture, showing off the ring he had given her. Their story fascinated me. I longed to know more about what Ruth's life had been like, the happy days, as well as the sad. I could picture Frank and her sitting right here, sharing iced tea, and watching the day draw to a close. Going to meet him had been a good decision. I decided to call him right that minute, and plan a trip to visit him again next week.

"Hi, Sarah! How nice to hear from you! I hope you're gonna tell me you plan to come visit soon?"

"That's exactly why I called, Frank. How would Saturday the 24th work for you?"

"I'm writin' it down right now. Remember, plan on havin' lunch here with me."

When I hung up, I felt better than I had all day, but within twenty minutes or so, I was once again feeling restless and unhappy. "Out of sorts," my dad would have said.

I ate a TV dinner, took a long, hot shower, and decided to go to bed early and read for a while. The reading part was a total loss. In complete disgust, I turned out the light. After a couple of hours of restless tossing and turning, I drifted off, then woke at 3:45, reaching for Mac.

Of course, he wasn't there. I was alone in my own cold and empty bed. I didn't like it. Worse, I hated it! I wanted to feel Mac's warm body next to mine. Hear his soft, even breathing. Smell his skin and his hair as he pulled me closer to him in his sleep.

Was this as good as it was going to get now? Could I give up what we had shared for the last few weeks and go back to dinner and hiking dates? The thought made me feel empty inside, and in spite of my resolve, I felt the tears begin. I buried my face in my pillow and cried in earnest. After a time, I grabbed some tissues from the nightstand, and blew my nose, trying to get a grip. Sobbing into my pillow like a teenager wasn't going to help anything. I needed to think about this situation—this ridiculously wrong, unhappy situation.

Yeah, I had always said I would take whatever I could get from Mac, because I loved him enough to settle for what he needed, rather than what I might want. But maybe I had been lying to myself. Maybe I'd never be able to accept our previous relationship being all we would ever have. Maybe I needed more, even if he didn't.

I got out of bed and washed my face, then padded downstairs in my long, white flannel gown. Sleep was over for sure, so I fixed a cup of tea and grabbed the afghan off the couch. I sat down at my table to wait for dawn to arrive and make everything better. The light of day is usually good for that.

I had been sitting for some time, tea long grown cold, when I realized I could hear the faint sound of a truck in the distance. I wasn't sure, but I thought maybe it had turned into my drive. My heart gave a little lurch. I went out on the porch, holding my breath and waiting. *Hoping.* In a moment, a wash of pale gold light bounced off the trees at the curve of my drive. Mac was coming for me! I flew down the steps and ran across the dark yard, nightgown billowing behind me, and bare feet leaving marks on the frosty grass.

The truck came around the bend and screeched to a halt. Mac leapt out, and ran to meet me. I launched myself into his arms, crying and kissing him again and again. He caught me around the waist and spun me in a full circle, crushing me to him, then carried me up the steps and into my living room, kicking the door closed behind him.

Saying my name over and over, he covered my face with frantic kisses. "Sarah, Sarah ... oh, my God, Sarah! Why did you leave? How could you go?"

Little desperate cries escaped me as I kissed him back. I couldn't get enough of the taste of him, and had to force myself to stop long enough to answer. "I thought this was what *you* wanted. Your privacy back."

"What? No ... *no!* My God, no! Privacy? This was the worst night I ever spent. I couldn't even *look* at that big empty bed, without you in it."

He bent over me again, kissing along my throat, and working his way back to my mouth, groaning, starving. I buried my fingers in his hair and pulled him closer to me, kissing him back desperately, drowning in the pleasure of it.

"I tried to wait," he gasped, "but morning was taking too long to get here. I couldn't stand it another minute. I needed you so much, Sarah! "

His mouth was rough and tender at the same time, on my throat, on my shoulders, everywhere at once. He groaned again, breath shuddering against my skin. "Nothing is right without you."

Burying his face in my hair, he inhaled deeply. "God, I missed that! The smell of your hair spread on the pillow next to me. You smell good, you feel good. I love you so much. Please don't do this ever again, Sarah. Not ever. Promise me."

"I promise! I was miserable, too. My bed was cold when it should have been warm, and I couldn't sleep without you beside me, holding me. I missed the sound of your breathing, your heartbeat. *Everything* was wrong."

I sighed, burying my face against his throat, kissing that hollow I love so much. "Staying apart overnight was a really bad idea, wasn't it?"

"The worst idea in the history of rational thought," he answered, leaving a trail of tiny licks and bites along my collarbone. "I have a better one. Never make me sleep alone again. Stay with me. Stay with me, *always.*"

He stopped kissing me and leaned back to watch my face. "Marry me, Sarah. Spend as much time here as you want—whatever makes you happy—only come back to me at the end of the day. That's all I'll ever ask. I belong to you. Say you belong to me, too. Say you'll stay with me forever, Sarah. Marry me."

Chapter 35
They Do Things Differently Here

THURSDAY, MARCH 15, 2012

I WAS WATCHING Mac sleep. Propped on my right elbow, facing him, I was totally mesmerized by the sight of his hard, lean chest, rising and falling in a steady rhythm. Sometime during the night, he had let go of me and rolled onto his back, right arm flung above his head, palm up. I studied the curve of those long, elegant fingers, the shape of the smaller bones in his wrist, a tracery of light blue veins just under the skin.

His hair was a sleep-tossed shock of ebony, falling in soft curls over his ears, and his stubble of morning beard accentuated the angle of his jaw. I smiled, heart filled to the brim with love for this beautiful man, and still not quite believing I could be waking up to this for the rest of my life. I was entranced.

He's so gorgeous, and he's mine. Mine, mine, mine.

With a wicked smile, I lifted the sheet just enough to peek underneath.

Oh, yes! Definitely all mine!

With a reluctant sigh, I put my palm against his cheek and whispered, "Wake up, Mac."

He turned toward me, reaching out and pulling me against him. I let him hold me for a moment, then whispered again, "Are you awake?"

"No."

"Why do I think you aren't being honest with me?"

"Am, too. I'm still asleep and dreaming I've got this hot chick in my arms, and she's naked. I have designs on her. Wanna hear more?"

"Too much talking. How about a demonstration? You should teach her what makes you happy first thing in the morning."

I heard the rumble of his soft laugh. "Class is in session."

Oh, my.

You'll have to take my word on this one—Mac is a very, very good teacher.

"ARE YOU STILL sure you want to do this, Sarah?" He finished buttoning his shirt, and turned toward me, eyebrows raised in question.

I smiled. "You changing your mind about your birthday present, Big Boy?" I was sitting on the edge of the bed, putting on my shoes.

"Not at all. This is exactly what I want. You and I together, always. But I just keep thinking it isn't fair to you. Don't most women want that whole big, fancy wedding thing, with all the trimmings?"

I gave him my best haughty expression. "Since when am I 'most women,' Mac?"

A slow smile spread across his face. "Since never, Sarah. You're not like any woman I've ever known. I'll try not to forget that again. Just be sure you know what you're getting into with me. I'm not easy, I know."

I stood and walked to him, sliding my arms around his waist and laying my head against his chest. "I don't need easy. I just need you, exactly as you are. I believe in us. We belong together. Now let's go get married."

So we did. Three days after Mac proposed to me, we drove to Asheville, and an hour and a half later, we walked out of the courthouse, husband and wife.

SATURDAY, MARCH 17, 2012

"MARRIED? WHAT DO you mean, married? You married Mac without—*without my ever even meeting him?* When? Where?" Jenna was sputtering, wide-eyed and nearly incoherent with shock. I knew she would be, but I also knew that when she calmed down, she would be happy for me. It might take a few minutes, though, judging by her reaction.

"I knew there was something strange going on when your Skypes got farther and farther apart. And I also knew you were hiding something from me, Sarah. Now I guess I know what it was."

In truth, she didn't. Marrying Mac was not something I had allowed myself to dream about very often over the last few weeks. But trying to keep from telling Jenna about Lloyd Carter's visit from Hell *had* been on my mind, and I knew I had sounded like I was hiding something during several conversations.

"But what I don't understand," she continued, "is why you didn't tell me you two were this serious? If I had known you were talking marriage, I would have been there for you,

you know that." She was almost in tears now, longing to be part of the huge, elaborate wedding that hadn't even taken place.

"I know that, Jenna. And I would have loved that, too, if I had been planning an actual ceremony. It didn't work out quite that way. It was very ... sudden."

"Too sudden to wait for me? What do you mean? How sudden?"

"Well, he asked me at 4:30 A.M. Monday morning, and we got married at 2:30 Thursday afternoon. See? Sudden."

Astonished, she stared at me, mouth agape, and no sounds at all coming out. This was such an unusual occurrence, I couldn't help myself. I laughed.

Jenna bristled. "Sarah! What on Earth is wrong with you? He asks you on Monday and you're married that Thursday? Didn't you ever hear of playing hard to get? And how is that even possible? What about getting a license, and the waiting period, and all that?"

I shrugged. "They do things differently here in North Carolina. What can I say? No waiting period. You bring in your ID, you pay the fee, and voila! They marry you."

"Just like that?"

"Just like that!"

"But why didn't you want a real wedding? You would have been such a beautiful bride. And I could have provided you with both flower girl and ring bearer, and been your Matron of Honor, too. I look great in taffeta! And Howie could have given you away." She paused to catch her breath. "It would have been really special," she added in a wistful voice.

I took pity on her. "Yes, it would have been very special to have had a big wedding with all of you here, Jenna. I would have loved to share it with you. But this was special, too. And it fit us better. Honestly, Jenna, neither of us wanted to wait one more day. We put it off until Thursday because that was Mac's birthday, and he said it was what he wanted for his present—for us to be husband and wife, and never be apart from each other, again."

She sniffed, looking mollified. "Well. That sounds romantic, I guess."

"Oh, if you think that sounds romantic, let me tell you about the proposal."

By the time I had finished describing that passionate, early morning dash into each other's arms, she was practically swooning, on board all the way, and eager to meet my new husband when her kids got out of school in June.

"What about his parents, Sarah? Have you met them?"

"His parents have been in Europe for the winter, so no, I haven't met them yet. We did talk to them, though. From what I gather, they're so happy that Mac found someone, I'd pretty much have to be an ax murderer for them not to like me. They'll be visiting us as soon as they return to the States. I'm kinda nervous about that, but Mac assures me they're very nice and will love me."

When she had finished asking all her questions about the wedding, I told her about Ruth Winn's life and Lloyd Carter's death. A severely edited version, of course. No ghosts mentioned at all, but there was enough gasp value in the details I did tell her to leave her open-mouthed, once again.

"Holy crap! You've been living there all these months with a dead body in your shed? I can't believe it, Sarah! Tell me you aren't still living in that cabin?"

"Well, of course not. I pretty much live with my husband, you know. He's old-fashioned that way. But he's helping me turn the cabin into a studio for my writing and painting. It's going to be perfect, Jenna. I love going down there to work. It's so beautiful and peaceful, and you'll love it, too, when you see it. All the bad stuff has been carted away and the grounds are clean. There isn't a trace of anything creepy left, I promise."

"Well, if you say so. As long as that Lloyd guy isn't hanging around to haunt you, or anything."

Oh, Jenna. If you only knew.

*

I HUNG UP shortly after that and went looking for Mac. I found him in one of his favorite places—sitting on the balcony off the living room, watching the stars wake up in the darkening sky. He turned as I came through the door, carrying two glasses of wine.

"Hello, Mrs. Cole. How'd Jenna take the news?"

I was still at that stage where being called Mrs. Cole made my heart flip-flop, and I felt a goofy grin spread across my face.

"Hello, yourself, Husband of Mine." I handed him his wine and sat down in the chair next to him. "She was completely shocked and aghast and sputtering all over the place. Typical for Jenna when something happens she didn't foresee. And she felt a bit left out, not having been offered a chance to help plan a big wedding. But she's happy now. And demanding to meet you as soon as possible."

"Hmmm. What happens if, heaven forbid, she doesn't like me?"

"Silly man. She'll love you. First of all, what's not to love? And secondly, she'll love you because you make me happy. No matter how crazy Jenna is, that's always the bottom line with her. She's a good person, Mac. I think you'll enjoy her, too."

We sat in comfortable silence, sipping our wine and watching night reclaim its power over day, one dark inch at a time. Rosheen was lying on the floor at Mac's side, and

Handsome jumped onto my lap, where he curled up, purring. I wondered if it was possible to be happier than I was at that perfect moment in time.

This I will remember all the days of my life.

The rising moon spread a silver shawl across the hills below. The damp, green smell of new leaves floated on the cool evening air, and somewhere deep in the woods, I heard the bark of a fox, making his rounds.

My Mac sat next to me, fingers entwined with mine, looking relaxed and at peace with the world. I wanted to paint this picture across the back of my mind in a perfect splash of memory I would be able to see, whenever I wished.

"Never forget this moment," I whispered. "Never, ever forget."

Mac smiled. "I was thinking the same thing." He lifted my hand and kissed my fingertips. "I don't ever want to forget the way I feel tonight, either."

MONDAY, MARCH 19, 2012

"I KNOW I SAID I'd let you work undisturbed today, but I figured you have to take a lunch break, right?"

I turned to see Mac standing on the cabin porch, picnic basket in hand. He was smiling through the screen door, waiting for me to invite him in. I gave him a fierce scowl, then burst into laughter at his crestfallen look.

"If you brought food with you, you're golden. Come on in."

He swooped in, kissed me soundly, then cleared the coffee table for the picnic hamper. In seconds, he had begun setting out cheese and fruit.

"Wow! Am I going to have a catered lunch every day? I could get used to this, you know."

With a wicked grin, he replied, "Not unless you come back to the house to eat, where I'm better equipped to take care of your needs. Food-wise, of course."

"Of course."

I sat down on the sofa, tucking my legs underneath me. "What's the occasion?"

"There doesn't need to be a special occasion for me to surprise you, Sarah, but it just so happens there is one, this time."

And surprise me he did. Kneeling down in front of me, he took my left hand in his. "I wanted to have this before we went to Asheville, but it wasn't ready until today." Then he slid an intricately carved platinum band onto my third finger, turned my hand over, and kissed my palm. "I hope you like it."

Speechless, I stared at the ring. It had an unusual and complicated Celtic knot design that was incredibly beautiful. "Oh, Mac. It's perfect. I love it!"

Before I could give him a proper thank-you kiss, he pulled an envelope out of the hamper. "There's more." He smiled and handed it to me.

Inside was a photograph of a whitewashed, thatched-roof cottage, with small, shaggy cattle grazing in an emerald green field nearby. A lone piper stood on a hill in the distance, silhouetted against a gray sky.

"We didn't have a traditional wedding, but there's no reason we can't have a traditional honeymoon. I thought maybe you'd like to go to Scotland. Or Ireland? London? Or would you prefer something tropical? Fiji or the Seychelles?"

Laughing, I flung myself on him, hugging and kissing him, all at once. "Yes! Yes to any of the above, but especially yes to Scotland. I've always wanted to go there!"

"I know. I pay very close attention to you, Sarah, in case you hadn't noticed. How would it be if we planned a trip for mid-summer? That way, you'd have a chance to meet my parents next month, and you'd be here when Jenna visits in June. After that, we'd be free agents for a few weeks, so we could go wherever you want."

Sharing cheese and grapes, we huddled over my laptop, while I Googled all sorts of places in Scotland. Mac took notes of everything we thought we'd like to see and do. It was all I could do to sit still long enough to finish lunch. "It's like all my Christmases have come at once," I said, admiring my beautiful ring. "I got fabulous jewelry, a dream vacation, and you, all in less than a week!"

"Am I at the bottom of that list, then?" He raised his eyebrows in mock alarm.

I grinned. "I saved the best for last, of course."

Smiling, Mac cleared away the remains of our lunch. "Good answer. And you got all your Christmases at once because you've been a very good girl this year. And because I love you so much. You do know that, don't you?"

"Yes, Mac. I do. I'd tell you the same thing, but you must be tired of hearing it by now."

He grew solemn. "I will never, ever get tired of hearing you say that to me."

I took his face between my palms, looked straight into his pale, blue eyes, and said, "I love you, MacKenzie Cole, with all my heart and soul. You are mine, and I am yours, from now until forever."

He kissed me thoroughly, and whispered in my ear. "You know, there is one small thing that makes me sad." He kissed me once again, then leaned back and looked at me with a wistful expression in his eyes. "I'm really going to miss calling you 'Sarah Gray.'"

AFTER LUNCH, I found I had lost my interest in writing about women in tight corsets being pursued by men in tall hats. I talked Mac into taking the rest of the afternoon off and going for a walk along the trail behind my cabin. Soon, we were sitting by the stream in the exact spot where we had first managed to have a normal conversation with each other.

"I love this spot," I sighed, leaning against Mac's shoulder, and watching the water churn by.

"I like it, too. I have very nice memories of some time spent here last fall, getting to know the beautiful Miss Gray." He put his arm around my shoulder and pulled me closer to his side, nuzzling my hair. "Little did I dream that two-hour conversation would lead to so many changes in my life."

Holding his hand, I traced my finger over his inner wrist, feeling the pulse beating just below the skin. Curious as to how his memories of that creek side meeting might differ from mine, I asked, "What do you remember most about that day?"

"Beside your silly cat assaulting my dog?" He looked off over the water, eyes on something only he could see, and then his mouth curved into a sweet smile. Turning back to me, he said, "I remember the way you looked before you knew I was there, bent over your sketch pad, concentrating so hard on your drawing. Your hair had blown loose and was spilling over your shoulder, and all around you, yellow leaves were floating down. You looked so beautiful, it made something inside me hurt. I almost backed up, so you wouldn't see me—so nothing would disturb the picture you made."

He tucked a loose strand of hair behind my ear, and went on. "I remember how nervous I was around you. I think I knew even then that you were bringing something new into my life that I wouldn't know how to handle." He kissed my temple. "What do you remember?"

Snuggling a bit closer to him, inhaling his clean, soapy smell, and feeling the solid warmth of him beside me, I smiled. "Easy. Your laughter after Handsome gave up trying to mutilate Rosheen. I'd never seen you laugh before, and suddenly, you were a whole new person.

"And I remember the way your hair wanted to fall into your eyes. You kept pushing it back with one hand, and it would tumble right back down again. The sunlight was coming through the trees in little, dappled patches, and every time you moved, it would shine on you. I thought I had never seen such beautiful, glossy black hair in my life."

"Hmmm. All my many outstanding physical attributes and you noticed my hair?"

"Oh, don't you worry, MacKenzie Cole. I noticed more than that."

"What else?" He coaxed. "Tell me."

"Well ... your hands. I thought I'd like to sketch them. You had picked up a leaf and were turning it over and over in your fingers, and it was sort of hypnotic. And I definitely noticed your eyes. They're unusually intense, you know, and I remember thinking they probably didn't miss much."

He tilted his head to one side, studying me. "I don't know whether that's true, but I don't think I miss much about what's going on with you." He paused. "Do you want to tell me about your book?"

"My book?"

His left eyebrow arched. "Sarah," he chided. "I don't have to be particularly observant to see that you aren't feeling as happy about it now as you once were. Is it writer's block? Are you stuck on a plot point? Would it help to talk about it?"

I sighed. "You see too much, sometimes. But you're right. I'm feeling a bit frustrated, I guess. I haven't been able to pick up the thread of my story again. It's just not working for me right now. First, I thought maybe the concept wasn't really any good, but I'm not sure that's the problem. It's more that I'm having an awful lot of trouble concentrating on it."

"Why is that? Are you comfortable writing in your cabin? Is there anything else you need? Would you rather we find a private spot in the house for you to work?"

"Oh, no. The cabin is perfect. I'm so glad you suggested turning it into a writing studio. It's peaceful, and comfortable, and I'm happy there. No, it's not the cabin. I'm just having trouble focusing on my story."

"Ah. Well, what *are* you focused on?"

Frowning, I wondered where he was going with this. When I didn't answer, he went on.

"I could be way off base, here, Sarah, but I don't think I am. I think the reason you can't focus on your Victorian romance is because your mind is filled with images of other people. I'm guessing that Ruth Winn, Frank Everly, and Lloyd Carter are occupying a lot of creative space in your head right now."

"I do think about them a lot," I admitted. "I can't help it. I've been trying to put them aside and get on with my book, but everywhere I look, something reminds me of how much Ruth and Frank loved each other, and the sacrifice she was willing to make to be sure Frank was safe. I often find myself imagining how Frank felt, finally moving on with his life, but never knowing what had happened between them.

"In my mind, I can see Ruth so clearly, sitting at my kitchen table, all alone, writing her letters. Pouring her heart out to a man who wouldn't read them until long after she was gone. I can't forget about them, for some reason. I don't want to waste time daydreaming about them, but I can't seem to help it."

He looked puzzled. "Why do you want to force yourself to finish a book you've lost interest in? Are you sure daydreaming about Ruth and Frank is a waste of time? Could it be that the story you should be working on is the one that's in your head right now, trying to get out? Is there any reason you can't put the Victorian novel to one side for a while?"

He shifted around to face me better, and ran a finger down the side of my face.

"I think in your heart, you really want to tell Ruth's story. It's obvious that she has touched something inside of you. Why not write about her life, and her love, and what she was willing to do to protect it all? The story has everything going for it—good and evil, love and hatred, life and death—I think you could do it. You've lived in her house. You've read her letters. You've met the man she loved. Hell, you've even met the man she hated and was forced to kill. Why not tell her story, Sarah?"

I just sat there, staring at him. Talk about feeling silly. I'd been struggling and fuming and looking for words that just wouldn't come, all for a story I was no longer interested in, filled with people I didn't care about any more. And all the time, the story I really wanted to tell—the story that had been handed to me like a gift from on high—was banging around in my head, day after day, begging to be written down, and being completely ignored.

Tears sprang to my eyes, and I ducked my head, blinking them back.

He pulled me closer, kissing my forehead. "Don't cry, Sarah. I didn't mean to upset you. Should I not have asked you about this?"

"No, of course not. I'm not upset with you. I'm thinking what a lucky woman I am to have a husband who cares about what I do, and whether or not it's making me happy.

And I'm astounded at how obtuse I can be at times where my own feelings are concerned."

Shaking my head in wonder, I smiled at him. "You are pure magic. You've reminded me that creativity can't be forced, and that the most important part of writing is to listen to what the heart wants to say. You're the best husband, ever!"

"Wow. And to think I was hesitant to mention it." He heaved a long, exaggerated sigh. "I suppose now you're going to tell me that you need to get back to the cabin and start to work."

"Yes, please!" I scrambled to my feet. "I have ideas ricocheting around in my brain like a pinball machine. I need to start making notes, now. And we have to go talk to Frank. I won't do this without his blessing, but I think he'll like the idea. Oh, can I use the information you found on Lloyd, with all the dates and charges against him? I'll need that for his part of the story. I wonder if Frank has any more pictures of Ruth. Maybe he would have kept one or two tucked away somewhere. I'll have to remember to ask him. But anyway, he'll have some of himself as a young man, I'm sure, and maybe some of Darcy's Corner, too." I stopped.

Mac's head was thrown back and he was laughing.

"What?" I demanded. "What's so funny?"

"You are, Sarah, babbling away! You're back to that woman I talked to last fall, in this very spot—full of enthusiasm and excitement and plans."

Tilting his head, he gave me a curious look. "Funny. She scared me then. Now, she just makes me realize that if we want something badly enough, we can make it happen. I've learned a lot from that woman, and I suspect she's not done teaching me, yet."

Walking back to my cabin hand in hand with Mac, I listened to his tales of summers spent here on Wake-Robin

Ridge, and I pictured him living out all the adventures of a young boy's heart. I could see that ten-year-old Mac in my mind's eye, running up and down these trails, climbing trees, and swimming in the pond by his secret falls. I imagined him learning to fish and hunt, sleeping in tents, and listening to ghost stories by a campfire at night. Someday I was going to write about that little boy, too, and how he grew to love these wooded hills so much. But first, I had another story to tell, and I couldn't wait to get started.

Mac went back to work, figuring he could still get a few things done before the afternoon was over. "Don't stay too late," he cautioned, as he told me goodbye. "I'll put some steaks on the grill when you get home."

I watched his truck disappear down my drive, then went back inside. Ideas for Ruth's story were pushing and shoving to get out of my head. I wanted to write them down, before they were scattered into the ether and lost forever.

The photo of the cottage in Scotland was laying by my laptop. I looked at it, marveling at the loving generosity of the man I had married. Running my finger over the carved designs on my wedding band, I thought about how lucky I was.

Ruth's life didn't have a fairy tale ending. I couldn't change that, but I could tell the world she had been here, and that she had given up everything for love.

Your voice will be heard, Ruth Winn. I swear it.

I sat down at my laptop and began to type.

Epilogue
One Year Later

"THIS MIGHT BE the most peaceful spot in the world," Mac said, his arm draped over my shoulder. We were sitting on a comfortable teak bench in a small glade on the north side of Mac's property. The enclosed area was roughly circular in shape and about twenty-five feet across, sheltered from wind and storm on three sides by various kinds of evergreens. In front of us, a small marble angel knelt protectively at the head of Ben's grave.

I smiled in agreement. "You may be right. I remember thinking it was a special place the first time I saw it, but having Ben here has made it even more so. It's like a little chapel."

The ground was carpeted with spring blooms in white, pale pink, soft blue, and deep red. Giant trillium, bluebells, bird's-foot violets, and my favorite, the lovely, wine-colored wake-robins were all in bloom. Mother Nature had laid out a bouquet of her best and most beautiful, and in my secret inner self, I believed it was special, just for Ben.

"Thanks to you, Sarah, I feel connected to him in a way I never have before. When I sit here with him, I can finally remember all the laughter and love he brought to my life."

I sighed, happy and grateful. What a long way we had come in the last year and a half. I had made the move of a lifetime, Mac had faced his own personal demons, and together, we had laid the ghost of Lloyd Carter. To ease our minds, Mac and I had spent the night of January 23 in his truck, watching the cabin from a safe distance. The peace of the winter night had not been disturbed. Lloyd's after-death reign of terror was firmly in the past now, and we weren't looking back.

Like any of us, we might face our share of troubles in the years ahead, but I knew in my heart that we would weather them all. We had each other, and that was so much more than many people ever found.

Mac's soft lips brushed my temple. "I checked Amazon this morning, you know."

"Did you now? And what did you find, MacKenzie Cole?"

"I found out I'm married to a best-selling author, whose book is getting rave reviews."

"Ah. And are you impressed by her?"

"I was impressed by her long before she wrote _Crying Don't Fix Anything_, but tell me, my talented wife, how does it feel to know you have created something that other people love so much?"

"I didn't really create it, you know. I just wrote it down. The story was all there."

"Baloney, Sarah. Some of the facts were there, but you created the story, all right. And filled in the gaps. And made Ruth and Frank and Lloyd come alive on the pages. Don't sell yourself short. You have real talent, you know, and I'm very proud of you."

I blushed with pleasure. "Thank you. And it does feel good to know that people are enjoying the book. Now to see if it was a fluke, or if I can do it again. I'm ready to start my next one, I think."

The success of my first book had been all I could have hoped for, and I felt that I had kept my promise to Ruth to make her voice heard. I glanced down at my right hand, where I wore her heart-shaped ring. Frank had sent it to me after reading the book, with a note that read in part, "Ruth would want you to have this. Consider it a gift directly from her to you. You have captured her heart and soul perfectly, and I'll always be grateful that you shared her letters with me."

I had poured so much of my own heart into writing Ruth's story that it was hard to let it go, but an idea for a new tale was beginning to take shape in my imagination, and I knew it was time to move on.

Mac, as always, was looking for ways to help. "Is there anything you need at the cabin, before you get started? How's the new desk working out? And the chair? Is it comfortable?"

I tilted my head and gave him a long look.

"What?" He asked. "Why such a serious look?"

"I was just wondering why you so often refer to yourself as 'difficult' or 'hard to live with.' You say it so frequently, you must believe it, but Mac? It's not true, you know."

He started to protest, but I held up my hand. "It's not. Maybe it was once, when you were struggling with how to live through grief and pain. Maybe then, okay? But that's not the real you. It never was. I live with the real you, and I've never known a kinder, more generous, and thoughtful person in my life. That's who you are, Mac. Not that other guy, hiding in his house, shutting everyone out, and trying to harden his heart against ever being hurt again.

"In spite of your worst efforts, you're a good man, and you are definitely not difficult to live with. You make me feel cherished and happy every single day of my life."

He sat looking at me in doubtful silence, but I persisted. "Believe it, Mac. Believe that we are both good and worthy people, with no more than the normal amount of human failings, and that we deserve our chance at happiness. I believe it with all my heart. Believe with me."

Giving me a hesitant smile, he at least appeared to be contemplating the possibility that he wasn't a selfish ogre after all. "You're a treasure, Mrs. Cole. My life will forever more be divided down the middle into Before Sarah and After Sarah. After Sarah is so much better."

"Now you're talkin'. How about some lunch?" I started to rise, then sat right back down. "Oh! Oh, Mac!"

"What is it? What's wrong?" He asked, eyes filling with alarm.

I took his hand and placed it against my rounded belly. "There. Do you feel it? Right there? The baby is moving!"

Mac sat very still, holding his breath for a moment, and then his face lit from within with a glow of wide-eyed wonder. "Oh, my God! Yes! I feel it!" His smile was ecstatic.

Leaning forward, he placed a kiss right over the spot, whispering, "Grow, little baby, grow. Mama and Daddy love you so much." And when he raised his head to smile at me, his eyes were glittering with unshed tears.

DINNER DONE, MAC and I sat on the living room balcony, enjoying that slow, still moment between daylight and dark, just seconds before the moon rises and works its magic. Mac had pushed his chair close to mine so he could hold my hand, and he was stroking the back of it, pausing now and then to nibble on my fingers.

"Are you still hungry?"

"Nope. I just like how you taste."

"Even after a year of tasting me?"

"Even after a forever of tasting you, I'll still like it."

Tilting his head to one side, he smiled as he studied me. "Look at you. You have no idea how beautiful you are, sitting there as radiant as an angel, and full of new life. My sweet Sarah!"

He kissed the palm of my hand, and turned to gaze out over the hills. "When I was a child, I believed in magic. Every summer, I would wander these woods, swim in the pond, watch the stars at night, and the sun coming up in the morning. It all felt like magic to me. But now I know what real magic is. It's us. Right here, right now."

I smiled, watching the moon continue its upward climb. It silvered each hill in turn, until it reached the balcony, then spilled its pale beams over us—a benediction from above.

I thought about the winding roads we had each taken to reach this spot, this moment where time spread out ahead of us, alive with possibility. Our child would grow up on Wake-Robin Ridge, and would become a part of the history of these ancient hills, just as so many who had come before had done. The circle would be complete, as it should be.

A chilly breeze had sprung up, and I shivered. Mac stood, helping me to my feet. "Too cool out here for you, now. Come to bed with me, Sarah. I want to hold you all night long."

And that's exactly what he did.

Author's Notes

The town of Darcy's Corner is a creation of my own imagination, as is Wake-Robin Ridge, itself. Both are neighbors of the very real town of Lake Lure, North Carolina, and the beautiful Chimney Rock, which stands as a sentinel, overlooking the town below. There are music festivals at Chimney Rock Park, but not exactly where I placed the one Mac and Sarah went to.

There is no Everly's General Store, though I wish there were. I'd love to browse the shelves and chat with locals at the Saturday Farmer's Market. And I'd love to see that breathtaking Halloween display of jack-o-lanterns! But Everly's, as I imagined it, is a combination of many small stores along various Blue Ridge mountain roads.

My descriptions of the wildflowers, streams, and waterfalls are composites of places I've visited on my rambles over the years. I wanted readers to see it all through the eyes of Sarah and Mac, as though they were standing beside them on Wake-Robin Ridge. The mountains of North Carolina are lovely beyond measure. I hope each of you gets a chance to visit for yourself someday, in search of your own secret waterfalls, quiet glades, and mossy green pools.

Happy travels!

About The Author

Marcia Meara is a native Floridian, living in the Orlando area with her husband of almost 28 years, two silly little dachshunds and four big, lazy cats. She's fond of reading, gardening, hiking, canoeing, painting, and writing, not necessarily in that order. But her favorite thing in the world is spending time with her two grandchildren, eight-year-old Tabitha Faye, and seven-month-old Kaelen Lake.

At age 69, Marcia wrote _Wake-Robin Ridge_, her first novel, and _Summer Magic: Poems of Life and Love_. She is currently working on her second novel, _Swamp Ghosts_, set alongside the wild and scenic rivers of central Florida. Her philosophy? It's never too late to follow your dream. Just take that first step, and never look back.

Stop by Marcia's blogs on book reviews and gardening to say hello.

Bookin' It: http://marciameara.wordpress.com

Who's Your Granny?: http://mmeara.wordpress.com